BOOKS 1 & 2 OF
THE JEFF RESNICK MYSTERIES

BOOKS 1 & 2 OF
THE JEFF RESNICK MYSTERIES

L. L. Bartlett

Copyright © 2014 by L. L. Bartlett
Murder On The Mind by L.L. Bartlett Copyright © 2005
Dead In Red by L.L. Bartlett Copyright © 2008
When The Spirit Moves You by L.L. Bartlett Copyright © 2011
Original Cover Design by Patricia Ryan

This is a work of fiction. Names, characters, places, and incidents are either the product of the author's imagination, or are used fictitiously, and any resemblance to actual persons, living or dead, business establishments, events, or locales is purely coincidental.

All rights reserved.
No part of this book may be reproduced in any form by any electronic or mechanical means (including photocopying, recording, or information storage and retrieval) without permission in writing from the author.

ISBN: 1940801044
ISBN 13: 9781940801049

Books by L.L. Bartlett

The Jeff Resnick Mysteries
Murder on the Mind
Dead In Red
Room at the Inn
Cheated By Death
Bound By Suggestion
Dark Waters
Evolution: Jeff Resnick's Backstory

Short Stories - 99¢
Evolution: Jeff Resnick's Backstory (these are not mysteries)
When The Spirit Moves You A Jeff Resnick Novelette
Bah! Humbug A Jeff Resnick Story
Cold Case A Jeff Resnick Story
Abused: A Daughter's Story

Writing as Lorraine Bartlett

The Victoria Square Mysteries
A Crafty Killing
The Walled Flower
One Hot Murder
Recipes To Die For: A Victoria Square Cookbook

Short Stories
An Unconditional Love

Love Heals
Blue Christmas
Prisoner of Love
We're So Sorry Uncle Albert
Panty Raid: A Tori Cannon-Kathy Grant Mini Mystery

Tales of Telenia (Adventure-Fantasy)
Threshold
Journey

WRITING AS LORNA BARRETT

The Booktown Mysteries
Murder Is Binding
Bookmarked For Death
Bookplate Special
Chapter & Hearse
Sentenced To Death
Murder On The Half Shelf
Not The Killing Type
Book Clubbed
A Fatal Chapter

After insurance investigator Jeff Resnick is viciously mugged, he discovers the resulting brain injury has left him able to sense people's secrets. When his estranged half-brother, Richard, takes Jeff to the family home to recover, Jeff's senses pick up clues to the recent vicious murder of a local banker. Despite Jeff's mixed feelings about his new sixth sense, he feels compelled to explore the banker's murder—using both his senses and his investigative skills, along with Richard's reluctant help. Against the gritty setting of wintry Buffalo, NY, and a tormented family history of his own, unraveling the truth threatens Jeff's—and Richard's—life.

MURDER ON THE MIND: ACKNOWLEDGMENTS

Over the years many people have read and commented on *Murder on the Mind*. Thanking them all would probably be impossible; however, several of my first readers immediately come to mind. Ed Whitmore, Alison Steinmiller, and Vivian Vande Velde gave me my first effective feedback, and for that I am truly grateful. For several years my critique partner, Liz Voll, had an opportunity to comment on my work. Guppy Marjorie Merithew was instrumental in editing the draft that snagged me the attention of my agent. And my staunchest cheerleaders are my current critique partners, Gwen Nelson and Liz Eng. I'd like to give a broad thank you to my Sisters in Crime chapter, The Guppies: The Great Unpublished, although that name is a misnomer as many of its members have achieved their dreams of publication. Thank you all for encouraging me in mine.

Murder On The Mind

The First Jeff Resnick Mystery

DEDICATION

For Ian,
the best brother in the world

Chapter One

Something walloped me in the gut. A hit without substance—without pain. It sucked me from the here and now to a vacant place where a hollow wind brushed my ears.

I waited.

There. In my peripheral vision: *Coming out of the mist. An animal. A deer. A buck.*

I blinked and was back in the bar, bending over the felt-lined table.

"You gonna shoot or not?" Marty growled.

My fingers tightened around the cue, which stopped their sudden trembling. I held my breath as I made the shot. The cue ball kissed the six and sent it into the left corner pocket. I straightened, trying to hide the unexpected panic churning my insides. "That's another five bucks you owe me."

Marty chewed the unlit stub of his cigar, fumbled with his wallet, and dug out a crisp five-dollar bill, slapping it onto the table. "Double or nothing."

Uh-uh. I needed to get out of there. To think about what had just happened to me.

"I'd love to, but I start a new job first thing in the morning." I snatched up my winnings and replaced the cue stick on the wall rack. O'Shea's smoky, blue-collar friendliness had been a haven from boredom and loneliness, reminding me of the taverns back home in Buffalo, only it was pool, not darts, that drew the Sunday night crowd.

"Go ahead, leave," Marty grumbled, gazing down the length of his cue. "But be back here—same time next week. Me and the boys are gonna win back everything you've taken from us." His break shot went wild. He should have stuck with darts.

"In your dreams," I said and shrugged into my leather bomber jacket.

"Are y'leaving so soon, Jeffrey?" Pretty Annie McBride, an Irish lass of about twenty-five with a killer smile, hefted a tray of drinks as she served a couple at a nearby table.

"Have to, darlin.'"

"An' when are y'going ta ask me out? I'm not getting any younger, y'know."

I eyed her appreciatively but considered my thin wallet. "Soon."

"I'll be collecting Social Security at this rate."

"Forget him, Annie," said Ian from behind the bar. "Find yourself a nice Irish boy." He winked at her.

"I'm half Irish," I countered to a round of laughter from Ian and the regulars. "My mother was an O'Connor—you can't get much more Irish than that."

"Never you mind them, Jeffrey," Annie said. "But don't wait too long, or I will find me some nice Irish lad." Annie smiled kindly and headed for the kitchen. I watched the door swing shut behind her.

Marty and another patron were already engrossed in a new game as I headed for the exit. "G'night, all."

A chorus of goodbyes followed as I left the pub.

I set off at a brisk pace, heading for my apartment three blocks away. A March thaw had melted the snow, but the temperature had plunged back to freezing and the bracing air soon cleared my head. The pub had been overheated and reeked of stale beer and sweat. No wonder I'd zoned out.

I thought of the cash in my wallet. Maybe my good luck at pool would stay with me when I started the job at Metropolitan Life. My unemployment benefits were about to end, so I'd been desperate to take the entry-level insurance claims job.

Hands stuffed in my pockets, I watched my feet as I walked. After I got that first paycheck, I'd ask Annie out. It had been months since I'd had any feminine companionship, and celibacy is highly overrated. I just hoped Annie's friendliness wasn't a put-on to get a good tip.

Traffic was sparse as I crossed Third, the sidewalk empty as I headed past the caged-in businesses that lined the street. I was usually cautious, but thoughts of the new job and what had happened at the bar distracted me as I dodged the miniature skating rinks on the cracked pavement. The next day would be nerve-racking. New names, new faces. Probably a backlog of case files, too.

"Hey, dude, got some spare change?"

A large silhouetted figure blocked the sidewalk.

Aw, shit.

A gust of frigid wind grazed my cheek. I jammed my hands deeper into my jacket pockets and tried to get past him.

"Hey, asshole, I'm talkin' to you!" The hefty teenager stepped into the lamplight, grabbed my jacket. Another figure emerged from the darkened doorway of a closed deli. Though shorter, the other kid brandished a worn baseball bat, looking just as threatening. I avoided his glare and the challenge in it.

In spite of the freezing cold, I broke into a sweat as I pulled away from the kid's grasp. "Hey, guys, I don't want any trouble."

"Then give us your money."

Damn. I'd just won fifty bucks at the bar and now a couple of two-bit punks were going to shake me down for it. But I'm not stupid.

I thumbed through my wallet. "You can have what I got."

"Is that all?" the shorter kid asked, slamming the bat into his palm. "You got a ATM card? We gonna go visit your bank."

"I've been out of work for months. There's no money left."

The big guy grabbed my left arm in a vise-grip. "Lester, why don't you introduce our friend here to Reggie."

Lester flaunted the wooden bat so that the logo burned into it was visible in the lamplight. A Reggie Jackson special, decades old but just as lethal as the day it was made.

"C'mon, guys, I gave you everything I had."

"Reggie wants to teach you a lesson," Lester said.

I took a step back, yanking my arm from the linebacker.

Across the street a hooker ducked into one of the doorways. Distracted, I almost didn't react as Lester swung the bat. I dodged, catching him with a satisfying kick to the groin. The bat went flying and he sank like the *Titanic*.

His friend snatched the bat, heading for me like a killing machine. I stepped back, raised my left arm to fend off the blow, but he caught me. The audible crack of bone sent me staggering. Skyrockets of pain shot up my arm.

The bat came down again, slamming into my shoulder, knocking me to my knees.

Icy water soaked through my jeans.

The bat came at me from the left, crashed into my temple, and my head hit the pavement. My vision doubled. Stupidly, I tried to raise myself as the bat connected with my skull once more.

Damn, I thought just before losing consciousness. I wasn't going to make it to my new job in the morning.

I drifted from painful reality, lost in some misty wilderness. I'd escaped one nightmare...but escaped to where?

Tangled sensations enveloped me—rising dread, irrational fear. The mist began to evaporate, and I focused all my senses on the emotion.

From out of the void a figure approached, surrounded by an aura of smothering emotions. Hatred, revenge—it spewed these and more. Unable to bear the torrent, I tried to turn away. The figure—a hunter—stalked its prey, but instinct told me I was not the quarry.

It paused in its search. The intensity of its rage choked me—kept me from taking a decent breath. I thought I'd pass out when the stalker moved away. Horrified, yet fascinated, I couldn't tear my gaze from the dark, retreating figure. What was being hunted? Why couldn't I see it, warn it?

The danger lingered.

I shuddered, afraid of the bizarre, gruesome death I knew was to come.

The figure faded into the surrounding emptiness, and I began to relax.

I was only dreaming, after all.

Chapter Two

"He's different," Richard said.

Hidden behind the butler's pantry door, my head half-shaved like a punk rocker, eavesdropping on a private conversation…yeah, I'd say I was different.

"Of course he is," Brenda said. "After what happened, I'd be surprised if he wasn't."

Broken arm, fractured skull. Emotional wreck. Working on paranoid, too. I leaned in closer, straining to hear.

"He's keeping something from me."

Richard didn't know the half of it.

"What?" Brenda asked, over the clatter of silverware dropping into a kitchen drawer.

"He mentioned nightmares back at the hospital. I should have pressed him on it, but I don't want to push him too hard. He still doesn't trust me." He fell quiet for a moment. "Something strange happened at the airport. I was looking for the claim checks. He knew they were in my wallet, but he hadn't seen me put them there."

"A logical place for them. Or maybe he's psychic," she offered offhand. The top dishwasher rack rolled out, glasses clinking.

Silence. I could imagine Richard's stony glare.

"I'll call UB Medical Center tomorrow," Richard said. "See if I can find a doctor to treat him."

"Then what will you do with him?"

"Nothing. He's here to recover."

"What if he wants to go back to New York?"

"Then he can go."

The dishwasher door closed.

"Bull," Brenda said. "You want him here. You want to turn his life around, remake him in your own image. But he's your brother, not you. For years he's made his own life without you. He'll need to make his own life again. Don't be disappointed when he no longer needs you."

Trust Brenda to be pragmatic.

"Do you want sausage or linguine for dinner?" she asked.

Tiptoeing back to my room, I closed the door. I leaned against it and closed my eyes, unsure what I was feeling. Panic came close.

Yeah, I was different.

I stretched out on the single bed in that shabby little room and thought about what happened.

After six months of unemployment due to downsizing, I'd been about to resume my career as an insurance claims investigator. Until the mugging.

Ten days later, I was four hundred miles away, in Buffalo, New York, moving in with my older half-brother and his live-in-lover. Broke and dependent on their kindness, I was lucky to have somewhere to go.

Dr. Richard Alpert hadn't changed much over the years. Silver now mixed with the dark brown hair around his temples, and in his full mustache. New lines creased his face, but along with the brains, Richard had the looks and, as sole heir, he now possessed the Alpert family fortune.

The flight from LaGuardia to the Buffalo-Niagara International Airport had taken fifty-seven minutes. With my skull-pounding headache, it felt like fifty-seven hours. Brenda Stanley, the pretty black woman behind the security barrier, waited for us. At thirty-four, a year younger than me, Brenda's an old soul whose eyes reflected the depth of her compassion. After a quick kiss and embrace with Richard, she turned to me.

"Jeffy Resnick, you look like shit. You need to gain ten pounds, and I'm just the one to fatten you up."

She was right about the weight loss. Ordinarily I'm just an average guy. Brown hair, brown eyes, and a respectable five-eight in height. More comfortable in denim than a suit and tie. Now my jeans hung from my hips. A sling hid the lightweight summer jacket—the only one Richard could find back at my apartment. A knit cap covered my partially shaved head.

Brenda frowned and, careful not to press against my broken arm, gently hugged me. She stepped back. "You two aren't fighting, are you?"

"Brenda," Richard admonished.

"Well, I know how it is when the old man and the kid get together."

Because of a twelve-year age difference, Richard and I had never been close. Our reunion in the hospital in New York days before had been rocky. We'd called a truce. Now to see if we could live with it.

"We're not fighting," I assured her.

"Good. You two get the luggage," Brenda said. "I'll bring the car around. Those parking lot thieves are gonna hit me up for five bucks. Highway robbery," she muttered, already walking away.

"Come on," Richard said, and started off, following the overhead signs to the baggage carousel.

"Why don't you marry Brenda and make an honest woman of her?" I asked, struggling to keep up.

"I've been trying to for years. She says it would break her mother's heart."

"Marrying a rich, white doctor?"

"It's the white part that's the problem."

Richard had filled me in on the most recent details of their lives. I'd met Brenda only once several years before, when they'd come to Manhattan on business. I liked her right away. They had been colleagues at The American Patient Safety Foundation, a think tank outside of Los Angeles, where Richard evaluated new medical equipment. Brenda was a registered nurse and his assistant, although neither she nor Richard had worked much with patients.

Budget cuts ended both their jobs and they moved back to the old homestead in Buffalo. With the inheritance, Richard didn't need to work and he wasn't sure what he wanted to do next. He seemed quieter, more introspective—if that was possible. I'd have to ask Brenda later.

We arrived at American Airline's baggage carousel already in motion. Suitcases, boxes, golf clubs, and skis slid past the already thinning crowd. Richard patted his pockets.

"They're in your wallet."

"What are?"

"The claim tickets."

A quick look in his wallet revealed the missing claim checks. Richard eyed me suspiciously. "Jeff, you were inside the terminal when the skycap gave them to me."

Was I? I shrugged. "Lucky guess. But you don't need them in the Buffalo airport. C'mon, let's go home. I'd rather barf in familiar surroundings."

***

"And on your right is the Vietnamese grocery store," Richard announced, sounding like a tour guide. He'd been giving a running commentary since we'd pulled out of the airport, while Brenda drove the streets like a native.

"Where's the snow?" I asked. It was, after all, March, and Buffalo is famous for chin-high drifts.

"It melted," Brenda said. "But it'll be back."

Shrunken dirty mounds of the stuff still littered the edges of parking lots and streets. I took in the seemingly endless ribbon of strip malls. "Video stores, head shops. It looks a lot shabbier than I remember."

"That'll change in a heartbeat," Brenda said. Sure enough, we approached the Grover Cleveland Golf Course, crossing the city line into Amherst, the suburb where Richard lived. The neighborhood dated back to the twenties, the houses built and maintained by old money.

Brenda turned right into LeBrun Road, driving slowly, letting me digest the neighborhood's changes. As she pulled into the driveway and parked the car, I got a good look at the house. The three-story brick Tudor looked the epitome of good taste. A gray slate roof and leaded bay windows overlooked the winter-matted carpet of lawn and the privet hedges bordering the sidewalk.

Richard retrieved the luggage from the trunk, letting me soak in the house. My nails dug into my palms.

"Come on inside," he called, sounding jovial.

"Can we go around front for a grand entrance?" I asked, taking my duffel from him.

"Sure." Brenda took out her key, leading the way.

I'd lived in that house during my teens and had never been through the front entrance, always using the back door, feeling like the unwanted guest that I was.

Inside the great oak door, the freshly waxed marble foyer shone, reminding me of a mausoleum. Brenda didn't like housework. They must have engaged a cleaning service. The house had been empty for years since Richard's grandmother's death. And though they'd been there for three months, the furniture in the living room was still shrouded in sheets.

I set the battered duffel on the polished floor and looked up the grand staircase. "Where am I bunking?"

"Grandfather's room," Richard answered.

Tension knotted my gut. "Your grandmother's probably turning over in her grave since Brenda moved in. You put me in the shrine, she'll positively spin."

"It's not a shrine," Brenda said. "I've been redecorating."

"Well, plant me somewhere before I keel over. Those pills don't put much of a dent in these headaches."

I picked up my duffel, forcing myself to follow Brenda up the stairs. Richard brought up the rear. With each step, a weird heaviness expanded through my chest. It was dread, wasn't it? Or maybe I was having a heart attack.

I paused near the top, dizziness sweeping through me. I leaned heavily against the banister.

Richard took the duffel from me. "Are you okay?"

I gave the barest of nods, forcing myself up the last step. My vision dappled, nausea churning inside me.

Brenda stood by the open door, like grande dame Leona Helmsley in one of her old Queen of New York ads.

I paused at the threshold.

Déjà vu.

I'd been there before.

But of course I'd been there. I'd lived in a room down the hall for almost four years.

Anger boiled out of the room before me. A vivid memory struck: Mrs. Alpert's blue eyes blazing, her lips clamped into a thin purple line.

It was her anger.

Panic gripped me. I backed away, nearly crashing into Brenda.

"Jeffy, what's wrong?"

"I can't go in there."

"Jeff?" Richard said.

"I can't stay in there."

Although she'd been dead for years, Old Lady Alpert's lingering presence was attached to her dead husband's bedroom. I tried to step forward, but my legs wouldn't move. A wall of betrayal stopped me.

"Jeff?" Richard repeated, his voice sounding wobbly.

I ignored him. "What about my old room?" I asked Brenda.

"There's no furniture—"

"What about Curtis's room?" Curtis Johnson, Mrs. Alpert's chauffeur, had lived in a room off the butler's pantry.

"We don't have sheets for a single bed," she said.

Hardly able to breathe, I stumbled away, groped for the banister and smacked into the wall, setting off explosions in my broken arm. I nearly tumbled down the stairs, collapsing on the bottom step.

Hunched over, I cradled my arm to my chest, rocking in rhythm with waves of pain. Tears of frustration, anger, and shame burned my eyes.

Richard brushed past me and crouched before me. "Jeff, what's wrong?"

I couldn't look him in the eye.

Brenda sat beside me, her hand resting on my shoulder. "You don't have to go in there, Jeffy."

I couldn't catch my breath—couldn't face her. "I'm sorry, Brenda. You went to a lot of trouble—"

"We'll fix you up with something. I'll hop over to Macy's and get you some sheets and a lamp. They'll be yours—nobody else's—and with no bad vibes attached to them, either," she said as though reading my mind. "Come on. You'll feel better after a nap." She pulled me to my feet.

I couldn't look at Richard—not yet. Brenda took my hand and led me through the house, winding through the kitchen and butler's pantry.

The door to Curtis's room squeaked open, a friendly, welcoming sound. Curtis taught me to play gin rummy and poker. He'd been a good friend to a lonely teenaged boy. The walls of his room were beige, in need of fresh paint. An old iron single bed with a white chenille spread was pushed against one wall. A battered maple dresser sat next to the empty closet. The bathroom housed a narrow shower, toilet, and a small sink. Though it resembled a cheap hotel room, the place embraced me.

I sat on the bed and shrugged out of my sling. Brenda took my jacket and hung it in the closet. I avoided Richard's physician's gaze.

"I don't know what came over me back there. I'm okay, Rich. Really. And the room is fine."

Richard set my duffel down. "Are you sure?"

"Yes," I said, forcing a smile. "This'll do fine. Besides, you said my stuff will be here tomorrow. Now bug off, will you, before I fall on my head and you make me go back to a hospital."

Richard looked ready to do just that, but then dutifully backed away.

Brenda stepped closer, squeezing my hand. "Welcome home." She kissed my cheek, ushered Richard out, and closed the door behind them.

The silence enveloped me.

My chest ached from the strain of suppressing so many emotions—with fear topping the list. I kicked off my shoes and stretched out on the bed, covering my eyes with my good arm.

Richard's ancient, nasty grandmother was dead. She couldn't reach out and grab me from the grave. I squeezed my eyes shut to blot out the memory of her hateful glare.

And then there was the dream….

Chapter Three

The dark figure was back, stalking its prey with a calculated viciousness. Terrified, the white-tailed buck ran blindly across a field of short-cropped hay.

I watched the hunter pull the cross-bow's trigger, let the arrow fly. It hit with a smart thwack, ripping through the deer's heart. The buck ran ten yards before dropping in the snow.

Confident, the hunter strode to the kill, hauled the animal onto its back, and crouched down. The wicked knife flashed in the waning light as the hunter gutted the carcass.

Sensations pummeled me. Startled fear, helplessness, and an overwhelming sense of victory. But the mix of emotions didn't gibe; the deer was goodness crushed, while the stalker radiated a sense of triumph, as though evil had been destroyed, instead of the destroyer snuffing out an innocent life.

I killed time putting away the clothes and toilet articles Richard had packed for me. Running out of things to do, I headed for the kitchen.

Brenda was alone at the counter. I took a breath to steady myself before entering.

She looked up from the sausage she tended on the stove. "Feeling better?"

I pulled out a chair at the table. "Maybe a little shaky. I could sure go for a sugar fix."

In seconds a glass of milk and a plate of chocolate chip cookies materialized before me. I ate three, feeling better with every bite. When I finished, I took the dishes to the dishwasher. Leaning against the counter, I dipped my right hand into my sling, scratching the skin around the top of the cast.

"It itches, huh?"

"I was gonna bend a coat hanger to scratch way down, but figured I'd end up a bloody mess."

She leaned across the counter to a ceramic crock filled with kitchen utensils and grabbed a chopstick. "Try this."

The stick reached my elbow from the top of the cast, and nearly as far from inside my wrist.

"Keep it," she said when I offered it back. "Just don't tell Richard where you got it. He'd tell you horror stories on infection and stuff. Doctors don't understand a patient's needs at all."

"So says the nurse."

"You got it, baby."

"Where is Rich, anyway?"

"In his study, where else?" Was there resignation in her voice?

I tucked the chopstick into my sling and glanced around the kitchen. "It's weird being here again."

"I can imagine." She adjusted the flame under the skillet.

"It looks pretty much the same."

She glanced around the old-fashioned kitchen. "Sort of like living in a museum. Still, maybe we can make it homey. If we decide to stay."

If? That wasn't the impression Richard had given me.

"I was surprised to hear you guys had come back here."

She covered the sausage and moved to the counter to chop celery for the salad. "No more surprised than me. Richard sold the condo and here we are. Most of our stuff is in storage."

I wasn't about to press her on what was obviously a sore subject.

"Rich's grandmother had a housekeeper and other help around the house. Do you do everything yourself?"

"No. A cleaning service comes in once a week. Cooking's fun, but even that's starting to wear thin." She sliced a tomato. "I've heard a few stories about Mrs. Alpert from Richard. I'll bet you could tell some, too." She looked up from her work, a mischievous glint in her eyes.

I took the bait. "Old Mrs. Alpert hated me. I was a constant reminder that Rich's mother was…" I considered my words carefully, "…not her choice of maternal material for her only grandson. The fact that I looked like our mother didn't help."

"So I heard."

"One Halloween a friend in the school's drama club loaned me the lead's costume from *The Headless Horseman*. I got a flashlight and the tall ladder from the garage…."

"You didn't—"

I grinned. "Around midnight I climbed outside her window and tapped on the glass until she woke up."

Brenda laughed. "God, you were a rotten kid."

"She screamed and woke up the whole house. She threatened me with reform school and made Rich come straight home from work at the hospital. I thought he'd kill me."

"What did he do?"

"Lectured me about the old lady's bad heart, but I always thought he was secretly proud of that stunt. Poor Rich, he always had to behave."

She smiled. "It means a lot to him that you're here, you know."

I fell silent, feeling awkward again. Why was it so easy to talk to her and so hard to relate to my own brother?

"Brenda, is something bothering Rich?"

"You catch on fast." She looked thoughtful. "It was harder for him to lose his job than it was for me. He'd worked at the Foundation almost eighteen years."

"I can identify with losing a job."

Her frown deepened. "It's more than just that." She was quiet for a long moment, then forced a smile. "Now that you're here, maybe we'll have some fun."

Did that mean there'd been a distinct lack of fun in their lives? It never occurred to me that Richard could have problems. Or was he living proof that money can't buy happiness?

I glanced down at the counter, noticing a large manila envelope with my name on it. "What's this?"

"I called the local brain injury association. Probably none of the info will apply to you, but it might give you some answers."

Back in my hospital room in New York, I'd been impatient with Dr. Klehr's explanations. The stocky man smelled of stale cigarette smoke and looked like he over-indulged on cheeseburgers and fries. We hadn't built a trusting doctor/patient relationship in the short time I'd known him. He and Richard had been exchanging professional pleasantries when I'd interrupted them.

"Can you just give me the bottom-line diagnosis?"

Nonplused, Klehr turned. "Mr. Resnick, you suffered a classic coup-contrecoup injury."

"Which means?"

"The injury occurred in a part of the brain opposite the point of impact. The injured tissue resulted from changes in pressure which traveled through your brain. Very simply, you've suffered some brain damage."

Klehr kept talking, but I didn't hear a word.

Brain damage? How could something like that have happened to me—be that wrong with me?

Dr. Klehr paused; I picked up the sudden silence.

"It sounds a lot more ominous than it really is," Richard said.

I'd looked at him in disbelief.

"You were lucky," Klehr continued. "The swelling was minimal. You haven't suffered seizures."

Yeah, that made me feel lots better. I couldn't get past that phrase "brain damage." Did that mean I'd never balance a checkbook again, or was I likely to go out and kill for kicks?

"What does that mean?"

"Memory loss, as you've already experienced. And you might notice a loss of emotional control. One of my patients cries at McDonald's commercials. You might get angry easily."

"Is this permanent?"

"Perhaps, but not necessarily."

"When will I know? How can I tell? When can I go back to work?"

He shrugged. "I wouldn't push it. An injury like yours takes time to heal."

"Weeks? Months?"

"We'll talk later. You've got enough to think about for now."

With a few parting words, Klehr left us alone. Richard chattered on, refusing to even consider worst-case scenarios.

I'd eyed him with distrust. He'd already known. Klehr explaining the extent of my injuries to me had been just an afterthought.

Was paranoia a side effect of a bruised brain?

I fingered the envelope, hefting its bulk. "Thanks, Brenda. I'll look it over later."

Much later.

***

After dinner, Brenda played barber, trying to even out my hair. It would do until it grew back in.

Later, with Richard safely holed up in his study and Brenda off to her meditation class, I sat alone in the spacious, well-lit dining room. The large manila envelope Brenda had given me sat before me on the polished oak table. The return address read: Brain Injury Association of Buffalo. That in itself sounded life-altering. Swallowing my fear, I tore open the flap, spilling the contents across the table.

Most of the brochures heralded the virtues of long-term care for family members suffering severe head injuries or strokes. Only a family with Richard's financial resources or fantastic insurance could afford those medical wonder-palaces.

Was Brenda trying to shame me into counting my blessings? No, she wasn't petty. Besides, thoughts like that painted me as a prime example of the self-centered personality changes indicated in one of the booklets.

After skimming the material, I was grateful I'd emerged from the mugging mostly intact. Still, two punks had taken my life—maybe my independence—from me. So what if it wasn't much of a life. It was a comfortable rut that, with the new job, just might've gotten better. The possibility that I might never again work in any kind of meaningful profession terrified me.

A little blue booklet caught my eye: a 'How-to-Handle' manual for families of the brain injured. As I skimmed it, the things that seemed to apply to me practically jumped off the page. Yes, I was irritable and overly emotional, as proved by my refusal to stay in the room Brenda had fixed for me. I was afraid of being permanently dependent on Richard. What if he tired of me? Where else could I go? How would I live until I could work again?

Sorting the pamphlets according to size, I set them in orderly piles and deposited them back in the envelope.

Aha, denial! Just as the manual predicted.

No, damn it. I had a choice—to just sit back and let life happen to me, or take my best shot at rebuilding a life. It would never be the same, but maybe that was for the best. The past five years held few memories worth taking out and polishing fondly anyway.

I stood too quickly, my vision suddenly dimming.

A spiraling abyss sucked me in—sickening me, shattering my new-found resolve.

The deer hung before my wide-awake eyes, swaying slightly in some unfelt breeze, its tawny hair catching the incandescent light from the lone bulb that lit the room. The cloying smell of sweet blood filled my nostrils. Then a voice in slow-mo repeated like a mantra, "Youprickyouprickyouprick—"

The chandelier's bright light was back.

I swallowed, nearly falling into my chair again. The muscles in my arms quivered in reaction. Moon-shaped grooves marred my palms where my fingernails had dug in.

If the dream could overtake me during my waking hours, I could be doomed to a life in the places described in the pamphlets I'd so cavalierly discarded only moments before.

Chapter Four

A white Bekins truck pulled up in front of the house at ten the next morning—a bright moment on an overcast day in mid-March. Before we left Manhattan, Richard had arranged for everything I owned to be packed and delivered. The arrival of my personal possessions was a tangible connection to my former life. A life where I'd been in control, responsible.

Brenda and I watched from inside the house as Richard directed the men to unload the cartons in the sun porch.

"I'll make coffee," Brenda offered, as Richard handed me the inventory.

I rested the pages on my cast, flipping through them with my good hand. Clothes, books, dishes, linens, various pieces of furniture. Obviously missing were items of quick cash value: my stereo equipment, binoculars, TV, personal computer, Nikon—and my gun. The guys who'd mugged me had taken my wallet and keys, then ransacked my place. The cops found fingerprints, but nothing would come of it in a city where scores of muggings or robberies happened daily.

My excitement vanished as I, a former insurance investigator, remembered I'd stupidly let my renter's insurance lapse. I'd had to let a lot lapse during six months of unemployment. Goddamn downsizing.

Richard watched me carefully, his eyes filled with pity. "Why don't we get that coffee?"

He clapped me on the shoulder and headed for the kitchen. I didn't follow. Instead, I waited until the last of the cartons were off the truck and the men started unloading the furniture.

My stomach lurched as two men in overalls struggled down the ramp with the shabby couch. Spray-painted Day-Glo orange stripes crisscrossed the back and cushions. The dressers, end tables, and every other piece of furniture were likewise marked. The movers stacked it all in the garage, save for the bed. I had that moved to Curtis's—my—room. Maybe steel wool and elbow grease would remove the paint.

The movers finished in record time. Richard appeared at the appropriate moment, opened his wallet and gave them a generous tip; then the big empty truck lumbered back toward Main Street.

"Do you want help unpacking?"

"Uh...maybe Brenda could give me a hand." I didn't want Richard to see all my crap—and that's just what it was—in the glaring light of day.

"Are you sure you won't have some lunch?" Brenda asked as she approached.

I shook my head, trying to pull loose the tape on the top of a box of underwear. Her fingernails were longer than mine and she easily worked one underneath, pulling the tape off. I opened the top, looked inside, and closed it again.

"What do you want me to do?" she asked.

"Restacking the boxes would be a big help. A lot of this should go right into the garage. The kitchen stuff—things like that. Maybe Rich can help us with those."

She reached for another carton and started working on the tape. "I think we have some box cutters in the kitchen junk drawer."

"Don't bother with that. It goes outside."

Brenda examined the unmarked sides of the box.

"It's the silverware," I explained.

She shook the box and was rewarded with the faint clink of knives, forks, and spoons. "How did you know?"

I shrugged, distracted, and attacked the tape on a box from the next stack. It came off, the top lifted—good, my bathroom stuff. The disposable razor from the hospital nearly cost me a pint of blood each morning.

Despite her size, Brenda had the strength of a longshoreman. She opened a box filled with towels. Wrapped among them were several framed photos, slightly bent and scratched, the glass missing, presumably smashed. One of them bore a trace of orange paint—Shelley, in happier times. I hadn't seen the photos in two years. Why had I held onto so many of my dead wife's possessions—still unable to part with them?

Brenda and I didn't talk much during the sorting ordeal. She'd hold up an item and I'd give her a yea or a nay. It wasn't long before the nay pile stretched three times higher than the yea pile. Luckily the garbage men would be around the next day.

Later, feeling weak and sick, I watched Brenda make my bed before she retreated. Napping on my own comfortable mattress gave me my first taste of security since the mugging.

When Brenda woke me for dinner, I staggered from my room like a drunk. Red wine accompanied the entree—corned beef, cabbage, and potatoes.

"What's the occasion?" I asked, stifling a yawn.

"St. Patrick's Day. Besides, it beats burgers any day," Brenda said, placing a huge helping on my plate. "I bought Irish soda bread to go with it. Dig in."

She served Richard and herself and they started eating. I poked at the cabbage with my fork.

Richard swallowed. "Is something wrong?"

"The night I got mugged, I'd been with friends at a pub." I pushed a chunk of potato around. "Nobody came to the hospital. Nobody called."

They stopped in mid-bite, glancing at each other. "Maybe they didn't know." Brenda reached over, clasped my hand. "You'll make new friends, hon."

I couldn't muster a reply.

They spent the rest of the evening cooking up plans to paint my room, trying to cheer me. I should have felt flattered, but the attention only depressed me. I wanted to be left alone.

By the time I said good-night, they looked more exhausted than I felt.

Darkness shrouded the cold, dank room, the atmosphere charged with dread. Fatigue weighed me down so I could hardly stand. Something nudged me from the side. I turned, hands outstretched to stop its gentle swaying motion. My fingers probed the softness, tried to curl into the lingering warmth, but the hairs were too short.

Hairs?

I fumbled in the darkness until encountering a sticky warmth—blood? Its sickly sweetness turned my stomach. Startled, I backed away until I could make out the still form in the shadowy room. A ten-point buck, dressed out—its genitals and internal organs discarded—and hanging to bleed. Its lifeless, glassy eyes bored into my own.

The back of my throat closed. I couldn't breathe, couldn't scream, as a wave of horror and triumph engulfed me, obliterating all rationality and what was left of my sense of self.

I awoke, nausea nearly choking me, stumbled to the bathroom and vomited. I sat, heaving, my head threatening to explode. Spent, I collapsed onto the cold linoleum. This had been no dream. This time I had stood alongside the dead buck, felt and smelled its death tang.

I couldn't stop trembling. I couldn't tell Richard something was terribly wrong. Not yet. Not when I had no understanding of what was happening to me.

***

Friday morning the three of us drove to one of those big franchise hardware stores to choose paint and buy brushes and drop cloths.

It felt good to be out among normal people, people who weren't sick—who hadn't had their brains bruised. There seemed to be a lot of them out and about. Retired men, women with small children, young adults choosing wallpaper, paint, vacuum cleaners.... Didn't any of these people work?

While Richard and Brenda debated the merits of natural versus synthetic paintbrush bristles, I strolled down aisles filled with build-it-yourself furniture, nails, screws, garden tools, ceramic tiles, and everything in between, until I landed in front of the rope and chain display. Synthetic and natural fibers came in various lengths and widths, prepackaged or ready to cut on large spools.

I crouched by a spool of Manila rope, half-inch width, by twelve hundred feet. The hemp felt splintery between my fingers. So…familiar. When I pressed it to my nose, the image of an old, dank, wooden shed or garage filled my mind.

In my dream the hanging deer had swung in a gentle, easy arc, but the light had come from a different angle….

I turned the rope over and over in my hand.

"Can I help you, sir?" asked an acne-scarred young man.

I dropped the rope and straightened. "No. Just looking, thanks."

As he walked away, I turned my attention back to the spool. The rope meant something, but I wasn't sure what.

"Oh, there you are!" Brenda said, coming up behind me. "Which one of these color chips do you like best?"

We started painting after lunch, though my broken arm kept me from doing much. After several hours of bad jokes and insults, the room looked better. Though Richard and Brenda said they couldn't smell paint fumes, I could—and it aggravated my headache, so that night I ended up sleeping on the living room couch.

My mind stayed on a circular track. What the hell was happening inside my head? The dreams and hallucinations were too real.

Then it came to me. A brain tumor. Caused by the severe blow to my skull.

What else could it be?

I stole into Richard's study, flipped through his medical texts until I found the symptoms. Yes, I suffered from drowsiness, lethargy, personality changes, impaired mental faculties.

I was going to die.

Awake half the night with worry, I wondered if I should draw up a will…then I remembered I had nothing of value to leave to anyone.

Richard and Brenda slept late the next morning. Brenda later told me it was a Saturday tradition for them to have a huge breakfast and skip lunch. Richard and I sat at the kitchen table while she made toast, then chopped vegetables and grated cheese for omelets. I waited for a conversational opening, but Richard buried his nose in the newspaper.

"Uh, Rich. I—I haven't been sleeping well."

He barely looked up from the sports section. "You're in a new place. Give yourself a few days." He continued reading an article on the Buffalo Sabres, absently grabbing a slice of toast from his plate.

"No…I mean, not since the mugging."

Richard looked up again, swallowing. "I can't prescribe something to help you sleep. I won't."

"That's not what I mean. What could make a person not sleep?"

He shrugged. "Anything weighing on your mind."

"Could someone with this kind of brain injury get a…a tumor?"

He folded the newspaper, setting it aside. "First of all, it would take months before you'd even notice symptoms.

I looked at your x-rays and believe me, I called in the best for consultation. It's my professional opinion that you're going to be just fine. What you need now is rest, and time to recover."

I took a deep breath. Richard was a good doctor. But....

"Then I don't understand it, because I don't feel the same any more. I'm...different."

"Of course you are; you suffered a trauma—" Brenda piped in.

I shook my head. "No. I don't mean the mugging. I mean *I'm* different."

Hadn't Richard said the same thing?

He pushed the paper aside, his eyes narrowing. "How?"

"I've been having these weird dreams."

Brenda looked up from her cutting board, but said nothing.

"The nightmare you mentioned in the hospital?" Richard asked.

"Yeah, that's when it started. I keep dreaming about a deer."

"A deer?" he repeated.

I forced myself to continue. "It's a bow kill, and it's hanging in a garage to bleed. But there're all these weird emotions tied to it: like triumph, and horror. Every time I dream about it, the emotions get stronger. One time it'll be a perverse sense of satisfaction, and then it'll be absolute terror."

Richard frowned. "I'm not a psychiatrist, but it could just be a reaction to being mugged. You were a victim, like the deer. You could've died."

"But that's not the worst of it. It's not just a dream any more. I've been having—" God. No going back once I said the word: "Hallucinations. When I'm wide awake."

Richard's stare went right through me.

"I might see it, feel it, smell it," I continued. "I live it. This thing—this deer—is hanging. In a garage. It's slit from stem to stern. And its eyes—"

I closed my own, remembering that nauseating, oppressive dread. "They're open and they're glassy and they're just so…dead. And whoever killed the buck feels tremendous triumph."

Richard's eyes were wide. There was definitely no turning back now.

"I hear these words, over and over: 'You prick, you goddamn prick,' and…." I let the words trail off.

"My God," Brenda muttered, dropping her paring knife into the sink.

Richard squirmed. Maybe the thought of a brain tumor wasn't so farfetched after all. "I don't have any pull at UB Med Center, but I have a few friends here in town I can call. If it'll make you feel better, we could—"

"No!" Brenda cried, diving for the newspaper. She thumbed through the thick pile, searching. "Didn't you see the headline? Weren't you listening to the news?" she said, her eyes wild. She spread the front page of *The Buffalo News* out across the kitchen table before us. The banner screamed: Businessman Found Dead in Bizarre Ritual Killing.

"What about it?" Richard asked.

"I heard it on the radio earlier. This guy was found in his own garage—eviscerated, hanging like a deer to bleed!"

Anxiety churned my gut.

"They've got no clues—nothing to go on," she said.

"What's that got to do with—?"

"Don't you think it's the least bit unusual that Jeffy has a dream—?"

"Don't start with that psychic stuff again," Richard warned her. "He just said it was a deer."

I wasn't listening.

Psychic?

Pure, blind panic hit me.

I wanted to puke.

The image was back.

I rested my head in my good hand, covering my eyes.

A man, a hemp rope cutting into his throat, swayed as though in a gentle breeze, his neck was twisted at an odd angle. Heavyset, about fifty-five or sixty, and naked. Rolls of fat hung like melted wax around his middle.

The rustle of paper stopped. "Jeffy?" Brenda pointed to a coarse-screened, head-and-shoulders photo of a man dressed in a business suit.

"That's him!"

"Who?" Richard asked.

"The man I saw hanging."

"You said it was a deer."

"No, I just saw him!"

"You had a vision, just now?" Brenda asked, excited.

I nodded. A vision. Much more acceptable than the product of a tumor, a nightmare, or a hallucination.

Brenda settled the paper on the table between us and started reading aloud. "Local businessman Matthew J. Sumner was found hanged Friday in his garage. The grisly scene...."

My fears about tumors instantly vanished. The murder took place somewhere else. In a field. I knew it had. I'd seen it. The deer must have represented this guy. My mind had given me a vision of something I could understand.

How the hell did it do that?

Why the hell did it do that?

And why had it started more than a week before the murder took place—when I was in a city more than four hundred miles away?

I skimmed through the story, desperate to find out the facts. But the police were giving out few details.

According to the ME, the Bison Bank vice president had been slain sometime late Thursday afternoon or early evening. Sumner was found hanging from a rafter in his own garage; his Cadillac Seville was missing. He'd been killed somewhere else, as evidenced by the marks on the body and lack of blood at the scene. His wife found him late Friday afternoon. She'd been visiting friends in Palm Beach the previous week. Funeral services were to be announced later.

I looked up. Richard's grim gaze remained fixed on me.

"This explains everything!"

"Calm down," he said.

"But I've got to do something about this."

"What?" He exploded from his chair to pace the floor. "What do you think you could possibly do?"

"I…don't know. But don't you see, it means I'm not crazy. I'm not—"

It didn't mean I wasn't crazy. I sounded crazy even to myself. Smoothing the newsprint, I stared at the photo of the dead man. He looked familiar.

Richard took his seat, his right hand methodically massaging his clenched left fist. "Jeff," he began, his tone reasonable—his physician's voice. "A head injury like yours can cause all kinds of problems. Make you believe all kinds of things."

"You mean I can't trust what I think? What I know?"

"It's something you should consider."

I continued to stare at the news story, read it over and over again, my conviction growing deeper with each new reading.

The tension in that kitchen was nearly unbearable. Finally Richard headed for the door.

"Where are you going?" Brenda asked.

"For a walk, before I say something we'll all regret."

Brenda watched him go and looked after him for a long moment. Then she took out the plastic wrap and started putting away the chopped vegetables.

"You believe me, don't you, Brenda?"

She nodded solemnly.

"What the hell is wrong with him? Does he think I want to know this stuff?"

She didn't answer.

"He's my brother—not my keeper."

"I think he's trying to be your friend." She sat down across the table from me and reached for my hand. "He's worried about you. He'll tell me I'm encouraging you in a fantasy."

"It's not a fantasy."

I looked down at the damnably familiar, yet unfamiliar, face of the murder victim. I considered asking her to help me, but what could she do? And I couldn't put her in a position where she'd have to choose sides.

And what if Richard was right? Was my willingness to accept the possibility of possessing psychic abilities proof that my thinking was skewed?

At that moment, I didn't know what to believe.

When Richard returned an hour later, his cheeks pink from the cold, Brenda and I sat at the kitchen table, listening to the radio's hourly newscast.

"Any new developments?" he asked.

I shook my head, wanting nothing more than to escape his scrutiny, yet defiant enough to stay. Ignoring us, he poured himself a cup of coffee, then disappeared into another part of the house.

The day dragged.

I sat on the sheet-shrouded couch and tuned in to Buffalo's all-news TV station, obsessed with finding out more details on the murder, yet little was forthcoming.

Richard kept circling back to the living room, watching me. Did he think he'd made a mistake bringing me home to Buffalo instead of committing me to a mental institution?

It was almost four when, despite the strain between us, Richard suggested we take a walk and I accepted. I needed to think, plan. Walking would also help me rebuild my strength, something I'd need if I was going to be involved in this thing—this investigation. As far as I was concerned, it was a done deal. Now, how the hell was I going to do it?

We started out at a leisurely pace, heading south. The trees were stark silhouettes against the white, late afternoon sky. Despite its proximity to Main Street, the neighborhood was quiet. It was hard to believe the student ghetto around the University's South Campus was only a mile or so away.

Eventually Richard broke the silence.

"How're you feeling?"

Not the question I'd expected. "So far, so good."

"You've only been out of the hospital for three days. You need time to heal."

I met his hard blue eyes. "I'm okay, Rich."

He paused, his gaze piercing me. "No, you're not. You've had a serious injury. I don't want you to push yourself too hard."

The set of his mouth gave away the depth of his concern. He exhaled a puff of breath. "Come on. Let's go home."

We didn't talk about the murder any more that day.

I hit the rack early but ended up staring at the ceiling for hours. The visions had stopped, replaced by unanswerable questions that circled around my head, keeping me from sleep. The biggest one was: why?

Why was this happening to me?

Chapter Five

The sun hadn't come up yet, but I'd already showered and dressed by the time the Sunday morning paper was delivered. I spread it across the kitchen table, grateful to study it in solitude. As I'd hoped, the top story was still the Sumner killing. Sumner was survived by his wife, Claudia, and three grown children, Rob, Diane, and Michael. There'd be no public viewing. Private interment would take place Monday morning.

Noises from another part of the house caught my attention. I decided to make myself scarce while Richard and Brenda breakfasted.

Back in my room, I sat on the edge of my bed. With eyes closed, I cleared my mind. The man in the newspaper picture was older than the face imprinted on my brain. Could I have met him? It seemed likely. But not in New York. It had to be years ago, when I still lived in Buffalo.

The newspaper said he'd worked for Bison Bank for over twenty-five years. Did I meet him at an early point in his career? I'd never had a bank account until I'd joined the Army. Maybe it had nothing to do with banking.

I thought back to my first summer job at Benson's car wash. I'd wipe down sleek Corvettes and angular Cadillacs, wishing for a junker of my own. Was Sumner a customer? I remembered the job, but not the people associated with it.

Damned frustrating, those holes in my memory.

Another summer I'd flipped burgers at some fast-food joint—anything to keep me out of the house and away from the crotchety old Alperts.

I let it go. Eventually it would come to me.

Despite my faulty memory, the bright morning invigorated me. On a whim, I decided to reconnect with the rest of the house, avoiding the kitchen and Richard and Brenda. It was soon obvious that only three rooms were in use: the kitchen, the study, and—I assumed—the master bedroom suite upstairs. Like the living room, much of the furniture in the other rooms was still shrouded in sheets.

Slipping into Richard's study gave me my first feeling of homecoming. The old leather-bound books had always attracted me. The dark-paneled walls lent a feeling of security. Years ago, Richard's wizened grandfather used to live behind the big mahogany desk. Sometimes we'd sit at opposite ends of the room and read the old man's books. He'd smoke his pipe, the sweet tang of tobacco filling my nostrils. The grandfather clock ticked loudly in the empty silence. Mr. Alpert and I weren't friends, but we weren't exactly enemies, either. I couldn't imagine Richard taking his place in the oversized, burgundy leather chair.

A set of the **Encyclopedia Britannica** filled the shelves behind the desk—the last edition available in hardcover, by their copyright date. Richard must've brought them from California. I pulled out a volume, intending to look up psychic phenomena, and quickly decided against it, shoving the heavy book back into the slot from where I'd plucked it.

It might be better to bungle my way through the discovery process with no preconceived expectations—or limitations.

Could I make it work for me? I picked up objects in the room, trying to zero in on previous owners, previous history.

A heavy glass paperweight was cold in my palm. The delicate wings of the butterfly encased inside seemed poised for flight, but I felt nothing odd or sinister. Likewise with the dust-free pipes and stand on the polished desk, sitting there as though waiting for old Mr. Alpert to strike a match.

But something had happened to me when I'd first entered the house. I'd been hit with cold dread and horror. Melodramatic, maybe, but that's what I'd felt. It was time to make another visit to the upstairs bedroom.

My sneakered feet squeaked on the polished floor as I rounded the corner. The hallway seemed to extend miles ahead of me, like a camera trick in an old Hitchcock film. The staircase, when I reached it, also seemed to have telescoped in length.

I swallowed and took a step. Okay. I was fine. On the second step, the sensation of alarm hit me and I knew something waited for me in old Mr. Alpert's room. I forced myself to continue upward and tried to think logically. Could the house be haunted? Oh yeah, the skeptic in me taunted, that made a lot of sense. Just as reasonable as visions of dead men and deer.

My legs were lead by the time I topped the stairs. The closed bedroom door taunted me. *Come on, chicken boy, face the worst.*

I took another step forward, but panic made me turn, and I nearly stumble in my haste to get the hell away. I wasn't up to facing whatever lingered in that room.

Not yet.

I grabbed my jacket from the hall closet and opened the front door. Outside the air was cold, and the blue sky was clear and incredibly normal. I felt calmer as I poked at the matted leaves around the shrubbery. Tulip spikes and the tips of daffodils protruded through the crusty dirt. The remnants of a hibernating garden lined the property. I followed it around to the side of the house and the driveway, facing the garage. Only drilled holes remained where a backboard had once been. When I was a kid, Richard and I had sometimes played one-on-one. Maybe it was still in the garage.

I went inside the large three-car structure, what had once been a carriage house, rediscovering the apartment above. The door opened with a painful creak. I tramped through the dusty galley kitchen, dining area, two bedrooms, living room, and small bath. I vaguely remembered a married couple—the housekeeper and gardener—living there when I was a teenager. My nose wrinkled in the musty, cobwebbed rooms. Old furniture, cartons of dusty books, gardening equipment, and other junk were still stored there.

A smile tugged at my lips, the seed of an idea forming, but it was too soon to hit Richard with any new requests.

Downstairs in the garage's empty bay, I studied the clutter of my own furniture and boxes. Some kind of organization was definitely needed. I pawed through the cartons. My old business cards surfaced first. I'd kept two sets, one with the company address, fax and phone numbers, and e-mail address, the other a calling card. Figuring I could still use those, I stuffed them into my coat pocket, along with a tape measure and a couple of half-used spiral notepads.

My next find was my old analog watch, with one of those Twist-O-Flex bands. I slipped it onto my right wrist, since the cast covered my left and ended at the knuckle line. I'd reset it once I got inside. I also found my out-of-date passport, grabbed an old pay stub, a canceled check, a bank statement—anything with my name and address on it, in case I needed to prove who I was.

I'd once considered being a private eye, investigating the field after my four-year hitch in the service—I had even earned an associate degree in criminal justice. But New York's mandatory three-year apprenticeship had been a major turnoff. I'd had enough of being someone's lackey in the Army. Plus private investigators' lives are damned boring. I couldn't see myself on endless stake-outs, spying on adulterous spouses, looking for runaway kids, or repossessing cars from people down on their luck.

The insurance field is boring, too, and guarantees mountains of paperwork. But the pay and the hours are definitely better, the income reliable, and the work inherently safer. Too many people own guns these days—and use them. Through my work in insurance, I'd known a couple of freelance PIs in the city. Quarterly taxes left them cash-starved with no benefits.

No, thank you.

I foraged until I came across my good suit, a shirt, and my lined raincoat—enough for me to get started. Closing the side door behind me, I headed for the house. Inside, I found my family tucked away in Richard's study.

"Uh, Brenda, where's the iron?"

She looked up from her book. "In the laundry room. Do you need some help?"

"No, thanks."

The dungeon laundry room was in the same place as in years before, although the appliances were brand new and top of the line. I tossed the clothes on the washer and awkwardly set up the ironing board. While trying my best to iron out the wrinkles, I ended up scorching my pants cuff. Moments later, I looked up to find Brenda standing in the doorway.

"I can do it."

"Oh, I know you can—when you have two good hands. But right now, you've only got one."

I let her take over. Now that my investigator's training was coming back, I wanted to look my best—trustworthy—when I interviewed witnesses. Having that goal made me feel whole again.

Richard showed up as Brenda handed me the freshly ironed dress shirt. I eased it onto a hanger, catching sight of his disapproving stare.

"Why don't you just say it?" I challenged.

"Oh, now you're reading my mind, too?"

"It doesn't take a mind reader to tell what you're thinking," Brenda muttered. She turned off the iron, set it on the washer to cool, stowed the ironing board, and stole out of the basement, leaving me alone with a man itching for a fight.

"Jeff, you're not well."

"I'm not sick, either."

"No, but you are recovering from a serious head injury. I think you should just slow down."

"I'm not exactly running around."

He eyed the suit. "No, but you can't just show up at the church and—"

"Now who's a mind reader?"

"I read the newspaper, too. You plan to go to the funeral."

"If I can get in. How else can I meet Sumner's family and friends?"

"Jeff, you can't just barge in, interfere with people's lives—"

"And I just can't sit around contemplating my navel twenty-four hours a day, either."

He followed me upstairs and into the kitchen. I laid the suit and shirt across one of the chairs, and sat down, not daring to look him in the eye. "You don't believe me."

Richard took the chair across from me. "I don't know what to believe."

"I don't know how to make you understand. It's like a nightmare, only it doesn't stop when I wake. I have no proof, just a strong feeling that what I know is true."

"Jeff, is it possible you're twisting the facts to support a delusion?"

"I knew that man was dead. I felt his death. Now I've got to prove to myself I'm not some kind of lunatic. But I can't. Not until I see the place. Not until I talk with the people who knew him. Not until I can put all the pieces together."

Richard stared at the table. "Okay. Then let's prove—or disprove—it together. Let me help."

I considered his offer. Was he only placating me? It didn't matter.

"Okay."

"Where do we start?" he asked.

"Tomorrow. At the funeral."

Chapter Six

Richard and I showed up at Christ the King Roman Catholic Church half an hour before the funeral Mass was due to start. We had to park on a side street three blocks away.

Days earlier, I had realized I was picking up the feelings of my fellow passengers on the plane. Yet, even with that experience under my belt, I wasn't prepared for the prickling sensations that radiated from the mob outside the church.

The murmur of voices vibrated through me like the buzz of a hive. The press of close-packed bodies seethed with a myriad of emotions. I penetrated the gathering, swallowing down sudden panic. Fists clenched, I gulped deep breaths of air so cold it scorched my lungs. Richard's eyes bore into mine. Was he waiting for me to freak?

I wouldn't give him the satisfaction.

Two policemen stood atop the church steps, keeping the horde of newsmen, photographers, and rubberneckers at bay. Private security had been hired, too. A man in a black overcoat checked the names of the mourners against a list on a clipboard. We didn't bother to check in with him—he wasn't about to let us in. With nothing much to see, I wandered through the crowd, eavesdropping.

Refused entry, a man spoke to a woman in low tones. "Matt and I were friends for over twenty years."

"There's no point hanging around," she said. "Maybe United Way will have a memorial service for him." She took the man's hand and led him away.

I scanned the crowd and seemed to recognize one of the reporters, who stood with a still photographer, but I couldn't place the face. I turned aside—didn't want him to see me in case he recognized me, knowing I'd feel foolish when I couldn't come up with his name.

Behind me a clique of young people stood huddled in a knot. "Do you think Diane even knows we're here?" someone asked.

"I've never been turned away from a funeral before."

"Like you've been to a million funerals," her friend said.

A white hearse turned the corner, waiting for the crowd to part so it could stop by the church's side entrance. I had to stand on tiptoe to watch as the funeral director and his associates escorted the bronze casket into the church. Where were the official pallbearers? This wasn't like any funeral I'd ever seen or been part of.

Richard glanced at his watch. "Mass will be at least an hour long. You don't want to wait until it's over, do you?"

"I don't know yet."

I should have done something. I should have asked people questions, but I didn't know who to single out—or what to ask. If the people standing outside the church weren't on the official attendees list, were they close enough to the victim to have known anything that would help me?

Richard stuffed his hands into his pockets. "Jeff, your cheeks are getting chapped. Your lips are practically blue. If I didn't know better, I'd diagnose you as cyanotic."

"Don't you mean hypothermic?"

"Come on, let's go home."

I looked back at the crowd. He was right. Coming to the church had been a complete waste of time. Besides, Richard looked frozen.

"You win, old man. We may as well go before the cold settles in those arthritic bones of yours." Truth was, I felt lousy, but I wasn't about to admit it to him.

As we neared the edge of the crowd, I broke through a ribbon of triumph—the same as I'd felt in the dreams.

I whirled and scanned the blur of faces around me.

The killer was there. Somewhere.

I shouldered my way through the mourners, heading for the barred oak doors, but my inner radar had already switched off.

Organ music blared from loudspeakers mounted on the side of the building. Pain lanced my brain as I rushed forward, searching for someone I couldn't even recognize.

The big doors banged shut behind a dark-coated figure. I dove for the brass handles, and a thick hand grabbed my wrist.

"Hold it, pal," the officer said sharply. "Unless your name's on the list—"

"I've got to get in there! It's an emergency!"

"What kind of emergency?"

I stared into the cop's skeptical face. "Who just went in?"

He glared at me.

"Please! It's important."

A hand grasped my shoulder. I spun around.

Richard. His eyes mirrored mine—an unspoken panic. "What is it?" he shouted over the music.

"The killer's inside."

He stared at me in disbelief. "Who?"

"I don't know."

I'd felt that presence, that gloating sense of triumph. Then the contact was gone—camouflaged by the mass of people still assembled on the steps, the trampled grass, and sidewalk.

***

Back in my room, I downed a couple of the little pink tablets and crawled onto my bed. My plan for the rest of the day was to keep a low profile. Richard hadn't said a word to me on the short ride home. Maybe that was good. Then again, I didn't like being condescended to either.

I closed my eyes and prayed for sleep, but my mind refused to rest. I couldn't stop thinking about what I'd experienced at the church.

If I was going to work on this case—and that's just what it had become to me—I'd have to approach it like one of my insurance investigations.

I got up, found a sheet of paper, and filled both sides, writing down everything I knew. Then, armed with a pair of scissors, I trucked out to the garage and the recycling bin to retrieve every newspaper article on the murder. I dumped the brain injury pamphlets in the trash, stashed the articles in the big Kraft envelope, and deposited it in my bottom dresser drawer.

A fat phone book sat on the kitchen counter. I grabbed it and settled at the table to make a list of numbers. First up was the public library. Richard hadn't offered me the use of his computer, and the Internet, and I wasn't about to ask. I'd never been a sportsman, so I knew next to nothing about deer hunting. I figured I'd better educate myself on the subject with some good old-fashioned books.

I called the Department of Motor Vehicles about a replacement copy of my driver's license. With no ID, I was a nonperson. I waded through the recording for what seemed like forever before speaking to a human being. Contrary to DMV lore, she was courteous and helpful. Good thing I'd gathered up so much potential ID. I'd need it to get a duplicate of my license.

Next on the agenda, I had to get started on the legwork before the trail got too cold. It was time to face the enemy.

Richard was in his study, parked behind the big desk, reading. He'd changed out of his mourning attire to yet another cashmere sweater and dark slacks, every inch the man of leisure.

I cleared my throat, feeling like a sixteen-year-old with a hot date and no wheels. "I need to borrow your car."

"Are you crazy? You've admitted having hallucinations, your arm is in a cast, making you a danger on the road, and you want to borrow *my* car?"

"How else can I get around?"

"Don't you think you've had enough excitement for one day?"

"Come on, Rich. I'm a good driver."

"I'll take you wherever you want to go." His expression darkened in irritation. "And where would that be?"

"The cemetery. Then Orchard Park."

"To do what?"

I shifted my weight from one foot to the other. "To talk to people."

"About Sumner? Why?"

"To find out who killed him, of course."

"How are you going to pass yourself off?"

"What's wrong with saying what I am—an insurance investigator." This was beginning to feel like an interrogation.

"Because you're not working for anyone at the moment. And misrepresenting yourself will cause trouble with the law."

I stepped closer to his desk. "What do you suggest I do? I know things about this case."

"It's not your case!"

"What if the police never find who killed Sumner? Look, I have to do something. I know things about the situation—things I can't explain knowing. Am I just supposed to sit around and do nothing while a murderer runs free?"

Richard's voice possessed that deadly, practiced calm so characteristic of the medical profession. "Tomorrow we'll go to UB and we'll—"

"No, damn it. And stop patronizing me. I don't need a psychiatrist and I resent the implication. I just need—"

Need what? It sounded crazy even to me.

"Just let me borrow the car."

"No."

"Then tell me how to get to Forest Lawn Cemetery from here and I'll walk."

Richard sighed. "I told you, I will drive you anywhere you want to go."

I grabbed him by the arm. "Then let's go."

***

Sometimes it seems like just about everything in the city of Buffalo is either directly on or just off of Main Street, and

Forest Lawn was no exception. We didn't talk much during the ride. I wasn't yet adept at judging my brother's moods. Was he truly angry or just annoyed?

We drove through the cemetery's back gate, and Richard slowed the car to the posted ten miles per hour down the narrow roadway. The tombstones stood stoically against the brisk March wind.

"Where to?"

I had no idea, hoping the funny feeling inside would guide me. "Take the next left," I bluffed.

Richard complied and we meandered down the single lane of asphalt, following the twists and turns through the older, more historical sections and then into the newer parts of the cemetery.

"This is hopeless, Jeff. How're you ever going to find Sumner's grave among all the thousands here?"

"Well, for one thing it'll be fresh."

Richard glared at me.

We came to another crossroad and I pointed to the right. Richard slowed the car as a lone woman dressed in dark sweats jogged toward us. Solidly built, with pink cheeks, she looked like she'd been out in the cold for some time. Richard muttered something under his breath, and I kept a sharp lookout, hoping I'd know Sumner's grave when I saw it. Instead, that weird feeling vibrated through my gut.

"There!"

A mound of freshly-dug earth marred a snowy hillock. The crowds had gone. No headstone marked the grave, just the disturbed ground and several sprays of frozen roses and carnations. Richard stopped the car and I got out. I walked up the slight hill, looked around, but saw no one. Good. I bowed my head and closed my eyes, concentrating—waiting for that funny feeling that had been guiding me, for some fragment of intuition to drift into my consciousness.

Nothing.

I frowned. The niggling feeling that had drawn me here was still strong, but whatever compelled me to come had not been the victim.

I heard the hum of a power window. "Well?" Richard yelled.

"I don't know."

The window went back up and Richard revved the engine.

I ignored him and walked around the grave. Many sets of footprints marred the light dusting of snow, but only one stood out in the freshly smoothed-over dirt. I stared at the prints. Someone had stood here for several minutes, judging from the depth of the prints. Someone in jogging shoes. I compared the print to my own foot and frowned. It was just about the same size. Lots of people jogged through the cemetery, so who would've noticed if one of them stopped at one particular grave for an inordinate period of time on a cold, wintry day? It was probably one of the mourners—maybe even the one I'd tried to follow into the church. Too bad we hadn't hung around until after the Mass. But then how would I have known what to look for?

I closed my eyes, concentrating again, hoping to suck up some residual…feeling, sensation—*something*.

I got nothing.

I looked down at the prints and placed my own feet on either side of them. I closed my eyes, my right hand balling into a fist. Yeah. Now I was getting something. Triumph? Yes, the person who'd stood here felt triumph over the dead man—the same emotion I'd experienced in the dream. Already I trusted these feelings...hunches?...as real.

And there was more.

Dread.

But dread didn't adequately describe it. Overwhelming despair made my eyes tear. The quack in New York had said a head injury fucked with your mind, and now I couldn't tell if the emotions bombarding me were my own or the dead guy's.

Suddenly something I'd felt so sure about only seconds before seemed insubstantial when I tried to analyze it rationally.

None of this was rational. But that didn't mean it wasn't real.

I took a breath and gathered my resolve. Okay, so what was I experiencing? I closed my eyes and thought about it. Cold, calculating, bean-counter mentality at work.

Thoughts that were not my own crept into my mind, lingering like a fog: *Youprickyouprickyouprickyouprickyouprick.*

Nothing new in that.

Try again.

Eyes closed, breathing steady, a myriad of sensations seeped into me. My fists clenched in righteous indignation. *That fucking prick had it coming to him.*

Then came the images.

Twilight.
Sumner's eyes bugged in terror.
Heart pounding.
A heavy object—a brick?—slammed into his temple. He went down.

Darkness.
The scene shifted. A baseball bat came at me—split my skull. I staggered, nearly fell.

"Jeff!" Richard's voice shattered the spell. "Are you okay?"

My hands shook. I stared at a trampled pink carnation. I'd learn nothing more here.

"Yeah."

Shoving my right hand in my coat pocket, I started for the car, grateful to get back to its warmth.

Richard studied me, waiting. "Well?"

"Well, what? I don't know anything I didn't know before. Being here's just convinced me that I need to look further."

"And where's that, Orchard Park?"

I flexed the fingers on my left hand as far as the cast allowed, desperate to warm them. "I have to start somewhere. Maybe his neighbors can tell me something."

Richard put the car in gear and headed for the exit. "I should've brought a book."

"You could just loan me the car," I said, struggling to fasten my seat belt.

"No, next time I'll bring a book."

***

The temperature had dropped ten degrees and dusk had fallen by the time I finished canvassing Sumner's upper middle-class neighborhood on Forest Drive, right in the Village of Orchard Park. No one answered my knock at quite a few of the houses. I didn't bother with Sumner's own house, which looked forlorn, although there were lights on inside the gray clapboard colonial.

Flashing my old ID had done the trick. None of the neighbors questioned my being there, but I learned virtually nothing. Sumner may have been gregarious in his public life, but the family didn't mix with the neighbors. They'd lived in the house for six years and kept to themselves. Sumner's children were grown, and no one paid much attention to the middle-aged couple's comings and goings. And besides, I was informed on more than one occasion, my potential witnesses had already spoken with the police and had told them everything they did—or didn't—know.

Though I'd given my card—with Richard's phone number scribbled on the back—to a few of the neighbors, I didn't expect to get any calls.

I opened the car door, climbed in, and again fumbled with the seat belt.

Richard squinted at me. "Any luck?"

"Looks like I froze my balls off for nothing." I glanced at the fuel gauge. "And you wasted a tank of gas."

Richard stared at me. "You look like shit. How do you feel?"

"Like shit."

Richard shook his head and put the car in gear as I sank back into the leather seat. The pounding in my head left me feeling vaguely nauseated.

"When did you start swearing? I don't remember you swearing so much," I said.

"You drove me to it. Now what?"

"I'll have to rethink my approach." Sumner was a businessman...a banker. "I'll have to talk to the people he worked with. But I can't use my insurance ID there, in case someone decides to check up on me." I glanced at my brother. "Where do you bank?"

He turned the corner. "All over. Grandmother didn't believe in keeping all her money in one bank—in case it failed. She got burned during the Depression. I never bothered to consolidate her holdings."

"Then you must have accounts at Bison Bank, right?"

"Yes," he answered warily, giving me a sidelong glance.

"How much—if you don't mind my asking."

Richard shrugged, his eyes on the road. "A couple million."

"Million? You inherited millions?"

Richard nodded, his eyes still intent on the road. "Of course."

I should've remembered that little fact. That I didn't was another example of my faulty memory. "How many?"

"Last year I paid taxes on the income from fifty-five million." He tore his gaze from the road. "Anything else you want to know?"

"If you've got that kind of money, what the hell are you doing living in Buffalo?"

"Because LA wasn't working out any more."

I sank back into the leather seat, ignoring the edge that had crept into his voice. "I guess someone with a few million on deposit wouldn't have any trouble getting me inside the bank. I mean behind the scenes, where Sumner worked. Right?"

"I can try," he said, resigned. He glanced at the dashboard clock. "I'll make some calls in the morning."

"Thanks. Could we hit the Amherst library on the way home? I kind of reserved some books in your name. Which reminds me, I need to go to the DMV and get an official ID. Then maybe the library will let me take out my own books."

He sighed. "No problem."

Meanwhile, dollar signs danced through my mind. I considered the hospital bill, the plane fare, and the movers. Richard could well afford to help me. So far there'd been no strings attached to the money he'd spent bailing me out, but how the hell would I ever repay him?

***

After dinner, I escaped to my room to do a little research. Despite the lingering headache, I forced myself to study the library books, and it wasn't long before I knew more than I cared to about bow hunting and field dressing game. From the description in the newspaper, that's exactly what had happened to Matthew J. Sumner.

The body had been shot through the back with an arrow. I didn't have to imagine the consequences of such an injury. My scrambled brains served me a graphic display of frothy blood spraying across stark, white snow. And the photos of gutted deer helped harden me to the vision of Sumner swinging from the rafter, his body looking more like a slab of meat than a human being.

While the newspapers hadn't mentioned mutilation—the severed and missing genitalia—it would be consistent with what I'd read about butchering Bambi. A bullet in the back of the skull would've been a quicker, neater death.

Settling back on the mattress, I did a little educated guesswork. Sumner was probably shot with a three-blade razor-sharp broadhead, carbon-shaft arrow from a compound bow. At least that's what the book's author recommended for greatest efficiency, speed, and accuracy.

I could get a look at the autopsy report at the medical examiner's office. In the case of violent deaths, such records are usually made public. The death certificate was also public record, but I didn't need to see that either.

I spread the clippings across the floor and bed and read and reread them all. The newspaper's speculation that the killer was some kind of crazed woodsman seriously differed from my own impression.

Most of the articles had been written by a Samuel Nielsen. Was he the familiar-looking guy at the church? I'd known a Sam Nielsen in high school. Could he be the same person? If so, it might be worth making his acquaintance again.

I picked up all the clippings and put them back in the envelope, then attacked the stack of parapsychology books. They weren't enlightening. Most of the information seemed anecdotal, rather than scientific. No wonder Richard remained skeptical. Besides, nothing seemed to apply to me.

All this investigating exhausted me. Would Richard be secretly pleased if I pushed myself beyond my physical limits and ended up back in the hospital?

To forestall that, I hit the sack early, but even after I'd turned out the light my mind continued working. I kept thinking about the weapon. I could call or visit all the archery supply stores and ranges listed in the phone book, but who said the killer had to buy locally?

I fell asleep to images of gutted deer and men, their dead, glassy stares focused on nothing.

Chapter Seven

The DMV was crowded when we arrived the next morning. Richard handed over the California title to register his car in New York State, and got his picture taken for a driver's license. After we filled out our respective paperwork, Richard flashed his identification and the poor patient—me—was given preferential treatment and escorted directly to the cashier. Did the good doctor get the same treatment in five-star restaurants?

They promised the licenses would arrive in about a month. Good old New York State bureaucracy. In the meantime, we were both given temporary paper licenses; mine looked lonely in my empty new wallet. According to the law I could drive again. Now if only I had a car.

Next step, the bank.

Being a large depositor had its benefits. Once inside Bison Bank, we sailed past security and headed for the executive offices. We stepped off the elevator on the tenth floor and Richard led the way to the reception desk. I followed, soaking up the layout as I went. Richard was learning. He'd made the appointment for lunchtime so I could snoop.

We paused in front of the receptionist, a skinny young woman with brassy blonde hair and a winning smile.

"Good morning. I'm Richard Alpert. I have a twelve-thirty appointment with Ron Myers."

The receptionist rose from her desk. "Right this way."

"Is there a drinking fountain around here?" I asked.

"Just down the hall, to the left."

"Thanks. I'll catch up with you, Rich." She nodded at me and led Richard away; I headed in the opposite direction.

Being lunchtime, the place was relatively empty. It didn't take long to find Sumner's old office. I could see by the frosted glass flanking the door that the light was on inside. I tested the handle. Unlocked. A quick glance around proved no one was in sight. I stepped inside.

The blinds were raised, giving a panoramic view of the city—not that Buffalo in March is all that attractive. Craning my neck, I could see the ice on Lake Erie shining in the distance. The peons in the tellers' cubes on the main floor would covet such an office. Cherry hardwood furniture buffed to perfection. Someone had already started packing Sumner's personal items into a sturdy cardboard carton.

I sat in the plush swivel chair, settling my good arm along the armrest, closed my eyes, and breathed deeply. I'd hoped to glean some insight into the man, but instead a memory from long ago surfaced, and I suddenly realized where I'd met Matthew John Sumner.

It was my mother's birthday, and the blue pressed-glass bud vase was the most beautiful thing my ten-year-old eyes had ever seen. I must've stood in Woolworth's gift section, staring at it, for more than five minutes, my attention completely focused on the $3.99 price tag. I had precisely $1.14 in my jeans pocket. I looked around and saw no one nearby. Slipping the vase under my jacket, I headed for the exit.

"I saw what you did."

My heart froze as I looked up into the stern face of the tall, hefty man above me. I'd never stolen anything in my life and now, on my first foray into crime, I'd been caught.

The man crouched down to my level, holding out his hand. Without a word, I handed over the vase.

"Why would a boy like you want something like this?"

I couldn't look him in the eye. "It's…it's my mother's birthday tomorrow. I don't have enough money."

"I see." He straightened. "Wait for me outside."

Being a frightened child, I did just what the adult told me to do. Minutes later, he came out of the store.

"Young man, you know it's wrong to steal."

Hot tears of shame stung my eyes as I nodded solemnly.

He handed me a paper sack. "Here. You give this to your mother on her birthday. But you have to promise me you'll never steal again."

Gaze focused on my feet, I nodded. He patted my shoulder. Without a word, I turned and ran all the back to our apartment.

I never stole again.

My mother had cherished that cheap piece of glass, but I couldn't look at it without feeling shame over how I'd obtained it.

Sitting in Sumner's chair, I pondered my debt to him. Our fleeting encounter some twenty-six years before had made one hell of an impression on my psyche. What else could explain the visions of his murder?

I left the whys for another time and forced my thoughts back to the present, studying Sumner's desk.

His Rolodex was fat and well-worn. Taking out my little spiral notebook, I jotted down any phone number that looked promising, including those of his children. The desk itself was already pretty much cleared, and the computer was switched off. Aside from the fact it was illegal, it was also unlikely I could tap into the bank's databases to check Sumner's files, and would he keep anything personal on his work computer anyway?

Several photos decorated the walls behind the couch: Sumner's wife, children, him receiving an award.

I sat back in the comfortable chair, grasping the arms, waiting for that funny feeling to come over me.

Nothing.

The file cabinets were locked, but the desk drawers weren't. I sifted through them and found the requisite pens, pencils, and other office supplies, along with a battery-operated razor, a toothbrush, and a tube of minty-fresh toothpaste.

The credenza's cabinets housed an assortment of trophies, paperweights, and award placards. Buried in back was a framed drawing of rainbows and colored balloons, crudely done in marking pens, like something a child might do.

I grasped the frame with my good hand and studied it. There was nothing special about it or the drawing, which looked to be done on heavy card stock. On impulse, I fumbled to remove it from the frame and found that it wasn't just a drawing, but a folded, handmade, one-of-a-kind invitation.

Come to a first birthday party for Jackie, January tenth, seven o'clock, three years before.

No address listed, so whoever sent it assumed Sumner knew where the party was to be held. But who was Jackie? It wouldn't be too hard to check the birth records for that date. I hoped the child had been born in the Buffalo area. I jotted down the date.

I slid the invitation back behind the glass, turned it over, and continued to study it. It must have meant a lot to Sumner, or why would he have framed it? Then again, why wasn't it on display any more? Why was it hidden?

Suddenly that queasy, unsettling feeling coursed through me. My fingers convulsed around the wooden frame as intuition flashed:

Nightfall.
Chest constricted. Throat closed on stifled sobs.
No!No!No!No!No!No!
A venom-filled voice—slow, draggy: "Get back in the car."
Rising panic.
Closed in. Dark. An unspeakable horror—

I dropped the frame as though burned, shattering the vision. Gasping for breath, I pulled at my suddenly too-tight collar. I sat back, wiped my damp right palm on my pants, willing myself to relax.

Fear. Got that in spades.

Raw terror. The world destroyed in a way that nothing could ever make right.

I frowned. These little nuggets of psychic insight were graphic, but not particularly helpful. At least not yet.

Unwilling to touch the frame again, I used a ruler to push it back into the cabinet, slamming the door.

"Can I help you?" An attractive redhead stood in the open doorway, her mouth pursed in annoyance. "This is Mr. Sumner's office. Unless you have a damn good reason to be here, I'm calling security."

"Sorry. I—" My mind raced, and in an instant I decided to tell the truth. "I'm waiting for my brother. He's meeting with Ron Myers. I didn't feel well, and the door was open, so I ducked in."

She looked at me with suspicion. Okay, so it wasn't the whole truth.

"I'll leave." I quickly rose and the room suddenly lurched around me. I grabbed at the file cabinet for balance, and the woman hurried to my side, grasping my elbow to steady me.

"Are you okay?"

"I need to sit." She led me over to the low couch. "This is embarrassing. I thought I was better, and now...."

She took in my lopsided haircut. "Were you in an accident?"

"Mugged. In New York."

"That happened to my sister Irene a couple of years ago."

Now that I had her sympathy, I might just get some information out of her. "My name's Jeff. Jeff Resnick."

"Maggie Brennan," she said, and offered her hand.

My fingers clasped hers, my gaze captivated by her deep blue eyes.

She wasn't what you'd call beautiful. Fine lines around her eyes hinted at years of smiles. The color of her eyebrows didn't match her auburn hair, cut in an out-of-date Dorothy Hamill kind of style, but it suited her. Her dark business suit made her look confident and competent.

"Umm. My hand?" she prompted.

Like a fool, I still clasped it.

"Oh, sorry." I pulled back my hand; the palm had gone moist again. "Did you say this was Mr. Sumner's office? Wasn't he the guy in the paper who—"

"Yes. Isn't it awful? I'm packing his personal things for his family."

"Did you know him?"

"Everybody around here knew Matt."

"I'll bet the bank practically had to shut down with everybody going to the funeral?"

"Not as many went as you'd think. The rules for time off are strict. A bunch of managers went, but nobody I know would waste a vacation day for a bastard like him." At my startled reaction, she quickly explained. "I can't believe I said that. I just meant that he could be hard to get along with—a perfectionist who expected daily miracles from his subordinates. But nobody deserves to die like that."

I indicated the photos on the wall. "He must've been devoted to his family."

"Devoted to bailing them out of trouble."

"Oh?"

She didn't elaborate. In the pictures, Sumner's children appeared to range in age from fifteen to thirty. No little tykes.

"Did he have grandchildren?"

"Not that I know of. His oldest son got married this past fall."

Okay. The invitation writer could've been Sumner's girlfriend, with a baby—his baby? If so, someone had to know about them. The question was who? But the woman standing over me wasn't the person to ask.

"Are you feeling better now? I can show you to Ron's office."

"If you wouldn't mind." I rose to my feet.

She closed the door behind us. As she led the way down the corridor, I noticed how nicely her skirt fit. She paused at a door, knocked, then poked her head inside. "Ron? I think I found your errant visitor." She held the door open for me.

"Thanks for your help." I offered her my hand again. She took it and I held on.

I liked Maggie Brennan.

***

Richard's bank advisor was more interested in talking about trust funds and estate planning than his murdered colleague. At my every attempt to change the subject, he'd jump in with some dull fact concerning loopholes and tax benefits Richard could enjoy if he'd entrust all his money to good old Ron. I didn't much care for the man, and I suspected Richard felt the same, although he gave me a few sharp glances when Myers's patience stretched thin. Eventually, I gave up.

From the bank we crossed the street and headed for The Extra Point, a sports bar lavishly decorated with local sports memorabilia—especially the Buffalo Bills. I'd lived away from Buffalo for a long time, and although they didn't win nearly enough, I still cheered for the team. I'd forgotten what they meant, not only to the city but to all of western New York. Didn't Richard say he had season tickets?

Seated under one of former quarterback Jim Kelly's jerseys, we ordered lunch, and my physician watchdog brother actually allowed me to have a non-alcoholic beer. I could only look longingly at his glass of the genuine article.

Over lunch, I filled Richard in on what I'd learned, leaving out my memory of meeting Sumner. He didn't seem impressed.

"I guess you didn't expect all this when you invited me to stay with you."

Richard set down his glass. "No."

"I thought things would be a little less hectic, too."

"Except for this psychic stuff, I expected you to be a lot more belligerent."

"Belligerent? You mean like when I was a kid?"

Richard blinked. "Why would you say that?"

"It seemed to me I was constantly in trouble. How about when I bugged your grandmother?"

He almost smiled. "Maybe. But getting you to talk was as hard then as it is now. In some ways, you haven't changed at all."

I didn't know how to reply to that.

"Belligerent, huh? Like those poor souls in the brain-injury rehab hospitals?"

"Jeff, I don't think you understand how serious your injuries are."

The chip on my shoulder grew bigger and heavier. "I'm not sick."

"Look, don't get angry—"

"I'm not angry. I'm adjusting—slowly—to everything that's happened to me. Let me do it my own way, okay?"

"Okay." He drained his glass. "Where do you want to go next?"

"The public library. I want to check the birth announcements in old copies of the newspaper."

"Has it occurred to you that you're going over the same ground as the police? What do you think you'll find that they won't?"

"I don't think they're looking into the same things I am. Besides, they're not likely to tell me what they know. By the same token, I'm not prepared to tell them what I know. At least not yet. Hell, Rich, I practically witnessed the murder."

He looked around, then lowered his voice. "Then go to the police."

"How can I convince them when I can't even convince you? And what am I supposed to tell them? 'Uh, I have a funny feeling about this murder.' They'd send me to a psych ward. Uh-uh, I can't talk to the cops until I have some kind of hard evidence. Now can we pay the check and get out of here?"

It took longer to find another parking space than to drive the two blocks or so to Buffalo's main library. True to his word, Richard brought his own book along. A heavy medical tome with a long, boring title. He sat and read for two hours while I gave myself one hell of a skull-pounding headache and a good case of vertigo whipping through the old microfilmed records.

I ended up checking two months' worth of newspapers for the names of children born the week before and after the January tenth date. I found three possibilities. John Patrick Ryan, Jacqueline Tamara Prystowski, and J. Matthew Walker. I hoped one of them was the Jackie I was looking for. Otherwise, I didn't know what I'd do.

I wrote down the names and addresses. Two of the announcements listed both mother's and father's names. The Walker kid's did not. Not that unusual these days.

Closing my notebook, I found my very bored brother and had him take me home.

Nausea kept me from eating dinner. I took two of the pink tablets and waited for sleep, the only haven of relief from the headache.

The memory of my only meeting with Sumner and the terror and horror I'd felt when touching that invitation kept circling through my aching head. I was onto something.

I was going to find Matt Sumner's killer.

Chapter Eight

I awoke late the next morning—perfect timing for calling Sumner's widow. I checked on Richard's availability first. Funny, my brother didn't seem to have a lot to occupy his days.

According to the newspapers, Claudia Sumner had been visiting friends in Florida at the time of the murder. Since she'd found the body, I wanted to talk with her while her memories were still fresh. When we spoke, I'd mentioned my former employer's name, carefully avoiding the fact that I no longer worked for them. Without that ploy, she'd never grant me an interview. Our appointment was set for one. In the meantime I hauled out the phone book. I wasted an hour trying to call the parents of the kids born January tenth. No luck.

Next I called the funeral home. No, they would not discuss the church guest list or any arrangements on the Sumner funeral. Instead, they referred me to their attorney.

Richard and I hit the road about twelve forty, giving us a twenty-minute window to get across town. We hadn't gone far when I pulled down the visor, inspecting my hair in the attached mirror. Maybe I should've asked Brenda to concoct some kind of bandage to cover my unusual haircut.

I'd explained to Mrs. Sumner about my...accident...so that when she saw me she wouldn't wonder what kind of nut case had come to visit her.

"What's the matter?" Richard asked, glancing over at me. "Are you nervous?"

I flipped the visor back into place. "Yes."

"Why? You interviewed six or eight people on Monday."

"Yes, but none of them was the victim's wife, and none of them found the guy hanging in the garage."

"Just what do you hope to learn?"

"I don't know. What I really want to do is get in that garage—"

"To see where it all happened?"

"Not the murder. Just the aftermath."

Richard made no further comment. He still didn't believe me. The logical part of me didn't blame him. The brain-damaged part of me was annoyed as hell.

"Look, after we finish here, I'll take you where I go and we'll get you a haircut," he said. "Maybe they can trim it up so that you don't look like a—"

"Psycho?"

Richard smiled. "Nonconformist."

"Thanks," I said, meaning it. The visor came down for another look. Definitely nonconformist.

Sumner's house appeared no different than it had before, except for the uniformed security guard posted at the bottom of the driveway. Mrs. Sumner had found it necessary to hire someone to keep the hounding press at bay.

Richard waited in the car while I checked in with the guard, who waved me through.

I walked past a late-model Altima. Mrs. Sumner's or a friend's? After climbing the concrete steps, I thumped the door's brass knocker. Seconds later it opened a few inches on a chain, as though she'd been waiting behind it. All I could see were a pair of sharp, gray, schoolteacher eyes.

"Mrs. Sumner, I'm Jeffrey Resnick. I called earlier."

"Can I see some identification?"

"Of course." My old insurance ID worked again.

She scrutinized the card. "I must confess I don't recall Matt having a policy with your company."

Then again, maybe it hadn't.

Just when I thought she'd slam the door in my face, she released the chain.

"May I take your coat?"

I waved off her offer and followed her into the house.

Claudia Sumner was an attractive woman of about fifty. Her short, permed hair was colored an appropriately light shade of brown, and her face was virtually unlined. Either she never had a care in the world or knew a skilled plastic surgeon. Petite and trim, she wore a beige cashmere sweater, matching slacks, and comfortable-looking leather pumps. I bet she never sat down in front of the TV with a bag of nachos and a pot of salsa.

She seemed to be alone in the house, with no friends or relatives in attendance for emotional support. In fact, her attitude was very businesslike, not at all the bereaved widow I'd expected to find.

She settled on one end of the overstuffed couch in the living room, motioning me into a chintz-covered wing chair. The furnishings stressed comfort. Antiques and expensive-looking porcelain figurines graced the shelves and tabletops.

Several framed photographs were scattered throughout the room, but they seemed to be exclusively of her children. No books or magazines, and no lingering aura of Matt Sumner, either.

"Are you working with the police?" she asked.

"I expect to share some information soon," I said, hoping I'd effectively evaded her question. "I'm grateful you agreed to talk with me. It must've been unpleasant to find your husband."

"I really don't care to discuss it."

"Can you give me some background on Mr. Sumner? His interests, perhaps?"

"The newspaper account was quite thorough. He was active in The United Way. In fact, he served as last year's campaign chairman. Matt truly cared about people."

Oh yeah?

"Did he have any enemies?"

She hesitated. "Not that I'm aware of. Matt was…could be," she amended, "very charming."

"Is it possible he might have had financial problems?"

"If you mean blackmail, no."

Her perfectly calm statement took me by surprise, but then she'd probably already been over this with the police. And if she was willing to be blunt, there was no reason for me to dance around certain issues.

"Did he have a girlfriend?"

The widow was not surprised by the question.

"Perhaps. He worked late a lot these past few years. I suspected he might be having an affair…but I guess I didn't want to know for sure. We lived a quiet, comfortable life."

Her cold gaze made me shudder.

"Did he ever mention Jackie?"

She blinked. "I'm sorry?"

"I ran across the name in conversation with someone at the bank."

"I know of no one called Jackie."

I got the feeling she wasn't exactly being candid with me. But then, I hadn't really expected her to.

"When did you last speak with your husband?"

She sighed. "Last Sunday evening. He said he had meetings all day Friday and I should take a cab home from the airport."

"Did you find him immediately?"

"No. I was home for about an hour. I'd unpacked my suitcase and thought I'd go to the grocery store. That's when I found him." She looked away, her eyes filling with tears. I wasn't sure if it was from grief or revulsion. I pretended to jot down a note, giving her a moment to collect herself.

"Who was the last family member to actually see your husband alive?"

She cleared her throat. "Me, I suppose."

"None of the children visited while you were gone?"

"I don't think so. Michael is in school is in Erie, Pennsylvania. Diane and Rob haven't lived at home for several years."

Which confirmed what the neighbors had said. "Do they live in the Buffalo area?"

"Yes, Rob does. Diane…." Her gaze narrowed. "Why do you want to know?"

"I'd like to speak with them, too."

She sat straighter in her chair. "I would prefer that you didn't, although I suppose there's no way I can stop you."

I changed my line of questioning. "Did your husband hunt?"

"Never. He could never kill anything."

Maybe not, but as a bank VP he'd had the power to ruin someone's financial life with the stroke of a pen.

"Did he have any other hobbies?"

"He golfed. He was quite good at it, too. He was to head a tournament in June. A benefit for one of his causes. At the moment, I can't think which one."

"That's quite understandable. How tall was your husband?"

She looked at me as though the question was ridiculous, but answered it anyway. "Five-eleven."

"And his weight?"

"I don't know. Maybe two hundred and ten pounds."

I jotted it down. "I'm curious; there were no calling hours at the funeral home. Was there a reason?"

She pursed her lips, her eyes narrowing. "You *are* curious."

I was afraid she was going to refuse to answer the question. Then she sighed. "To be perfectly honest, Mr. Resnick, I want to put this whole unpleasant ordeal behind me. You can understand that, can't you?"

"What about his friends? Wouldn't they—?"

"I telephoned those people I deemed necessary. The church was full of our friends and his colleagues. There was no need to subject my family to a media circus."

A plausible explanation, yet how could she know of all the people whose lives her husband had touched? How many would have showed up to pay their respects, people who were genuinely sorry to hear of his passing?

I tried a different tack. "I understand you'll be selling the house."

She called my bluff without blinking. "As a matter of fact, a real estate agent will be here later today."

She really was eager to move on.

And then my mind went completely blank. I couldn't think of a single question that didn't involve finding the body and the entire grotesque situation. She picked up on my hesitation.

"I'm curious about the insurance policy, Mr. Resnick. Can you tell me how much it's worth, and who the beneficiary is?"

Every muscle in my body tensed. "I'm just the investigator, ma'am. I'm not at liberty to discuss such matters."

"But surely you have an idea? Can you give me the policy number, or the date it was issued—anything to help me trace it?"

"I'd be glad to get back to you on that."

Her gaze was steely. "I'd appreciate it."

It was time for me to get to the real reason for my visit. I pretended to consult my notes, posing the question as though it had no real relevance. "May I have a look in the garage?"

Again her eyes narrowed in irritation. "I suppose. Although there's really not much to see. I had a cleaning service come through this morning." She got up from her seat.

I followed her through the house to a utility area. She pointed to the door. "I hope you'll forgive me if I don't follow you."

"I quite understand." Besides, I didn't need a companion for this phase of my investigation.

The double garage was cold, the only illumination coming through the frosted glass on the door to the back yard. I flipped the light switch to my left and a lone bulb lit the empty space I was already familiar with. I'd heard crime scenes, especially where a homicide had been committed, are filled with an aura of anger, desperation, and pain. This place was no different, but Sumner's murder had not been committed here.

With no cars parked inside, the garage seemed cavernous and unnaturally tidy. The police had probably gone over every inch of it in search of evidence. Still, Claudia Sumner had been correct; there was little out of the ordinary to see.

Matching bicycles hung from laminated hooks near built-in storage cupboards. No gardening equipment cluttered walls or shelves, yet I suspected that under the remaining snow the yard was perfectly landscaped and attended to by experts. A garage door opener stood silent vigil over the room. The newspaper stressed there'd been no forced entry. The killer could've used the remote to get in. No mention was made of it being found.

Except for rope marks on the joist where the body had hung, and a brown stain on the concrete, now scrubbed almost clean, there was nothing of interest to see. But the lack of visible evidence didn't mean there was nothing for me to experience.

Closing my eyes, I tried to relax, to open myself to whatever psychic pipeline was feeding me information. In seconds that sick wave of anger and triumph filled me. Fear and a strong sense of revulsion swirled in the mix, but the queasy feelings I received were not from Matt Sumner. From the start, I'd gotten next to nothing from the victim.

Clearing my mind of distracting thoughts, I concentrated, trying to conjure up the image of the deer running across a barren field.

Instead, the vision that appeared before my mind's eye wasn't the tawny buck, but a naked, middle-aged man in bare feet, stumbling across the snow, racing for his life. The pronounced thwack of the arrow leaving the bow jarred me. Sumner's anguished grunt of shock as the arrow connected with its target left my stomach reeling.

The vision winked out. I let go of the breath I hadn't realized I'd been holding. It wasn't so bad now. I was already learning to distance myself from the other's fear—to experience it, but not make it my own.

But maybe that wasn't the way to go. Maybe I needed to delve deeper, immerse myself in that sense of terror to truly understand what the witness had seen, felt. Yet my own sense of fear—survival instinct—kicked in. Someone had literally butchered Sumner, while another terrified someone had watched. I wasn't willing to experience that first-hand.

I remembered that god-awful feeling of despair I'd gotten from the invitation in Sumner's office, muted now that I had no catalyst to reignite it. What was it…?

And then it hit me: Betrayal. Stark, maddening betrayal. Why?

Because the same thing could happen to me.

A thrill of horror washed through me, leaving me clammy with cold sweat.

Needing to do something, I dragged a stepladder across the floor. Once positioned, I climbed. Hauling my left arm and cast onto the joist helped me maintain balance as I reached the top rung. Looking down at the beam, I examined the rope marks. Minute fibers, embedded in the wood, still remained.

I shut my eyes, rubbed the fibers between my thumb and forefinger, making it a Zen experience to become one with the rope. Stupid as it sounds, it worked. The killer's rope was old. It had sat coiled in a dark dank place for a long time before being used—the same impression I'd gotten at the hardware store.

Replacing the ladder against the wall, I pulled out my tape measure and checked the height of the joist from the floor. Sumner was five-eleven, so his feet would've hung anywhere from six to ten inches above the ground.

I had no need of the police photographs. With only a little effort I could see a mental picture of every detail. I forced myself to confront the image of Sumner, hanging.

He looked so...dead, his skin tone a flat, bluish white. Yet his opened, unseeing, cloudy eyes seemed to follow me. I looked away.

Heart pounding, I circled the phantom body. Sumner's neck had been broken, probably after death. The rope around his throat had rubbed against his ears and dug a visible groove into his skin. A bruise darkened his left temple, and I found myself absently touching my own, where the baseball bat had collided with bone. We'd both been attacked by a right-handed assailant.

The entrance wound in Sumner's back was puckered and blood-blackened. My gaze traveled the length of his body; his genitals were missing, all right. Had the killer kept them as a souvenir?

Sumner's chest cavity was empty, his sternum gouged and every organ gone. The ribs were totally exposed, reminding me of a rack of ribs ready for the barbecue. Bruises marred his shins, and both feet were crisscrossed with cuts, probably received while attempting to escape his murderer across the crusted snow. The bottoms of his heels showed scrape marks, and dust particles clung to his back and buttocks. Had the cops found skin cells on the floor where he'd been dragged across the concrete?

I looked away and the vision was gone. The bloodstained floor drew my attention. The murderer would have to be pretty strong to haul Sumner around, transferring him from the crime scene to his home, hoisting his rigor-stiffened body to hang, and all without leaving a single fingerprint or other clue. There was cruelty in leaving the body for his wife to discover, as though the killer were rubbing her nose in the crime.

The light bulb was missing from the garage door opener. After the murderer strung up the body, he'd probably wanted the garage dark when he opened it to leave. Had the lamppost been on that night? Surely someone had to have seen *something*.

I turned. Claudia Sumner stood behind the storm door. She'd waited for me—watched me—her arms crossed over her chest in annoyance.

"Thank you for your help, Mrs. Sumner."

She opened the door and reached to touch the garage door control. With a hum and a jerk, the door slowly rose.

"Good day, Mr. Resnick."

As I headed down the driveway, the door started its slow, steady descent.

I was glad to reach the car and Richard's friendly face.

Chapter Nine

"The pot's empty."

Brenda and I looked over our sections of newspaper to stare at Richard.

He turned his coffee cup over to show us it, too, was empty.

"I made supper," Brenda said, her voice flat. "And washed up."

"I can't get the filters out with only one set of fingers," I said, showing him the limited range of motion my cast allowed.

Richard scowled, let out a breath, and got up to make a fresh pot.

Evenings had fallen into a pattern. After dinner, we'd sit around the kitchen table drinking coffee and reading the paper which we hadn't gotten to in the morning. Later, I'd try to stay out of Richard's and Brenda's way. Things seemed strained between them, and no doubt my presence was a contributing factor. Then, for as long as I could concentrate, I'd reread the newspaper articles on the murder, or maybe glance at the library books, before going to bed. A boring lifestyle, but I wasn't up to much more.

The coffeemaker chugged and Richard took his seat again.

The front doorbell rang.

The various sections of the papers were lowered again as we glared at one another for long seconds, daring each other to answer it.

It rang again.

Without a word, Richard pushed back his chair and disappeared down the hall.

I turned my attention back to the financial page and felt sorry for old Rich. It seemed like he was doing all the fetching and carrying lately. Did a man as well-educated and professionally situated as my brother feel degraded by such trivial matters?

Brenda got up to pour herself another cup of coffee as Richard returned with grumpy-looking man in tow.

"Jeff, this is Detective Carl Hayden. He'd like to speak with you." He didn't bother to introduce the plainclothes cop to Brenda.

My stomach suddenly knotted. I recognized the name from the newspaper articles. Hayden was the lead investigator on the Sumner murder. He was big—about six-four, maybe two hundred and fifty pounds—and he looked pissed. With a crew-cut and heavy-featured, he reminded me of a slow-moving freight train—deadly, and not to be underestimated.

"Detective Hayden." I offered my hand, which he ignored.

"Would you like some coffee?" Brenda asked politely, but her body language belied her solicitous words as she eyed the cop with suspicion.

Hayden shook his head, all business, turning his full attention to me. "Sir, Mrs. Claudia Sumner called Orchard

Park Police Department this afternoon. She said you'd paid her a visit."

"Yes, sir." I figured I'd better be as polite as he was. After all, I didn't want to be charged with obstructing justice, if that's what he ultimately had in mind.

"You told her you were an insurance investigator. But she doesn't deal with The Travelers."

Neither did I, any more.

"Sir, do you now work for Travelers?"

I carefully considered my answer. "No."

"Have you ever worked for that company?"

"Yes."

"In Buffalo?"

"No."

I hoped my curt answers wouldn't bug him, but I didn't want to give him any more information than I had to.

"Mr. Resnick, just what is your interest in Mr. Sumner's death?"

"How did you track me down?"

"The DMV. Mrs. Sumner's security guard took down the license plate number of the car you arrived in. Please answer my question." He was polite but firm.

"Like everybody else, I just want to know what happened to him."

"Everybody else doesn't pass themselves off as insurance investigators and visit the bereaved," Hayden said evenly. "Where were you on Thursday evening between the hours of four and eight o'clock?"

"You can't suspect Jeff," Brenda cried.

"I was with them." I nodded toward Richard and Brenda. "All day, all evening."

"We can vouch for him," Richard added. "Detective Hayden—" He turned the cop aside and spoke quietly. "My brother recently suffered a rather severe head injury, which can account for—"

"Richard!" Just what I needed—to be branded a nut.

Listening intently to Richard, Hayden looked at me over his shoulder, his expression grim. When he turned back to me, it was with no hint of sympathy.

"Mr. Resnick, I'd appreciate it if you'd refrain from visiting the Sumner family; they've suffered enough. And it would be unfortunate for you if they decided to press harassment charges. Besides, the Orchard Park PD is capable of solving this murder without outside interference."

Defiance flashed through me, but I kept my mouth shut.

Hayden nodded at Richard and Brenda, then headed back the way he'd come, with Richard struggling to keep up.

"Of all the nerve," Brenda said.

"I haven't stepped on anyone's toes," I said, but she wasn't the one I needed to convince. I was out of the hospital on Richard's say-so. As my next of kin, and a physician besides, Richard held all the power. I wasn't sure of my rights should he decide to have me committed, or—

I forced myself to breathe evenly. No way could I let paranoia get the better of me. It made me react like those brain-injury case studies in the pamphlets.

Footsteps approached. I must have looked panicked because Brenda moved closer and put a hand on my shoulder. "It's okay, Jeffy. Everything's okay."

Richard's face betrayed no emotion. "We need to talk," he said, his voice calm, his attention fixed only on me. He took his seat at the table across from me.

I felt like a kid who'd been caught spying on a skinny dipper. I hadn't done anything wrong. Not really. Certainly nothing *too* illegal.

He composed himself and I wondered if he assumed that stance before telling patients they had only weeks to live.

"Something's not right with you, and I don't believe it's physical."

"Why? Because I know about this murder?"

He nodded. "I'm having trouble dealing with this whole situation."

"You're having trouble? What about me? I feel like I'm going crazy. It's like the inside of my brain itches and I can't scratch it. My whole life is fucked up because of a couple of street punks who needed crack money."

Richard remained controlled, rational. "Just what do you know that you didn't read in the paper?"

My voice rose. "I know that a man was murdered."

"Everybody knows that."

"I know he was killed in a field. I know that a little kid witnessed it."

"What little kid?" Brenda asked.

"Jackie."

"The kid on the invitation you saw in Sumner's office?" Richard asked.

"Yes."

"And how did she witness it?"

"I don't know—*he* just did."

They were both staring at me; Brenda aghast, Richard incredulous. But the impact of my words had only just hit me. Until that moment, I hadn't known Jackie was a boy or what he'd seen, but I was as sure of it as I was about my own name.

"If you don't want to talk to me or Brenda, I think you should talk to someone else," Richard said, his voice deadly calm. "You need professional help to get over the trauma of your…accident."

"It wasn't an accident—it was an unprovoked attack. A robbery. And they got a whole lot more than just my money. They took my life!"

"Which proves my point. You need to work through this anger. Until you do, your subconscious is going to keep harping on it, which is why you're obsessing on this murder."

"No." Our gazes locked. "I know what I know. I had those dreams in the hospital before Sumner was murdered."

"Do you actually believe you have psychic power?"

"Whatever's happening to me is real. It's not a psychotic reaction, or a delusion, or something I'm making up to get attention."

"You must admit your behavior has been a little strange."

"How so?"

"The fact that you can't go upstairs, for one."

Just thinking about it filled me with dread. "It's because of your grandmother."

"Oh, so now you think the house is haunted?"

"Richard!" Brenda chided.

He whirled on her, eyes blazing. "Stay out of this."

"Just who do you think you're talking to?"

"Him!" He turned back to me. "Well?"

"I don't believe in ghosts—but there's something of her up there. It's leftover anger—rage. I don't understand it, but it's there and it hurts like hell." I changed the subject.

"What happened to the sympathetic doctor I spoke to the other day, the one who wanted to help me? Now, because the police have got wind of my investigation, you want to shut me down, hide me in a closet, and pass me off as some kind of brain-damaged fool!"

I bolted from my chair. I didn't have the stamina for an extended battle with Richard.

"Where are you going?" Richard demanded, following me through the house.

"Out." I grabbed my coat from the hall closet, struggled to get it over my cast, and opened the front door.

"Jeff."

"Let him go," Brenda said, as I stormed out into the cold.

"Jeff, come back!" Richard called after me again.

I stalked off toward Main Street, my breath coming out in foggy wisps. The cold air felt good, cleansing. With every step I felt empowered, even though I hadn't won the argument.

The Snyder business district was to the right. I headed for it.

Biting my lip in frustration, I faced the reality of my situation: Richard had lost all patience with me. That meant no more lifts around town. No more getting me in places like the bank. The strings were now firmly attached, and I would either have to play the game his way...or get back on my feet. To do that, I needed a job.

The answer seemed simple, but was I physically ready to work? The headaches weren't as bad, but they still came daily and probably would for some time. I couldn't even remember how much longer I needed the cast on my arm. I had no money and nowhere else to go. I'd paid taxes—I might be eligible for Social Security. But how long would it take to get it, and what was I supposed to do in the meantime?

I paused, looking around. Where the hell was I going, anyway? In the back of my mind I remembered a cozy little bar up ahead, next to the fire station.

The penetrating wind made me huddle deeper into my unzipped jacket. What was the name of that tavern? Oh, yeah, McMann's. Richard had taken a few hours off from the hospital to take me there on my eighteenth birthday. My first legal drink. We'd stood at the bar, sipping our beers, surrounded by a bunch of old geezers, and shared a fleeting moment of camaraderie. Afterwards we'd returned home to find Richard's grandmother waiting for us. Her shrill voice cut my soul as she ranted about our alcoholic mother.

I'd been a forgotten bystander as Richard argued that as my guardian he could take me where he wanted, do exactly as he saw fit. It hadn't occurred to him that on that date I could legally make my own decisions. That same night I decided I'd enlist in the Army at the end of the school year.

Richard tried to talk me out of it—he wanted me to go to college. But I wouldn't listen and traded one four-year sentence for another. I wanted to get away from that old woman the way I now wanted to get away from him.

The wind whipped around me and I stopped dead. Déjà vu dragged me back to the night of the attack. The circumstances were the same: a lonely street, a bitter cold night. Panicked, I looked ahead and behind me, expecting two shadowy figures.

There was no one.

I started off again, slower, my feet crunching on the crusted snow once more.

It was time to play devil's advocate. What if Richard was right? Could some injured, twisted part of me be fooling me into thinking I knew things I couldn't possibly know?

No.

I'd seen Sumner's face in my mind before Brenda showed me his picture in the newspaper. I don't know why I was blessed—or was it cursed?—with this knowledge, but I trusted it. If I didn't believe there was a reason for this happening to me, it would drive me crazy.

A look around my surroundings helped me get my bearings. Up ahead the lights of my alma mater, Amherst Central High School, illuminated an entire city block. On really bad days, Curtis the chauffeur would drive me there... unless Mrs. Alpert rose early. Then she insisted he be at her beck and call. She always picked the stormiest days.

I hated that old woman with a passion I've never felt since, and I'd wanted to get out of that house so badly....

Why did it always come back to her?

Forcing my thoughts back to the present, I continued walking.

A bakery sat at the crossroads. What had been there years ago? I'd already walked past the Snyder fire station before realizing something was wrong. Hadn't McMann's been right there? The fire station looked big and new and had obviously been expanded to sit where that quaint little tavern had been.

Confused, I glanced around me. The cold seeped through my thin-soled shoes. I was too far from home to start back without first stopping to warm up. All the little stores were dark and the night seemed to be closing in.

An elderly woman peered through the bakery's plate glass window. She'd rubbed a hole in the condensation and motioned to me. I looked around. There was no one nearby. She *was* beckoning me.

I waited for a car to pass before crossing the street, not knowing why I felt drawn. She met me at the door.

"Come in—come in. It's too cold to be out on a night like this."

I entered and she threw the dead bolt behind me, sending a shiver up my back. She led me to the rear of the shop, the aroma of fresh-baked bread and cakes was still heavy in the warm moist air.

A storeroom acted as a buffer between the storefront and the actual bakery; a bare bones affair, not much more than stacked crates and boxes, a card table, and a couple of chairs. On a shelf over a sink sat an ancient hot plate—a dangerous arrangement, but the old woman seemed unconcerned. She filled a saucepan with water and turned the burner on high. Taking two cups from the shelf, she carefully measured cocoa from a canister.

"All I have is instant. Not very good, but it warms me."

"Look, I don't want to put you to any trouble—"

"It's no trouble."

In her late seventies and heavyset, she moved stiffly, as though with arthritis. Her accent was Polish, her wrinkled face careworn, but her eyes were bright and loving—an odd assessment coming from me. I don't take to people right off. Yet her whole demeanor encouraged trust, like you could tell her all your troubles.

Why had she invited me here? I was a stranger—a man. She should be afraid of me—instead, I was leery of her.

I shoved my good hand into my jacket pocket, feeling self-conscious. "What am I doing here?"

"You look like you need to talk. I need to listen. Sit," she said and ushered me to a folding metal chair, taking one on the opposite side of the wobbly table.

"You here all alone?"

"Yes."

Why didn't that question frighten her? I could be an ax murderer, for all she knew.

"My son—he's a big shot with his own business downtown," she said. "He wants me to move to Cheektowaga to live in one of those old folks' homes. But I like living over the shop."

"I lived over a bakery when I was a kid."

"The bread smells so good in the mornings, yes?"

"That was the only good part about living there."

"That's not true. I'll bet there were many good things. You just don't want to remember."

"Why do you say that?"

She shrugged theatrically, her smile enigmatic. "I've been waiting for you."

"For me?"

"For a week. Maybe two."

"But I've only been back in Buffalo a week."

"But it's good now that you're here, eh?"

I shook my head. "I should have stayed in New York."

"There's nothing for you there. Here you have a girlfriend, your family."

"I don't have a girlfriend. My brother is my only family."

"See," she said, the creases around her eyes doubling, her smile warm.

I leaned back in my chair. This was too creepy.

"You need to talk," she repeated. "I'm here to listen."

"Why would I tell a stranger about myself?"

"Maybe I understand—maybe I'll tell you something about yourself you don't know. Maybe I'll tell you something about yourself you already know."

The hair on the back of my neck bristled. "Like what?"

"Give me your hand."

She didn't wait for me to offer it. She grabbed my right and her creased hands caressed mine; and more chilling, her clear brown eyes seemed to look into my soul. Finally she shook her head and gave me back my hand. "First I'll tell you about me; then you can decide if you want to tell me about you. My name is Sophie Levin. Look." She pulled back her sweater sleeve to reveal a tattoo of faded numbers.

"Buchenwald?" I guessed.

"See, you know."

"A good guess."

She shook her head. "No, this you know. Like lots of other things you know, eh?"

I wasn't sure how to answer.

The water began to boil. She got up, poured it into the cups, and stirred. Then she disappeared into the shop and came back with a *placek*. I hadn't tasted one of those sweet crumb loaves in years. She cut thick slices and put them on napkins from the shelf, and set one in front of me.

"Now, I'll tell you how I survived the camp. I would volunteer for the work groups. I did anything they said. Dig holes, bake bread—anything. And I knew when to be away from the barracks. To stay was to die."

"How did you know?"

She tapped her temple. "I knew. Like you know. For me there are colors. Everyone has colors that surround them. I would watch certain guards and when their color was black, it meant death. I knew to stay away. Right now you are red. Very angry. Your brother—don't be hard on him. He loves you, you know."

Was she nuts? "How do you see these colors?"

"Not with my eyes, with my mind. It's not wrong, it's not bad. Just different. You see things a different way, too. But then you always have."

"No."

She shook her head, dismissing my protest. "Of course you did. I can tell you many times—but it's better you remember yourself. Little things. Finding lost things. Waiting for a letter—a phone call."

I hesitated, afraid to ask my next question.

"Are you...psychic?"

She shrugged. "I just see colors...and then I know. You feel things, deeply. Before this happened...." She reached across the table, traced a finger down my shorn temple, "...you never let yourself. Now you have to. The plug is pulled—the feelings leak out—other people's feelings find you. It's very hard for you, but good things will come of it. They will," she insisted. "But sometimes things will seem worse because you can't understand them. Sometimes it's hard to understand."

I wanted to believe her. Hadn't I just been telling myself the very same things? Yet suddenly I was as skeptical as Richard.

"I don't know what you're talking about."

She thought for a moment. "You like to take photographs, eh?"

I nodded uncertainly. How could she know these things?

"You take a picture—it's there, in your camera. Even when it's not developed—it's still there."

"A latent image?"

"Yes. These things you know, it's a latent talent. You always had it, but it wasn't developed. Now you can develop the pictures in your head. You can see them when others can't. You can know things when others don't." Did she even know about digital photography?

"My brother wants me to have tests—" I began.

"How will knowing the science of it help you? If they can even tell you."

That was pretty much how I felt about it, too.

"Still, you must be careful," she warned. "Believe what you know, and be watchful. Even innocent situations can hide great danger."

She held out her hand. "Now, tell me about me."

Reluctantly, I clasped her warm fingers, felt her pulse thrumming rhythmically through the skin and found her smile encouraging.

"Well?"

"You're a nice lady. You want to help people." I didn't know what else to say.

She took back her hand and frowned. "You'll get better at it." She picked up her cup and took a sip. "Not bad for instant, but better with marshmallows. That's what my granddaughter says."

She launched into a monologue about her grandchildren, giving me a chance to digest what she'd said. I think she knew I wasn't listening, but she seemed to like to hear the sound of her own voice.

She was right. I'd always been good at finding lost objects. I assumed it was a matter of remembering where you'd last seen the missing item. That and begging help from St. Anthony. Were emotions the psychic key for me? I remembered returning home from school and knowing, before I opened the apartment door, when my mother would be passed out drunk in front of the TV. And I'd learned early to keep the hurt, anger, and humiliation inside. It was the only survival mechanism I'd found to help me cope.

Most of what I knew about Sumner's murder hinged on emotions. Those of the killer—and that of a witness. I'd felt anger and triumph and terror, all mixed up.

I looked down at my empty cup.

"It's time for you to go," Sophie said, rising. "My son would be upset if he knew I entertained a gentleman here." She patted my shoulder. "It's a long walk home. I'd let you call your brother to come get you, but my phone hasn't worked all day. The bar down the street has a pay phone. You can call from there."

I followed her back into the shop. Fat snowflakes fluttered and settled on the empty parking spaces outside.

"That's okay. I think I'll just head on home."

"Oh, no—it's too far to walk in the snow. You're not as strong as you think. You must promise me you'll go to the bar." Something about her tone made it seem like an imperative.

"Okay, I promise."

"Good."

She clasped my hand and I nearly staggered at the burst of unconditional love that suddenly enveloped me. I looked into her smiling, wrinkled face, and suddenly didn't want to leave.

"Can I come back and visit you again?"

She shrugged. "Sometimes I'm here. Sometimes I'm not. It's best you come at night. Alone."

"Why?"

"It's just best." She winked at me. "Good-bye, Jeffrey."

She locked the door behind me, and waved. As I headed down the sidewalk, I realized I'd never introduced myself. I looked back. The shop was dark, but a light blazed in the apartment overhead.

My anger toward Richard had waned, but the sour feelings it evoked lingered as depression settled in.

I had other things to think about. Like what had inspired Sophie to direct me down the road instead of going home?

Curiosity got the better of me.

I headed for the bar.

Chapter Ten

The glow of a neon beer sign drew me half a block to a working-class sports bar called The Whole Nine Yards. Its dry warmth enveloped me as I pushed open the heavy glass door. A scattering of patrons watched a basketball game blaring on the tube. Football jerseys, hockey sticks, pennants, and signed photographs dotted the walls, but the budget for decor was a lot less than at The Extra Point downtown. It had the feel of a business on a downslide.

Sophie had been right. The bar actually *did* have a pay phone, but I avoided it. I had no intention of calling Richard.

The bartender interrupted his conversation with an older man at the other end of the bar when I took a seat. Weariness clung to him. I guessed him to be the owner, who looked like he'd been on his feet all day. "What can I get you?" he asked.

I considered my nearly empty wallet and my belly full of cocoa. "Club soda."

His expression said "no tip," but he poured me a glass from the well soda trigger. "That's a buck."

I put a five-dollar bill on the bar. He grabbed it, rang up the sale on the old cash register, gave me my change, and went back to kibitzing.

Four bucks—my total net worth. I'd have to nurse my drink for a while, but that was okay. I was willing to park here for a couple of hours.

I'd tended bar for a while after my stint in the Army; I could do it again. Sure, a part-time job at a place like this, within walking distance from Richard's house could work out. But who'd hire a broken-armed jerk who couldn't lift a case of beer or hold a lime to cut garnishes?

My mind wandered back to the ugly scene back home. Richard's house was not my home. It was a place to stay until I got back on my feet; at least that's what he'd said at the hospital.

The memory of that conversation came back to me.

He'd been gone all day, leaving me alone in that cell of a room. We hadn't had many meaningful discussions since I'd awakened from the coma two days before. Still, I'd gotten used to him being in the background.

"So, where've you been all day?" I'd asked, when he finally showed up that evening.

Richard settled his coat over the back of the room's only chair. "I had things to do."

"Business? Sightseeing?"

He straightened, as though tensing for battle. "Getting estimates from movers to take your stuff to Buffalo."

"Look, I never said—!"

"I know what you said. I was only getting estimates, okay?" He hesitated before continuing. "I spoke with your apartment manager."

My insides squirmed.

"Your back rent's taken care of."

"But I owed—"

"I said it's taken care of."

I was about to spew like Vesuvius when he interrupted me again. "The last few times I've seen you, you've been distant and pissy. Have I done something to offend you?"

"The cultured, refined Doctor Alpert never offends anyone."

"Then stop acting like you've got a stick up your ass and tell me what's eating you."

"All right, you want an answer—the problem's you. You being so goddamned rich makes me feel like I'm shit. You're always shoving it down my throat and I'm sick of it!"

That wasn't even remotely true, but it sounded good and fit my mental state at the time.

He stiffened. "I'm sorry my financial status offends you, but I'm still your brother. I care about what happens to you, you dumb shit. Why else would I be here?"

He'd never spoken to me in anger. I'd never known him to swear.

"Guilt," I shot back. Richard blinked, taken aback. "Yeah, guilt—for the way your family treated our mother. Maybe you're only here for me because you weren't there for her!"

Richard looked away. My words had hit a nerve, all right, though I knew indifference hadn't kept him from knowing my mother and me. The legal maneuvers his grandparents used to keep my mother from him had cut him off from us, too. Yet I couldn't admit that to him in the heat of anger.

"Neither of us can change the past. But, in case you hadn't noticed, we're all the family we've got. When will it penetrate your thick skull that you're important to me?" He paused. "You never told me about Shelley until it was all over. Christ, your landlord told me you'd lost your job. Why didn't you call—why didn't you come to me?"

"Rich, you can't take care of me the rest of my life."

He spoke slowly, holding back his own anger. "I'm offering to help you 'til you get back on your feet. No strings attached. If you're too damned proud—" Richard broke off, struggling to regain his composure.

"Look, I don't want to fight about this. That's the last thing you need right now. All I ask is that you seriously consider coming back to Buffalo with me—at least until you recover. After that, you can do as you please."

I'd exhaled raggedly, defeat seeping into me. Sick, hurting, and broke, I had nowhere else to go.

"Okay. I'll consider it."

Neither of us spoke for long minutes, then Richard grabbed his coat.

"I'm going to find something to eat. Want me to bring you a sandwich?" I shook my head. "Okay. See you later, right?"

"Yeah, right."

Richard shuffled toward the door, but paused. "I'm sorry, Jeff. I hoped things could be different." Genuine regret colored his voice. I felt like a heel. Then he was gone.

I sank back in the bed. Dr. Klehr said a head injury like mine can lower all defenses. He'd been right. For the first time since my wife's death, I buried my face in the pillow and let the tears flow—like I had all those years ago when my mother died, when I first found myself totally on my own. It took a while before I could think rationally.

So, I'd finally told Richard off. Instead of feeling better, shame burned within me.

I hauled myself out of the bed, my arm aching. Leaning against the window sill three floors above the street, I stared at the bleak winter sky. The shit was just piling higher and higher.

Richard was right. What kept me in Manhattan, anyway? No job, no significant other, no close friends. The city held nothing but bitter memories. Richard was the only family I had. He was all I had on my side—if I hadn't just blown that, too.

A noise at the doorway interrupted my thoughts. I turned to see Richard, hands thrust into his coat pockets.

"I—I came back to apologize."

"What for?"

He inched closer. "Because maybe part of me thought I could come down here and play savior for you. It was arrogant of me. I'm sorry." Eyes downcast, he stared at his polished shoes. "I guess I still think of you as that skinny fourteen-year-old kid who desperately needed a home."

This was a Richard I'd never known—had never bothered to get to know.

He met my gaze and continued. "I came here because I'm sincerely worried about you and thought I could help. I hoped that after all these years maybe we could be friends. I don't know about you, but I can always use another friend."

My throat tightened until I thought I might choke. "That's funny. I was just thinking the same thing."

Richard moved forward, his arms open to capture me in a hesitant, gentle hug. And for the first time in my life, I hugged him back. Then suddenly we were standing face-to-face, embarrassed and uncomfortable.

"Please come to Buffalo. There's nothing for you here. Besides, I've got Bills season tickets, and Brenda hates football."

"Okay, but I've got to have my own space. And when it's time to leave, I don't want an argument."

Richard raised a hand. "Fine."

A cheer broke the quiet—and the buzzer signaled the end of the first period on the bar's TV.

I took a sip of my club soda. I owed Richard a lot, yet bitterness gnawed at me because the tentative trust I'd put in him—and he'd shown in me—had been so easily erased.

I couldn't let Richard browbeat me. If I didn't pursue my own investigation, Sumner's murderer might go free. And then there was the small boy who'd witnessed that terrible crime. It was his mental SOS, his fear, I'd experienced—not Sumner's. I'd never gotten anything from the victim—as though he had expected to die....

The door opened and closed and the light tap of footsteps interrupted my reverie. "Do you have a phone?" a woman asked.

The bartender pointed. "Over there."

I looked over my shoulder, surprised to see the woman from the bank. She dropped a couple of quarters in the slot and dialed a number off a card in her hand. She caught my eye and I looked away.

I gazed into my drink. My arm itched. I wished I'd brought the chopstick.

A minute or two later, she joined me at the bar. "Hi, remember me?"

"Maggie Brennan."

She nodded and sat down on the stool beside me. "And you're Jeff."

She remembered.

"Car trouble?" I guessed.

"I hit a pothole. My right front tire blew. And wouldn't know my cell phone is dead."

I proffered my broken arm. "I'd like to give you a hand, but—"

"That's okay. Triple A will be here in a while."

"Can I buy you a drink instead?"

She eyed my glass. "I'll have what you're having."

I caught the bartender's attention. "A club soda—with a twist—for the lady." Somehow, she didn't seem surprised by my order. Moments later, the bartender put a fresh napkin on the bar and set down the glass. I left another dollar for him and indicated a table in the back, away from the noisy TV.

Maggie draped her coat over the back of the chair that I'd pulled out for her, then sat down. "Thanks. I'm taking a writing class at Daemen College. I was on my way home when I hit that damn pothole. I've never even been in this place before. I'm glad you were here."

"But you don't even know me."

She shrugged. "At least you're a familiar face. Hey, you got your hair cut. It looks good."

I raked a hand over my head. "Thanks. I'll feel better once it all grows in. In the meantime, I don't feel so much like a freak."

She gave me the once-over. "You don't look like a freak."

"But what if you'd walked in here and hadn't known me, and I'd tried to hit on you?"

"Would you?"

I felt a smile tug at my lips. "Maybe."

She took a sip of her drink. "You told me a fib the other day."

"Me?"

"You acted like you were sick."

"It wasn't much of an act. If you hadn't caught me, I really would've keeled over." I gazed into her pretty blue eyes. Something about them inspired tranquility.

"What were you really doing at the bank?"

I stared into my glass. The bubbles on the side had just about dissipated. "Hanging out with my brother."

"Doctor Alpert? But your name's—"

"Resnick," I supplied, and she nodded. "We're half-brothers. Bet you wouldn't know that by looking at us." She frowned, and I regretted the smart remark. I looked back down at my glass and sobered. "Okay, I'm looking into Matt Sumner's death."

"Are you a cop?"

"It's a personal matter. Can you tell me more about him? Who his friends were? How he spent his time away from work?"

She leaned back, her face growing cold. "I didn't know him well, and I didn't want to know him any better."

Great. My only remaining source on the man had just dried up.

Her expression softened. "But, maybe I'd like to get to know you a little better."

I gave her what I hoped was a reassuring smile. "That would be nice."

The corners of her mouth rose—a really nice smile.

"So, tell me about yourself," I said.

"I'm thirty-nine and not ashamed of it. Depressed some days, but not ashamed. Like everyone else these days, I'm overworked and stressed-out. I'm also divorced and childless. How about you?"

"I'm an unemployed insurance investigator, a widower, and currently sponging off my wealthy older brother."

"Widower?" she asked, as though not hearing the rest. "I'm so sorry. How long ago?"

"Two years."

She hesitated, curiosity getting the better of her. "H... how—?"

"Cocaine. At first she'd have a hit or two on weekends. Then it was a couple of times a week. I worked late—trying to keep my job while downsizing went on all around me. She got fired as a travel agent when she was arrested for selling coke to an undercover cop. After that, she promised me she'd stay clean, but she was already too far gone. Six months after she left me, the cops found her dead in a bathroom at Grand Central Station. Shot execution-style. They figured she tried to rip off her supplier."

Hey, I'd told the entire tale—albeit much abbreviated—and hadn't gotten angry. I was making real progress.

"How awful for you." She tapped the cast on my arm. "You said you were mugged?"

"All I remember is that baseball bat coming at me. They took my wallet, my keys, ransacked my apartment, took everything I had that was worth anything, and ruined just about everything else."

"Oh, Jeff!" Again, the compassion in her eyes captivated me.

"Anyway, my brother rescued me and here I am." My God—I was spilling my guts to a virtual stranger—but she was so easy to talk to. I leaned back in my chair. "Sorry. I didn't mean to dump all this on you."

She took a sip of her drink. "My husband was gay. Only he didn't tell me that until we'd been married eight years. After he left, I'd get myself tested for AIDS every six months. I didn't know anything about his secret life, or how many men he'd been with."

I nodded. "Came the end, Shelley would sleep with anyone for cocaine. It scared the hell out of me. For a while, celibacy was my way of life."

She reached across the table to shake my hand. "Amen."

Her fingers were warm. I held on longer than was absolutely necessary. Our eyes met and an odd sensation passed through me, an unexpected sense of well-being, yet my heart pounded.

"Um…my hand." She smiled. "Didn't we just go through this at the bank?"

Embarrassed, I relinquished my hold and felt a tug inside me. She hadn't told me everything. But then why should she?

"You live around here?" she asked.

"Down on LeBrun. I'm just staying with Rich until I get back on my feet."

"Doctor Alpert is older than you, isn't he?"

I nodded, draining my glass. "Twelve years. My mother was a staunch Catholic. She married well the first time. Richard's father was handsome and an heir to millions. He didn't expect to die young and leave his wife penniless. Mom had a nervous breakdown and ended up in the State hospital. They didn't even have the decency to put her in a private hospital."

"Who?"

"Richard's paternal grandparents." I shook my head. "While Mom was in the hospital, they got legal custody of Rich, saying she was unfit."

"Where do you fit in?"

"Years later, Mom married Chet Resnick, a Jewish dry cleaner. He left us when I was four. My mother wouldn't talk about him—except to say he gambled and drank. I heard he was dead."

"So, how did you and your brother ever get together?"

"He found out Mom had cancer and came by the apartment the Christmas before she died. He was in his first year of residency at the time." A lifetime ago. "She was really proud of him. He was curious about us, said he'd like to get to know us. But two months later, Mom was dead. He took me in."

"How long did you stay?"

"Four long years." I paused. "Can't we talk about something else?"

She nodded and took another sip of her drink. "You said you were looking into Matt's death. What does that mean?"

"Right now, nothing. Claudia Sumner sicced the cops on me. Now I won't be able to talk to their kids."

She studied my eyes. "This is really important to you, isn't it?"

"Yeah. It is."

"Why?"

Because I got whacked on the head and now I know things I'm not supposed to know, and I've seen things I wasn't supposed to see. And I'm probably crazy or stupid—or both—and I have a ridiculous debt to repay to Matt Sumner, but I have to find out the truth for myself.

"It just is."

Guilt darkened her eyes. "I didn't tell you everything I know about Matt. I mean, I don't know what might be of use to you. But I like you. You seem…trustworthy."

"And I'm not even wearing my sincere suit."

Her smile disappeared. "This may not be important, but Matt recently fired one of the loan managers. The police have been digging around and it came up. To tell you the truth, I'd almost forgotten about it."

"What happened?"

"They said Don Feddar was approving loans without the proper documentation. There was a big blow-up and Matt fired him."

"How long ago was this?"

"Just before Christmas."

"That's a possible motive for murder."

"But Don's a sweetheart. He's not capable of doing what was done to Matt."

"That's probably what people thought about Jack the Ripper before his first crime." She conceded the point. "Does this guy have kids? A little boy named Jackie?"

"I think he has three daughters." She looked up, her attention caught by flashing yellow lights in the parking lot. "Hang on. The tow truck's here." She snagged her coat and went out to talk to the driver.

I watched while the guy changed her tire. It wasn't until he finally climbed into the cab to leave that she came back into the bar. Her cheeks were pink and her hair was wind-blown. She looked terrific.

"Well, I guess I should get going. Do you need a lift?"

I didn't want to go home. I didn't want her to go, either.

"Sure."

I took our empty glasses over to the bar, left a two-dollar tip for the bartender, then shrugged back into my jacket. Outside it must've been twenty degrees as a light snow still fell. Maggie unlocked the passenger side door of her Hyundai and I got in.

The drive to LeBrun was awkward. I'd felt so at ease with her in the bar, yet now I was tongue-tied. I studied her features in the strobing lamplight as she navigated through the slick streets. Why couldn't I think of something—anything—to say?

She turned onto my street, slowing. "It's halfway down," I told her. "There."

She pulled into the driveway, then turned to me. It seemed like she wanted to say something, but she didn't speak. So I did.

"Can I call you?"

She reached for her purse, her smile radiant. Tearing a sheet from a notebook, she jotted down her number. It took all my willpower not to kiss her right then. I took the paper from her. "I'll call."

Then I was out of the car, standing in the silent falling snow, watching her little blue car pull out of the driveway. She waved before she started off toward Main Street.

Hot damn, I liked Maggie Brennan.

Chapter Eleven

I knew when I showed up for breakfast the next morning that it wasn't the time to announce I'd made a couple of new friends. Brenda and Richard weren't speaking, and I more than half suspected I was the cause.

Richard announced he'd made an appointment for me at UB Medical Center with an orthopedic specialist for that afternoon. I didn't argue.

Plaster is old-fashioned. My new physician gave me the option of a fiberglass cast—in designer colors, no less—or a removable plastic-and-Velcro brace. I chose the latter, glad to be rid of the anchor-weight cast. An x-ray showed my ulna to be healing nicely.

No one mentioned sending me to a shrink.

Even so, I wasn't feeling cocky as I left the doctor's office. Something was definitely up with Richard.

We walked in silence back to the car. Richard had accompanied me to the clinic, and sat in the waiting room until I'd finished. He didn't ask how things had gone.

He touched the button on his key fob and unlocked the car doors before walking around to the driver's side, and climbing in. He turned the key in the ignition and cleared his throat. "Anywhere you want to go?"

I shook my head. "Let's just go home."

Snowflakes began to fall, dancing on the windshield before being blown away, replaced by new ones. I gazed at the traffic whizzing by and remembered what Richard told Brenda days before: "He's different."

He was right, I was different. And I looked at everything in a new, harsher light—especially myself.

I didn't like what I saw.

Minutes later we were home. Richard stopped the car in the driveway, letting me out before he parked the Lincoln in the garage. I started for the house, but paused. I couldn't let this go on. Pulling up my collar, I waited for him. Although it was only three o'clock, the sky had darkened to the west—a storm was brewing.

The garage door closed and Richard came out the side door, shoulders slumped, head down. He looked as bad as I felt. He glanced up, surprised to see me.

"Wanna take a walk?"

He took in the sky. "In the snow?"

"Why not? Besides, I want to talk."

He blinked at me. "You never want to talk."

"I never had a crack in my skull before, either."

"Do you think that makes a difference?"

"Yeah, I do."

Richard shrugged. "What's the point?"

The defeat in his voice scared me. "Are you giving up on me already?"

"No. It's just—I don't like things being so awkward."

"That's kind of what I wanted to talk about."

We started down the driveway at a snail's pace. Awkward was a good description for how I felt. And he was right. Expressing myself was something I'd never been good at.

I took a breath for courage.

"Back in New York I said something I'm not proud of. That you're always rubbing my nose in the fact that you have a lot of money. It isn't true. You've never treated me with anything other than kindness. In return—"

"Jeff, don't—"

"Let me finish. In return, I've been an ungrateful son of a bitch, too proud to accept your generosity gracefully. I'm sorry."

"You're my brother. You've been through hell."

"Well, I just wanted to say thanks. I've asked a lot of you and…I have a feeling I'll be asking more before this is over."

"You mean this stuff with the murder?"

I nodded.

He forced a smile, but his eyes were still troubled.

For all I seemed to know about Sumner's death, I was unable to read anything on my own brother. It was time to risk it all. "What's going on with you and Brenda?"

Richard's gaze remained fixed on the sidewalk ahead. A muscle twitched in his jaw. "I wish I knew."

How arrogant was it of me to think he'd be preoccupied by only me and my problems.

"Once my arm heals, I could be out of your hair in a month or so."

He looked at me, his eyes pained. "Are you going to abandon me, too?"

"What do you mean?"

He looked away. "Brenda's thinking of going back to LA. Something about the climate here not agreeing with her." His voice sounded shaky.

Major guilt trip. "Oh, man, Rich."

"It's not your fault. This has been brewing for a while—ever since we came here."

"I don't understand. When we got off the plane, she seemed so glad to see you. I could feel she really loves you."

"We've been together a long time," he admitted. "She knows I love her. I know she loves me. But she says we don't have a life here—that I'm ashamed of her. That's bullshit."

"Is it a race thing?"

"I don't know. Maybe."

"Well, do you ever take her out?"

"Where? This is Buffalo, for chrissakes."

"There have to be some nice restaurants. Toronto's only ninety minutes away. Go to a movie, join a country club, I don't know."

"It goes deeper than that. A lot deeper."

"How?"

"She says I don't trust her any more. That I used to ask for her opinions—that I trusted her judgment. She says I don't any more."

"Why?"

"Mainly because I haven't been supportive of you and this psychic crap. She fell for it hook, line, and sinker."

"These things are really happening to me."

His voice was gentle. "I know you believe that. But things are different here. Buffalo's a working class town. I've heard it called a city of no illusions." He paused. "Maybe she's right. I was open to more possibilities back in LA. We dabbled in so many things at the Foundation. Our team collaborated with Stanford on experiments with extrasensory perception. We studied a psychic with frightening psychokinetic powers.

Things like that don't exist in Buffalo—certainly not with my own brother."

I wasn't comfortable talking about that. "Maybe you're going through a mid-life crisis. You could sell the house, go back to LA."

"No, I belong here. I can't explain why, but I can't leave again. And because of that, I'm going to lose Brenda."

"I think you need a job—both of you."

"It's not that simple."

"Isn't it? Here I am, wondering if I'll ever work again. I'm thinking maybe I could tend bar—something part-time. Something where I won't fail. Damn it, Richard, you're a doctor. And you're good."

He shrugged. "I used to be. But I don't want to start a practice at this stage of the game."

"How about volunteering somewhere? There's gotta be clinics just crying for someone with your talent to work gratis. You could probably name your hours, do as much or as little as you please. But you've got to do something. You've worked too hard to just let your skills—and Brenda—slip away."

He nodded, but I could see he wasn't convinced. We walked half a block in silence.

"Thanks," Richard said finally.

"For what?"

"A different perspective. Maybe I do need to get back to work. And maybe I have been ignoring Brenda. Maybe if we did something together...." His words trailed off, but he seemed to warm to the idea.

An inch or more of snow had fallen in the short time we'd walked, covering the sidewalks, the wind whipping it into peaks. Fooled by the premature darkening of the sky, a few of the street lamps flickered to life. Lights were blazing in the house as we approached, welcoming us.

Once inside, Richard clapped me on the back before disappearing into his study.

After I showed Brenda the brace, I grabbed a cup of coffee and parked myself by the phone. Thanks to a helpful library aid and the city directory, I tracked down the employers of several of the three little Jackies' parents and talked to the two fathers. Neither admitted knowing Matt Sumner, but then why would they? One hung up on me. I needed to talk to Maggie. Maybe she could check to see if any of the parents had accounts with Bison Bank. And it would give me an excuse to call her.

Donning a sweatshirt, I wandered out to the sun room—a misnomer on that chilly, dark day, but a great place to think. I borrowed Brenda's portable radio, listening to mellow jazz while I froze my butt off watching the wind make snow sculptures. The winter storm watch had turned into a full-blown blizzard, and the snow began to drift out on the driveway. I was glad I didn't have to drive in this weather, although I'd have to get the hang of it if I decided to stay in Buffalo.

The thought didn't seem as appalling as it had just a week ago.

In addition to the weather, the hourly newscast reported that the police had found Sumner's car in a mall parking lot in Erie, Pennsylvania—the same city where his youngest son went to school. Interesting. Seeing the car was a pipe dream. The cops would impound it, though they wouldn't find much to further their investigation. It's harder to get a decent fingerprint than most people think, and I suspected the murderer hadn't been stupid enough to leave them.

Eventually Richard came out and hauled me in for dinner. He and Brenda were back on speaking terms, albeit extremely polite.

Afterwards, I volunteered to clean up the kitchen. Being one-armed, the job took longer than I thought. By the time I finished, every pan was clean, the table was wiped, and the floor had been swept. Maybe I could find employment as a domestic. Meanwhile, I must have glanced at the phone a hundred times, trying to work up the courage to call Maggie.

Finally, I punched in the seven-digit number I'd memorized the night before. It rang once. Twice. Three times. I was sure an answering machine would kick in when a breathless voice answered, "Hello?"

"Maggie? It's Jeff Resnick. Is this a bad time?"

"No. I just came in from walking the dog." She sounded pleased. She might not be after I begged my favor. "How are you? How's your arm?"

"Better. Some snow, huh?" I wasn't showing her my most articulate side.

"Yeah. But, it's late in the season. It'll probably melt in a day or two."

"Yeah." A lengthy silence followed. "Uh, I'm a little out of practice. You know, with this dating stuff."

"Yeah?"

"So, you want to go out?"

"What did you have in mind?"

"Well, that's kind of a problem. See, I'm not working, and I might not be for a while. I don't have a car, either."

"Oh."

"Did I just blow my chances?"

I envisioned her smiling. "Well, my mother wouldn't say you were a hot prospect, but I've always rooted for the underdog, so you haven't blown it. Yet."

I might now. "Could you check on something for me at the bank?"

She hesitated. "Does this have anything to do with Matt Sumner's death?"

"Yeah."

"Are you using me? I mean, I could still do whatever it is you want, but do you really want to get to know me better, or are you just feeding me a line?"

"No. I think you're nice. I'd like to get to know you better. I don't have any friends in town." My foot was jammed so far into my mouth it would take major surgery to remove it.

Silence, then she laughed. "Okay, what do you want?"

She listened patiently while I explained the situation.

"Because of privacy laws, I can't give you specifics. I can let you know if they've got accounts or loans with us, but that's it."

"That's all I need. Thanks."

"Okay. What about going out? Can you swing lunch? Dutch treat?"

"Yeah. Where?"

She gave me the address of a place close to the bank and we agreed to meet the next day.

I found Richard and Brenda in the study. As usual, Richard sat behind his desk, his nose buried in a book. Brenda had parked on the leather couch by a lamp, doing some kind of needlework. They both looked up as I knocked on the door jamb.

"I need a favor tomorrow. A ride. I sort of have a date."

Brenda's eyebrows rose. "A date?"

"I met this lady at the bank the other day. We're going to lunch tomorrow. I thought maybe you two could go out, drop me off, then pick me up later."

"You mean you don't want us to join you?" Richard asked. There was a lightness in his tone that had been absent for days.

"No!" This wasn't my night for conversation. "I mean, sure, if you want. But—"

"No one's taken me to lunch in ages. Richard?"

He smiled at her. "Sure."

I figured I'd better make a fast escape before my foot became permanently lodged in my mouth. "Thanks."

***

Richard dropped me at Ted's Place, a little diner across the street from the main branch of Bison Bank in downtown Buffalo. He and Brenda were headed to a much more upscale restaurant down the street, where linen napkins and salad forks were standard at every place setting.

I stood in the cafe's crowded entryway, waiting for a table to open. The place smelled of bacon, coffee, and greasy fries, and was an obvious favorite with downtown office workers who'd donned heavy coats and boots to trudge past thigh-high snow banks to get there.

A waitress seated me in the last booth. As I perused the menu, Maggie flopped down across from me.

"Hi! Sorry I'm late. Did you order yet?"

I shook my head. "Good to see you."

She struggled out of her bulky down coat and set it beside her on the bench seat. She wore a navy knit sweater over a dark wool skirt. The thin gold chain around her neck made her look dressy yet casual.

She glanced over the menu. "I'm starved. I had to shovel the driveway, so I didn't have time for breakfast, and nobody brought in doughnuts. God, I hate winter."

"I guess I shouldn't mention that some guy in a pickup with a plow did our drive about six this morning."

She stuck out her tongue at me, then went back to the menu. The waitress showed up with steaming coffee pots—regular and decaf—in each hand. We ordered, Maggie settling for chicken salad, and I asked for beef on weck—rare roast beef, piled high on a salty, caraway seeded kimmelweck roll, served with a Kosher dill, sinus-clearing horseradish, and au jus. For me a New Orleans po boy or a Philly cheese steak sandwich would never beat Buffalo's beef on weck.

After the waitress had gone, Maggie opened her purse and took out a sheaf of folded papers. She looked around, decided it was safe to speak, and motioned me closer. "I could get fired if anyone found out about this." She handed me the pages.

"I won't say a word."

The first was a typed list of the three names I'd given her. The Ryans had a VISA account with the bank, the Prystowskis had none. Under the third name was a lengthy paragraph, which I skimmed.

Sharon Walker had no current accounts with the bank, but her father's construction business had many loans with Bison Bank over the previous two decades. The text concluded with a terse statement: Walker Construction had gone bankrupt three years before. At that time, Sharon Walker headed the company. Matt Sumner was the executive in charge of those loans. I wondered if that alone could get Maggie fired, and swallowed a pang of guilt. As I stared at the Walker woman's name, something in my gut twisted.

I shuffled through the next several sheets, photocopies of Sumner's appointment calendar the week of his death. Interesting.

"I had to do some digging on that third name. I threw in the calendar as a bonus. Hope it helps."

I folded the papers and put them into my coat pocket. "Thanks. I really appreciate it."

"No problem," she said, but sounded nervous and quickly changed the subject. "Hey, your cast is gone."

"The brace is better. And I only have to wear it another twenty-seven days." I took a sip of my coffee. "You never told me exactly what you do at the bank."

"I'm an administrative assistant—a glorified title for secretary, except that I have a secretary. She does all the piddly work, I deal with the directors and handle the more complicated assignments—like coordinating this conference, which is driving me nuts." She paused to sip her decaf coffee. "I've been there fourteen years. The way things are going, with so many banks consolidating, you never know how long you'll last."

"A familiar story. I worked my way up to supervisor, only to be busted back to field investigator, then out the door, after a major re-engineering at Travelers. Thinking about it depresses the hell out of me."

The sandwiches came, but I was more interested in listening to Maggie than eating. She seemed nervous and began to chatter.

"If you need a dentist, my brother-in-law has a practice in Tonawanda. He's wonderful. Totally painless."

"Totally?"

"Well, it depends on how well you take care of your teeth."

"Do you live in Tonawanda?"

She shook her head. "Out in Clarence. Me and my dog, Holly, a golden retriever. I got her for Christmas a couple of years ago. She's a big dog and needs to be walked at least once a day. Then there's the yard work." She rolled her eyes, making me laugh.

We talked while we ate: the Buffalo Bills, the weather, how she dabbled in interior decoration as a hobby. Occasionally she'd look down at her plate, bite her lip like something bothered her. Then she'd find another safe topic and start again.

The check arrived and I grabbed it. Brenda, bless her heart, had slipped me a twenty.

Maggie donned her jacket and pulled a white knit beret over her hair. I stood to follow her and pay the check at the register.

"Bye. Thanks for lunch," she said, took a few steps, and turned back. She gave me a quick hug before hurrying out the door.

People crowded past me on their way in or out, but I hardly noticed. I just stood there and smiled.

***

I wasted the rest of the day with mundane tasks—namely laundry. After dinner, I returned to my cramped room. I needed a desk. I needed more space. I needed my *own* space.

I studied the copy of Sumner's calendar Maggie had given me. The daily register was broken down into half-hour increments. Most of the entries were downright cryptic. Maggie had included a Rosetta-stone-like key for me. Merrill, R1010C translated as a meeting with Bob Merrill in Conference Room 1010. Most of Sumner's appointments had been right at the bank, the entries made in neat, fat, girlish script—the secretary's, no doubt. The last entry for Thursday, four thirty, was made in a messy scrawl, which I assumed to be Sumner's own hand. According to the newspaper, he left the bank about four o'clock and was never seen again.

I stared at the entry: Ron. Ron Myers? He was a colleague on the same floor. Surely the cops had talked to him—and every other Ron in the building. I'd have to ask Maggie.

My mind wandered to thoughts of Sumner's remains... or lack thereof. According to the deer hunting book, the internal organs were usually left in the field. Hunting season in western New York State occurs in the fall, when only a deep frost is expected. It had snowed less than an inch in Amherst the night of the murder; it may have snowed more than that on the outskirts of town, and since then we'd had a major snowstorm. I couldn't remember the weather patterns in and around Lake Erie to know just where the snow belt lay. Instead, I thought about the steaming pile of organs left in the cold night air. What if the raccoons hadn't gotten them? What if...?

Richard didn't have a map of western New York, but he said Brenda had one on the back seat of her car—a Buffalo atlas, which included all of Erie county. My shoes were snow-caked from trudging through the ever-forming drifts to retrieve it. I sat at the kitchen table and flipped through the atlas pages, with no idea where to start looking.

Brenda shuffled into the kitchen on slippered feet. Although it wasn't late, she was dressed in a blue quilted bathrobe. "Is that from my car?"

"Yeah. Rich said I could—"

"Okay, but I want it put back where it belongs. You want some hot chocolate?"

"Sure."

She got the milk out of the refrigerator and heated it in a saucepan on the stove. No instant stuff for Brenda. She had a cylinder of Ghirardelli sweet ground chocolate and cocoa, and scooped teaspoons of the stuff into large mugs.

I turned my attention back to the atlas, still with no clear idea of what to look for. The pages flipped past. Whole sections of the book were devoted to the outskirts of Buffalo. I ran my hands over the paper, hoping for some kind of impression.

Brenda plunked a steaming mug, heaped with fluffy clouds of Reddi-Wip, in front of me, taking the adjacent seat. I took a sip. Better than the cheap stuff, for sure.

"What're you doing?" she asked, took a sip, and ended up with a whipped cream mustache.

I kept fanning through pages, running my hand over the type—waiting for…something. "I'm looking for Sumner's guts."

"Are you kidding?"

"No, I'm not."

She wiped her lip with a paper napkin. "What will you do if you find them?"

"I have no idea."

She took another sip, watching me as I continued to run my hands over the pages. "What are you hoping to come up with?"

"I'm not sure. But as far as I know, the cops haven't found his insides. What do you know about DNA testing?"

She looked thoughtful. "I'm sure they took tissue samples during the autopsy. It would be easy to match them." She glanced down at the page in front of me. "If you find them."

My index finger rested on the town of Holland. "I think I already have."

Chapter Twelve

"You want to what?"

To say that Richard wasn't enthusiastic about my plan was definitely an understatement.

"I'm pretty sure I know where to find the rest of Sumner's remains, but I need your help."

His eyebrows drew close in consternation.

"Think of it as archeology, Rich."

"Do you realize how much it's snowed in the past week?"

"It's in the country. Snow blows away in an open field. I'll bet we can find it easy."

Skeptical doesn't begin to describe the expression plastered across his features.

I awoke early the next morning. Too psyched to eat breakfast, I wandered around the house, waiting for Richard and Brenda to get up. I dressed in my oldest jeans and sneakers. The only pair of boots I owned were more suited for line dancing than foraging through deep snow. With no heavy jacket, I dressed in layers—cotton, flannel, and wool—and hoped I wouldn't freeze to death. That was unacceptable to Richard, who, when he finally got up, loaned me one of his jackets—easily two sizes too big. I talked him out of cashmere and into flannel, but when he reappeared in his grungies, he still looked like a walking advertisement for Neiman Marcus.

By raiding Richard's bar and the broom closet, I'd collected a plastic grocery bag filled with tools that might come in useful, and plunked them in the back of Brenda's Altima. I figured Richard wouldn't want the back seat of his beautiful Lincoln cluttered with broom, shovel, and the like, and Brenda was accommodating, as usual. She informed us she intended to read up on frostbite remedies while we were gone. She had no desire to spend the better part of the day in subfreezing temperatures.

It was after eleven when we finally started out. The day was bright and sunny. As Maggie predicted, the snow was melting and the roads were clear and dry as we headed south. For the first time in what seemed like ages, I felt good. Useful. Richard drove the twenty-some miles in silence, making me glad to have the radio for company.

We passed naked trees, closed ice-cream stands, and mile after mile of snow-covered fields. One thing was apparent: the road was not well-traveled.

The perfect place for murder.

The Holland town line sped past. "Slow down, will you? I'm not exactly sure where we're going."

"Does anything look familiar?" Richard asked.

I shook my head. "I've got no mental picture of our destination, just a funny feeling in my gut, which, I'll admit seems pretty insubstantial."

Richard slowed the car. Instead of looking at the countryside, I concentrated on the thrumming inside me.

"Stop!"

"Here? It's the middle of nowhere."

"We're getting close."

Plow-piled mounds of dirty snow flanked the road. The shoulder was virtually nonexistent. Richard parked as close to the snow as possible before activating the hazard flashers.

"If this car gets hit, you're going to explain it to Brenda. Not me."

I closed my eyes and concentrated. That shaky feeling inside grew more pronounced.

"What is it you feel, anyway?"

"I don't know how to describe it." I frowned, thought about it for a moment. "It's like being a Geiger counter. But instead of a noise, I have this tense feeling inside me. Like a guitar string tightened too much." That didn't come out exactly right, but he seemed to accept the explanation.

I got out of the Altima, opened the rear door, and took out the grocery bag, shovel, and broom.

Richard surveyed the waist-high snow. "This isn't going to work."

"Of course it will. Beyond the road, the snow can only be a foot or so deep." I knew I was being optimistic, but I didn't want him to crap out on me before we even got started.

We struggled over the snowbank, and I took the lead. The shoulder sloped into a gully and, because of the drifted snow, it was hard to tell where the terrain became level again. After only a couple of feet, I realized that thanks to my bum arm, my center of gravity was off. My foot caught in the crusty snow and I went down. I rolled onto my right side, protecting my already-broken left arm. The air turned blue and I'm sure Richard learned a few new curses to add to his growing repertoire.

He crouched beside me. "Are you okay?"

I glared at him. "That's some great bedside manner."

He frowned, helped me to my feet, then thrust the broom at me. "Here, use this as a walking stick."

I jabbed the pole into the snow, taking a tentative step forward. I wished I'd thought to bring sunglasses; the glare was unrelenting. Shading my eyes, I looked around to get my bearings. "This way."

We started off to the southwest, and it was anything but easy going. Traffic passed behind us on the road, but the winter landscape before us was absolutely desolate. It took almost ten minutes to walk some twenty yards; my feet were wet in less time than that. The ice-crusted snow broke around the toes of my sneakers in jagged hunks. I looked back and saw that, instead of a straight line, we'd made an uneven path. No wonder people get lost in the desert.

"Why I ever agreed to come along…" Richard muttered behind me.

"You won't let me drive, remember."

"I could have stayed in my nice, warm house. But, no, I'm trudging through snow—"

I listened to him gripe for the next five minutes. It took all my self-control not to turn around and clock him. As it was, if we found nothing, I was sure he'd start filling out the commitment papers for me when we returned home.

That funny feeling vibrated right through me. I stopped, gazed around us at the crystalline snow. "This is a good place to start digging." I nodded toward the shovel.

"You want me to dig?" he asked, incredulous.

I rubbed my broken arm. "Well, I can hardly do it."

If looks could kill, I'd have been as dead as the object of our search. Grumbling, Richard thrust the shovel into the snow. I watched as he cleared a one-foot square patch and found nothing. He started shoveling around that small area, pushing aside the snow until there was only flattened grass underfoot. Nothing. Nothing. Nothing.

Minutes later, he'd cleared an area about the size of a back yard pool.

"Take a rest," I said, and he gratefully leaned on the shovel. Although in good shape for his age, Richard was not used to physical labor. His flushed cheeks and labored breathing were accompanied by a thin film of sweat across his forehead.

"This is useless," he puffed. "Like looking for a needle in a haystack. A wild goose chase. A complete and utter waste of time."

"Can you come up with any other clichés?"

I took the shovel from him. We were close to finding it—very close. Awkwardly, I tried to scoop away the snow, but it was just too heavy.

"Don't," he told me, grabbing for the handle, which I held onto. "How're your feet?"

"They're okay."

"They're wet. It's below freezing. You'll get frostbite. Let's call it quits."

"No." Stubborn, I tried again. This time I managed to move some snow, but not enough to make a difference.

"Stop." He took the shovel from me. "I'll give you five more minutes, then we're heading back to the car." He meant it. But I didn't have to wait five minutes.

Richard jabbed the snow and hit something solid. "What the hell?"

"That's it!" I fell to my knees, scooping away snow with my good hand. Fumbling with the grocery bag, I brought out the hand brush and removed the last of the snow from the dark, icy mass. Richard paled as I handed him an ice pick. "You can have the honors."

Richard knelt beside me in the snow, then carefully chipped away at the mound. He stopped after about a minute, studying it.

"Well?"

He pointed to an ice-encrusted protrusion. "See this, it's a pancreas."

"Human?"

"It sure looks like it to me." He straightened, looking at me expectantly.

"I think I'm ready to warm up my feet now."

We gathered our things, all but the shovel. I rubbed it down with my snowy glove to remove any stray fingerprints. We left it standing in the snow to mark the spot, and trudged back to the car.

I noted the odometer reading while Richard made a U-turn, then we headed back toward Holland. "Now what?" he asked.

"I guess we report it."

"How do you report something like this?"

I hadn't thought of that. "Do you have a lawyer here in Buffalo?"

"Yes."

"Before we do anything, maybe you should call him. I don't want to be interrogated by the cops without one. Hayden already warned me off. When he finds out what we've found—"

"We?" Richard echoed.

"You were there, too."

His expression was grim. "What if we reported this anonymously?"

"Smart move. Otherwise how are we going to explain this? 'Uh, hi, I'm a nut-case fresh from the Big Apple. I found these guts on the side of the road.'"

He was not amused.

"And I'll tell you something else. Who do you think will be the prime suspect?"

Richard stared at me. "You, of course."

I shook my head. "I'm not the expert on anatomy."

It took a moment for that statement to sink in. He blanched. "Jesus."

I consulted the atlas. "Take the next cutoff. We have to get out of the area fast. Someone might remember the car. Course the California plates will confuse the cops for a while," I said, thinking aloud.

"We are going to report it, aren't we?"

"Sure, but I'd rather wait until we get back to Buffalo. From a pay phone, if we can find one. Then we'll hide Brenda's car in the garage." I stopped myself. "Do I sound paranoid?"

"Just a little," he said and smiled. He was quiet for a while. "I owe you an apology."

"What for?"

"You knew where to find...." His words trailed off. "I didn't want to believe you."

"Yeah, but you humored me."

"I was determined to prove you wrong once and for all. But this—this is creepy."

"Tell me about it. You're not the one it's happening to. But if you want the truth, I didn't know if we'd find them. On a gut level, I trust these feelings, yet I'm afraid to. I'm afraid to look like a fool. I keep hoping this blasted insight will just go away."

It was after two when we returned to Amherst. I dialed 911 from a pay phone in the parking lot of a grocery store. Disguising my voice with a lousy Texas accent, I told them where to look, and hoped like hell they'd take me seriously. If not...I suppose it wouldn't matter; finding frozen viscera wasn't going to solve the case. But it was a stepping stone for me. It was time to start adding things together.

***

I found Richard staring out his study window, sipping a dark Manhattan. Under my arm was the dog-eared Kraft envelope.

"Is the sun over the yardarm?" I asked.

"It is for me. It's not every day I find that kind of buried treasure."

"I can't wait to see the six o'clock news." I sat down behind his desk, moving his papers, books, and mementos aside. He watched as I spread out the newspaper clippings, my notes, and everything else I'd collected on the Sumner murder.

"I've got some ideas on who the killer is, but I want to bounce them off a neutral party."

"I don't know how neutral I can be, after this morning."

"Well, I figure we're in this together now, right?" He didn't say no, so I took that as assent. "You read the newspaper profile of the killer?"

"Yes."

"What do you think?"

"I don't have an opinion."

I handed him the clipping and he read parts of it aloud. "The assailant is probably between the ages of thirty-five to sixty, strong, an active outdoorsman or hunter. No known motive."

"I think they're wrong. I think the killer is little Jackie's mother."

"Which little Jackie? Which mother?"

"Sharon Walker. I have this funny feeling…and lately my funny feelings have been correct."

"What do you know about this woman?"

"Virtually nothing. She had a child on January tenth four years ago. I know her father had business dealings with Sumner. I know her father's company went bankrupt. That's it."

"That's what your friend, Maggie, told you, right?"

I nodded.

"How can you conclude she murdered him with just that?"

"I can't. That's why I have to find a way to prove it." I sat back in his chair. "Obviously there's no paper trail to lead the police to her."

"You mean checks, love letters—that kind of thing?"

I nodded. "That invitation I found in Sumner's office may be the only thing he kept."

"Are you sure it came from her?"

"Am I positive?" I thought about it for a moment. "No. But it seems likely."

"So what's her motive for murder?"

"I have no idea. But I'll find out."

Richard took a deep swallow of his drink and pulled up a chair beside me. "Okay. What've you got in mind?"

I savored the moment; he was hooked.

"First of all, a trip to the library downtown. They should have all the newspapers on microfilm or CD-ROM for the time when Walker Construction went under. I can lift names and interview the former executives or employees. If I can get a fix on this woman without tipping my hand—"

"But aren't her former co-workers likely to go straight to her and warn her about you?"

"Not if I can find a disgruntled employee or two. Someone with an ax to grind is likely to tell me the dirt that went on before the company collapsed."

Richard took another long pull on his drink. "This really is a nasty business you're in."

"Murder is a nasty business, and I think Sharon Walker killed Matt Sumner. And she did it in front of her son."

"You said that before. How do you know?"

"I kept getting all these feelings: fear, triumph, horror. It took me a week to sort it all out. The emotions came from all of them at the time of the murder. Somehow I got caught up in it. What's weird is I started feeling all this before Sumner was murdered. And, let me tell you, it's bad enough to have your own fears without experiencing somebody else's."

Richard studied me. "I still think this would make a fascinating study. You really should let UB's Psych Department—"

"No way! I'm not going to be anyone's guinea pig."

"Oh." He sounded disappointed.

"What do you have in mind?"

"I keep thinking about my grandmother. What is it you sense upstairs? What is it of her that's left up there? And why is it in my grandfather's room?"

"I've been wondering about that myself—trying to work up the courage to face it."

He downed the rest of his drink in one gulp. "Well, I'm fortified. Let's go."

This wasn't how I'd planned to spend the rest of the afternoon. But I found myself following in his wake, glad it was still daylight. I didn't think I could face the old lady in the dark of night.

I started up the stairs, dread closing around my chest. Richard paused at the landing. As I topped the last step, he reached for my elbow to steady me. "Maybe this wasn't such a good idea," he said.

Panic churned through me. I was tempted, really tempted, to run back down the stairs. But—

"If not now, it'll still be waiting for me tomorrow or next week."

My words sounded a whole lot braver than I felt.

Richard opened the bedroom door. The sun had disappeared behind the trees, leaving the room gloomy with shadows. Because I was prepared, whatever loomed inside did not reach out for me. I took a steadying breath and entered. The furniture was mahogany, just as I remembered it from glimpses years before. A faint odor of fresh paint still clung to the off-white walls. The new carpet was beige wall-to-wall. The room was pleasant, neutral, with absolutely no soul of its own. I stood in the center and concentrated. Murmuring voices echoed. Something that wasn't from the here and now?

"Well?" Richard asked.

I cocked my head, listening. "I hear something. Like voices behind a wall." I walked around the room and paused at a highboy, ran my hand across the top. The dread grew stronger, threatening to choke me.

Bright light flared behind me.

I whirled to find the shadows replaced by morning sunlight flooding through the windows. The rose-colored cabbage-flowered wallpaper was back. Mrs. Alpert stood in the doorway where Richard had been only moments before. Dressed in a drab wool skirt, with a crisp white blouse under a navy sweater, she looked like an ancient, stern librarian. She leaned on the cane in her right hand; in her left she clutched a piece of paper. Her bloodshot eyes bulged in anger; her paper-white skin was wrinkled ten years beyond what I'd ever seen.

"What is this?" she nearly screamed, her thin voice shrill in the virtual silence.

I turned to see what she was looking at. Old Mr. Alpert stood in front of his closet, fastening a cardigan, his skeletal, heavily veined hands fumbling with the buttons.

"None of your business," he said, and closed the door.

"You bought her flowers, didn't you?"

"Yes, I did. It's the least I can do for her now. Goodness knows I should've done more for her in life."

"How dare you say that to me? She took my boy. She stole him!"

"And you stole her child."

Dizziness rolled over me as I realized who and what they were arguing about.

The scene wavered, images colliding like a double-exposure. I could just make out Richard standing where I'd left him in the open doorway. His mouth moved, but I couldn't hear what he was saying.

As Mrs. Alpert stepped between us, the past obliterated him.

She leaned heavily on her cane, spittle flying as she spoke. "I took what was mine. Flesh of my flesh."

"You destroyed her—drove her insane."

Furious, she came at him, smacked him on the arm with her cane. "How dare you talk to me like that!"

Old Mr. Alpert glowered at her for a long moment, then without a word turned for the closet. He took out a suitcase, set it on the bed, and opened it. He crossed to the dresser.

"What are you doing?"

"Packing." He took out shirts, set them in the suitcase, then turned to another drawer, taking out underwear and socks.

"Where do you think you're going?"

"California. To visit Richard."

Torrents of her anger drilled through me, made my head pound, my pulse race. All these years later, that old, fragile-looking woman still scared the shit out of me.

"Why?" she demanded.

Mr. Alpert turned toward his bathroom. "Because I can't take being with you any more. I don't want to be with you any longer."

Her hand crumpled the paper; then she dropped it onto the floor.

He crossed the marble threshold between the carpeted bedroom and the ceramic tiled bathroom.

She followed.

I did, too.

Oblivious to her, Mr. Alpert reached into the bathroom cabinet for his shaving gear. Her face twisted as she hauled back and slammed the cane against his skull. He went down as though pole-axed.

I jumped forward to stop his fall, but he passed through my hands. His temple smacked the side of the claw-footed tub and he crumpled on the floor.

Mrs. Alpert glared down at him, watching his scarlet blood pool on the cool white tile. Her smile was thin-lipped and triumphant.

She turned for the bed.

I followed and watched as she returned the old man's clothes to the highboy, then placed the suitcase back in the closet. Without a backward glance, she headed for the hallway and closed the bedroom door behind her.

Seconds ticked by.

Mr. Alpert lay unmoving on the bathroom floor.

The emotions tied to that incident still clung to these rooms: the old man's despair at betraying my mother, his wife's fury at my mother for stealing the affection of Richard's father—her only child.

The crumpled paper the old woman had discarded lay at my feet. I bent down and picked it up. Smoothing it out on my knee, I read the typed script, an invoice from Mankowski's Florist Shop: $35 for flowers, placed on Plot 58975, Elizabeth O. A. Resnick.

The room shimmered back into the present.

I stood upright again—back where I started. The overhead light blazed. Richard gripped my shoulders, gently shaking me. I took in a sharp breath, staring into his worried blue eyes.

"Jeff? Jeff, snap out of it!"

Brenda appeared in the doorway. "Richard Alpert, what have you done?" Then she was between us, her arms wrapped around me. I let her steady me. "It's okay now," she soothed. "It's over now."

I took a ragged breath and suddenly realized I was okay. No residual anger, fear, or hatred remained. The room was just like any other in the house. I wiped at my eyes and coughed.

"Are you all right?" Richard asked. "Christ, Jeff, what the hell happened? You were practically catatonic."

I cleared my throat, pulling away from Brenda. "Have you got any Irish whiskey?"

Ashen-faced, Richard nodded, then disappeared.

I collapsed onto the edge of the bed.

Brenda joined me. "Are you okay?"

"Yeah." I ran a hand through my sweat-dampened hair. "She killed him, Brenda. Old lady Alpert whacked the old man over the head—killed him right in the bathroom."

She rubbed my back like a mother comforting a child. "I knew something bad happened here."

I looked at her, confused.

"I always got bad vibes in this room," she explained. "But not like you. My grandma would've said you've got the second sight."

"You, too?"

She shook her head. "Not like you." She rose from the bed and opened a drawer in the dresser, took out a yellowed piece of paper. "I found this while we were redecorating. I don't know why, but I never showed it to Richard."

A cold shadow darkened my soul. The same florist bill I'd seen only minutes before.

"I can't tell Richard. He loved the old hag."

"Then don't."

"He's already asking—"

"He doesn't have to know everything."

She was right.

Richard arrived with a highball glass filled to the brim with ice and good sipping whiskey. I wondered how he'd managed to get all the way upstairs without losing half the glass's contents.

I tasted it and coughed. "Damn fine."

"What the hell did you see?" he demanded.

I glanced at Brenda. Her nod encouraged me to explain.

"The day your grandfather died, he had an argument with your grandmother. About this." I handed him the aged invoice.

He studied it. "She found out."

"Found out what?" Brenda asked.

"Grandfather always bought Betty flowers on the anniversary of her death. Before his arthritis got too bad, he used to go to the cemetery. I drove him a couple of times." He looked wistful. "He was a good man, Jeff. The only father I ever knew."

"At least you *had* a father figure." That came out sounding a lot worse than I'd meant, but Richard had the grace to ignore it. As a kid, I'd had none of the privileges Richard had. But for all the advantages of wealth, I bet he was nearly as miserable as me. We had more in common than I thought.

The light outside continued to fade, the shadows growing more dense.

"Anyway," I continued, "they argued and she...she went off in a huff. He...uh...slipped in the bathroom."

Brenda gave me a comforting smile, but Richard was looking at me, not her, and didn't see.

"Are you going to be all right?" he asked.

I took another sip of that damn fine whiskey. "Sure."

"Then let's get out of here," Brenda said. "It's close to dinner time and I can use some help in the kitchen." She rose from the bed and left us. I heard her soft footfalls on the stairs.

Richard looked around the room, apparently caught up in his memories. He seemed content with the shorthand account I'd given, which satisfied me. I had no desire to destroy whatever illusions he had of his little old grandmother.

I took another sip of my drink.

"Aren't you still on medication? You're not supposed to be drinking," Richard admonished.

"Are you going to report me to my doctor?" I stood. "Come on. Brenda wants help in the kitchen. Think we got any cheese and crackers?"

"I expect so." Richard led the way.

I took one last look around the room. I'd faced and conquered my fear. I felt like Neil Armstrong on the moon: one small step—and one giant leap toward getting my life back.

Chapter Thirteen

We sat down to eat dinner watching the kitchen TV. The top story on the six o'clock news was indeed the anonymous tip the cops had received on where to find the last of Sumner's remains. The reports sounded so sanitized. The man was viciously killed, gutted like a deer, and the news media tiptoed around the truth. I suppose they were looking out for the tender sensibilities of children in the audience, but was the reality of Sumner's murder that much worse than the violent fantasy of network dramas?

A brown-eyed blonde reporter with big hair from Channel 7 stood by the roadside with a live report. We even saw our shovel. I was surprised she didn't try to interview it. She hinted it was the murderer who'd tipped the cops.

Yeah, right.

After dinner, I went back to my room to draw up a research list for the library, but found I couldn't concentrate. I tried going over the news clippings, with the same results, and instead toyed with the idea of calling Maggie. I thought about her a lot lately. I wondered what her apartment looked like, where she shopped for groceries, what she liked to do on cold winter evenings, if she slept in flannel or nothing at all.... And I wondered if it was too soon to call her again.

I had to force myself to think of other things. Something bothered me about my first visit to Sumner's neighborhood—nobody seemed to have seen anything the night the body was dumped. People usually want to be helpful, especially in a murder investigation. Of course, I hadn't spoken with all the neighbors. If I had my own car, I might've spent a day tracking down everyone.

Someone had to have seen something the night of the murder.

Stretching out on my bed, I realized that so far I'd been pretty timid in pushing this investigation. Not my usual style. But I'd been busted down to field investigator, and then unemployed for so long. And that stupid mugging.... Richard's reluctance to believe in me hadn't helped, either. But ultimately, the problem was mine. So what was I going to do about it?

I'd been a damned good investigator, so why was I holding back? Despite my success earlier in the day, I knew I couldn't depend on my funny feelings to solve the case. I had to do some real, hard-nosed digging. I wanted to talk with Sam Nielsen, the reporter from *The Buffalo News*, and I needed to make my peace, or at least attempt it, with Detective Hayden.

I hauled myself up and headed for the kitchen. Searching the cabinets, I found an unopened package of rainbow chip cookies. I stared at the drawing of the little hollow tree. My mother had drilled into me that you should never, ever take cookies from an unopened package when you hadn't paid for them yourself. Despite the fact that Richard's millions could buy a lot more cookies, the rule still applied.

I closed the cupboard door and again longed for my own car, so that I could go buy my own cookies, or nachos, or beer. Having no money put a definite crimp in that scenario. I hadn't owned a car in years, although I'd always kept my license current. In Manhattan, a car was pointless; murders occurred to protect parking spaces. But occasionally Shelley and I would rent a car and spend summer weekends at quaint little bed-and-breakfast inns in Cape May or head for the Green Mountains of Vermont.

I shook my head clear of the memories, then realized I'd remembered something good about my time with Shelley. Two years after her death, it still hurt to think about her.

Standing in the middle of the kitchen, I realized that for the first time since the mugging I felt downright bored. I truly was on the mend. I looked around and caught sight of the phone book on the counter. What I really wanted was to call Maggie.

And say what?

Instead, I found myself flipping through the white pages, searching the columns of six-point type. I already knew Sharon Walker's name wasn't there, but there was a James M. Walker listed at an East Aurora address.

My finger traced back and forth under the name. All I had to do was pick up the phone, call old Sharon, and maybe we'd have ourselves a real nice conversation. Excuse me, ma'am, did you kill Matt Sumner?

A glance at the wall clock reminded me it was getting late to pull that kind of a stunt. The worst that could happen was she'd hang up.

What the hell. Grabbing the phone, I punched in the number.

One ring.

Suddenly nervous, I wished I'd taken time to write a script. Hello, Ms. Walker, I'm taking a survey.

No.

Two rings.

Maybe she wasn't home.

Three rings.

I hoped to God she wouldn't use the phone's call-back feature—or have caller ID.

"Hello?" A woman's voice.

Ready or not.

"Hi, this is Ken with Niagara Associates. I'd like to ask you a few questions about the Buffalo media."

For a moment she said nothing. I heard a TV in the background. "A survey?"

So far so good.

"Do you regularly read *The Buffalo News*?"

"On Sunday. I get it for the coupons."

Had I expected a quaver in her voice? Maybe some kind of intuitive message that screamed she was Sumner's murderer? Instead, she sounded like any ordinary person answering an annoying phone call.

"May I ask your favorite local television and radio stations?"

"Well, I watch Channel 7 news at six o'clock most nights. And I listen to WMJX in the mornings."

Time to risk it all. "How do you feel the local media has covered the Matt Sumner murder?"

A long silence followed, and then I heard a click.

I replaced the phone on the hook, knowing I'd pushed her too quickly. I'd gotten no insight and didn't know anything I hadn't known before.

Stupid. Definitely a tactical error. After all, the news had been filled with our little treasure hunt. Had I inadvertently tipped her off that she had not gotten away with murder, and that someone was now hunting the hunter?

What if I spooked her into leaving the area? Or worse, what if my call pushed her into doing something potentially lethal to someone else?

Suddenly, taking the timid approach to my investigation seemed a lot smarter than pushing things—or potentially dangerous people. And yet, I never asked the woman's name. What if the telephone number had been reassigned? Maybe I'd never even spoken to Sharon Walker.

Antsy, I wandered over to the refrigerator and looked in. The six-pack of Canadian Ice beer looked inviting, but I wasn't supposed to drink while on medication. I'd already pushed my luck with the whiskey earlier. I needed to get some non-alcoholic beer to tide me over. Such thoughts reminded me once again of my transportation—and monetary—deficit.

Brenda's key ring hung on a decorative brass rack near the door. Their bedroom and Richard's study were in the back of the house, away from the garage. I could sneak Richard's car out. They'd never hear a thing.

Instead, I headed for the study. Richard was still up, reading from some leather-bound medical tome.

"Don't you ever sleep?"

He glanced at the grandfather clock across the way. "It's not even ten o'clock."

"I know, but if you were asleep I could steal your car and joyride around town."

He looked at me with suspicion. "Where do you want to go?"

I shrugged. "Somewhere for junk food. To hang out."

"Hang out where?"

"Maybe Orchard Park."

He sighed, letting the book slam shut. "Why?"

"I want to see Sumner's neighborhood at night. See whose lights are on. Nothing special."

He looked...resigned? Maybe he still felt guilty for goading me into confronting my fears upstairs. He shoved the book aside, stood, then neatly pushed in the chair. "Okay. Let me tell Brenda."

"Ask if she wants to come."

That cheered him. "Okay."

I went back to my room, changed into some shoes. By the time I found my jacket, Richard was waiting for me in the kitchen.

"Brenda said she isn't into male bonding. But if we get wings, to bring some home for her."

We trudged out to the garage and stamped the snow from our shoes before getting into the Lincoln. In a minute or so the big car's heater kicked in and we'd reached Main Street. Richard turned right, heading for the Thruway.

I watched the streets flash past. Traffic was light. We'd make it across town in no time, which was good, because through the power of suggestion, the thought of spicy Buffalo wings began to get to me.

Richard pulled into the turn lane. "Why do you really want to go to Sumner's neighborhood?"

"I don't know. I keep thinking about it. I feel like I need to be there. Tonight."

"You're not expecting the murderer to return to the scene of the crime, are you?"

"It's not the scene of the crime. And no, I don't know what to expect. I just expect…." Anticipation gripped me. "Something."

He turned onto the entrance ramp. "Do you want to get something to eat first?"

"What did you have in mind?"

"I didn't want anything until Brenda mentioned wings. Now that's all I can think of."

I laughed. "How about on the way back?"

He nodded, his gaze still fixed on the road.

"Things seemed to have thawed between you and Brenda. Is everything okay?"

"We're negotiating."

"What does that mean?"

"We're going to look for ways to expand our horizons."

"You don't sound thrilled."

"Right now I'm willing to try anything to please her. Besides, like you, she thinks I need a job. She's been calling clinics and gathering information. She's got it in her head we're going to volunteer as a team."

"What do you think about that?"

"The idea's still too new. I haven't had a lot of hands-on experience in a long time."

"Is that why you've been burying your nose in books?"

He laughed. "It can't hurt to brush up."

The conversation petered out. I considered telling him about my call to Sharon, but what good would it do? I could berate myself without his input.

Richard took the Orchard Park exit. We drove in silence to Sumner's quiet neighborhood. The roads were empty on this snowy March night. In fact, as still as death.

At ten-fifteen we rolled slowly past the Sumner place. Lights blazed in the living room and other parts of the house. Was Claudia home alone, or had she gone out, leaving the lights on a timer to fool burglars?

We went to the end of the street. Richard pulled into a driveway to turn around. "Now where?"

"Can we stay a few minutes? I feel like I have to wait for something."

"Another psychic message?"

"I don't know."

He looked jittery. "We can't just park. Someone's bound to call the police. I mean, the neighbors have to be nervous after what's happened."

He had a point.

"I'm probably making more out of it than I should. I just felt like I should be here tonight."

He nodded and started down the street, putting on his left turn signal, even though there was no one behind us. I too looked both ways for oncoming traffic and saw a man and his dog jogging farther down on Freeman Road.

"Turn right, will you? I want to catch up with that jogger."

In seconds we were moving parallel to a guy who looked to be in his mid-thirties. I hit the power window control. It slid down with an electronic hum, the cold air blasting in.

"Sir? Sir?"

The man looked straight ahead, picked up his speed. The dog barked, but he yanked it along with him.

"Sir?"

He glanced over to me. "I don't want any trouble."

His words startled me. Hadn't I said the same thing to the muggers just weeks before?

"I'm investigating Matthew Sumner's death. Do you jog this neighborhood on a regular basis? Maybe you saw something."

He slowed and Richard braked along with him. He stopped beneath a street lamp, giving us the once over.

"What do you want?"

I got out of the car, handing him my business card. "I'm investigating Matt Sumner's death," I repeated.

He examined the card and gave me another quick once-over.

"Did you jog around this neighborhood a week ago Thursday?"

"I run most nights."

"Do you know where the dead man lived?"

He looked down the road. "Back on Forest. The gray house with the ornamental cherry trees out front."

I nodded. His dog, a big, happy black Lab with a wet nose the size of ripe plum, sniffed my coat. He yanked the leash and the dog sat.

"I jog down all these streets on a regular basis. I try to get in three or four miles a day, so I pretty much know the neighborhood. Who parks in their driveway, who parks in the garage. Stuff like that. One night, a couple weeks ago, there was a strange car in that driveway. I figured they had company."

He didn't even have to describe it. Just as he spoke, I could see it. A dark, full-sized station wagon, with a chrome roof rack. I couldn't tell the make or model; it was old, but looked to be in good shape. Snow lazily drifted to earth in big flakes, covering the driveway. I wondered if the police had noted the tire tracks or if the snow had melted before Claudia Sumner had discovered her husband's body. I tuned back into his description.

"—wagon. It was black, or dark red. Something like that. The funny thing is, it was backed right up to the garage door."

"Did you see anyone?"

He shook his head. "The garage door was down. At the time, I didn't give it much thought."

"What time was this?"

He let out a breath. "I usually start out about eight thirty, so it would've taken me about fifteen minutes to get there. Maybe eight forty-five."

I looked at my watch. "You're late tonight."

"One of the kids is sick. The whole day's been shot."

"Have you talked to the police about this?"

"I didn't think it was important."

"Would you be willing to?"

He shrugged. "I guess. But what good would it do? I didn't see anyone and I didn't see the license plate."

"The cops like to be thorough. Your name, sir?"

"Paul Linski. I live a couple of blocks from here over on Cherry Tree Lane." He gave me his phone number, and I told him the police would be in touch. I patted the dog, and Linski waved as he took off down the road.

I got back in the car.

"You knew," Richard said. "When you were talking to him, you already knew what he was going to say."

"When he said he saw the car, I knew it was a dark-colored station wagon. If I can find some pictures online or at the library, I might be able to pick out the year and model."

Richard put the Lincoln in gear then pulled into a nearby driveway to turn around. "This is too weird. *You* are too weird."

"Thanks. I love you, too." Satisfied with what we'd accomplished, I turned my thoughts to a more important issue.

"So where's a good place to get wings?"

Chapter Fourteen

My first call Sunday morning was to check the central library's recorded message for their hours. The second call was to Maggie.

Nervous as a teenager, I punched her number. The phone rang four times. Didn't she ever pick it up on the first ring?

"Hello?" She sounded breathless again.

"Hi, Maggie. It's—"

"Jeff! Good to hear from you."

"Am I interrupting anything?"

"No. Just rushing around getting ready for Mass at noon. It's Palm Sunday. I'm going to the Basilica in Lackawanna. Want to go? I could come pick you up."

"I haven't been to church in years. I wouldn't know what to do any more." A funny feeling welled inside me. Apprehension? I wasn't sure. "Anyway, I've already made plans to go to the library this afternoon."

"How about next Sunday? It's Easter."

"Let me think about it. I thought you lived in Clarence. Why go to church all the way out in Lackawanna?"

"I grew up there. I love the Basilica; it was my parish. Have you ever been there?"

"No. A sinner like me probably wouldn't be welcome."

"Don't be silly. Besides, they've been restoring it for years. It's worth it just to see the gorgeous art and stained glass."

"I'll think about it. But I would like to see you again."

"Make me an offer."

We settled for lunch on Tuesday.

***

Richard and I turned Brenda loose in the home decorating section of Buffalo's Central Library, then we attached ourselves to the machines in their archives. We were able to backtrack Walker Construction's downfall from articles in the financial section of *The Buffalo News*.

We split up the work. Richard looked into the company's history, while I concentrated on the people.

Watching Richard work, I realized he would have made a damn good investigator. He thrived on digging through minutia—a necessary evil. No wonder he missed his research job.

We lost track of time. The librarians literally had to bully us off the equipment to get us out. By that time, we were starved. We found Brenda in the main lobby, loaded down with coffee table books. It took no persuasion at all to convince her to go out for an early dinner. We settled on the Red Mill, because Brenda thought its paddlewheel looked quaint.

Richard and I brought along our research to compare notes. His pages were well-organized, and he bucked the old physician's cliché by writing in neat script. Mine looked no different from what I'd done in high school—haphazard. But I could read them, and that's all that mattered.

After ordering drinks, Richard settled a pair of reading glasses on his nose and shuffled through his notes. "Walker Construction's financial problems began after they contracted to build a shopping mall on the outskirts of Cheektowaga," he began. "The land was purchased, but the permits were delayed time and again when environmental studies got bogged down in red tape. They'd already ordered extra equipment and building materials, but every time construction was slated to start, something else would crop up to halt work.

"Another shopping mall was proposed on a site on Walden Avenue," he continued. "Despite the same delaying tactics, Pyramid Construction weathered the bureaucratic storms better than Walker. Walker Construction's loans were called, penalties were levied, and the company was strangled. They ended up laying off fifty percent of their workforce under Chapter Eleven bankruptcy. That was the beginning of the end."

"I got the names of five company officers, including acting company president Sharon Walker," I said. "I want to interview as many of them as possible. It might take a few days."

"What did you learn about Sharon?"

"She took control of the firm after her father's fatal heart attack in the midst of the bankruptcy proceedings. I found the others in the city directory or the phone book. Now I have to figure out exactly what I want to ask them."

"Not bad for an afternoon's work," Brenda said.

The waitress arrived, forcing us to consider the menu.

"I was busy, too," Brenda said after we'd ordered. She produced a handful of glossy brochures. "Richard, you never told me there's a ton of great stuff to do in Buffalo. Did you know there's a theater district downtown? And the Albright Knox Gallery. It probably isn't the Huntington, but won't it be fun to find out?"

I remembered Richard's comment days before about broadening his horizons. Instead, he looked like a deer caught in the headlights of a speeding car. I tried not to smirk, but I was glad it was him and not me.

* * *

I awoke the next morning with the beginning of one of my skull-pounding headaches, and immediately popped two of the little pink tablets. I was getting low. I'd have to get Richard to write me a prescription.

After fortifying myself with a cup of coffee, I got on the phone. Charles Nowak had been Walker Construction's vice-president, so he probably knew just about everything there was to know about the company. When I called his home, his wife gave me his work number and suggested I contact him there. He was now a sales rep with a competing construction company.

But I didn't want to concentrate on only those at the top. While I had her on the phone, I told Mrs. Nowak I was working on a fraud investigation. Did she know of anyone whose actions might've led to the downfall of the company? She tried to be discreet but dropped one name: Ted Schmidt, a former employee who'd been caught stealing and selling heavy equipment. He'd gone to jail for at least a year. That was all she knew.

I called and talked with Nowak, explaining the situation and making an appointment to see him later that afternoon.

Next I tried the Orchard Park Police Department. Detective Hayden was out, but expected back at eleven. That gave me a couple of hours to kill.

I knew from experience that cops—and nosy reporters—often believe they know who killers are, but don't have enough proof to make an arrest. Before I visited Detective Hayden, I decided to try and see Sam Nielsen. He had to know more about the case than had appeared in the paper. My problem was getting him to spill it. I might have to dangle a carrot of my own in front of him. But what? No way did I want him to know how I knew what I knew.

Richard didn't seem to mind adding another destination to the day's itinerary. To prepare myself for the meeting, I donned my sling and combed my hair to de-emphasize the shaved areas of my skull. It didn't help: I still looked like a shock therapy patient.

Brenda came in with the mail just as we were about to leave. "There's a letter for you, Jeffy."

I took the envelope from her, opened it, and smiled: my Federal Income Tax refund. The post office had delivered it to my old address, but my landlord had forwarded it to me.

"It ain't much," I told Richard, "but I need to cash this."

"No problem. We'll stop at a bank this morning."

Despite the gray skies, Richard seemed in good spirits. Once we hit the road, I broached a subject that had been on my mind for days.

"Rich, when can I drive again?"

"When you're better."

"Who's going to decide that? You, me, or some other doctor?"

"Right now I think I'm a better judge than you. You're not ready."

"I feel fine," I lied.

"You don't look fine. Have you seen the dark circles under your eyes? And you're paler than snow."

I pulled down the mirror on the passenger side visor and had a look. Okay, so there were circles under my eyes. I hadn't been out in the sun in nearly seven months, was I supposed to look like some tanned and healthy beach bum?

"I have a lunch date tomorrow with Maggie. I'm trying to get to know the woman; I can't have you tagging along forever."

"I don't mind driving you around. I'll drop you off at the restaurant and, when you're ready to leave, you can give me a call and I'll come get you."

I let out a breath. He was being obstinate. Or maybe I was. "Can you give me a timetable? If I was your patient, how long would you make me wait before I could drive?"

"If you were my patient, I'd order bed rest. Unfortunately, I'm only your brother, and you're notorious for ignoring my advice."

"Richard!"

"Another three or four weeks. Jeff, don't be so impatient. You nearly had your head caved in. Give yourself time to heal."

He was probably right, but I was ready to get on with my life…whatever it ended up being.

Richard dropped me off in front of *The Buffalo News* building, intending to find a parking space. He said he'd hang around the lobby until I came down. I didn't anticipate being inside too long.

I managed to slip by a security guard and found the crowded newsroom bustling with ringing phones, lively conversations, and reporters at their computer terminals hacking away at the news of the day. A tall young woman in a very short skirt told me where to find Nielsen's desk.

I immediately recognized him as the reporter I'd seen at the church. Over the years Sam had lost most of his dark, wavy hair, but he was the same guy I'd known at Amherst Central High. We'd never really hit it off. To him I was just some nerd with a camera, while he'd been Mr. Popular and the editor of the yearbook. My self-esteem, low as it currently was, was still higher than it had been more than eighteen years before. I marched up to his desk and introduced myself.

"Sam Nielsen? I'm Jeff Resnick. I've been reading your stories on the Sumner murder case. I hoped I could have a few moments of your time."

He pointed to the empty chair next to his desk. "Sit down." His face betrayed no hint of recognition, which was just as well. "What's your interest in the case?"

"I'm an insurance investigator—currently unemployed. I was recently mugged," I said, hastily explaining my infirmities. "I'm trying to—" I gestured with my right hand, as though I'd forgotten what I wanted to say.

"Polish up your skills?"

"Exactly."

"What have you come up with so far?"

"Not a whole lot. I talked with his neighbors, his wife, some of the people he worked with."

"Guy was a first-class prick, right?"

"He hasn't been portrayed that way in the paper."

"No," he admitted. "He was friends with the editor in chief. That's colored our reports a bit. But you want a relatively prominent murder victim portrayed in a positive light, at least if you want the crime solved. If the public doesn't care, then someone who knows the truth might not come forward."

"And your editor wants the crime solved."

"You got it." He scrutinized my face. "What did you say your name was? You look familiar."

"Jeffrey Resnick."

He shook his head. "Can't place you. But it'll come to me."

"The whole situation reads like something out of the *National Enquirer*."

"Hey, don't blaspheme in the news room," he warned good-naturedly.

"I'm curious. Your stories haven't mentioned what happened to Sumner's wallet and car keys. Were they found in the car?"

"In the glove box."

That in itself was unusual. "Anything missing?"

"Just the cash. About seventy dollars. This case has got to break soon. Somebody knows something. Somebody tipped the cops on where to find the victim's—"

"Guts," I supplied.

"Yeah. It's just a matter of time before the whole thing breaks."

"You obviously have an inside line on what the police know. Are they close?"

He shrugged. "They're too busy arguing jurisdiction. The body was found in Orchard Park, but he was murdered in Holland."

"Have they narrowed down a list of suspects?"

He shook his head. "They keep running into dead ends. But I've got a feeling about this one."

"A hunch?"

"Yeah. You depend on them in this job. Whoever told them about the murder site is going to lead them straight to the killer. Guaranteed."

"Hey, Sam, got a minute?" a voice called.

Nielsen glanced over his shoulder, recognized the speaker, then turned back to me. "Excuse me." He got up, joined the man out in the hall, both turning their backs to me.

I glanced at the reporter's desk. A fat file folder labeled Sumner sat among other clutter.

Nielsen was deep in conversation.

I flipped open the file. Scribbled notes, typed pages—one askew. A photo copy—the letterhead said Amigone Funeral Home. I almost laughed, remembering the absurd name for the local chain of family-owned funeral homes, not for the first time wondering if their clients asked themselves…am I gone?

Nielson was still talking.

I reached over, slipped it out, set it on top. It was the list of funeral attendees—two columns of neatly typed names, with one exception. Hand written, wedged between Mr. and Mrs. Michael Tessier and Clarence Woodward, was the name I'd hoped to see: Sharon Walker.

She hadn't been included on Claudia Sumner's original list. Someone had added her name at the last minute. Interesting.

I closed the folder just in time. Nielsen turned back, took his seat again.

"Sorry about the interruption."

"No problem." I stood. "I won't take up any more of your time. Thanks for talking to me."

He grabbed a business card from the top drawer of his desk. "If you come up with something, give me a call."

"I'll do that."

His gaze remained fixed on my face. "Are you sure we haven't met before?"

I shrugged. "Thanks again."

***

We crossed into the village of Orchard Park and found the Orchard Park PD located in the Municipal Center, a brick structure with a faux-colonial facade. We parked and headed inside. Detective Hayden was in. The receptionist first called him, then ushered us through a series of halls to his office.

Hayden sat behind a big ugly steel-and-Formica desk, littered with stacks of case files, papers, and official-looking garbage. He held a mug of coffee in one hand and a jelly doughnut in the other. Confectioners' sugar clung to his upper lip.

"Are you two joined at the hip?" he asked, eyeing Richard.

"Are you really the stereotypical cop who drinks coffee and eats doughnuts?" I shot back.

Richard glared at me. "I have the car," he explained.

Hayden pointed to the two chairs in front of his desk. "Sit. I checked with NYPD. You really were mugged."

"You couldn't tell?" I said, brandishing my broken arm.

Hayden shrugged. "So why'd you want to see me?"

"The Sumner murder."

He leaned back in his chair. "Of course. Dig up any clues?" His sarcasm bugged me.

"Only his guts."

He looked skeptical. "That was you, huh?"

I pulled out my notebook, giving him specifics that hadn't been mentioned in the media. "We called 911 from the grocery store parking lot on Kenmore Avenue at one forty-seven on Saturday afternoon. The remains were found on Route 14, two-point-three miles south of Vermont Hill Road."

His skepticism dissolved. "Yeah?"

"We left our shovel out in the field. It was made by the Hawking Company."

His expression turned absolutely grim as he sat up straighter. "How'd you find…them?"

"Then the uh…viscera…matched Sumner's DNA?"

"Yeah. Now answer my question. How'd you know where to look?"

"This is the part you're not going to believe."

Chapter Fifteen

"Why come to me?" Hayden demanded, after I'd told him about the dreams and how they'd intensified once I returned to Buffalo.

"You're in charge of the investigation."

"What do you want? Publicity—your name in the newspaper?"

"That's the last thing I want. I want to find out who killed Sumner and bring that person to justice."

Hayden snorted. "Now you sound like the Lone Ranger."

I got up. "Come on, Rich. I don't need this shit."

Hayden leaned back in his chair. "Now let me give you a scenario. Say a doctor, an expert on anatomy, held a grudge against a bank official. And say this doctor had considerable holdings at the bank. Let's say he also had an accomplice, perhaps his younger brother—"

Richard's eyes blazed, but he held his temper in check.

I didn't.

"My brother is not a surgeon, and he's not a butcher. And neither of us could hit the broad side of a barn with a bow. If you're too narrow-minded to listen to what I have to tell you, so you can catch a goddamn murderer, you can just go fuck yourself, Hayden. Let's go, Rich—"

"Wait. Tell him about the jogger."

"What jogger?"

I had to take a breath to quell my anger. "I found a potential witness for you. One who may have seen the killer's car the night of the murder. But, if you're more interested in spinning fantasy—"

Hayden's eyes betrayed his interest. "You got a name?" I gave it to him. He made a note. "Anything else?"

I sat down again. "What do you think of the murderer's profile they printed in the paper last week?"

"We're working on some leads," he said evasively. He turned and rummaged through a cabinet behind his desk, then handed me a black plastic rectangle: a garage door opener. "Okay, Mister Psychic, get any vibes off this?"

"I can't plug into this stuff like tuning a radio, you know."

"Try," he said. "We recovered it with the victim's car."

I clasped the remote, closed my eyes, and waited. What was I supposed to get? A lot of people had probably handled it. How was I supposed to single out the killer?

But I did get something.

An impression.

A figure, dressed in a dark hooded sweatshirt and dark jogging pants. I couldn't see the face. The killer had pressed the button, and the garage door had slowly risen. Then the killer had jumped into the station wagon, pressed the button again, and the door descended. The station wagon roared to life and the remote was tossed onto the empty passenger seat.

I shook my head, handing it back to the detective. "Sorry."

Contempt shadowed his eyes, but I wasn't about to try to qualify my impressions to give him ammunition to shoot me down. He put the remote back in the cabinet.

"Anything else?"

I shook my head and Richard and I stood.

"I'll call this Linski guy."

I headed for the door. "You do that, Detective."

"And I'll be sure to call you if I need you. I know where to find you."

The cold air outside seemed fresh and clean next to the overheated clamminess of the station. I breathed deeply.

"Thanks for defending my honor back there," Richard said.

I shrugged it off.

"Are you okay?"

"Just pissed."

"Why didn't you tell him about Sharon Walker?"

"He doesn't believe me. But, after he talks to Paul Linski, he might cut me some slack. And maybe in a couple of days I'll have something concrete to give him."

"You got something from that remote, didn't you?"

"Yeah, but I couldn't tell if it was Sharon. Maybe after I meet her, I'll know for sure."

"When are you planning that?"

"I don't know. First I want to find out more about her."

He pressed the remote to unlock the car door for me then headed for the driver's side. I looked behind me. Hayden stood at one of the station's windows, staring after us.

***

We stopped at a branch of Bison Bank and cashed my check. Having my own money almost made me feel like a contributing member of society. That elation was brief, however, thanks to the headache hovering on my fringe of awareness. It threatened to take center stage until we had chicken sandwiches at a fast-food joint in Niagara Falls. Richard explained the biochemical correlation between headaches and an empty stomach over a second cup of coffee.

Thanks to my windfall, I was able to pay for our lunch, an extremely small gesture of thanks for all Richard had done for me, but it made me feel better.

Afterwards, we headed for Keystone Construction. We were a couple of minutes early, but Charles, "just call me Charlie," Nowak was waiting. A stocky, balding, good-natured man, he looked every one of his sixty-plus years. Richard waited in the reception area while I met with the former Walker Construction V.P. Sitting in one of the two chairs facing his desk, I wondered if my tiny cubicle back at Travelers in Manhattan had been so mundane.

"Thanks for taking time to see me," I started after the introductions. "I'm looking into the relationship between Matt Sumner and the demise of Walker Construction to see if there might be a connection."

"I've been reading about his murder in the paper." He shook his head. "It's terrible. But why do you think the two are connected?"

"I can't go into that right now. But I hoped you could shed some light on his connection with Walker."

"Sorry. I didn't know the man personally. Big Jim Walker dealt with him on a one-to-one basis. He died several years ago."

"That's when his daughter took over the business, wasn't it?"

He nodded.

"How long have you known Sharon Walker?"

"Since she was born. Jim and I started the business together. We were friends since we were kids."

"I'm curious. Why didn't you take over when Jim Walker died?"

"Jim had the majority interest in the business. He left everything to Sharon. She felt only she could follow in his footsteps, and she's not one to delegate authority."

"I take it that wasn't in the company's best interests."

"Not when we were hoping to build the Broadway Mall." He shook his head. "Sharon burned a lot of bridges when the company was in trouble. She tried to keep it from falling apart, but she just didn't have the experience. And she wouldn't listen to anyone who did."

"Are you still in touch with her?"

He shook his head. "I don't think she talks to anyone from the company. She and her son live in that old, rundown house out in East Aurora. It's all she had left after the bankruptcy. She's got enough money to make ends meet, thanks to a trust fund, but that's about all."

East Aurora. That confirmed it. I'd definitely spoken with Sharon on Saturday night.

"Did she have much contact with Matt Sumner at the bank?"

"Yes. Matt worked closely with Jim and our comptroller. I know he felt as bad as the rest of us when the company failed. He did everything in his power to keep us afloat."

"Did you all socialize with Sumner?"

"Not me. But Sharon did for several years. She was engaged to his son."

"Oh?"

He nodded. "Five or six years ago."

"I understand Rob Sumner married someone else last fall."

"I wouldn't know that. Jim was disappointed when they broke up. He liked Rob. Being an only child, Sharon was used to getting what she wanted, when she wanted it. I don't think that set right with Rob's family—particularly his mother."

"Was Matt Sumner fond of Sharon?"

He shrugged. "I really don't know."

"Would you know if Sumner cheated on his wife?"

Nowak blinked, startled by the question, but answered it anyway. "I don't know for sure. But there were rumors."

"Such as…?"

He shook his head, unwilling to speculate. I tried another question. "I understand Walker Construction had other troubles during the bankruptcy. Do you know where I can find Ted Schmidt?"

"I suppose he's out of jail by now. He cost the company a couple hundred grand. Maybe it wouldn't have saved us, but we wouldn't have gone under as fast, either."

"Getting back to Sharon, was she friendly with anyone in the office?"

"Not really."

I frowned, frustrated. Then it occurred to me; Sharon would never confide her problems to a man she saw as a rival for control of the company. "How about any of the women?"

"She might have talked with Lucy Kaminski. She was Big Jim's secretary for over twenty years."

"And when Sharon took over—?"

"She worked for Sharon."

"Do you know how I could get in touch with her?"

He took out the telephone book, flipped through the pages, jotted down a number and address on a piece of paper, and handed it to me.

"You wouldn't happen to have a photograph of Sharon, would you?"

He looked thoughtful. "As a matter of fact—" He reached behind him into a file drawer. "I used to have this on the shelf over there. I put it away when the glass broke."

He handed me a framed eight-by-ten photo of a group shot. Charlie stood with a woman who matched him in age and size, presumably his wife, next to a tall, rugged man and a teenaged girl.

"Big Jim was my best friend for almost fifty years."

"This is Sharon and her father?"

He nodded. "Maybe ten or twelve years ago."

Sharon had been athletic-looking, with long, mousy brown hair. Dressed casually in jeans and a sweater, she wasn't pretty, but her blue eyes sparkled. In the photo, she looked at her father with love and admiration.

"Were they close?"

Nowak nodded.

I traced my finger over the picture of Sharon. Her face seemed familiar to me. An image flashed in my mind—a woman, jogging. My eyes slid shut and the memory came back to me as clearly as when I'd actually experienced it. A woman had jogged in the cemetery the day Sumner was buried: Sharon. She must have just left the grave as we approached. No wonder the killer's vibrations had been so strong.

I opened my eyes to find Charlie Nowak staring at me. Embarrassed, I handed back the photo, cleared my throat, and asked a few more questions, but I didn't expect any other revelations. He'd already been more cooperative than I could've hoped. Still, I was glad when the secretary interrupted us with an important call. I saw myself out.

"Well?" Richard asked once we were outside.

"Definitely worth the trip." We got in the car and I told him about Sharon's broken engagement and that she lived in East Aurora, just down the road from Holland where Sumner had been killed. "I've got to talk to Sharon's secretary."

"What's next?" Richard asked.

"I'm going to see Maggie for lunch tomorrow. I need to talk with Ron Myers at the bank again, too, if you can help me out with that. I don't think that entry on Sumner's calendar referred to him, but if the police have questioned him about it, I want to know whatever he told Hayden." I rubbed at my temples.

"Still got the headache?"

"Yeah. They haven't been so bad for the past couple of days. But today...God, I feel rotten."

"I told you, you're pushing yourself too hard. You won't be happy until you end up in the hospital again."

I didn't want to argue with him and sank back against the seat and headrest. But I had one more place to go. "I want to stop at the bakery."

"What bakery?"

I hadn't told him about my friend Sophie. "On Main Street in Snyder. There's someone I want you to meet."

"Are you sure you're up to it?"

"It's on the way. Just head for home." I hoped I'd doze off, but had no such luck. I opened my eyes a few blocks from the storefront and got my bearings. "Just up ahead, on the right. It's the place with the blue sign."

Richard pulled into the half-empty lot. "So who am I going to meet?"

"A cool old lady. She told me to trust this empathic stuff."

Richard didn't roll his eyes, but he looked like he wanted to.

The place looked different in daylight. More modern. And I didn't remember all the wedding cake toppers on display on the shelves behind the glass case that served as a counter. A chunky, middle-aged man stood behind the cash register ringing up a sale as we entered. My head was pounding. It was an effort to stand, to think. But I needed to connect with my new friend and mentor so I waited until the customer ahead of me started for the door before I stepped forward.

"Hi. I'm looking for Sophie."

"Who?"

"Sophie Levin. I met her here last week."

He shook his head. "Nobody here by that name."

"Older lady—with a Polish accent."

Again he shook his head. Richard looked at me doubtfully.

"She lives above the shop."

"You must have the wrong place. No one's lived upstairs in years. We don't even rent it out. It's our office space."

That funny feeling was back in the pit of my stomach. "Did she ever live here?"

"No one's lived upstairs—not since the last tenant died some ten years back."

"Was she electrocuted?"

He shrugged. "I dunno. That was before we bought the property. Can I interest you in some fresh bread? We've got a nice rye."

"No, thanks."

Richard nudged me. "Come on. Maybe the place you're looking for is in the next block." He sounded like the placating professional again.

The man behind the counter merely shrugged.

We got back in the car.

I'd met Sophie—spoken with her. She wasn't a figment of my imagination.

So where the hell was she, and why was I so confused?

Chapter Sixteen

Tuesday dawned gray and cold. The headache was still with me. I couldn't even remember if I'd joined Richard and Brenda for dinner the night before. The evening was just a blank.

My breakfast consisted of three pink tablets. For a while it seemed to quell the pounding. What kept me going was the thought of seeing Maggie again.

Richard called Ron Myers and begged a favor—an appointment for me at eleven. Since Myers was actively campaigning for Richard to deposit all his money with Bison Bank, he was more than happy to grant me an interview, hoping to solidify a deal.

Meanwhile, Brenda had scheduled an appointment for her and Richard to look at a clinic downtown. She was hot for them to volunteer their time and skills somewhere, but he didn't seem enthusiastic. I couldn't tell what was going on with him. What he said he wanted and what he really wanted seemed to be two different things.

I was putting on my shoes when Brenda ducked her head inside my door. "There's a phone call for you."

"Female, I hope," I said, thinking of Maggie.

"No such luck."

Who the hell could be calling me?

I followed her into the kitchen and picked up the extension. "Hello."

"What's going on?" It was Sam Nielsen's voice. "Suddenly you and your brother are suspects in the Sumner murder case."

My mouth went dry. "How did you get this number?"

"Directory Assistance."

"I'm not listed."

"Your brother is. I remembered your face five minutes after you left my office yesterday. The geeky photographer on our school yearbook. You still play basketball?"

"Yeah. Tell me why we're suspects."

"More your brother. The rumor around Orchard Park PD is that you're some kind of psychic."

Holy Christ. Hayden hadn't promised he wouldn't talk about me. I'd just assumed….

Nielsen was still speaking. "—that it was you who found Sumner's body parts out in Holland. Possibly put them there. Do you want to comment?"

"No."

"How about off the record?"

My hand tightened around the receiver. "Why should I believe you?"

"I protect my sources."

I didn't know what to say. I had to warn Richard. We needed to contact his attorney—to cover our asses.

"Hayden seems to think you haven't told him all you know," Nielsen continued.

Maybe I should've told the cop more. Maybe—"What makes you think I'll tell you?"

"Picture this headline: Psychic Finds Sumner Remains. That's not the kind of information you want circulated, now is it?"

The pounding in my head increased. I'd been back in Richard's life a couple of weeks and already I'd ruined it, just when he'd returned to Buffalo, getting ready to resume his career. "What's this going to cost me?"

"Just information."

"Like what?"

"You got a suspect for the murder?"

"Nothing concrete."

"We could help each other." He sounded sleazier than a Vegas lounge lizard.

"I don't have enough facts to make an accusation."

"We could work together to get the evidence. Come on, Jeff—we're old high school buddies."

"I remember you, too. You thought I was a geek, and now you want my cooperation?"

"My editor's on my case. He wants a new angle—now," Nielsen said.

I swallowed. To placate him, I'd have to throw him a tidbit. "Concentrate on Sumner's former lovers."

"You think a woman did that to him?"

"Doing the deed and responsibility for it aren't necessarily the same thing."

"Sounds like a long shot to me. Come on, Jeff—give me a name."

"I can't. Not yet."

Nielsen was quiet for a few moments. "All right. I'll give you a couple of days to think about that headline. How it could change your life. I'll be in touch."

The connection was broken.

I hung up the receiver and stared at the wall phone.

Richard ambled into the kitchen. "You about ready to go?"

I turned to face him, feeling shaky, and leaned against the counter for support.

He frowned. "What's wrong?"

"Hayden told a reporter that we found Sumner's remains. This guy, Nielsen, wants me to tell him what I suspect or he'll go public that I'm a…that I can sense…." I couldn't finish the sentence.

"Jesus," he muttered.

"If we don't leave now, we're going to be late," Brenda said as she entered the kitchen. She stopped, took in both our faces. "What's wrong?"

"Maybe we should consult a lawyer."

Richard nodded.

While he drove, I relayed the story to Brenda. By the time I finished, she looked as grim as I felt.

They dropped me off at the bank at ten fifty-five. Richard said to call him on his cell phone when I was ready to leave. I told him to just meet me outside the bank at one, after I had lunch with Maggie.

Speaking with Nielsen had shaken my confidence. I no longer felt up to talking with Myers, but I had an hour to kill before I was to meet Maggie. I reported in with the receptionist who'd greeted Richard and me the week before. She ushered me into Myers's office.

I'd arrived right on time, but he was engaged in what turned out to be a lengthy phone call with an important client. He motioned me to sit and I took in his office as I waited. I tried not to think about screaming headlines in seventy-two-point type and studied the objects decorating Myers's workspace. Several frames sat on his desk, but I couldn't see the photographs. His office faced east, on the opposite side of the building from Sumner, with a view of more office buildings. Obviously he wasn't as important as Matt Sumner had been.

Finally Myers hung up. "Sorry about that. How can I help you, Jeff?" His smile and enthusiastic handshake didn't conceal his true motivation—to get his hands on more of Richard's millions. He saw me as a means to an end. The feeling was mutual.

"I don't know if my brother explained the situation, but I'm investigating Matt Sumner's death." The muscles along his jaw tightened at the mention of Sumner's name. I'd definitely touched a nerve.

Myers said nothing.

"I understand the police have already spoken with you. Your name was on his calendar the day he died."

"I never even saw him that day." Myers stopped himself, as though afraid to offend me.

"I don't think you had anything to do with his death," I assured him. "I hoped you could tell me more about him."

"Just what are your credentials, Mr. Resnick?"

I met his wary gaze. "I'm an insurance investigator." And please don't ask for proof, I mentally amended.

He didn't, probably figuring a millionaire's brother had no reason to lie.

Myers sat back in his chair, the strain around his eyes visibly relaxing.

"What do you want to know?"

"I'm getting conflicting pictures of him. He was a saint or a sinner, depending on who you talk to."

"He was that. A saint and a sinner."

"How so?"

He eyed me critically. "Look, whatever I tell you is in confidence, right?"

"Absolutely."

He took a steadying breath. "Matt treated some of the staff like dirt. Particularly the women. He could be a real jerk. He had this way of making you feel like you were shit, and grinning all the while. He really turned on the charm with the clients. His smile, his manner with them was worth a million bucks. In fact, it was worth more than that to the bank."

"I'm particularly interested in his relationship with the people at Walker Construction."

"You mean Sharon Walker." It wasn't a question.

I nodded, surprised he knew her by name.

"Matt and I worked closely with the lawyers to pound out a settlement. Sharon and the company comptroller visited often during the bankruptcy proceedings."

"What's your impression of her?"

"Tough. She wore all the right clothes, but something about her didn't fit the image she tried to project."

"Was she overly friendly with Sumner?"

He shrugged. "Matt always had a woman on the side. I suppose she could've been one of them. I know he talked his son out of marrying her. If he had a relationship with her, he never said. He didn't brag about those things, but everyone knew. Sometimes he'd show up with other women at company functions. He'd introduce them as clients. Claudia knew; she didn't care. She had his money. That's all that mattered."

"What was his relationship with his children?"

"Rocky. The youngest was in rehab a couple of months ago. An alcoholic at sixteen." He shook his head. "To be a success in this business, you have to put in one hundred and ten percent effort. Matt put in more. He sacrificed his family life for the job. But then my wife divorced me last year for the same reason. She took the kids and moved to Ohio. Now I've got nothing but this job." Regret colored his voice.

"What about the charity work Sumner did?"

"Company-directed. I work with a camp for kids with cancer. Matt had United Way and leukemia. Sometimes we're given three or four charities and we delegate. Those with the most seniority get the high-profile charities. The company looks good and it's a tax write-off."

I thought of Sumner's glowing obituary and frowned; only P.R. after all.

"I understand Sumner went out of his way to help Walker Construction during the bankruptcy," I said.

"He originally approved those loans. The deal we cut netted half the bank's outlay, but we still lost millions. No, he didn't go out of his way to help them."

That conflicted with what Charlie Nowak said, but it had a ring of truth. "Did he ever speak of Jackie?"

Myers shook his head. "Was she another girlfriend?"

"I don't know." I remembered something Maggie mentioned to me at the bar. "How about the guy he fired at Christmastime. Don...Don—"

"Don Feddar," he supplied, and shook his head. "It's too bad what happened to him. I'm not at liberty to discuss it, but you might want to speak to him yourself. He's in the phone book."

I nodded. Thanks to the ache in my head, I couldn't think of anything else to ask. "You've been very helpful, Ron."

"Your brother means a lot to this bank. If we could get our hands on all his money—"

I forced a laugh. "You're an honest man. I'll mention it to him, but I can't guarantee anything."

"I can't ask for more." He offered me his hand. "Let me know if I can do anything else for you."

"As a matter of fact, I wouldn't mind having a look at Sumner's office. Just to get a feel for the man."

He hesitated—seemed to weigh the value of pleasing me—then shrugged. "No problem."

He led me down the hall to the office. Except for the furniture, the room was stripped. Maggie had done a good job of removing everything personal.

"I have a lunch meeting in a few minutes. You can just shut the door when you're done," he said.

"Thanks."

"Let me know if I can be of any more help." Myers shook my hand again before leaving.

I took in the bare walls. Although devoid of his possessions, there was still a lot of Matt Sumner left in the room—much more than there'd been in his own home.

Head pounding, I moved to the leather chair, sat down, and closed my eyes.

I wondered if those pills I'd been taking had lost their effectiveness. I reached into my jacket pocket and took out the prescription bottle. Three tablets remained. I took out two, choking them down without water.

A glance at my watch told me I had ten minutes before I was supposed to meet Maggie. I leaned back in the chair and looked out the window. A typical cloudy day in Buffalo. Years ago, the seemingly perpetual gray skies had depressed me; now they seemed familiar and I realized with some surprise I was starting to feel at home here again. Would I still feel that way if Nielsen made good his threat?

I couldn't afford to waste the time Myers had given me and, straightening in the chair, I began my search. I opened the desk drawers. Empty. I went through the credenza—nothing there either. Yet I couldn't shake the feeling I'd missed something.

I checked under the couch cushions, and down the sides of the chairs. Nothing. I was about to give up when I thought to look under the desk. Bingo! Caught between the center drawer and the desk frame was a mangled envelope. With some careful maneuvering, I managed to extricate it. I sat in Sumner's chair and smoothed the crumpled paper on the desk. The return address on the upper left-hand corner said Roche Biomedical Laboratories. It was empty, and was postmarked two days before the murder.

Chapter Seventeen

A secretary gave me directions to Maggie's office. She greeted me with a sunny smile that almost made me forget how crappy I felt. She had on a navy suit with a powder blue blouse, and the same gold chain around her neck. It made her look like a high-powered executive. Despite my own office attire, I felt like someone you might avoid on the street.

"Hey, I thought we were going to meet downstairs."

"I'm a few minutes early. I can wait."

"Thanks. I'll be right with you."

I took one of the chairs in front of her desk and she turned back to her computer. She made a call, switching back and forth between two databases as she spoke. The fact that she was busy gave me the opportunity to think up various topics we might discuss over lunch. Only, with my head about to explode, I didn't feel like talking. I didn't feel like eating or even thinking. At that moment the whole lunch idea seemed like a big mistake.

"Sorry about that," Maggie said at last. "I'm in the middle of organizing a conference and it's turning out to be a bitch."

She grabbed her coat and we headed for the elevator. A minute later we were waiting for the light to change at the corner outside the bank. A ripple of pleasure shot through me when she grabbed my hand as we crossed the street. Her gloved fingers curled around mine and held on tight.

We ended up at a pizza joint around the corner. I wasn't interested in food, but Maggie ordered us a small pepperoni and mushroom pizza and a couple of Cokes. My broken left arm rested on the table as I rubbed my forehead with my right hand.

She touched my sleeve. "Are you okay? You don't look well."

"Since the mugging, I get these miserable migraines." I braved a smile. "I have to admit you're the bright spot in my day."

She smiled. "How's your case going?"

"I have a few more people to talk to."

"You're really treating this like a job. Have you thought about doing it for a living?"

"I did. I was an insurance investigator, remember?"

"No, I mean being a cop. Or a detective. It's never too late to start over."

"'Fraid not. In fact, I thought about being a bartender. Just until I figure out what I want to do. My brother's been on my back. He says I shouldn't even think about work for another few weeks."

"He's a doctor. He should know."

"He's my big brother and he still thinks of me as a fourteen-year-old kid." That came out sounding a whole lot angrier than I'd meant. "Don't listen to me. I don't know what I'm saying."

She changed the subject. "Have you had a really good fish fry since you got back to Buffalo?"

I shook my head. A mistake.

"You've got to have one on Good Friday and I know the perfect spot."

"I'd like that."

"Great. I'll pick you up at your house about six."

"Good. You can meet Rich and Brenda, too."

Her expression darkened, but amusement flashed in her blue eyes. "Uh-oh. Meeting the family already?"

"Hell, you've met Rich before."

"As a client, not a person."

I had to smile. "And you have to call him Richard. He hates being called Rich."

"You call him that."

"I know."

"Are you sure you're not still fourteen?"

I shrugged and she grinned.

"Hey, you've got to go to the Broadway Market, too."

"My mother and I used to do that every year when I was a kid." I managed a smile at the pleasant memory. It was one of the few traditions we'd observed.

"I'm taking my mother-in-law on Friday."

"Mother-in-law? I thought you were divorced."

"Yes. I got the house, but Gary's mother, Lily, lives in the downstairs apartment. She takes care of my dog when I'm at work. It's a great arrangement."

Our pizza arrived and Maggie doled out pieces for each of us. The aroma made me feel sick. Maggie dug in with gusto. She wiped her mouth with a napkin. "Mmm. This is great. Aren't you having any?"

"I'd like to...but I don't think it's a good idea right now. Don't let me stop you. Enjoy." I took a tentative sip of my Coke. Much as I wanted to be with her, I was counting the minutes until I could get out of there and go home to my bed. I took out my prescription bottle. The last tablet. I downed it with a swallow of Coke.

She ate slowly and in silence, watching me, looking more and more worried as time went on.

"Sorry I'm not better company," I apologized.

"Hey, if you don't feel well, you don't feel well. I wish there was something I could do. Do you want me to call your brother?"

"He'll pick me up at one o'clock." I took another sip of my drink. Coke is supposed to help settle your stomach, but its sweetness sickened me. I pushed the glass aside.

The waitress came by. "Is everything okay?"

"Can you wrap this?" Maggie asked.

"Sure thing." She took the leftover pizza away.

"You want to take it home for later?"

I shook my head and winced. The waitress returned with a brown paper bag and the check. I fumbled with my wallet and pulled out a ten-dollar bill. My vision doubled; I couldn't even see the amount on the slip of paper. "Is this enough?"

Maggie took the money and the check from me. "It's fine."

"No doubt about it. I make a great impression. Broke, sick...a real winner."

"It's refreshing to find a man with vulnerabilities. I can't tell you how many macho jerks I've met in the past five years. Come on."

She grabbed my arm, pulled me up, and helped me on with my coat. Then she paid the check and, with her arm wrapped around mine, guided me back across the street. She parked me in one of the chairs in the bank's overheated lobby, then made a quick call to her office from the receptionist's desk. Moments later she took the chair next to me. "I'll wait with you until your brother gets here." She took my hand and squeezed it reassuringly.

Embarrassment doesn't begin to cover what I was feeling...except at that moment I felt so awful I would've accepted help from the devil himself.

When Richard's silver Lincoln pulled up in front of the bank at three minutes past one, Maggie helped me to my feet and steered me toward the door. "Want me to go out with you?"

"No, please. I gotta have some dignity."

"Okay." She squeezed my hand again. "I'll see you Friday night, right?"

"I wouldn't miss it."

The cold air hit me like a left hook, making the ten or so feet from the door to the car seem more like a mile. I practically crawled onto the back seat.

"How'd your lunch go?" Brenda asked as the car took off into traffic.

I sank back into the seat. "Fine."

My voice must have sounded strained, for she turned to look at me. "Are you okay?"

"I've been better."

I could see Richard's eyes glance at me in the rear-view mirror. "I got us an appointment with my lawyer in twenty-five minutes. Are you up to it?"

No, I was tempted to wail, but he wouldn't need to consult an attorney if it hadn't been for me. "Sure." I closed my eyes and sank back against the leather upholstery, hoping I could survive another hour.

***

Richard's late grandfather had been a partner in the local attorneys' office that still handled Richard's affairs. Morton, Alpert, Fox, and Jemison had been, and still was, one of the most respected firms in town. That they'd kept the old man's name years after his death reaffirmed the respect he'd commanded.

Daniel Jemison, son of the last of the original partners, was about Richard's age. Dressed in a drab gray suit, white shirt, and dark tie, the trim, sandy-haired lawyer didn't impress me as a man with much imagination. Throughout Richard's narration, Jemison's face remained impassive; only a raised eyebrow now and then betrayed he was even listening. I sat hunched in my chair, massaging my forehead, wishing the steady thumping would stop.

When Richard finished, Jemison swiveled his chair to gaze out the window, which overlooked the First Niagara Center, home of the Buffalo Sabres hockey team. We waited for long moments before he finally spoke.

"My advice is to go home and devote yourself to TV reruns."

I glanced at Richard in the adjacent chair. He looked as baffled as I felt.

"I beg your pardon," Richard said.

"Don't do anything. Don't even leave the house if you can manage it."

I leaned forward in my chair. "But I know—"

"Whatever you 'think' you know is immaterial, Mr. Resnick. There are any number of possible litigants who could drag you into court. The woman you suspect. The police. Any of the people you've interviewed. It wouldn't hurt for you both to leave town—lose yourself in a big metropolitan area: New York, L.A. Let this whole situation blow over."

The pain in my skull flared.

Richard stood. "Thanks, Dan. And thanks for seeing us on such short notice."

Jemison rose. "Always a pleasure." He shook hands with Richard, but I turned away before I'd have to.

I shuffled out the door to the reception area.

Brenda put down a magazine, rose from her seat, and joined me as I headed for the elevator. "You look awful."

"That's just how I feel."

"Did it go badly?"

"You'll have to ask Rich. I just want to go home."

Richard had joined us by the time the elevator arrived. We rode down in silence with several others. The walk to the parking garage seemed like miles. Several times I almost stumbled on the sidewalk. It was only Brenda's steadying grasp on my arm that kept me upright. I tried to catch a glimpse of Richard's expression, but he kept a pace or two ahead of us until we got to the car. He opened the back door and helped me in. A minute later, he'd started the car and we headed home.

I shut my eyes, concentrating all my energy on controlling my gag reflex. I was determined not to throw up on Richard's beautiful leather upholstery. I heard them conversing quietly, but couldn't spare the effort to listen.

It seemed a long time before Richard pulled up the driveway and stopped the car by the back door. Brenda helped me into the house, and I waved her off as I staggered to my room. I pulled off my raincoat, the tie came next, then I blindly fumbled with the belt at my waist. I kicked off my shoes and walked out of my pants, all the while ripping open the Velcro fasteners on the brace, and dumped everything into an untidy pile on the floor. Then I crawled onto my bed, wrapped myself in the spread, and collapsed.

My pulse pounded through my skull. Sound and light were my enemies as I huddled into a ball of misery, pain, and despair. I hadn't felt this bad since I'd regained consciousness back in the hospital after the mugging.

I heard a faint rustle and cracked an eye open far enough to see Brenda picking up my clothes, hanging them on hangers. "Hon, you really shouldn't take off that brace."

"Not now," I murmured.

"Are you going to be sick?"

"Maybe."

She bent low by my bedside. "If you can't get to the john, the wastebasket's here. Okay?"

I tried to nod and ground my teeth against the nausea. Then she was gone.

It's scary that a headache can be so thoroughly incapacitating. This was worse than the worst hangover.

I lay there, barely breathing, as even that sound jarred my brains. It seemed like hours before I dozed off. At some point I found myself in the tiny bathroom, worshiping the porcelain god with the dry heaves, but the next thing I knew, it was dark and Brenda was back in my room. The light from the hallway gouged my eyes like knife thrusts.

"Jeffy? You want some dinner?" she asked, her voice gentle.

I groaned. "No."

"How about soup?"

It seemed like she'd asked me to explain a complicated math problem rather than answer with a simple yes or no.

Then Richard crouched beside me, his face only inches from mine. "When was the last time you took your medication?"

I had to think about it, and thinking was an effort. "Lunch time. I—I ran out."

"Jesus," he swore, and then he went away, too.

Sometime later, I came to again and found the bedside lamp blazing. I covered my eyes with my hand, surprised to find my face damp. Sweat? Tears? I wasn't sure.

I barely managed to raise myself from the oblivion of misery. Richard hovered somewhere above me. I heard him talking, but caught only fragments. "Ease the pain…non-narcotic…better by tomorrow.…"

A needle pricked the inside of my right arm. He kept on talking, his voice a soothing croon, and I sank back into a fog bank of exquisite pain.

Whatever that magic syringe contained must have done the trick, for although I tossed and turned all night, plagued by dreams of teenagers wielding baseball bats and clubbing me senseless, I did sleep. When I woke the next morning, the pain was bearable.

At some time during the previous day, someone had taken off my dress shirt and the brace was back on my arm.

They'd taken good care of me. Now I needed to find out if Richard intended to throw me out on my ass. I couldn't blame him if he did.

I stumbled from my bed and found a navy velour robe draped across the top of my dresser. I put it on, awkwardly knotting the belt at my waist.

I must have looked a sight when I staggered out into the kitchen and found Richard and Brenda seated at the table with the breakfast dishes still in front of them. "Any coffee left?" My voice sounded as husky as a chain-smoker's.

"Sit down. You really want coffee? How about some hot chocolate?" Brenda asked.

I sat. "I'll take the chocolate." Settling my weight on my good arm, I closed my eyes, breathing shallowly.

"You want something to eat?" Richard asked.

"I'm not ready for food."

"Are you going to live?"

I squinted up at him. "You tell me."

Instead he got up, grabbed a white paper bag off the counter, and took out a whole pharmacy of new and different drugs, setting them in front of me. His expression was stern, but his voice was gentle. "I'm telling you this as your concerned brother and as a licensed quack. Don't fuck with your health."

I blinked, surprised at his choice of words.

"Did you ever read the instructions that came with your prescription?"

"Of course. Well, kind of. Only what was on the bottle."

"Do you know what happened yesterday? You overdosed. Every pill you took made the headache ten times worse. You can't pop those things like candy. There's a regimen involved when taking this stuff."

"Well, I didn't know." It sounded lame, even to me. The whole episode should have terrified me, but I'd instinctively known that Richard would be there for me, that he'd take care of me. Exactly what I hadn't wanted only weeks before.

"I can't take care of you," he continued, as though reading my mind. "I'm too emotionally involved. I've arranged for someone at the UB clinic to see you on Monday." He took two of the pills from one of the bottles. "Take these now. We'll go over the rest of the routine when you can think straight."

"Yes, sir," I murmured with respect. He spoke to me like I was a five-year-old, but I was too tired to complain, and ready to do just about anything so not to endure a repeat of the previous day. Brenda put a small glass of water in front of me and I downed the pills.

"Did anything break on the Sumner case yesterday?"

"Jeff!"

"Rich, I gotta know."

"No. Nothing happened. No one was arrested."

Brenda placed a steaming mug before me and took her seat.

I took a sip of chocolate, avoiding both their gazes. "Sorry I crapped out on you yesterday. We should've talked about…." I wasn't sure how to finish the sentence.

"About Dan's advice?" Richard said.

I nodded. "I'm sorry I dragged you into all this, Rich. I—"

He held up a hand to stop me. "I've had a day to think about it. If you want to continue looking into Sumner's murder, I won't stop you. Hell, how could I?"

"But, Jemison said—"

"I know this is important to you. I just want you to consider the consequences if you continue with your—" It cost him to say it. "—investigation."

I thought carefully before answering. "I keep asking myself, what're the consequences if I don't? I *know* what I *know*. I can't explain to you why I feel obligated to keep looking for answers. I just have to do this."

He didn't say anything for a long moment. Then, "Okay, then let's talk about what you're going to do today—which is nothing," Richard said.

"No argument there," I said, glad he'd changed the subject. And I didn't do anything else that day but rest. I managed to drink the whole mug of chocolate before crashing for a three-hour nap. For lunch, I kept down an entire bowl of soup. By Wednesday evening I began to feel almost human again and choked down at least half the dinner Brenda served me. I watched the evening news, glanced at the newspaper to look for anything new on the Sumner investigation, and was in bed and asleep by eight o'clock.

Thursday morning, I was ready to go back to work.

Chapter Eighteen

Brenda had scheduled another clinic visit, so the two of them were gone before ten o'clock. Meanwhile, I started the day by checking the newspaper to see if Sam Nielsen had made good his threat to write about me. He hadn't. Yet.

Next I got on the phone, checking with the library, the ever-handy City Directory, a patient library assistant, and the local phone book to find the Walker employee who'd been prosecuted for theft. I found four Theodore Schmidts. I narrowed the field to two. On the last call I hit pay dirt. The woman who answered said Schmidt was her boyfriend and I could find him at his job any time during the day.

After that, I called Rob Sumner's house. No answer. I'd have to try again later.

I retrieved the piece of paper Charlie Nowak had given me days before, and dialed Big Jim Walker's secretary's home number. It rang several times before an older woman answered. "Lucy Kaminski?"

"Yes."

"My name's Jeffrey Resnick. I'm investigating Matt Sumner's death. Charles Nowak gave me your name and thought you might be able to tell me—"

"I'm sorry. I didn't know the man."

"But you did work for Sharon Walker."

"Oh, yes. Sharon was engaged to Mr. Sumner's son. But that was years ago."

"Could I come out and talk to you about—?"

"Oh, I don't think so," she interrupted once again.

"Would you speak to me over the phone?"

I pictured her pursing her lips, trying to decide if she should continue the conversation. "I really don't like discussing such personal matters with strangers."

"Of course, you're right," I admitted, backpedaling. "Mr. Nowak said you worked for Jim Walker for over twenty years."

"Twenty-five years," she said with pride.

"Did you retire when the company went under?"

"Yes. It was very sad," she admitted, and launched into a detailed remembrance—just as I'd hoped she would. I made the appropriate oohs and ahs when necessary, and waited patiently until she was ready to talk about what I wanted to hear.

"Everything must've changed when Mr. Walker died."

"Yes. The company went downhill fast. Sharon just didn't have the feel for the business end of things."

"It must've been hard for her—caring for her son and all."

"I know I'm old-fashioned, but if she'd just left running the company to the men, we'd all still be employed. And that poor child. She left him with a babysitter from early morning until quite late in the evening. A mother really needs to be with her baby when he's that small. Once or twice she brought him to the office when the babysitter was sick."

"Did she neglect the boy?"

"Who am I to judge?"

I took that as a definite yes. "Did she ever speak about his father?"

"Never." Her tone changed. "It was very strange. There were four women in the office. We wanted to give her a baby shower, but she refused. She got very angry about it. I think she was embarrassed because she wasn't married. She knew Big Jim would've been disappointed."

"I take it they were very close."

"Yes." She paused. "Oh, dear. I've said much more than I intended. And I don't see what all this has to do with Mr. Sumner's death."

"At this point, I'm just looking into his business affairs."

"I suppose he helped when the company went through bankruptcy, but that didn't save our jobs." I could certainly identify with that.

I made a few sympathetic remarks and ended the conversation.

My limousine picked me up at eleven-thirty and the three of us took a lunch break at a local family restaurant before Richard and I dropped off Brenda at home and started off again. Brenda had given me a point-by-point comparison of the clinics they'd already visited, but old Rich was quiet during her recitation. I could tell the clinic they'd visited that day had not met with his approval. Not that he talked about it to me.

We found Ted Schmidt at Mount Olivet cemetery, behind the controls of a backhoe digging a grave. I watched his precision with the scoop as it gouged the partially-frozen earth, making a hole the exact size of a casket.

It gave me the creeps.

Schmidt was about my age, dressed in work clothes, a heavy jacket, and a yellow hardhat. I waited until he finished the grave before I approached him.

"Ted Schmidt?"

"Who wants to know?"

I handed him one of my cards through the open window on the cab. "I was hoping you'd speak with me about Walker Construction."

His eyes flashed. "Hey, I did my time. I don't need to be hassled about it anymore." He shoved the card back at me.

"I'm not here to hassle you. I'm looking into a possible connection between Walker Construction and the murder of Matt Sumner of Bison Bank."

The anxiety in his face eased. "The guy they found gutted in his garage?"

I nodded.

"Cool," he said with an eager smile. He turned off the big machine and jumped down from the cab. "What do you want to know?"

"Anything you can tell me."

He took off his work gloves. "I didn't work in the office, but I heard what was going on. We all knew the company was going under. Management was hiding assets, so I figured I'd grab my share before there wasn't anything left to get. Only I got caught."

"Did you know Sharon Walker?"

"Everybody did. She could handle anything on the site. Run a backhoe, drive the trucks, dump a load of gravel as good as me. But she forgot all that when she went into the office."

"So she was kind of a tomboy growing up?"

"She was the son old man Walker never had. He even called her Ronnie. First day of trout season, deer season, those two were gone."

I remembered the reference on Sumner's calendar on the day of his death: Ron. And she was a born hunter, too.

"Was she good to work with?"

"Before she went in the office, yeah. Just like one of the guys. After her father died and she took over, she started wearing high heels and suits with frilly shirts. She became one of those Feminazis. You know, bossing everybody around. Thinking she was hot shit."

"I take it she was the one who had you arrested."

His anger flared anew. "The lousy bitch." He jabbed his finger in my face to emphasize his words. "Other people were doing the same as me—looking out for themselves—but who did they prosecute? Me!"

Schmidt spewed venom against Sharon and Walker Construction for another ten minutes, giving me his personal opinion on each and every member of management, and the company's personnel policies. Obviously time in jail had done nothing to cool his hatred toward the company. I was grateful to finally escape.

"You okay?" Richard asked as I got in the car. His tone betrayed his amusement.

"I don't think I'll need my ears cleaned for a long time. He reamed them out nicely."

"You should've seen yourself, Jeff. He was shouting in your face and you were bending back so far I thought you'd fall over."

"But would you have rescued me if he'd really gotten physical?"

The lines around Richard's eyes crinkled. "I've got the cell phone. The police are as near as 911."

"Thanks for your concern. Hey, can I use this thing to call Rob Sumner's house?"

"Sure."

I dialed. Still no answer.

"What now?" he asked.

"I haven't talked with the guy Sumner fired. If we could stop over there, I could get that out of the way, too." I took out my notebook and found the address. As it turned out, it was in the neighborhood and minutes later we pulled into the driveway. As usual, Richard had come prepared, and hauled out a bulky medical text to read while I worked.

I rang the doorbell and waited. A rusting Reliant sedan sat in the driveway, so I figured someone had to be home. Finally the door opened. A harried-looking man of about forty stood before me. Dressed in jeans and a flannel shirt with the tails untucked, his bare feet were stuffed into worn slippers. A wet dishtowel adorned his shoulder and a screaming baby straddled his left hip.

"Yeah?" he demanded.

I handed him one of my cards. "Don Feddar? My name's Jeffrey Resnick. I'm looking into Matt Sumner's death, and—"

"Too bad he didn't die sooner. We'd have all been a lot better off!"

I wasn't sure how to reply.

"Can we talk?"

He nodded at the baby. "If you can stand her crying."

He gestured for me to enter. I followed him through the house. Toys were strewn about the place. Dust bunnies thrived in the living room, and the kitchen floor looked like it hadn't been mopped in months. He sat the baby in the high chair and cleared a stack of laundry off a chair for me.

He tossed my card on the table without looking at it. "I'm currently a house husband," he said, shoving a teething biscuit at the baby. She grabbed it in her chubby hand and stuffed it in her mouth. Her cries faded to whining. "I haven't worked since December twenty-third. Wasn't that a nice Christmas present for the wife and kids?"

"I heard. That's why I wanted to talk to you."

"You wanted to know if I murdered him, right? If I was going to do it, I'd have done it months ago. And no, I don't hunt."

"I heard the police already grilled you."

"Grill is right. They had me down at the station in Orchard Park for six hours a couple days after the murder." He shook his head, sat down, and continued folding laundry. "I told them, the night Matt was murdered I was at Tracy's dance recital. She's my oldest. I got over a hundred witnesses. I took the video of all the kids. I'm duping copies for a bunch of the parents. Anyway, it didn't matter to the cops that I have an alibi. They figured I could've had someone else do the deed. Yeah, and how was I supposed to pay for it?"

A little girl about three, dressed in a miniature jogging suit with Sesame Street characters marching across her shirt, came into the kitchen. She latched onto Feddar's leg. "Daddy, I don't feel good." He grabbed another teething biscuit from the box on the table and handed it to her.

"I heard you got fired for approving loans without proper documentation."

Feddar nodded. "Matt disputed that the signatures on the loans to Walker Construction were his."

"He accused you of faking his signature?"

"It was my word against his, and he was a vice president. Lying bastard."

"Was that the first time it happened?"

He shrugged "Upper management only cares about their own—and the bottom line."

It sounded like run-of-the-mill corporate bashing to me, but I didn't doubt him. I'd seen some pretty ruthless managers in the insurance business, managers who'd denied claims on a whim. It sickened me, but I was a small cog in a big machine. That's why I was sacrificed when others with less experience were saved.

"Could Sumner have had it in for you?"

The little girl dropped her biscuit on the floor and tried to climb onto his lap. Feddar kept pushing her down, but she wasn't easily deterred.

"I don't think so."

"Was he friendly with others in management?"

"Only to the extent that it involved business. I don't know what he did in his spare time, other than—" He broke off, looked at his children. "F-U-C-K-ing any woman desperate to get out of the secretarial pool, although it wasn't so bad the past few years. He was afraid of a sexual harassment lawsuit."

I thought about Maggie having to work under those conditions.

"He'd gone as far as he was going to go in the company," Feddar continued. "I got the feeling he was bored. I know he had a younger woman on the side for several years, but he saw other women, too."

"Did he brag about it?"

"No, but I know she had a child. I heard snatches of conversation. I got the feeling he was fond of the kid. Hard to believe a snake like that could have a heart buried under all that flab. That softness for little kids was one of the reasons he did so much charity work. Katie here is prone to ear infections—she's got one working now. Matt always asked about her."

"How old is she, three?"

"Three and a half."

Jackie was four—only a few months difference.

"I got the impression Sumner didn't get along with his own children."

"That's true. He couldn't accept teenage rebellion. He was a strange man. He did a lot of good—raised a lot of money for good causes, but he could be such a bastard, too."

"Daddy, you said a bad word. I'm gonna tell Mommy," the little girl scolded.

"He did have a certain charm, though," I pressed.

"Oh, yeah. Never forgot a name or a face. It worked well for him in business and in his charity work. He could remember how much a contributor gave from year to year. That was a big part of his success. He could flatter you and make you believe lies were truth."

"Could he have been blackmailed?"

"Matt was too smart for that. He would've found a way to wheedle out of it."

The baby's biscuit was soft and gummy and she methodically smeared it through every inch of her sparse hair. Feddar picked up the child at his knee and draped her over his shoulder. She quieted, wrapping her small fingers around the folds in his shirt.

"Did he drink?" I asked.

Feddar laughed. "He couldn't handle it. I once saw him fall face-first—drunk—into a plate of linguine. That was at a Christmas lunch, and we'd all had a few. Funniest thing I ever saw, but no one dared laugh. One of the women felt sorry for him and drove him home. He came on to her in her car. Needless to say, that was the last time she played Good Samaritan."

"I'm getting an uneven picture of this guy."

"He missed his calling. He should've been an actor. He was a sleazebag, but it was amazing to see him charm women. He was good with all the clients, and if he wanted to encourage young talent at the bank, he'd do it. If you went to his alma mater, he practically kissed your ass."

"Where was that?"

"Notre Dame."

"You didn't go there?"

"Hell, no. Buff State."

"Daddy, I don't feel good," the little girl murmured.

"I know, sweetie," he said and patted her back. "The only good thing that's come out of all this is that I spend more time with my kids. But I'm not much good at housework. My wife is supporting us now, but when my unemployment runs out, I'll have to find something. We can't live like this and keep the house."

I nodded. If Richard hadn't rescued me, I might've become another statistic on the homeless front.

I thanked Feddar for his time, and made a hasty exit.

The day was winding down, and I was tired. I used Richard's cell phone and finally got hold of Linda Sumner, Rob's wife. When I explained I was looking into her father-in-law's death, she suggested I come over about six-thirty, after Rob came home from his job as assistant manager of a pizza parlor.

With nothing else to do, Richard and I headed for home to kill an hour before going out one last time. It gave me time to write up my interviews with Kaminski, Schmidt, and Feddar. I missed my computer. I had writer's cramp by the time I snagged my chauffeur to leave.

At precisely six-thirty we arrived at the little duplex on the fringes of Kenmore. I pressed the doorbell and waited. Finally Rob Sumner jerked open the door. While I'd seen a picture of him in his father's office, it had obviously been taken several years earlier. He looked about twenty-eight, with a beer gut years in the making. His close-set eyes and sullen expression reminded me of a schoolyard bully.

I introduced myself, but he didn't invite me inside. Despite the cold, he stood in his shirtsleeves—his hands jammed into his jeans pockets.

"My mother warned me you might be by to badger me."

"That's not my intent. I'm looking into your father's death. I hoped you could clarify a few things."

He scowled. "What do you want to know?"

"When did your relationship with Sharon Walker end?"

"What difference does that make?"

"I'm looking into the connection between the Walker Construction firm and your father."

"You think someone at Walker could have murdered Dad?"

"It's possible."

He thought about it for a moment, then answered. "Sharon and I went together for a couple of years. I met her at a party my dad threw for some of his clients. She came with her father. We got to be friends. We went out for about two years."

"When was this?"

"Six, seven years ago."

"Did you have her added to the list of those allowed in the church?"

"Why would you need to know that?"

"Do you know who the father of her child is?"

"No, I don't! And what's more, I don't care. Look, what's this got to do with my father's murder?"

"Do you still have a relationship with her?"

He took a step forward, forcing me back. "Hey, I don't need you coming around here saying things to upset my wife."

I kept my voice level. "I only told your wife I was looking into your father's murder."

His eyes flashed in outrage. "I don't need any more trouble."

So, there was trouble in newlywed paradise.

"What kind of trouble, Rob? Do you know something you haven't told the police? Did someone threaten you?"

"No," he shouted, but his furtive glance convinced me he was lying. "Look, don't bother us again. Or next time—!" He raised a fist, shook it at me, then stormed into the house.

I stared at the closed door for long seconds before I turned and walked down the driveway and climbed into the car.

"I was ready to call 911 that time," Richard said. "What was he so steamed about?"

"I'm not sure. But you know, I got a funny feeling he was covering up something about his father's death. He knows—or suspects—something. And I swear he lied to me about the timing of his relationship with Sharon Walker." I let out a long breath, leaning back in the seat. My conversation with Rob had shaken me more than I cared to admit.

Richard backed the car out of the driveway. "You look beat."

"I feel beat—like I put in a whole day."

"You did." He headed for home, down streets that, despite the gathering gloom, were beginning to look familiar again.

"Look, tomorrow's Good Friday—a holiday for most of the city. Why don't you take the day off, too?" Richard said. "Relax—have some fun. Is there something you'd like to see or do now that you're home? Niagara Falls? Toronto maybe?"

I thought about it for a moment, remembering Maggie's suggestion. "Well, I would like to go to the Broadway Market."

Richard shrugged. "Sure." He looked puzzled. "Why?"

I looked at him, incredulous. "You mean you've never been there on Good Friday?"

"I don't think I've ever been there."

"I guess I shouldn't be surprised. It is a working-class haven."

"Now let's not get nasty," he said, his amused tone making me smile. "Seriously, Jeff. Take a day off. Will it really make a difference?"

"Probably not. And from everything I've found out, the victim deserved what he got."

"It's not your place to judge."

I made no comment. But if what he said was true, why had God, or the fates, dragged me into this whole mess? Sumner's small act of kindness—buying that crummy vase for my mother's birthday—had indebted me to him. An out-of-proportion debt, but a debt nonetheless. I suppose no cosmic rule said I had to like the truth I uncovered. And deep down I knew this little mystery had kept me going. Without it, I might've given up entirely.

"A day off?" I repeated, the idea beginning to appeal to me. "Okay, Rich. You've got a deal."

Chapter Nineteen

The morning started with sunny skies and warm temperatures, the kind of day that makes you mistakenly think winter's gone for good. As a kid a trip to the Broadway Market on Good Friday had been a tradition for me. Though grown, I was no less delighted.

Richard seemed nervous about taking the Lincoln to that part of town, but Brenda didn't seem to care, so we took her car. Cars jammed the side street, waiting to get in the ramp garage. We circled around, looking for a place to park, and ended up on the roof.

We walked down three flights of stairs and entered the Market. Young and old people of all ethnic backgrounds packed the seedy-looking warehouse space. The market's worn, concrete floors and walls of peeling paint couldn't dispel the holiday spirit.

Stalls and kiosks were scattered across the floor and clustered around the edges of the room. Vendors sold wooden Ukrainian Easter eggs, tacky ashtrays, cigarette lighters and other trinkets, Lotto tickets, and Easter plants. We passed meat counters where people lined up four or five deep, waiting to buy their holiday roasts or fresh Polish sausage.

You don't mess with a woman bent on shopping, and Brenda had a purpose. Richard and I were soon separated from her in the crowd. I wandered the place in a pleasant fog, comparing the present-day Market with the one I remembered. Paranoia struck when I remembered Sophie Levin's warning about danger in even innocent situations. I found myself searching the crowd for a woman with a small boy. Not shadows of my past, but Sharon Walker clutching her crossbow, dragging her young son behind her.

Pausing at a candy counter, I studied the offerings. "Are you getting anything for Brenda?" I asked Richard.

"She doesn't go in for that kind of silliness."

"Well, if you don't buy her something, I will. Then I'll look like a hero on Easter morning."

He frowned, then bought her a two-pound box of assorted chocolates. But he made me carry the bag so she wouldn't suspect anything.

By the time we caught up with Brenda, she was loaded down with grocery bags—more food than the three of us were capable of eating. "That's the beauty of owning a freezer," she quipped. "Now what else do we have to get?"

"A butter lamb," I said.

"Which is?"

"Butter in the shape of a lamb. It's a Polish Easter tradition," Richard explained.

"What are the pussy willows for?" she asked, seeing a woman pass by with an armful of them.

"Dingus Day," Richard said.

"Yeah. You buy them and hit Richard with them on Easter Monday. Then you go to a tavern, drink beer, and have fun."

She looked skeptical. "Why?"

"It's Polish tradition," Richard said.

"But you're not Polish," she said.

"I'm half Polish," I said.

"Well it doesn't show," she teased good-naturedly. "Oh, eggs! We have to get eggs."

"What for?" Richard asked.

"Coloring, of course. And we have to get the dyes, too."

Richard looked at me and frowned.

"You can be such a stuffed shirt, Richard," Brenda said. "But Jeffy and I are determined to have fun."

"I'm not opposed to having fun. I'm just not very artistic."

"You don't need to be, my love." She patted his cheek and he faked a smile. Then she started off in the direction of a poultry stand. "It's all settled—egg coloring after lunch. Wait until you see what I got. We'll have a feast guaranteed to clog your arteries."

We got the eggs, and the dyes, and started for home. And lunch was a feast. Brenda laid the cold cuts on a platter and we made deli-type sandwiches out of ham, tongue, sliced beef, bologna, and liverwurst. She bought Polish rye bread with caraway seeds and set out a jar of horseradish that brought tears to the eyes and cleared our sinuses. For dessert, she bought fresh *placek*—that wonderful, sweet, crumb loaf—and sugar cookies, which tasted terrific with hot, strong coffee. I ate more in one sitting than I'd eaten in months. For the first time in a very long while, I felt happy, and it was the company as much as the good food.

After eating too much, we all felt logy. I volunteered to clean up while Brenda and Richard headed for the bedroom and a nap. I was glad to give them a chance to be alone. I'd been monopolizing too much of Richard's time.

I hit the mattress, too, but sleep didn't come quickly. I kept thinking about Sharon Walker, her crime, and the small boy who'd witnessed it. And wondered what in hell I could do about it.

* * *

I must've dozed off, because the next thing I knew noises from the kitchen woke me.

Brenda sat at the table. The eggs were in a shallow bowl, already boiled and cooled. She measured water into four old-fashioned glasses. "Hey, Jeffy, sit your butt down and let's decorate these eggs."

"Coffee," I rasped. "Got any instant?"

"Not in this house. I'll make some while you fix the colors and start dunking."

I read the directions and dropped dye tablets in the glasses. Then I picked up the transparent wax crayon that came in the package and took an egg in hand.

"What're you going to draw?" she asked.

"An Easter cross."

"Draw flowers, too."

"But all I can make are dumb-looking tulips."

"Just make it pretty."

She brought over two steaming mugs. After two weeks, she knew just how I liked my coffee. We sipped our coffee and dipped eggs like a couple of contented children. I debated spoiling the mood, but something had been nagging me.

"Brenda, why don't you and Richard get married?"

The joy of the moment left her face. She stared at the glass of blue colored dye, taking her time to mull over the question.

"Jeffy, there's a lot of guilt involved when you love a white man," she said, her voice soft. "Some of the worst racists I know are African-Americans. Some in my own family."

"Your mother?"

She nodded. "For most of my life I've worked in the white world. Two—possibly three—other people of color worked at the Foundation in Pasadena, but that's all. I know I was hired as a token black, but that's where it ended. I worked damn hard and I earned every cent of my pay. And I was paid well. I don't need Richard's money. I have my own and I spend it."

"You didn't answer my question."

She frowned. "I was married before. To a man of color. He abused me. He felt emasculated because I had a better-paying job than he did." She stopped, pursed her lips. "It's more a woman thing than a race thing. I'm a person. I won't be a man's property ever again."

"But Rich isn't like that."

"I know. But it's been hard coming to Buffalo. It's a conservative, blue-collar town. And this is a very white neighborhood. It would be difficult for Richard to live here with me as his wife."

"He loves you."

"It's more complicated than just love."

I hesitated, almost afraid to voice my next question. "Are you going to leave him?"

Her eyes flashed in anger; then she shook her head and picked up another egg, carefully dipping it into the glass of dye. "You're braver than your brother. He's afraid to ask that question."

"Don't leave him because of me. I'll go before I let that happen."

Tears brimmed her eyes. She reached for my hand. "Jeffy, nothing you could do would come between us. You could be the glue that ultimately holds Richard and me together." She smiled at my puzzlement. "It's okay, you don't have to understand. I don't even understand. But, like those visions you have and hold as truth, I hold this as truth."

I didn't know what the hell she was talking about, but then we were hugging each other and I felt better.

"What's going on?" Richard asked, entering the kitchen.

Brenda and I pulled back, looked at one another, and smiled.

"Nothing," I said and took another sip of my coffee. "Nothing at all."

"Sit down and draw a caduceus," Brenda told Richard, the somber spell broken.

"What on earth is that?" I asked.

"The medical symbol. A snake and staff," he explained, taking his seat. He turned to her. "And why would I want an Easter egg with a caduceus on it—if I could even draw one?"

She held up one of the eggs decorated with my artistry. "Because this is the sorriest example of an Easter egg I've ever seen. You have to be better at it than your brother."

He shrugged and picked up the wax crayon. "It's blunt."

"So sharpen it." I handed him a paring knife. "Hey, guys, I'm going out with Maggie tonight. Should I tell her about this psychic stuff?"

"Yes. If it's going to make a difference, you want to know before you get too involved," Brenda advised.

"Just do what feels right," Richard said. He frowned at the crayon. "How am I supposed to draw something as complicated as a caduceus when the crayon is clear wax and I can't see what I've drawn?"

"Draw a tulip. It's easier," I said.

Richard's artistic endeavors were no better than mine, I noted with satisfaction, but the egg-coloring project was a success if only for the fun we had.

We finished about five, which gave me an hour before Maggie arrived.

I showered and changed and found myself sitting on the stairs by the front door like a dog awaiting its master. I admit it, I was looking forward to my night out. Since I still had cash left from my tax return, the evening would be on me—not her.

With time on my hands, I thought about Rob Sumner. He knew—or suspected—a lot more than he'd let on. I prayed for sudden insight so I'd know what part—if any—he'd played in his father's death. Not that I believed he participated in the murder, but I couldn't shake the feeling he was somehow involved, however indirectly.

And perhaps Sharon's next victim?

Now where did that come from?

I was still pondering different scenarios, with Rob at the center, when the doorbell startled me. I jumped to my feet and opened the door. Maggie stood on the steps, poised to ring the bell again. Her unzipped, iridescent, down jacket seemed to waver between lavender and blue.

Dressed in jeans, boots, and an emerald green sweater, she looked terrific.

"Hello!" She took a step forward and gave me a quick peck on the cheek. "Good to see you looking better."

"Glad to be feeling better." I held on longer than absolutely necessary, soaking up that wonderful, peaceful aura she seemed to emit. I stepped back. "Come on in."

"Sorry I'm late. Lily had a crisis. She ran out of whiskey and her boyfriend was coming over. Elderly love."

I suppressed a smile.

She looked around the grand entry hall. "Great house. I could kill for a tour."

"It's not mine, or I'd say yes. But I'll bet Brenda could be talked into it. Come on. They're in the study." I didn't bother to take her coat as we were going to leave in only a few minutes. Maggie followed me through the long corridor to the opposite end of the house. Richard sat behind his desk; Brenda was on the couch facing the fireplace. "Rich, Brenda, this is my friend Maggie Brennan."

Richard stood. "Hi, Maggie, I think I recognize you from the bank." He held out his hand to shake hers.

Brenda came up behind her.

"This is Brenda."

Maggie turned and blinked, momentarily startled. I may have forgotten to tell her Brenda's black. "Oh. Nice to meet you," she said, extending her hand.

"We've heard a lot about you. I understand interior decoration is a hobby of yours?"

"Yes. You have a lovely home."

"In desperate need of updating. Would you like a tour?"

Smiling, Maggie glanced at me. "I'd love one."

The women disappeared and I scowled at Richard. "Well, I won't be eating dinner for a couple of hours."

"Have a seat," he said, gesturing me into the empty wing chair in front of his desk.

He took his own seat and started flipping through pages of what looked like bank statements. "Counting your millions?"

Richard frowned. "Take my word for it, having a lot of money is a burden."

"I could get used to it."

"I doubt it. I'm forty-seven years old. Brenda doesn't want to get married, and she certainly doesn't want children. So what am I going to do with all that money in one lifetime?"

"Give it away."

"I've been meaning to. Grandmother got burned by a bogus charity. I guess that's why I'm stalling. I haven't even invested the money, much to my accountant's dismay. It just keeps growing, even though most of it just languishes in bank accounts."

"Give it away," I repeated. "Make it a business. Check out every charity. If it's legitimate, send them money."

"I'd have every charity in town kissing my ass."

"Give it anonymously."

He looked thoughtful. "Maybe."

"Just leave me a million or two, okay?"

"I thought you liked your independence?"

"I do. And I'm kidding."

He shrugged, the barest hint of a smile on his lips. "I'll leave you a million anyway."

"Don't hurry and die on my account. I kind of got used to having you around."

"Seriously, Jeff, years ago I offered to send you to college. That offer's still open. Or I'll set you up in business, if that's what you want."

"Look, Rich, you could buy me my own insurance agency, or a McDonald's franchise, but then it wouldn't be mine. It wouldn't be something I'd earned."

"I can lead you to the road to success. You'd have to stay there on your own. You'd do it, too. You have integrity, Jeff. And my offer stands."

"Then how about a compromise? I'm going to need transportation to find a job. Maybe in a couple of weeks we could go look at cars. But I'll pay you back. It's important to me to pay my way. Understand?"

He smiled. "Too well. You're as bad as Brenda." He collected the papers in front of him, put them into a file folder, and deposited them in his desk.

"What about you? What do you want to do?"

He shrugged. "Brenda's got her heart set on volunteering at a women's clinic. But a clinic that also handles abortions is a little too high-profile for me. I want to help people, but I don't want to be a target."

"How about opening your own clinic?"

He shook his head. "All my money wouldn't be enough to fund it. Plus the logistics are beyond comprehension. That's why we've looked into working for an established clinic."

"Do you really want to volunteer your time?"

"I might like to work at UB's clinic. And maybe teach."

"What does Brenda think?"

"I've bored her with it for so long she cringes at the mention of UB. But I always thought of the place as home. I know that sounds silly, but I do."

"No sillier than having visions and trying to solve murders. In fact, it sounds a helluva lot saner to me."

"The problem is nothing can compare with my job at the Foundation. I worked with some of the greatest minds and computer equipment." He shook his head ruefully. "So much of my life was tied up in my work that I didn't have time for anything else—except Brenda, and she shared that work."

"So, you're not a shrink."

"No, but I've done my share of counseling other people."

Including me, I thought. "So what stage of grief are you in now?"

"Acceptance. Thanks to you."

"You mean my pitiful life made you realize how good you've got it?"

He looked stricken, until he realized my sarcasm held no animosity. "Actually, yes."

I shrugged. "I'm glad one of us got something out of this experience."

He leaned back in his chair. "Give yourself time. It's taken me a year to get this far."

"Then talk to Brenda about UB. She's cool."

He smiled. "You're right, she is."

Maggie's boot heels tapped on the parquet floor. Laughter preceded their entrance.

"Are you ready?" I asked Maggie.

"Sure." She nodded at Richard. "Hope to see you again soon."

Brenda and Richard waved to us as Maggie backed out of the driveway, making me feel a bit like a kid out on a first date. She headed toward Main Street, then turned right, heading away from the city. "Where are we going?" I asked.

She gave me a wry smile. "Nowhere fancy. Just good, cheap food."

Chapter Twenty

"What do you recommend?" I asked, peering at Maggie over the top of my laminated menu.

"The fish fry, of course."

Mike and Ann's Tavern wasn't fancy. Plastic flowers in plastic vases decorated each table. No one seemed to mind—every seat was taken. But it wasn't only the good food that had attracted Maggie.

"I'm allergic to cigarette smoke," she explained. "This was the first smoke-free bar I came across. That doesn't matter now that the laws have changed. But this is still the best place I know for a fish fry."

"I had a feeling you didn't like being around smoke."

"Who does? If I'm exposed to it for even a few minutes, I suffer for days. I just have bad lungs."

My eyes wandered down the front of her sweater. I wasn't disappointed in what I saw. She cleared her throat and I looked away, pretending to study the daily specials.

The beer-battered haddock, fries, coleslaw, and fresh-baked rye bread were excellent, and the portions were generous. Too generous for me. Maggie assured me her dog would do justice to the leftovers.

We talked while we ate. Maggie had so many interests and amusing stories to share. In comparison, I felt like the dullest man on earth. I gave her the rest of my history—how I'd lost my job at Travelers, then used all my savings just to survive. I told her about landing the new job and how life was on the upswing until the mugging.

It seemed like every sentence I uttered began with, "I used to...." I used to play racquetball. I used to dabble in photography. I used to target shoot.

I used to have a life.

"My sister Irene says you're a loser. That I should run away from you as fast as I can."

My stomach tightened. She'd said the words with such lightness that it almost sounded like a joke. But her sister might be right.

"Then why didn't you cancel tonight?"

Maggie's gaze held mine. "Because the day I met you, when you shook my hand, I felt—" She stopped, as though having trouble putting her thoughts into words. "I felt something."

I had, too. I liked it. I wanted more.

She hesitated, then reached across the table and touched my hand, reigniting that same spark of something inside me once again.

We sat there, amidst the dinner crowd bustle, staring at each other. Smiling at each other. Studying each other. Then a shadow darkened her deep blue eyes. She released her hold, reached for her coffee cup, and lowered her gaze. "There's something I should have told you."

I swallowed dryly. "Oh?"

"Matt and I were...together for a while."

Oh shit. And I'd told Nielsen to concentrate on Sumner's ex-lovers. I worked at keeping my voice level. "You had an affair?"

She placed the cup back in its saucer and toyed with her spoon. "It was right after Gary left." Her face seemed to crumple. "When your husband leaves you for another man, you feel like a failure as a woman. Matt and his never-ending string of compliments made me feel desirable again. But it wasn't long before I felt pretty darn cheap."

For a moment I thought she might cry. Then she took a breath and straightened in the booth. "Matt took advantage of me when I was vulnerable. I'm not making excuses for myself. I should have known better. When I finally realized what I'd allowed to happen, I was angry. I broke it off and Matt took his revenge. He got me transferred back to the secretarial pool where I started. It took me four years to move up to the top floor again, and he made my life hell once I made it back, too."

Her anger and resolve, stretched across the expanse of table, touched me. "Why didn't you tell me this sooner?"

She wouldn't look at me. "I didn't want you to think less of me."

I studied her troubled face as she tried to distance herself from the hurt.

"I don't think less of you. I think less of him."

Her smile was thin-lipped and embarrassed.

I needed more from her. But how could I get it without seeming as big a jerk as the man who'd used her? "What about Sumner's children? Ron Myers said the youngest son has a drinking problem."

"Michael went to rehab after he showed up drunk at school toting a loaded gun. I'm the one who made the arrangements to get him into a place near Albany. Matt's daughter, Diane, is the only sane one in the family."

"What's with Rob?" I asked. "When I spoke to him yesterday, he was pretty hostile. I got the impression he really didn't want anyone looking into his father's death. Like he might've known something about it."

"I don't know. Matt was great at damage control. I wondered if Rob got caught stealing or maybe selling drugs a couple of years ago. He was in some kind of trouble, but it all blew over."

"Did Sumner confide in you about such things?"

Maggie shook her head. "He didn't respect me—or any other woman. I once heard him tell one of the guys that women were only walking twats. I know that's vulgar, but that's what he was."

I frowned. The more I learned about Sumner, the more my revulsion grew. But I needed to find out more.

"I'm trying to get in Sumner's head—get a better understanding of him. Does that make sense?"

She nodded.

"Then tell me, where does one have a clandestine affair in Buffalo?"

"We'd meet at his condo. I don't think Claudia knew about it. I don't know if he owned or rented it. It might even belong to the bank. You wouldn't believe the assets they have."

Someone dropped a couple of quarters in the jukebox. Elvis began singing "Suspicious Minds."

Maggie leaned forward, and spoke louder. "I found a duplicate key in his desk while cleaning out his office." She patted her purse beside her. "I don't know why, but I took it."

My eyes widened as a whole range of possibilities blossomed in my mind.

She smiled coyly. "Wanna take a drive?"

***

The condo was in a tract of ubiquitous clones in Tonawanda off Sheridan Drive. If you came home drunk on a Saturday night, you'd probably never find your own place.

Maggie parked in the short drive and killed the lights and engine. No porch lamp shined at number three twenty-two. It wasn't much to look at. A double garage took up most of the front of the place. The entrance was a white steel door. A round, leaded window was the only source of natural light on the south side of the first floor, although double dormered windows were centered on the story above.

We got out and I looked around. No neighbors peeked out to watch us. Not even a barking dog cut the silence.

Maggie headed for the front door, stuck in the key, and reached for the handle.

A sick feeling welled in my stomach.

"Wait! Do you have gloves?" I met her on the steps, could hardly see her eyes in the dark.

"What for?"

"If the cops haven't been through here already, we don't want them finding our fingerprints when they come."

"Good idea," she said, and pulled a pair of knit gloves from her coat pocket. I held the cuff of my right glove between my teeth and pulled it on my hand, as she fumbled with the key in the lock.

The condo was dark. I waited until she shut the door behind us before patting the wall in search of a light switch. I found it, and a crystal chandelier flashed to illuminate the entry. I took in the stark white walls, tiled entry, carpet and sectional furniture in the room straight ahead: the place reminded me of a hospital. No art or photos decorated the hall. To the right, a staircase led to the loft above. The place felt cold, like no one had been there in weeks.

We wandered into the living room, Maggie flicking on switches as we went. A cathedral ceiling soared some twenty feet above us. Rectangular skylights, like black eye sockets, reflected the glow of track lighting. A black-and-white modern-art painting decorated the space above the white mantle. A companion piece of corporate art hung near the dining table. The rest of the walls were blank. A natural-looking fake fern filled the cold hearth. A stereo cabinet held audio equipment, but few CDs. The black box of a TV sat on a pedestal across from the couch, its remote the only clutter in the room.

"Not much personality, is there?" Maggie commented. "It hasn't changed a bit since I was here five years ago."

"Apart from the style of furniture, it's not much different from Sumner's house."

I ventured farther into the sterile room to look over the breakfast bar and into the galley kitchen. "What's through that door? The garage?"

She nodded.

"And upstairs?"

"Two good-sized bedrooms. A terrific bathroom. It's got a double shower and Jacuzzi bath. There's a hot tub on the deck." She walked over to the French doors. Beyond her I could see the lights of the condos on the next street.

"The basement opens out to the back courtyard. Matt had a wet bar down there. It's got a pool table, too. Wanna see?"

I shook my head and looked around the room once more. Too bad I couldn't touch anything. I just hoped I'd suck up whatever residual essence remained of Sumner by other means.

I closed my eyes, breathed deeply, opening myself up to the place. Tendrils of something nudged at my brain.

Maggie and Sumner had made love here. He'd touched her. Maybe memorized her every curve.

A wave a jealousy washed through me.

Don't think about it.

But I couldn't stop. It ate at me.

I squeezed my eyes shut tighter.

The tendrils grew stronger. I wasn't sure just what it was I was getting—but I was definitely getting something. Fear, maybe, but unlike what I'd felt before. I concentrated and the feeling swelled. Yes, another's stomach-churning fear.

"Are you okay?" Maggie asked, worried.

Everybody seemed to be asking me that question on a regular basis. I let out a long breath and forced a smile. "Yeah. Let's look upstairs."

Maggie led the way, turning on more lights as we went. It seemed to enhance my newly awakened senses, the fear expanding with each step.

"This is the guest room," she said, adopting a real estate broker's cadence, "but I doubt anyone's ever stayed here."

Like the living room, it was a study in black and white. The headboard and matching dresser were ebony enamel. A white spread covered the mattress, and sheepskin acted as a throw at the left side of the bed, its ivory softness a contrast to the stark white carpet. No night tables with bedside lamps for reading comfort. No books, either. No decorations on the walls. I opened the closet door. Nothing. Not even coat hangers.

"Next is the bathroom. I'd kill for one like this," she said and flipped on a switch.

Chrome and tile sparkled like something out of a builder's brochure. Except for a box of tissues, there was nothing in sight to indicate anyone lived here. I opened the medicine cabinet and found an electric razor, toothpaste and a single toothbrush, mouthwash, cologne, a can of men's hair spray, and a half-empty box of condoms. Old Matt liked to be prepared. A drawer in the vanity held a dozen new toothbrushes—no doubt for use by Sumner's lady guests—and an unopened box of disposable cups. Freshly laundered white towels sat neatly stacked in the linen closet.

"I take it Matt didn't spend a lot of time here."

"It didn't take him long to climax," she said, sarcasm filling her voice. She cleared her throat. "The master bedroom's got a king-sized bed, a down comforter and—" I felt her tension rise.

I left the bathroom and saw a hand towel on the threshold between the master bedroom and hall. A dark smudge marred its pristine state. "What's wrong?"

She wrinkled her nose. "Do you smell something?"

I did. A flat, coppery odor I recognized.

"Stay here," I told her and headed down the hall.

I hit the light switch. Blood—like paint on a blank canvas—splattered the walls by the right side of the bed.

"What is it?" Maggie called.

I moved to the far side of the bed, careful not to tread on the footprint stains that ruined the carpet.

Claudia Sumner lay huddled on her side, naked, the top of her head blown clear away.

"Jeff?" Maggie cried, fear threading her voice.

No gun was visible. Where were Claudia's clothes? Was her car in the garage?

My gaze drifted to her face as phantom images of Shelley's murder exploded in my mind. But it was Claudia's blood, brains, and bone sprayed across the walls, floor, and bed.

The room was suddenly too hot, making it hard to breathe. I backed away, hoped to hang onto my stomach contents long enough to reach the bathroom.

I brushed past Maggie and threw up in the sink. Coughing and gasping, I ran the water until I could catch my breath.

"What did you see?" she cried. "What's in there?"

I wiped my mouth on my sleeve.

"Claudia."

Maggie's eyes went wide with fear. "Is she...dead?"

I nodded. "Hours ago. Maybe even yesterday."

Maggie took a ragged breath, her eyes wild, and backed away, crashing into the wall, then bolted for the stairs.

"Wait!"

I caught her at the landing, grabbed her sleeve.

"We've got to get out of here!" she wailed, and tried to pull away.

I pushed her against the wall, pinning her with my body.

"Listen to me. We can't panic. Do you hear me?" She shook her head, terrified. "Maggie, listen to me." I clasped her chin. "We've got to turn off the lights. We've got to make it look like we were never here."

"I'm going to lose my job. My God, we could go to jail!"

"No one has to know we were here. We wore gloves. It's going to be okay."

But she covered her face with her hands, weeping. I pulled her close and let her cry on my shoulder. I smoothed her hair in rhythm with her sobs. "It's okay, Maggie. It'll be okay. I promise."

"How? How can it ever be right?"

I had to come up with something. Some answer. She was depending on me.

I drew back, looked her in the eye.

"Have you ever done any acting?"

Since I'd already reported one find to the cops via 911, I figured I'd be pushing my luck to try it again.

Fifteen minutes later, in the parking lot of the same grocery chain where I'd previously found a pay phone, I wrote Maggie a script. She practiced it three times, speaking lower, slower, sounding sexy as hell.

We stood under the glare of a mercury vapor lamp, clutching the phone between us, Maggie transmitting her fear like carrier waves. She pressed the touch-tone pad. It rang twice.

"Please listen," she said calmly. "I'll only say this once. There's a body at three twenty-two Maiden Lane. Claudia

Sumner, wife of Matthew J. Sumner. She was shot. Today, possibly yesterday. Please send someone."

I pressed the switch-hook and our eyes locked. "You did great, Maggie."

A tear rolled down her cheek. "Let's get the hell out of here."

* * *

Maggie eased the shifter into park and turned off the engine. We hadn't spoken in the ten or so minutes it had taken for her to drive me back to Richard's house. The silence continued to lengthen.

Finally Maggie let out a sigh. "I feel like a criminal and I'm not guilty of anything."

"Technically, we're guilty of breaking and entering."

"Oh, shit." She sank back against her bucket seat.

"The question is, who else knew about the condo? And what was Sumner's wife doing there—naked and dead?"

"Waiting for a lover?" Maggie suggested. She, too, had seen through Claudia's facade of the faithful wife. "But who'd kill her and why?"

"Probably the same person who killed Matt. Maybe for the same reason." I wasn't ready to tell her what I thought about Sharon Walker.

Her gaze was fixed on nothing, her brows furrowed with worry.

"Don't think about it," I said.

"How can I stop?"

"You just have to."

We both had to.

"What if someone saw us? What if—"

"If the neighbors saw or heard anything, the cops would have been swarming the place. We did them a favor. It could've been days—maybe a week—before some poor cleaning lady found her."

"I'm glad I didn't look. Have you ever seen anything like that before?"

The memory of my trip to the morgue to identify Shelley's body would be with me until I died.

"My ex-wife was killed the same way. But I didn't see her until the coroner had cleaned her up. This was a lot worse." I knew I'd have nightmares for weeks.

"I wish I'd never found that damn key," Maggie said and turned her face away. "I'm sorry. This isn't how I'd planned to end the evening."

"Me, either."

"I like you, Jeff, a lot. But after what happened tonight, I—"

She didn't have to say the words. I already knew. "You don't want to see me."

"I'm not saying it's forever. Give me a few weeks and maybe we can try again. It's just…."

I cupped her chin, turned her face toward me, and leaned across the shifter, pressing my lips against hers. There was no passion in her response; neither was there revulsion. Maybe we *could* try again in another couple of weeks. Maybe.

Chapter Twenty-One

Claudia Sumner's untidy death kept me awake and staring at the ceiling for a long time. She must have known all about little Jackie. Otherwise why was she so interested in finding out the beneficiary of the fictional insurance policy I'd mentioned when I'd met her? Did she wonder if her husband had changed his policies—maybe even his will—to include his lover and bastard child?

Ron Myers said Claudia loved money. She also loved her children. How far was she willing to go to protect them and their inheritance? If Sharon confronted her—demanding Jackie's share of Matt's estate—Claudia could have been foolish enough to argue with her about it, not knowing she was Matt's killer.

Sumner's tryst with Maggie had happened at the condo five years before. Little Jackie was now four years old. Had Sumner bedded Sharon immediately after Maggie had broken it off? If so, Sharon would have known about the condo. It fit the time line. Had she lured Claudia there? Her death fit the pattern of humiliation, too. Sharon had taken Sumner's clothes before killing him. That she'd do the same to his wife made sense, as well. And killing Claudia at the condo, where

Matt had slept with all his side dishes, was the ultimate degradation.

I got up late and found Richard and Brenda at the kitchen table still reading the paper. "Morning," I called, shuffling toward the coffee pot.

They looked at me over the tops of their respective newspaper sections. "Good morning," Richard said. Did I detect a sliver of ice in his tone?

"Did you have a good time last night?" Brenda asked.

"Uh…yes and no." I grabbed a cup from the cupboard and poured myself some coffee.

"There's been a development in the Sumner case," Richard said, folding the front page of the paper to show me the banner headline. "They found his wife murdered."

I gulped my coffee. "Yeah. I know."

He studied my face. "How do you know?"

I considered lying but decided against it. "Who do you think found her?"

"Jeffy!" Brenda cried.

"Christ, now what kind of trouble are you in?" Richard asked.

"Nobody knows it was us."

"Us?" Brenda said.

"Maggie was with me." I explained how she'd found the duplicate key to the condo in Sumner's office. I left out the part about Maggie's affair with the dead man.

"I don't see how they can connect either one of us."

"Oh no?" Richard turned and grabbed a Post-It note from the counter. "That reporter called three times last night. You snuck off to bed before I could give you the messages."

"Uh…thanks. I guess. I'll call him later."

They gave each other worried looks, but Richard shook his head and they both found places other than me to look at. Finally Brenda refolded her section of newspaper. "Tomorrow's Easter Sunday; we really should go to church."

"Church?" Richard echoed. "But we never go."

Brenda shoved the Life & Arts section's color spread in front of him. "The paper says there's a Basilica in Lackawanna. Look at these pictures; the statues and stained glass look terrific. Its design is supposed to be based on St. Peter's in Rome. And it sure wouldn't hurt you couple of sinners to go." With that Brenda got up from the table, clearing away some of the dishes.

"But you're not Catholic."

"The two of you are. Maybe it'll rub off on me."

Richard scowled. "What time?"

"Noon." Brenda looked at me. "Want to come?"

I shrugged. "Sure." Besides, Maggie had said the Basilica was her parish. Maybe I'd see her there.

The phone rang. Richard's scowl deepened. "I'm not answering it."

"Me, either," Brenda said.

I got up, picked up the receiver. "Hello."

"Jeff." It was Sam Nielsen, sounding insufferably pleased. "You've been avoiding me."

"No, I haven't. I just wasn't home when you called last night. Why have you been annoying my family?"

"Me, annoy anyone? Ha! I was just wondering if you heard about Claudia Sumner?"

I didn't answer.

"A woman called 911. Do you know who?"

No way was I going to implicate Maggie. Some part of me still hoped I had a chance of being with her. "I read about it in the paper."

"That's not what I asked."

Damn him. He was going to hound me until I gave him something more. "Look, I've just moved back to Buffalo and I don't have any wheels. I need to make a few more inquiries. Are you available this morning?"

"Name the time and place."

We agreed to meet in an hour. I hung up the phone to find Richard and Brenda staring at me. "Do you think that's a wise move?"

"I've gotta get him off my back. If nothing else, I'll bore him to death."

Brenda let out a sigh but said nothing.

"And I'd like to go to East Aurora this afternoon, if you don't mind driving, Rich."

"Why?"

"To meet Sharon Walker."

Brenda sat down at the table again, her eyes flashing. "No, Jeffy. Don't do it."

"Why not?"

"Because from what you've told us, she's a vicious murderer. Maybe she killed Sumner's wife, too. I don't want you to be next."

"She's not going to kill me. I'm not stupid enough to accuse her."

"What will you say to her?" Richard asked.

"I'm not sure. I figured I'd just wing it."

"Wing it?" Brenda asked.

"Then what?"

"Then I'll go to Detective Hayden with everything I've got on her. It's up to him to decide if he wants to pursue it. I'll wash my hands of the whole thing once I talk to him."

Brenda crossed her arms over her chest. "Amen!"

***

A shiny black SUV with the license plate HOTNEWS pulled up the driveway exactly on time. I headed for it and slammed the door after I got in.

"Where're we going?" Nielsen asked.

"Do you like pizza for breakfast?"

"Not since college. Why?"

"We're going to the joint where Rob Sumner works."

"What for?"

"To talk." I gave him the address. "Put this sucker in gear and let's go."

"You don't expect him to show for work the morning after his mother was murdered."

"Of course not. But that doesn't mean I can't talk to his co-workers."

Nielsen shrugged, backed out of the driveway, and headed for Main Street. "Why the interest in the son? Do you think he's involved?"

"I don't know. Something in his attitude makes me suspicious."

"Is this a psychic insight?" he asked with more than a hint of contempt.

"It's a gut reaction. I've got years of investigative experience behind me. I've worked in the field for the last fourteen years."

"I did some digging on you. You had a pretty good career going."

"And it would've continued, if I hadn't been mugged."

"As of yesterday, NYPD hadn't made any headway on that."

He had done his homework. "I didn't think they would."

Nielsen palmed the wheel as he turned onto Transit Road. "Do you want to tell me how this psychic stuff works?"

"No."

"Aw, come on, Jeff. We're old school pals."

"I've forgotten a lot since I had my brains scrambled, but I know for a fact we were never friends."

"That could change."

"Why?"

Nielsen braked for a red light. "Because if you've got genuine psychic abilities—"

"Less than a minute ago you were sneering at the idea."

"I admit I'm a skeptic."

"And I can't put on a show for you. This stuff is hit or miss."

"So you were scamming Hayden?"

"No. Sometimes—and only sometimes—I seem to tune into people's emotions. The rest of it just kind of happens."

"And this only started after the mugging?"

"Yeah, and I hope like hell it goes as fast as it came."

Nielsen pulled into the pizza parlor's nearly-empty parking lot. The OPEN sign was still dark, but lights burned inside the building. "How are we handling this?" I asked.

"I'll just watch you in action."

I glared at him for a moment, and then got out of the car. He tagged behind me. The shop's door was unlocked and we stepped inside.

"We don't open for another half hour," said a teenaged girl mopping the entryway.

"I'd like to speak to the manager."

"That's me," said a harassed-looking man of about forty, coming up from behind the girl. His nametag read Dennis Sloan. "Are you interested in the assistant manager's job?"

"No." I introduced myself, ignoring Nielsen, and pulled out one of my business cards. "I'm here about an employee, Rob Sumner."

"Ex-employee."

Interesting that Linda Sumner wasn't aware of her husband's current employment status. Just where had he been going every day, when he should have been working?

"I'm looking into Matt and Claudia Sumner's deaths. Can you give me some insight into Rob's character?"

He scrutinized my card. "I can't tell you why he was let go—corporate policy."

"What can you tell me about him?"

Sloan took a half-step back and crossed his arms over his chest, his expression stony.

"When was he fired?"

"Two weeks ago."

Just about the time of his father's death.

"I understand he's not very responsible—or reliable," I said. "And maybe he drinks a little too much. He expects other people to clean up his messes." I thought about Rob's parents, and wondered if Claudia had slipped her son money to keep him afloat until he found another job. "He's also got a violent streak."

Sloan's eyes flashed, and his mouth went tight. "No comment."

He didn't need to say a word. "Thanks for your help." I couldn't keep the sarcasm out of my voice.

We went back outside and headed for Nielsen's car. "That went well," he said.

I could've decked him. He opened the driver's door as a rusty Ford Escort pulled into the lot, parking in the spot farthest from the entrance. A tall, skinny kid dressed in the franchise's standard uniform got out. On impulse, I jogged over to meet him.

"Can I talk to you for a minute?"

He looked at me suspiciously. "What about?"

"Rob Sumner." I handed him my card as Nielsen joined us. "I'm investigating his parents' deaths. What can you tell me about Rob?"

"He's an asshole," the kid answered without hesitation.

"Why'd he get fired?"

"He was balling one of the waitresses in the storeroom after hours."

Good old Rob—following right in his old man's footsteps.

"He was already on probation for beating up my buddy, Gene," the kid continued. Reticence wasn't his problem.

"Gene was another employee?"

"Yeah, until that bastard Sumner got him fired last month."

"What happened?"

"Rob said Gene was stealing money from the girls' tip jars. But it was Rob who took the money—Gene saw him. After Mr. Sloan fired him, Gene came back to have it out with Rob. He didn't know the guy's a psycho. He broke Gene's nose—really messed up his face."

Sloan watched us from the restaurant's plate glass door. I nodded in his direction. "Don't let him give you a hard time for talking to me. The First Amendment says you're entitled to an opinion, kid. Thanks for the information."

I headed back to the SUV with Nielsen trotting to keep up. "You got some good stuff. Why don't you don't look happy?" he asked.

I waited until we were inside the car and he started the engine before answering. "Rob Sumner threatened me the other day. At the time I didn't take it seriously." I looked down at the sling surrounding my broken arm and thought about the throbbing in my skull that never really went away. "Maybe I should."

"It's a tough game you're playing," Nielsen said. "Or maybe I should remind you that it isn't a game. Just keep in mind how Sumner was killed and what happened to his body afterwards."

I turned to stare at him. He didn't have the clue what I knew—what I'd seen. And I wasn't about to tell him.

Chapter Twenty-Two

Richard cut over from the Thruway to Route 400, heading southeast. The ride so far had been silent, and though I couldn't pick up on anything Richard felt, I could tell by his body language that he was nearing the boiling point.

"What if you're wrong? What if it wasn't her?" he blurted at last. His fingers, wrapped around the steering wheel, were white. I held onto the envelope of evidence I'd brought along nearly as tightly.

I glanced across the seat. "I'm not wrong."

"You haven't even considered the possibility that someone else could've killed Sumner."

"I don't have to."

He kept his gaze fixed on the road. "I don't like this. I don't like it one bit."

As I gazed out at the colorless countryside, doubt crept into my thoughts. A week before, Richard had suggested I might be twisting the facts to support a delusion. That accusation still haunted me.

"Okay, Rich, say Sharon wasn't the murderer. There're only three other possible suspects."

"That you know of," he shot back.

I ignored him. "Claudia Sumner, for one. With her husband conveniently out of the way, she was eager to get on with her life. She liked money and seemed to know about every one of his insurance policies. She knew of his affairs and she was conveniently out of town at the time of the murder. Nice little alibi. I got the impression that her life would improve with Sumner out of the way. No doubt she'd planned to find someone else who could maintain the lifestyle she obviously enjoyed. That is, if he wasn't already waiting in the wings."

"Of course, the fact that she's been killed, too, eliminates her from the running."

"You got that," I agreed. "How about her son? Rob Sumner and his father didn't get along. Rob had been in some kind of trouble several years before. Maggie thought it might be drugs. She wasn't sure."

"What else?" Richard asked, giving me a quick glance across the seat before turning his gaze back to the road.

"Rob's former girlfriend had been screwing his father. Not pretty, but that would've been ancient history—hardly worth killing his father for years later. Rob lost his job around the time his father was killed—but that was no motive for murder, either."

"Strike two," Richard said. "Although, from the looks of his house, Rob wasn't living the good life."

"No," I agreed, "and he cheated on his wife only months after their marriage. A chip off the old block. He stole tips from waitresses who made less than minimum wage, and he's got a violent streak that's easily aroused. He may not have killed his father, but once the will's read, he'll probably profit from his father's death."

"Who else?"

"Don Feddar, the guy Sumner fired before Christmas. He might have had a motive for murder, but he also had an undisputed alibi for the evening of the killing. And he certainly couldn't afford to pay anyone to do it for him. Strike three and out."

We were silent for a minute or two. Richard finally broke the quiet. "Everything you've said to count out the other suspects sounds totally logical. But have you used logic to support your theory that Sharon killed Sumner?"

"I *know* what I *know*," I said, but he was too intent on driving to notice the glare I gave him. "However jumbled the original vision was, I'd known about the murder before it happened. I knew the murderer had stood at the grave on the day of the funeral. Something directed me to the murder site and the victim's last remains. The same thing compelled me to go to Sumner's neighborhood where I found the jogger who'd seen the killer's car. I also knew the killer had handled the garage door opener."

"All intangibles," Richard muttered, waving a dismissive hand at me.

"Hey, I sensed the killer at the funeral and at the cemetery; that's why I was so sure that the killer had sent Sumner the invitation to the child's birthday party. That was the first real evidence that led me to Sharon Walker. Her son was born on January tenth—same as the invitation. Sharon Walker was engaged to Rob Sumner before her child was born. Sharon Walker had business dealings with the murdered man. Sharon Walker was a skilled hunter. A skilled hunter killed Matt Sumner."

"There're lots of skilled hunters around here."

"Oh, come on, Rich. A good investigator relies on his instincts. And, damn it, I know Sharon Walker murdered Matt Sumner."

"Your belief in her guilt isn't hard evidence. In the eyes of the law, she's innocent until proven guilty. Have you found enough to take to the police?"

I sank back in my seat. "I don't know." I studied the scenery flashing past the window, caught sight of a house number. " It should be close now."

Richard braked, pulling over to the shoulder of the road.

Sharon lived on the outskirts of town, but I knew the place before I saw the numbers tacked around the front door. The gloomy skies added to the air of neglect that hung around the old farmhouse. Ancient forest-green paint was sun-blistered and peeling, half the shutters were gone from the windows, and the gutters around the front hung precariously from the edge of the roof. Four steps led to a rickety porch. A good gust of wind would probably knock it down. The detached garage looked forlorn at the end of the long rutted drive. Sticks and bits of trash covered the matted lawn. In the driveway sat a maroon Chevy Caprice station wagon with a chrome roof rack. Richard pulled his car up behind it and shut off the engine.

We got out and I headed straight for the wagon. The driver's door had been painted over in a slightly different color, probably covering an advertisement for Walker Construction. I touched the tailgate and a shudder of revulsion ran through me as conflicting visions of Sumner lying in the back of the car seemed to explode behind my eyes. I had it: She'd driven the barely conscious man to Holland. After she'd killed him, she'd loaded the body into the back of the car once more and taken it to his home. And all the while she'd felt powerful and dangerous. It had excited her.

"Well?" Richard asked.

I nodded, letting out a ragged breath, needing to clear my head of the remaining web of strong emotions. "He was in there all right. After he was dead, she…covered him with a dark blanket."

To the right of the car, away from the house, sat a dilapidated barbecue. Bricks had fallen from it in a waterfall of debris.

The muddy ash pit beckoned. I picked up a stick and poked at the grayish goo, turning up swatches of scorched fabric. "She must have burned his clothes here." I dislodged scraps of different materials from out of the muck.

Richard held out a clean handkerchief and let me settle the fabric evidence onto it, one at a time; then he carefully folded it and put it into his coat pocket. He glanced over his shoulder at the house.

"Someone was just at the window."

"Was it her?"

"I only saw the curtains move."

I looked back down at the ash pit, suddenly afraid—and not just for myself. This woman had already committed one—probably two—terrible crimes.

"Maybe you should wait in the car. Two of us could be intimidating. I don't want to push her into doing something stupid."

Richard didn't look happy. "Whatever you do, don't provoke her."

"That's the last thing I intend to do."

He nodded and turned, heading back to the Lincoln.

I crossed the twenty yards of brown lawn to the house, climbed the porch steps, knocked on the door, and wondered what the hell I'd say to the woman. I waited about thirty seconds before knocking again.

Time dragged.

It would be smarter to just forget the whole thing.

What if she remembered my voice from that prank call the week before?

I was about to try one last time when the door was wrenched open.

"Yeah, what do you want?"

Dressed in stained gray jogging pants, sweatshirt, and sneakers, her bleached hair cropped short, Sharon Walker was overweight and unattractive, her expression haunted. Not at all like the photo of the young girl I'd seen only days before.

She wasn't what I would've expected of Matt Sumner's lover—or Rob's.

"Ms. Walker? My name's Jeffrey Resnick and—"

"I know who you are."

"Did Rob Sumner call you?"

She crossed her arms across her chest. "Yes. What right have you got to say that Matt was killed by somebody at Walker Construction? What right?"

"I didn't say that. I told him I was looking into his father's dealings with Walker Construction."

"Why?"

I chose my words carefully. "There seems to be a question of impropriety."

"Even if it was true, which it isn't, what difference could it possibly make now? He's dead. My father's dead. Walker Construction is dead. It doesn't matter any more."

A small boy, about four years old, pushed forward, attaching himself to her leg. He looked like a miniature version of Matt Sumner.

"Is that Jackie?" I asked.

"His name's Jimmy. He was named after my father."

"Was he once called Jackie?"

"What were you doing poking around my car and my yard? You're trespassing on my property. I have every right to call the cops and have you arrested. Now get out of here." She turned to go back inside and I grabbed her arm.

"Wait—!"

A second became an eternity as the vision of what she'd done—all the triumph, the horror, and the fear—hit me as hard as being clobbered with that baseball bat.

I saw them—standing by the barbecue, arguing—Sumner waving a letter at her. She screamed at him while the little boy cowered in terror behind her. My hand tightened around her forearm, but I couldn't move as the vision shifted.

Claudia Sumner had pleaded for her life—but Sharon made her kneel on the condo's virginal white carpet, held the snub-nosed revolver to the base of her skull, and pulled the trigger.

"Let go!" Sharon yelled.

Overlapping images of Sharon and Sumner—Sharon and Claudia—assaulted me, squeezing the breath from my lungs. Feelings of fear, anger, and triumph bombarded me.

The boy leaped forward, punching me on the thighs. "Leave my mommy alone, you bad man."

Her face twisted in fury, Sharon wrenched away from me, shoved me, and sent me tumbling backward down the steps—only the rickety rail saved me. She grabbed the boy, turned, and slammed the door. The deadbolt clicked in place.

Muscles quivering with shock, I pulled myself upright. Gasping for breath, I forced myself to move—to get the hell out of there.

I headed for the car, breaking into a jog for the last ten yards, yanked open the passenger side door and scrambled in.

"What happened?" Richard demanded.

"Go! Now!"

The tires spun in the gravel as he gunned the engine. The Lincoln jerked down the drive and onto the highway heading west. Numb, I sat there, staring at nothing, the fingers of my right hand clamped around the door's hand grip just to keep from trembling.

"Jeff!" Richard's voice was stern.

"She killed him, all right," I blurted. "He showed her a copy of the lab report. The one that told him the hair sample he'd provided did not match his DNA exactly. And he knew. He knew! So he came out to her house to confront her. He told her she wouldn't get another dime out of him. If she wanted money, she could go to the boy's father. She could go to Rob for money."

"Good grief," Richard muttered.

The images began to sort themselves out in my head.

"She bent down and grabbed—" I had to concentrate to understand. "She grabbed a brick from the barbecue and slammed it into his skull. The kid went berserk. She thought she'd killed Sumner. When he wasn't dead, she flipped out—decided to have some fun with him. She's strong. She dumped him in the back of the station wagon, took him out to Holland, cut off his clothes with her deer-skinning knife, and let him squirm in the snow, all the time taunting him. He didn't believe she'd actually do it. He begged her to stop, but she only laughed. The kid got out of the car and ran across the snow—shrieking, crying. She screamed at him to get back in the car. The kid was terrified. She crouched down, cut Sumner free, and told him to run. Then she took aim with the bow."

"Jesus. You got all that from just touching her?"

"More." I shuddered again, frozen to my toes. "I have to assimilate it."

He pulled into the parking lot of a diner along the road. By then my initial panic had subsided. I grabbed my envelope and followed him inside. At nearly three in the afternoon, the place was deserted. Richard pointed to a booth near the front, and a waitress in a white uniform and black apron came to the table. "Coffee and apple pie for both of us," Richard said.

"*A la mode*?" she asked hopefully.

"Plain."

She frowned, but hustled off.

"I don't want anything," I said.

"Shut up and do as I tell you for once."

I shut up.

The pie was typical diner fare. The filling oozed out of the crushed crust, making it look as though someone had sat on it. It was stale, too. The coffee was bitter.

"What else?" Richard prompted.

"Sharon was screwing both of them. Rob because she thought she loved him, Matt because she wanted to save her father's construction company."

"Did Rob know at the time?"

"I don't know. But his father paid her, supported the boy. Something must've happened." I thought about it for a moment and realized what I'd seen for myself. "Sumner noticed the boy had his wife's nose. To confirm his suspicions, he had the kid's hair DNA tested, comparing it with some of Claudia's as well as his own. Because it matched factors from both of them, the test proved it was Rob, not Matt, who fathered Sharon's son."

"How do you know that?"

I pulled out the wrinkled envelope. "I found this in his desk the other day."

Richard studied it. "This doesn't prove anything." He handed it back.

"Not by itself. But it wouldn't be hard for the cops to get a copy of the letter. Our Ms. Walker had strung Sumner along for over four years and, with the gravy train about to end, she wasn't about to let him have the last word."

"What about Sumner's wife?"

"Sharon went after his estate. No way was Claudia going to let her have any of the money. But she'd underestimated Sharon. Thought she could reason with her."

I sipped my coffee. "It bothers me that Rob Sumner called her. Told her I might be out to visit her. Why would he do that?"

"Maybe he's afraid of her," Richard suggested. "He, of all people, knows what she's like. He may suspect she killed his father—and his mother."

"He knows something," I agreed. I thought about it for a moment. "Maybe he wants her to get caught. She's practically living in poverty. She could go after him for child support now that his father isn't paying her. Maybe he wants her out of the way. So he called her to make her angry—"

"At you," Richard finished. "He may have deliberately set you up as a target."

"How? Sharon only knows my name. The cops and Sumner's family know I don't work for the insurance company. But only Detective Hayden and Sam Nielsen know where I live. I haven't left much of a paper trail here in Buffalo…yet." That last word seemed to hover over the table like a prophetic curse.

We sat in silence for long minutes. Dishes clattered in the kitchen. Static-laced Muzak came from a speaker in the ceiling.

Richard indicated the plate in front of me. "Eat up."

I did my best, but neither of us could finish.

"Where to?" Richard asked once we were back in the car.

"Let's get this envelope of stuff to Detective Hayden. After that, I don't want anything more to do with Sharon Walker."

***

It was Hayden's day off. I tried his home phone number and found him in. He wasn't exactly happy to hear from me, but told me to come over anyway. He lived in one of the older neighborhoods in Orchard Park.

Two boys' bicycles, covered in fresh mud, were clashed on the soggy ground in the front yard. The basketball hoop over the garage door had no net. It started to rain as I knocked on the side entrance door. Richard looked morose and huddled into his jacket. I knocked again, and a matronly woman answered. "Mr. Resnick? Won't you come in? My husband is in the den."

The tidy, dated kitchen reminded me of a set from a sixties sitcom. The aroma of meat loaf and boiled potatoes filled the air. An unfrosted chocolate cake, cooling on wire racks on the counter by the sink, added to the sense of unreality. We followed her through the orderly house to the den. She ushered us inside and closed the door behind us.

This was obviously Hayden's domain. Family photos were scattered over the walls, including a large color portrait of Hayden, his wife, and two preteen boys. Bowling trophies shared shelf space with a clutter of books, magazines, and other memorabilia.

"Still joined at the hip, I see. Sit," Hayden commanded. "I don't like my weekend interrupted," he warned without preamble.

"With any luck, you'll never see me again after today." I handed him the envelope.

"What's this?" He lifted the flap and dumped the contents on his desk.

"My case against Sharon Walker."

"Who?"

"The woman who killed Matt and Claudia Sumner. It's kind of a long story. I hope your meat loaf will keep."

I repeated what I'd told him at the police station earlier that week, catching him up with the events that had occurred within the past few days—leaving out the part where Maggie and I found the second victim. While I spoke, he pawed through the envelope's contents. He didn't ask where I got the copy of Sumner's calendar, and I wouldn't have told him. Richard handed over his handkerchief with the fabric swatches.

Hayden leaned back in his Naugahyde swivel chair. "All circumstantial. You haven't got a thing I can go to the DA with."

"I know that. But once you subpoena the lab report, that alone should give you a new angle to investigate."

He picked up the envelope. "Where'd you get this?"

"Sumner's office. It was jammed behind one of the drawers in his desk."

"And what were you doing there?"

"I had permission. Ron Myers can vouch for me." I waited, and when he said nothing, "Well?"

"Well, what? There's nothing here. No case."

"Will you at least look into it?"

"Yeah, but it won't come to anything. Guaranteed. Sumner slept with a number of women, but he was usually discreet. He was being blackmailed. He withdrew fifteen hundred dollars from his savings account every month for the past four years. That is, until this past month. He didn't pay and was killed for it."

"It wasn't blackmail. He considered it child support."

"Whatever," the detective said.

"And you don't think a woman could've killed him?"

"Arranged to have him killed? Certainly. Doing it herself? That's another matter, especially considering how it was done."

"Don't be such a chauvinist, Hayden. This isn't the turn of the century, and Sharon Walker is no dainty little female. She can probably bench-press more than all three of us put together."

"That doesn't prove a thing."

"Then what about her car? It matches the one Paul Linski saw."

"By his own admission, he doesn't know for sure if he saw it on the night the body was dumped."

"What about the carpet fibers? She carted Sumner from Holland to Orchard Park in the back of her station wagon. There had to be fibers on his wounds, in his lungs, or under his fingernails."

Hayden continued to glare at me.

I let out a long, quavering breath, trying to hold my anger in check. I'd wasted my time and his.

"Well, you keep all that stuff, Detective. It isn't doing me any good." I stood. "And if the case is still open in a year or two, maybe you'll be willing to take it under consideration. Come on, Rich, let's go." I paused at the door. "And thanks for telling Nielsen about me. My tax dollars at work."

I opened the door and started back through the house. Mrs. Hayden stood at the counter, assembling her layer cake. I walked past but heard Richard murmur, "Nice to meet you," on his way out. He always did have good manners.

The door closed behind him and he followed me to the car. The drizzle had turned into a steady downpour. We got in the Lincoln and sat.

Richard turned to me. "I'm sorry, Jeff."

"What for? I didn't really believe he'd go for it. To tell you the truth, I'm surprised he didn't throw us out." I took a breath to steady my shaky nerves. "I've done my civic duty. I reported what I know about a crime. If Hayden chooses to do nothing about it, it's out of my hands."

"I just hope you haven't set yourself up as a target."

Me, too, I thought.

Richard silently fumed for most of the ride back to Amherst, more depressed about the situation than I was. It was time to lighten the mood.

"Did you see the basketball hoop on Hayden's garage?" I asked.

"Yes."

"Whatever happened to ours?"

He frowned. "Grandmother had it taken down the day you left for the Army."

"But you put it up."

"I did it for you. She never bothered to ask me if I'd like to keep it. It was shortsighted of her."

"Why?"

"It made it easier for me to take the job in Pasadena. That stupid basketball hoop was the tenuous connection I had with you. She wouldn't understand that you could mean something to me. When it came down, it was the first step toward my freedom."

"I don't get it."

"I was just a possession to Grandmother. She'd won me from Betty. She saw your leaving as another victory. The job in California was my way out, but not without a lot of guilt. I wasn't there when Grandfather died, and I wasn't there when she died two years later, alone. Curtis found her in her bed."

"Did you come back to Buffalo?"

He shook his head. "What was the point? There was no one to come home to. I made all the arrangements by phone. I've never even been to her grave," he finished quietly, his gaze locked on the road ahead, his expression unreadable.

I remembered then what Brenda had said to me the day I'd returned to Buffalo: *It means a lot to him that you're here.*

"You think we could get another one?" I asked.

"Another what?"

"Backboard. I won't be in this brace forever. It might be fun to play some one-on-one again."

He risked a glance at me, his smile tentative. "Sounds like a great idea."

I think we both knew then that I wasn't ever going back to Manhattan.

Chapter Twenty-Three

That evening, I spent over an hour out in the garage, rummaging through my boxes. The cold and damp seeped through my jacket. I was ready to give up my search when I finally found what I wanted. I scrounged some tissue used in packing my stuff, and wrapped the small object. I hoped Richard would like it.

I also tramped through the loft apartment again and decided I'd wait until my arm was completely healed before asking Richard if I could live up there. Once I got a job, we could work out some kind of rental agreement. I wanted my own space; I needed a place of my own. But I didn't want to go too far, at least not yet.

That wasn't the end of my evening, however. I had one more little mystery to solve. Without a word to Richard or Brenda, I set out on foot, headed down the neighborhood's backstreets for Snyder. The brisk wind was at my back and the clouds overhead were heavy and threatening. I needed to talk—but not to Richard, or any other physician or academician at his old stomping grounds of UB. There were still so many things I didn't understand about this crazy new ability I seemed to have acquired—like why had I been blessed with it? Only one other person understood my predicament.

I crossed the parking lot to the darkened bakery and pressed the buzzer at the side of the door, held it for long seconds at a time. After a minute or so, a light came on in the back of the shop, then a large silhouette shuffled toward the door.

"Stop already!" came Sophie's muffled voice through the glass as she flipped open the lock. "Come in before you let in all the cold."

"Where have you been? I came to see you the other day and they never heard of you."

"You didn't come at night. Alone." Her tone was belligerent. Then she shrugged theatrically, as if that was explanation enough. "So, why'd you come now?"

"I need to talk to you."

She nodded and motioned me to follow her into the back room once again. "Instant coffee all right?"

I nodded, taking my seat at the card table. She filled the same saucepan with water, set it on the hot plate above the sink. I remembered that, days earlier, the baker had sidestepped my question about electrocution.

"Don't you think that's a dangerous arrangement?"

She gestured. "This? I'm always careful." She measured the coffee into cups. "So, you found the killer. I knew you would." We'd never even discussed my case. How did she know? "How can I help you now?" she asked.

"What do I do next?"

"It's in God's hands now."

"That's not the answer I was looking for."

"Who says I have answers?"

"I guess you don't, because you seem to answer most of my questions with questions."

Her eyes crinkled as her lips drew into a self-satisfied smile. Then she shrugged. "Tell me all about it."

She listened patiently, serving the coffee as I told her about Sharon, Sumner's and Claudia's grisly deaths, and all the other prominent players in this little drama.

"You know who did it—you told the police. So what's the problem?"

"The problem is Sharon should be punished for what she's done and nobody seems to care!"

Sophie frowned. "You don't think she's being punished every time she looks at that child?"

"What if she takes her anger out on the kid?"

"That could happen. Jeffrey," she said reasonably. "As long as one person knows the truth, she hasn't gotten away with anything."

"But I don't want to be the sole guardian of that truth."

She smiled tolerantly and patted my hand. "Trust."

"That's your advice? Trust?"

"Things have a way of working out the way they are meant to."

"Unfortunately, too often these days people literally get away with murder."

She shook her head sadly. "That's not all you wanted to ask me, is it?"

"No."

"Now that you believe, you want to know why, eh?"

"Yes."

She shrugged. "Maybe you're just lucky."

"You call this lucky?" With a gesture, I reminded her of my partially shaved head.

"Aren't you doing what you always wanted to do?"

I blinked in confusion. What the hell was she talking about?

"You always wanted to help people," she said. "You just never knew how."

"How will finding Sumner's killer help anyone? It doesn't even help him—he's dead."

"Maybe you'll help that little boy. The one you were worried about just now."

"I don't even like children."

She shook her head. "Everybody loves children. Even you."

I wasn't going to argue.

"What does it matter why you have it? You have it. Now you have to learn to live with it," she said.

"You sound just like my brother."

"He's a doctor—he should know."

"Now you sound like my—" Girlfriend, I'd wanted to say, but that wasn't going to happen now.

Sophie smiled. "I told you, things have a way of working out the way they were meant to." She glanced at the clock on the wall. "Time for you to go."

I got up and followed her through the shop, feeling like a child who'd just been scolded. "Will you be here the next time I come by?"

"Maybe. Maybe not. Here, take a *placek* home for Easter breakfast."

I hefted the loaf. It felt real enough. "Thank you."

She drew me into a hug, kissed my cheek, then pulled back, held my face in her warm hands. "Good things will come of this. They will," she insisted. "Now, take care walking home. Stay on the sidewalk where there's lots of light. I'm too old to have to worry about you."

She radiated a sense of peace and deep affection. I recognized it, understood it. But again I wondered: why me?

"I'll be careful," I promised, and kissed her goodbye.

The lock clicked into place and she waved before turning and heading for the back room once more. I watched as first that light went out, and a minute later the light above the shop burned.

The bakery sign over the door looked shabby, in need of repainting. Was it the same one I'd seen the other day? I couldn't be sure. Maybe I didn't want to know. Tucking the *placek* under my arm like a football, I turned and started for home.

I followed Sophie's instructions and stayed on the sidewalk under the intermittent flare of the street lamps. The long walk home gave me plenty of time to think. Maybe that was my problem—I was thinking too much.

A car whizzed past, splashing dirty water my way. I checked traffic before cutting across Main Street, anxious to get off the busy road and leave behind the stench of exhaust fumes. I headed down a quiet side street, pausing at the corner to pull up my jacket collar against the damp night.

Turning left, I picked up my pace, in a hurry to get back to the warmth of my room, where I could lie awake for endless hours, thanks to my jumbled nerves. Frustration nagged at me. The fact that Detective Hayden wouldn't consider my evidence against Sharon Walker reinforced the reality that I had virtually no control over any portion of my life, and probably wouldn't for weeks, possibly months.

I refused to take the thought any further. Frustration could also be a byproduct of my present physical condition. Before the mugging, impatience had never been a problem.

I knew that damned feeling of impotence would eventually pass, but it couldn't come soon enough for me.

Richard's driveway was in sight when I heard the roar of an engine, saw blinding high beams as the car barreled toward me. It fishtailed on the wet pavement and jumped the curb. I leaped into the privet hedge, out of its path, an instant before it would have nailed me.

Heart pounding, I rolled onto my knees, watched the speeding car recede into the night, its taillights glowing. Some trained investigator I was—I couldn't tell the make or even the color.

I brushed uselessly at my muddy jeans. The adrenaline surge that had coursed through me seconds before was already waning. Probably a drunken teenager out joyriding, trying to scare pedestrians.

Or it could've been Rob Sumner.

Or worse, Sharon Walker.

No! They couldn't know where I lived. And how would they have known it was me on the street at eleven o'clock at night? Dressed in dark clothes, I could've been anybody out for a walk.

Okay, maybe the sling on my arm was a dead giveaway.

Maybe.

I groped in the blackness, found the *placek*. One end was crushed but still salvageable. I stormed off across the lawn for the house. There was no point in even mentioning this little mishap to Richard and Brenda, yet I couldn't dismiss it entirely.

I hated feeling afraid.

***

Easter Sunday I awoke to the sound of rain pelting against my bedroom window and strained to reach my watch on the bedside table. Eight thirty, lots of time to get ready to go to the Basilica. Best of all, I awoke with no headache, so despite the gray start, it looked like it might turn out to be a good day.

I showered and dressed, and smelled bacon and fresh brewed coffee as I headed for the kitchen.

"Happy Easter," Brenda called and leaned her cheek in my direction for a kiss.

"Happy Easter," I said. "Where's Rich?"

"Straggling."

"Good. I have something to give him. Just a little thank you. You think I need to wrap it?"

"A present?" she asked, her eyes widening in delight.

"It's not much."

When I didn't offer any other information, she said, "I'm sure it'll be just fine without it." I could tell she wanted to know more, but she didn't ask and I didn't volunteer the information.

The *placek* still sat on the counter and I grabbed a knife from the drawer, cut a slice from the undamaged end, and plopped it on a plate.

"Where'd that come from?" Brenda asked.

"Just something I picked up."

I sat at the table, grabbing the front section of the newspaper. No headline screamed of Sharon's arrest. It was stupid to have thought there might be. I'd only told Hayden about her the afternoon before. Warrants and such take time. In the unlikely event he had gone after her, it wouldn't have gotten in the paper yet anyway. Nielsen hadn't written about me either. Again, yet.

Despite Sophie's advice to trust that Sharon would be nailed by the cops, I thought about Sam Nielsen's offer. If Hayden didn't act on my evidence within a week, I'd call the newspaper and tell the reporter everything. He promised he protected his sources, and my revelations might force Detective Hayden to take Sharon Walker seriously.

That decided, I studied the national headlines. I couldn't get excited about the latest threat to peace in the Middle East and grabbed the comics instead. Richard came in about the time I finished *Hagar the Horrible*.

"I see you're stimulating your mind," he said in greeting, brushed past me to Brenda, giving her a perfunctory kiss, then stood back, his chest puffed out. "Coffee, woman!"

Hands on her hips, she gazed at him speculatively. "You know where the cups are."

I tried to stifle a smile—impossible—turning my attention back to the paper. In a moment, a steaming cup of coffee appeared in front of me. Richard brought out the sugar bowl and creamer.

"Thanks."

"You're looking chipper this morning," he said, doctoring his own coffee. "And dare I say it, you even look healthier?"

"It's because my heart is true." I poured milk into my cup, stirred it, and took a sip. "Good coffee. You could be in a commercial, Brenda."

"They couldn't pay me enough," she said, and started breaking eggs into a bowl. "Fried or scrambled?"

"I'm just going to have this *placek*," I said.

"You don't eat enough to keep a bird alive," Brenda said, but I knew she wouldn't force feed me, either.

"Scrambled, please," Richard said, grabbing a piece of the paper.

"How come we're not eating those hardboiled eggs we colored on Friday?" I asked.

"They're just to look at," Brenda said.

"It's a waste not to eat them. I could make deviled eggs after Mass."

"Okay, but I want to take a picture of them first. Richard, where's our camera?"

Richard's nose was buried in the newspaper. "It's around here somewhere. I'll find it later."

Brenda nodded toward Richard, her eyes nearly bulging. I frowned, not comprehending. 'The present,' she mouthed.

I nodded. "Uh, Rich. Have you got a minute?"

I waited for him to put the paper down—at least ten seconds. He seemed impatient.

"Now that all this stuff about the murder is more or less over, I wanted to thank you for helping me out, carting me around, being patient, and a good brother, and all that crap."

Okay, so I'm not much of a speechmaker. I took the tissue-wrapped packet from my pocket, handed it to him.

He blinked at me. "You shouldn't have," he said automatically.

"It's not much. Just something I thought you might like."

Puzzled, he studied my face for a long moment. Brenda came up behind him, watching. He fumbled with the wrapping and pulled the beaded chain from the tissue.

"Ivory's not politically correct any more, but what the hell."

"It's a rosary, isn't it?" Brenda said.

"It belonged to our mother. Your father gave it to her. It meant a lot to her."

He stared at it for a long time, his expression unreadable. He ran his thumb over the beads. "I never had anything of hers. I don't even have a photo of her."

I reached over and clapped him on the shoulder. "Well, now you've got something. I think I can dig up a picture, too."

"It's beautiful," he managed, his voice husky.

"I should've given it to you years ago. I mean, it came from your father, not mine. For whatever it's worth, I know she loved him a lot. She loved you a lot, too."

"Thank you." He cleared his throat, his watery eyes still fixed on the rosary.

"Happy Easter, Rich."

***

We were late. The ham was in the oven and I already had my coat on when Richard remembered the candy he'd bought Brenda two days before. I didn't mind the delay. If we missed the beginning of the Mass, it wouldn't be a tragedy.

Richard had the Lincoln waiting in the driveway when Brenda and I came out of the house. As usual, I got in the back seat. A funny feeling crept through me as I fastened my seat belt and the car started down the drive.

"Wait a minute, Rich."

He braked. "Did you forget something?"

"Something's not right." I looked up and down the street, but I didn't know what to look for. Tire tracks gouged the lawn in front of the hedge. Was my unease tied to the car that nearly hit me—could have killed me—the night before?

"We're already late," Brenda reminded us.

Something lurked nearby. Something....

"Okay," I said. "Let's go."

He started off toward Main Street. I couldn't shake the feeling that I should be wary, but I didn't know why and tried to ignore it.

"Did you read the newspaper article on the Basilica, Jeffy?" Brenda asked.

"Nope. Don't know a thing about it."

"It's called Our Lady of Victory Basilica," Richard said. "Only a few cities in the U.S. are so graced by a basilica."

"So how did one end up in Lackawanna?" I asked.

"It was built with the pennies of Polish immigrants back in the nineteen twenties," Richard lectured, "and was the dream of Father Nelson H. Baker, who headed the Homes of Charity. An orphanage, home for unwed mothers—that kind of stuff. He wanted to build a shrine to the Blessed Virgin."

"Kinda snowballed, huh?" I said.

"A basilica is one step up from a cathedral," he agreed. "Anyway, since building a big church isn't a miracle, the Vatican couldn't make him a saint, which is what the locals wanted, so he was posthumously given the title of Apostle of Charity. Decades after his death, he's still revered."

"Did you make all that up?" Brenda asked, giving him the fish-eye.

"No. I went online and read it."

Brenda scowled. "Sounds more like you memorized it for a sixth-grade oral report."

"She's just astounded at your phenomenal memory, Rich."

"Naturally," he agreed as we stopped for a red light. Traffic was light, but I looked around anyway, searching for…I don't know what. I still had that uneasy feeling in my gut. Probably the *placek*.

We arrived at the Basilica about fifteen minutes late for the Mass. The church's large parking area was full on Christianity's number one holy day, so we left the car on the street. The rain had ended, but the skies were still threatening. Braving the gloom, we walked the block or so and entered the main entrance. It was Brenda's turn to recount the newspaper account on the Basilica.

The place was packed. The fire marshals would've had a field day if they made a spot inspection. The pews, and every square inch of floor space, were jammed. To sit, we should've arrived an hour or more before the Mass.

I felt dwarfed by the soaring ceiling overhead, awed by the church's grandeur and sense of holiness. The newspaper hadn't exaggerated the amount of gilding, frescoes, and stained glass that seemed to decorate every square inch of walls and ceiling. Life-sized marble statues representing the stations of the cross lined the right and left aisles. The choir was situated somewhere high above us at the back of the church, sounding like the proverbial heavenly host, and accompanied by a magnificent pipe organ. An usher bustled us down the left aisle, directing us to stop under the station of the cross titled: "Jesus Meets His Afflicted Mother."

"Wow, this place is gorgeous," Brenda whispered, and received a stern shush from Richard.

The singing stopped and the priest began to speak. I studied the altar and the oversized statue of Our Lady of Victory, her arm wrapped protectively around Jesus, depicted as a small boy. It reminded me of little Jackie... or Jimmy. No one had protected him from the terrors of life.

The priest droned on. It would take a long time just to get through Communion. Coming here had not been a good idea.

The air was close. I started to feel claustrophobic. As the choir broke into song, the woman beside me dropped her umbrella. I stooped to pick it up when a sharp ping sent marble shards flying from the mantle only inches from my head. I whirled to see Sharon Walker sixty feet from me across the church. Still dressed in the grubby jogging suit and a lavender ski jacket, her arms were extended in front of her, clasping a handgun, her eyes feral.

The muzzle flashed and Richard shoved me, knocking me into the woman beside me.

The choir still sang as bedlam erupted. Worshipers screamed, crashing into each other, struggling to escape. Sharon shouldered her way through the panicked crowd, heading for the back exit.

Stunned, I looked around. Richard was on his back, his beige raincoat stained scarlet. Brenda jerked with his tie, fumbling to open his shirt. "Call 911," she screamed. "Call 911!"

I fell to my knees. "Rich?"

"She must've followed us—" he gasped, already deathly pale. "Don't let her…get away."

Torn, I didn't know what to do. The singing had stopped, replaced by terrified screams reverberating around the vaulted ceiling.

"Brenda'll take care of me. Go!" Richard said.

His fingers clutched our mother's rosary. I gave his hand a squeeze and pulled away.

Then I was on my feet—smashing into people, pushing past them, heading for where I'd last seen Sharon, relying entirely on my newly awakened sixth sense.

She hadn't gotten away. People jammed the exit to the parking lot, but I turned left, away from the crowd, heading down the stairs and into the church basement.

Sharon had bypassed the bottleneck upstairs, planning to cut through the warren of rooms under the main floor and get out the Basilica's front entrance. I had to stop her. Not because the police wouldn't eventually catch up with her—but because she'd shot my brother. If he died, I'd kill her myself—my own brand of justice.

I had nothing left to lose. I was tired of being a victim.

Dodging into the open doorway, I took in the rows of pews that faced a lectern in the large white empty space.

No Sharon.

I ducked to the right into the ladies' room.

No one.

I didn't check the stalls—I'd lived with her aura for weeks. I could almost smell her.

The door at the far end of the long corridor was closed—locked? She was trapped.

What about her gun? In westerns, a handgun held six rounds. What make did she have? How much ammo did it carry? She'd fired twice. Was it a semi-automatic? Did she have a full clip?

A sign over the open doorway read: Father Baker's Rooms. I crossed the threshold, the floor changing from white ceramic tiles to dated green-and-yellow asphalt squares. The bedlam upstairs masked my movements. I was close—the hairs on the back of my neck acting like radar.

"Give it up, Sharon! I've already been to the police. They know you were blackmailing Matt. They know about the lab report. They know Jackie is Rob's son, not Matt's."

"Liar!"

Bang!

I ducked behind the wall. Now all I had to do was keep her talking until the police arrived. For all I cared, they could take her out with a SWAT team.

"You told Matt you named your son John Matthew after him because he promised to help you with expenses. In return, you said you wouldn't tell his wife. But something went wrong. He told you he wouldn't give you any more money."

"He owed us—he was Jackie's father."

"Grandfather!" I corrected.

Bang. Another shot slammed the mahogany woodwork.

"You're bluffing! You have no proof!"

"I know about the letter from the lab that tested Jackie's hair. The cops know, too."

Bang!

"And they know about Claudia. You figured with her out of the way, Jackie would get his fair share of Matt's estate. You wanted Matt's money."

"He owed it to us. He ruined our business."

"You ruined it with bad management."

Silence.

I tried another tack. "You followed me here."

"Damn right!"

"How'd you find me?"

"Rob's brother-in-law is a cop. He tapped into the DMV files for your address."

Bastard.

"You did everything right until today. I knew you killed Sumner, so you came after me. But you were stupid to try it in such a public place."

"Shut up!"

Bang.

Five down. What if she had another clip? Dumb move. If I was smart, I'd just wait her out—I had all the time in the world.

But Richard didn't.

All that blood....

My anger flared. "You shot my brother, you stupid bitch."

"Like I care. I've got nothing to lose."

"What about your son?"

No answer. She hadn't considered the boy. Maybe she never had. She'd killed Sumner in front of little Jackie.

Then realization hit: the woman was crazy. Not temporarily deranged, as defense attorneys love to claim, but certifiably insane. I'd touched her madness the day before and never even recognized it.

"You tried to run me down last night, didn't you?"

No answer.

"You played right into Rob's hands. Did he tell you to come after me?"

"What're you talking about?"

"Rob told you about me, knowing you'd try some asshole stunt. He wanted you to get caught."

"Rob cares about me—he loves me."

"Then why'd he marry Linda? Why didn't he tell Matt that Jackie was his son? How come he's never helped you raise the boy? Because he doesn't give a shit about you or his kid!"

Silence.

Then it hit me: Sharon had only ever loved one person. Someone who'd loved her in return.

"What would your father say about all you've done?"

Her anger rose—I could feel it.

"He was so proud of you. But you let his company fail. Then you tried to save it by sleeping with your fiancé's father. You got knocked up by Rob and told his father the child was his. When he found out the truth, he cut off the money. So you murdered him—right in front of Jackie!"

"Shut up!"

"Then when I found out, you tried to kill me, but you botched it by missing me and shooting someone else—in front of hundreds of witnesses. Now you're trying for thirds. Stupid, stupid, stupid!"

"Shut the fuck up!"

"It's a good thing Jim Walker's already dead, because this would've killed him!"

She fired six times.

The hammer clicked onto an empty chamber.

I flew into the side corridor, tackling her, slamming her onto the spotless floor as she struggled to reload.

The gun went skittering.

She dived for it, dragging me with her.

Though shorter than me, she was stronger, with two good arms. I grappled to hang on, but her legs flailed and she clipped me on the jaw. Stars exploded before my eyes. I couldn't let her get that gun, but I was tiring. She kicked me loose and scrambled for the gun.

Sirens wailed. Was it the police or an ambulance?

On my knees, I dove for her back as she scooped up the gun. Grabbing a fistful of her short hair, I body slammed her—smashed her face-first into the floor. Blood spattered the gaudy tiles and she wailed, struggling to buck me loose.

I rammed her skull against the floor again and again, running on autopilot until her struggles subsided. She lay still, panting, as blood puddled around her battered face. I grabbed her gun, checked the clip.

She'd somehow managed to reload it.

I staggered to my feet, wiping sweat from my eyes. My broken arm ached and I swayed, afraid I'd pass out.

Running footsteps thundered. A uniformed cop popped into the open doorway, his service revolver aimed right at my face.

"Freeze! Put the gun on the floor. Now!"

With exaggerated care, I did as he said.

"Flat on the ground!" he ordered.

It took no persuasion—my knees buckled. Seconds later, he had me spread-eagled on the floor, patting me down. He wrenched my arm.

"Watch it, it's broken! I'm wearing a brace. She shot my brother upstairs. She killed Matt Sumner."

"Shut up!"

More running footsteps advanced—the rest of the troops had arrived.

Chapter Twenty-Four

By the time the uniforms had taken me back upstairs, my hands were bound with the heavy plastic strips cops now use instead of handcuffs. The ambulance bearing my brother had already left. A beefy patrolman shoved me into the first pew.

No one knew anything about Richard. No one would tell me anything. Someone hollered that Hayden was on his way. The church had been cleared, with witnesses being interviewed elsewhere. Another team of paramedics had arrived and departed, carting Sharon away, accompanied by a police escort.

I hadn't been in a fight since my high school days. I'd never hit a woman. I'd been determined to prevent her from ever hurting anyone else—so why did I now feel so ashamed?

Sharon's bloodied face, twisted with anger, was such a contrast to that of the statue of Our Lady of Victory, which towered above the church's gilded, ornate altar. Some sculptor unknown to me had captured in stone the embodiment of true compassion. I prayed to the Virgin in an endless litany, *Don't let Rich die. Please don't let Rich die.*

"Strange to see you without your other half," Hayden said from behind me.

I turned and glared at him. "She shot him. Now are you convinced I was right?"

Hayden had the decency to look embarrassed.

I steeled myself to ask the next question. "Is my brother still alive?"

Hayden looked grim. "He was when they left here."

"Thanks," I said. At least he was being straight with me. "Can you take these off? I only beat up the bitch, I'm not planning to hurt anyone else."

"Did a number on her, too, I hear. Thompson!" Hayden called, and the uniformed cop came over and removed the restraints. Hayden sat beside me on the pew. "Tell me about it."

I did.

"Well, the witnesses confirm she shot your brother. After they finish with her at the hospital, she'll be booked. Then we'll look into the rest of it. Here," he handed me a set of keys. "One of the patrolmen gave them to me. The black lady with your brother asked him to see that you got them."

I stared at Brenda's ring with keys to the house and both cars. Richard's Lincoln was still parked on one of the side streets.

"Thanks."

"They took him to ECMC," Hayden said.

"Where?"

"Erie County Medical Center. Used to be called Meyer Memorial."

I nodded. "I know the place."

"You can give us a detailed statement tomorrow." He clapped me on the back, a gesture that almost resembled friendship. "I know where to find you, right?"

"Yeah, right."

Hugging my broken arm, I got up and headed for the back entrance.

A block from the church, I found Sharon's station wagon. The little boy was asleep on the back seat, his tear-streaked face at peace. He didn't know his mother would never come for him.

The driver's side door was unlocked. I opened it and poked my head inside. "Hey, partner."

The boy blinked awake, unafraid of me. "Go away."

"Remember me, sport?"

"You're the bad man who wants to hurt my Mommy."

"That was a misunderstanding. Do you know any policemen?"

He shook his head.

"I know a cop who'd love to meet you. He's got a shiny badge. Want to see it?"

He shrugged.

I offered him my hand.

The boy looked at the empty driver's seat. "My Mommy's not coming back. Is she?"

"Not right now."

The boy looked back at my outstretched hand. His eyes had a dull cast to them. He'd seen more of life than a kid his age should. Reluctantly he took my hand.

We walked in silence to the Basilica. One of the uniformed officers recognized me and let me cross the police line again. We entered the cavernous church. The detective spoke with the priest in front of the main altar.

The kid held my hand tightly while I spoke to Hayden, cowed by the building's size and grandeur. The pitch of his fear was familiar—I'd been living with it for weeks.

I crouched down in front of him. "Jimmy, Detective Hayden will take you downtown. You'll be okay."

"Where's my Mommy?"

I looked up at Hayden, who towered over us. "Don't worry, kid," the burly man said, "we're taking care of her. Did the Easter Bunny visit your house today?"

The boy shook his head.

"Well, he came to the police station, and I think he left something there for you."

With Sharon's son in good hands, I once again headed for the exit. It was then I saw the rack of row upon row of dancing candlelight. I turned for it and thought of Richard. I'm not religious, but right then I needed God on my side.

My throat tightened as I stuffed money into the slot in the brass box. My hand trembled as I lit the candle. I watched it flicker and steady before I turned and started for the car without a backward glance.

I retrieved Richard's Lincoln and struggled to remember the way to ECMC. I got lost and had to stop at a mini-mart to ask directions. Once there, I parked the car in the hospital lot. I'd been eager to drive, but not under these circumstances. I yanked the keys from the ignition, pocketed them, and sat with my fingers wrapped around the steering wheel. Would Richard ever drive it again? I'd only just found my brother. What would I do without him?

I was wasting time, yet fear kept me from moving. Brenda was alone. She probably needed me…I knew I needed her.

I hadn't needed anyone for years.

I got out, locked the door, and went in search of her.

The emergency room wasn't crowded—major mayhem seemed to be taking a holiday on this most holy day. I found Brenda sitting alone in the far corner of the waiting room, my mother's rosary beads wrapped around her fingers. She saw me and stood. After a quick embrace, she pulled back.

"How's Rich?"

"They had a hard time stabilizing him—he lost a lot of blood. There was a closer hospital, but they said it was better to bring him here. They're more experienced with gunshot injuries." Her voice was so quiet, so lost.

I motioned for her to sit and she took her seat once more. She bit her lip. "I'm scared, Jeffy. I'm a nurse and I know everything that can go wrong."

I reached for her hand. "You know they'll do everything they can." I was quiet for a moment. "He's going to make it."

"Do you know this for sure?" she asked.

I couldn't lie to her. "No."

She fingered the rosary beads. "I'll have to seriously rethink this marriage business. I've lived with your brother for seven years. I know him as well as I know myself. But when he came in here, I was nothing more than a friend. I'm a nurse, and they won't tell me anything. His blood is under my fingernails, and they won't tell me anything."

"Well, they'd better tell me."

I got up and headed for the information desk, with Brenda tagging along behind me.

The receptionist wasn't helpful. Having a different last name than the patient was not an asset. I'm surprised she didn't ask for a blood sample for DNA analysis before one of the nurses took pity on us. She made a phone call and found out Richard had been taken to surgery only minutes earlier. Being short-staffed because of the holiday, the surgeon hadn't had time to come out and speak with us. The bullet had ripped through Richard's right lung, causing vascular damage.

"Why don't you go upstairs to the surgical waiting room?"

A TV crew barged through the emergency room entrance. Brenda's eyes widened in panic.

"Is there a way—?"

"They know the drill," the nurse said, eyeing the cameraman. "They're not allowed anywhere near the surgical unit."

Brenda and I followed her directions to the third floor, which was even more quiet than the emergency room. The two of us had the small room to ourselves and settled in for a long wait.

We took turns sitting, pacing, sitting. We didn't talk much. The TV bolted on the wall was tuned to CNN, the newscaster's voice an annoying monotone. I couldn't turn it off, so I hit the mute button and occasionally glanced at the news in mime.

Over and over I relived those terrible seconds at the church. Sharon Walker's skill with a handgun equaled her skill with a bow. If I hadn't stooped to pick up that stupid umbrella, she would have nailed me with the first shot. At least then Richard wouldn't have had to suffer for my... what? Stupidity? Stubbornness?

Please don't die on me, Rich.

Time dragged.

After the first hour, the numbness around my brain cells wore thin. I hunched over on the uncomfortable couch, my thoughts going in circles.

Exactly four weeks ago it had been me in a hospital emergency room. For four days I was a comatose John Doe. No one had worried about me. No one had known. No one had cared.

Four scant weeks ago, my brother had been a stranger. Now I could only grieve for the wasted years when I'd rebuffed his gestures of friendship.

You can't die on me, Rich. You just can't.

I never believed in fate, but the random pattern of my life didn't seem so random any more. Was it preordained that I return to Buffalo? Was it inevitable that crime should continue to touch my life? Shelley murdered by a drug dealer; me beaten and left for dead by a couple of crackheads; Richard shot by a murderer I was chasing. My life's path seemed to follow a downward spiral. If the pattern continued, then Richard was as good as dead.

No!

I looked across the small room at Brenda. Lost in her own thoughts, her gaze was vacant, her eyes haunted. She and Richard had shown me such generosity. Richard had shoved me aside—taking the bullet meant for me. I swallowed a pang of grief. It took me thirty-five years and this tragedy to make me realize how much I needed—loved— my brother.

Anger raged through me. Why hadn't I been warned about this? What good was this psychic crap if it didn't work for me? Sophie said good would come of it. Yeah, then why was Richard being punished?

Some cosmic force had brought me back home, had shown me Sumner's death, compelled me to find the murderer, and I never had a clue or a vision or even a funny feeling that Richard could be in any danger because of it. Sumner was a liar and a cheat. Why was it so important that I find his killer, risking my brother in the process?

Brenda got up and wandered over to the window. She peeked through the slats in the narrow blinds, her expression placid. "You know," she said, breaking the quiet. "Richard wouldn't volunteer at a women's clinic because of the potential for violence. Instead, he gets shot in church. Does that make any sense?"

I let out a shaky breath. "It's all my fault. If I'd never come back here this wouldn't have happened."

Her eyes flashed. "Jeffy, don't do this to yourself. You made Richard happy. He hasn't been happy for a long time."

"You could've fooled me. He's been preoccupied, depressed—"

"He was worse before you came home. Now he wants to go back to work. He's talking to lawyers about unloading some of that money. He's getting back to being his old self—the man I fell in love with. It's because of you. Can't you see how special you are? What you mean to him—to us?"

No. I couldn't.

The minutes dragged.

Four o'clock.

Five o'clock.

I was about to swear that time had absolutely stood still when an Amazon of a nurse, dressed in surgical scrubs, approached. Her expression was sour, no-nonsense, and short on compassion. Brenda and I were instantly on our feet.

"We had another gunshot emergency," the nurse said succinctly. "Doctor Elliott had to go directly back into surgery. He asked me to speak with you. Mr. Alpert came through the surgery well. His vital signs are good and he's in recovery now."

"Can we see him?" I asked.

She looked directly at me. "Next of kin only."

Brenda's gaze shifted. "That would be you."

"No." I grabbed her hand. "We're family. We're going in together and no one's going to stop us."

The nurse straightened to her full height. "You want to tell that to security?"

Brenda shook her head, her eyes filling with tears. "You're wasting time, Jeffy. Just go!"

I clutched her hand, experienced the conflicting emotions roiling through her.

The nurse heaved an exaggerated sigh, and I realized her gruffness was only a facade. "Okay, both of you. But only for a minute." She pointed her finger right in my face. "One. Minute." She turned on her heel.

Hand in hand, Brenda and I jogged to catch up with her.

I'd never been in a recovery room before, never seen anyone fresh out of surgery. Swathed in a sea of white sheets, Richard looked ghastly, his skin tinged an odd green. Startled, I paused. Brenda's grip on my hand tightened—she pulled me closer to the gurney. A cardiac monitor beeped in rhythm with his heart. IV bags hung overhead.

My stomach tightened. This was me, four weeks before.

As though sensing our approach, a groggy Richard opened his eyes.

"My two favorite people," he rasped. We both reached for his hand. He captured one or two fingers from each of us.

"How do you feel?" Brenda whispered.

"Horrible."

"You'll be okay," I said, trying to keep my voice from cracking. "The shoe's on the other foot. When you get home, I can bully you around."

"Don't even think about it."

My throat tightened. Sorrow and remorse threatened to choke me. "Why'd you do it, Rich? Why'd you shove me aside and make yourself a target?"

He squeezed my fingers ever so slightly. "You're my kid brother...I couldn't let her hurt you." His eyes closed and he was asleep.

Brenda and I hung around the hospital for another three hours until Richard was taken to his room—the best in the hospital—and sleeping peacefully.

We took the elevator downstairs, exited, and walked straight into a mob of reporters with video and still cameras.

"Give us a quote!"

"What's your relationship with Sharon Walker?"

"No comment," I said, pushing Brenda through the crowd.

I thought we'd successfully left them behind when a voice called out, "Jeff Resnick!"

I turned: Sam Nielsen, his eyes bright with anticipation, waited.

Though I might regret it, I made my decision. "Give me an hour to shower and eat, Sam. I'll call you at your office."

"Exclusive," he demanded.

"Yeah." I turned, took Brenda's arm, and guided her away.

The clouds were gone, the crescent moon a slash of pure white light in the cold, dark sky. We pulled up our collars against the cold and, hand-in-hand, headed for Richard's car.

Chapter Twenty-Five

It's true what they say about doctors being the worst patients. Once Richard started feeling better, he became cranky and bossy—totally unlike his usual self. But Brenda and I suffered through his moods, keeping him company from the time visiting hours started until the nurses threatened us with the hospital security forces to get us out at night.

Maggie visited several times, bringing him flowers and us care packages. Her presence forced Richard to be almost as nice as usual. Brenda and I bought a chess game at the toy store before visiting one day, and that kept Richard—and me—occupied for hours on end, while Brenda patiently worked on her needlepoint or read magazines.

Sharon Walker wasn't as lucky. No one came to visit her in jail. Three days after her arrest, the cops found her hanged in her cell. Hayden called me even before the press was notified to ask if I'd seen it coming. I hadn't. Once the cops had taken her away from the church, I didn't give the woman more than a passing thought. I wondered if the guilt trip I'd laid on her about her father had influenced her that much. Had I inadvertently caused her death?

I didn't like to think about that.

They buried her in her family's plot at Mount Olivet Cemetery. Some macabre part of me wondered if Ted Schmidt had dug and then danced on her grave.

The police found enough evidence at her house to convict her, and although he was only four years old, her son turned out to be a credible witness to Sumner's murder—for all the good it did. In my mind, justice had more or less been served.

Sharon had no other family and true to form, Rob Sumner did not claim his child from Social Services. I felt bad for the kid. I hoped little Jackie—or Jimmy, as his mother had called him—would be placed in a foster home where he'd find some semblance of a normal life. Maybe one day be adopted. Toward that end, after I told him what happened, Richard called his lawyer and set up a trust for the kid, assuring psychiatric help and anything else the boy needed. It was the first step in what Richard called "unloading some of that damned money."

The kid would probably have a better life without Sharon.

Yeah. Sure he would.

As a result of Sam Nielsen's newspaper articles, I received several job offers; two were from crackpots, one seemed genuine. That is, until I inquired about their health care benefits and outlined my particular problems, then they no longer wanted to interview me. The answering machine took the bulk of the crank calls.

I stopped by the bakery—twice—for more placek and conversation, but Sophie wasn't around. I wasn't about to give up on her. I'd just have to keep trying.

Spring sunshine warmed the air six days after Richard was shot—the day he was released from the hospital. The crew from the sporting goods store had only been gone five minutes when the Lincoln pulled up the driveway. Richard and Brenda were late getting home from the hospital.

Richard got out of the passenger side of the car, looking pale, but smiling. Other than his arm in a sling, there was no outward sign of his near-death experience.

I greeted him with a basketball tucked under my still-healing arm.

"Looks great," he said, indicating the new backboard over the garage door.

"Yeah, and in another couple of weeks we can use it." I dribbled the ball on the driveway, tried a one-handed lay-up shot and missed. The ball bounced once and rolled away from me.

"Yeah," I repeated, embarrassed, "another couple of weeks."

Brenda got out of the car and joined us; her body language said she was wired. I looked at the two of them, sensing something was definitely going on.

"What's up?"

Richard glanced at her. "Do you want to tell him, or should I?"

In answer, she peeled off the leather glove on her left hand, flashing a large diamond ring. "We stopped at the jewelry store on the way home. Isn't it gorgeous?"

Delighted, I took her offered hand, noticing how the sunlight reflected off the many-faceted stone. "Nice. Congratulations." I stopped myself. "No, you get best wishes," and I leaned forward and kissed her cheek. "You get congratulations." I shook Richard's hand. "When's the date?"

"Oh, who knows," Brenda said and laughed, "but sometime soon. And we want you and Maggie to stand up for us. Then we're going to Paris for a honeymoon. Won't that be great?"

"Yeah, it will." A swell of wellbeing coursed through me. On impulse, I drew them into an awkward group hug."

"It really will."

***

*Bartlett presents her second supernatural mystery featuring Jeff Resnick, a down-and-out insurance investigator who acquired hard-to-control psychic powers after sustaining brain injuries in a mugging. Jeff is now living with his brother, Richard, in Buffalo. Better but still weak, Jeff is struggling to adjust to his strange new abilities. While minding his own business in a local bar, he's asked by the bartender to look into the murder of his cousin. Jeff instantly gets a flash of a red, rhinestone-studded high-heeled shoe. Add to that the visions of bloody hands, and he knows he must take the case. Richard insists on helping him, and Jeff acquiesces even though he remains mired in guilt over putting Richard in the line of fire yet again. Their investigation leads them into a world of fetishes and drag queens. Jeff risks his health and possibly his life, but knows he must continue, or someone he cares about will be in danger. Bartlett's hero is complicated and mesmerizing, making for a gripping and energizing mystery. – **Booklist**

DEAD IN RED

Dedication

For Frank

DEAD IN RED:
ACKNOWLEDGMENTS

Every author I know has a group of friends who read and critique her/his work, and I'm no different. My first readers come from my Sisters In Crime Chapter, The Guppies. My thanks to Nan Higginson, Marilyn Levinson, Liz Eng, Elizabeth Becka, Sheila Connolly, and especially to Sharon Wildwind for their comments and suggestions.

Thanks also go to Michelle Martin and Judy Stock for their expertise on running small bakeries; Hank Phillippi Ryan gave me pointers on journalism, and Michele Fowler shared her knowledge about theater and wardrobe. D.P. Lyle, MD, provided his expertise in medical matters. (Likewise, Sharon Wildwind, RN.) Any errors in that respect are definitely of my own making. I can't forget my staunchest cheerleaders and critique partners Liz Eng and Gwen Nelson, nor my agent Jacky Sach and editor Hugh Abramson.

Thank you all!

Chapter One

My footsteps echoed on the pavement that cold night in early March. Huddled in my old bomber jacket, I dodged the mini skating rinks that had once been puddles on the cracked pavement. Preoccupied. By the creepy thing I'd experienced only minutes earlier. By thoughts of a new job. Of the fifty bucks I'd just won playing pool at the little watering hole near my apartment. Five months of unemployment had cleaned me out. I was on a roll and determined not to let anything spoil it.

Then two imposing figures stepped out of the darkness, demanded money. I gave them what I had. It wasn't enough. One of them grabbed me, decided to teach me a lesson.

Not if I could help it. I yanked my arm back, kicked one of them in the balls—and paid for it.

Backlit by a streetlamp, I saw the baseball bat come at me, slam into my forearm, delivering a compound fracture that sent skyrockets of pain to obliterate my senses.

Couldn't think, too stunned to move as the bat slammed into my shoulder, knocking me to my knees.

The bat came at me from the left, crashed into my temple, sent me sprawling. My vision doubled as I raised my head and the bat walloped me again.

"My cousin's dead."

The voice brought me out of my reverie, or rather the nightmare memory that claimed me at inopportune moments.

Tom Link's bottom lip quivered and he looked away. Heavyset, with a barroom bouncer's countenance, I hadn't expected him to reveal any trace of what I was sure he would call weakness.

My fingers tightened around the cold pilsner glass as something flashed through my mind's eyes: The image of a sparkling red, woman's high-heeled shoe.

I tilted the glass to my lips to take a gulp of beer. Bursts of insight—if that's what they are—bring with them a certain creep factor, something I doubted I'd ever get used to.

I concentrated on breathing evenly as I sipped my beer and waited for Tom to continue. It isn't often a bartender confides to a customer. I know. Years before I'd spent time on that side of the counter, listening to the stories of lonely men—and women—who had no other confidants.

Tom wasn't just a bartender at the little neighborhood sports bar that teetered on the verge of going under—he was also the owner of The Whole Nine Yards. I'd been patronizing the unassuming place for the past couple of months, getting the feel of it, a part of me hoping I could one day be a part of it.

I'd heard about but hadn't known the murdered man—Walt Kaplan. He'd opened the bar early in the day, whereas I'd never been there before eight p.m.

"How can I help?" I asked.

Tom's gaze shifted to take in a group of regulars crowded around the large-screen TV bolted to the wall, before turning back to me. "You said you used to be an investigator—"

"Before I got my head caved in," I said, referring to the mugging I'd suffered some three months before. I'd read about Walt's murder in the paper, but Tom probably knew more about it than the news had reported. "What happened?"

Lips pursed, Tom ran a damp linen cloth over the old scarred oak bar. "Walt worked here part-time. He left here on Saturday afternoon and never came back." His worried brown eyes met mine. "Your name's Resnick. We're *landsman*, Jeff. Would you be willing to look into it? I'll pay you."

We weren't "*landsman*." I was a lapsed Catholic, not Jewish, but now wasn't the time to dispute that. Besides, the idea intrigued me. I'd been hanging out at the little neighborhood tavern with the idea of eventually asking Tom for a part-time job, and now he was offering an employment opportunity far different than what I'd anticipated.

"What about the cops? Don't you trust them?"

"I've been robbed four times in the last twelve years. Did they ever catch the guys? No."

Part of me—the smart part—knew if I accepted his offer I'd be sorry. Another part of me wanted to jump at the chance to feel useful again. I tried to keep my eagerness in check. "Tell me more about Walt."

Tom's jowls sagged. "You woulda liked him. He was a lot like you."

My stomach twisted. "How so?"

A small smile twitched Tom's mouth. "Quiet. A loner. He wasn't one to talk about himself. You've been coming here for a couple months now and I know your name and what you used to do before your accident, but that's all."

He had me pegged there. Spilling my guts to strangers wasn't in my program. At one time I'd been a top insurance investigator, but office politics weren't my forte. I screwed myself one time too many and ended up on the unemployment line. On the eve of starting a new job, I'd been mugged by a couple of street thugs. The resulting brain injury had changed my life forever.

"The newspaper said Walt was found by the Old Red Mill. That he was stabbed and had apparently been robbed."

Tom nodded. "His wallet was missing. So was a big diamond ring he always wore. His father gave it to him when he graduated from high school. I went to the mill. Nothin' much to see but some crime tape." His gaze met mine, hardened. "But you'll get more than I did."

Get more? The words made my insides freeze. How did he know? I could count on one hand the people who knew I was—that I could…

Cold sweat broke out on the back of my neck. The word "psychic" didn't really apply to me. Since the mugging, I'd been able to sense strong emotions. Not from everyone I met—but sometimes from those who were no longer alive. Sometimes I just knew things—but not always. It was pretty much haphazard and damned disconcerting when it happened. And often these feelings and knowledge brought on migraines that so far drugs hadn't been able to quell.

Tom's gaze bore into mine.

"Get more?" I prompted, afraid to hear his answer.

"Being a trained investigator, I mean."

I heaved a mental sigh of relief. "Yeah."

"When can you start?"

As a teenager I'd ridden my ten-speed all around Snyder and Williamsville and could still recall some of my old routes. The area behind the Old Red Mill had always been weedy, with a steep embankment that loomed near a rushing stream. No way would I risk my neck to take a look in the dark. "Tomorrow morning."

Tom nodded. "It wouldn't hurt for the regulars to get to know you. Dave"—he indicated the other bartender drawing a beer at the brass taps across the way—"doesn't want Walt's early shift. You up to working here at the bar three or four afternoons a week?"

I looked at my reflection in the mirrored backbar. My hair had grown back from where some ER nurse had shaved it, but the shadows under my eyes and the gaunt look and sickly pallor were taking a lot longer to fade. I'd been living with my physician brother for the past three months. While I was grateful he'd rescued me, allowing me to recover at his home, I was tired of the enforced inactivity he'd insisted upon. The idea of actually having something to do and somewhere to go appealed to me.

"I'd like to try."

"Okay. Show up here about eleven tomorrow and I'll give you a run down on how we operate." He turned, took a cracked ballpoint out of a jar and grabbed a clean paper napkin, on which he scribbled a few lines. "This is what you have to do. I don't need workers' comp or the IRS breathing down my neck."

My hand trembled as I reached for the napkin. Who would have thought that a part-time job in a neighborhood bar would make me so nervous? A warm river of relief flooded through me as I read the short list. "I can do this. Thanks, Tom."

***

"A bartender?" My half-brother, Richard Alpert, looked up from his morning coffee, his expression skeptical. His significant other, Brenda Stanley, lowered a section of newspaper to peer at me. The three of us sat at the maple kitchen table in the home Richard's grandparents had built decades before in Buffalo's tony suburb of Amherst, the egg-stained breakfast dishes still sitting before us.

"I need a job."

"Okay, but why a bartender?" Richard asked.

I'd been rehearsing my answer for an hour. Now to make it sound convincing.

"I've done it before. It's pretty much a no-brainer, which is something I can handle right now."

Richard scowled, studied my face. Being twelve years older than me, he's felt the need to look after me since the day our mother died some twenty-one years earlier. Back then I was an orphaned kid of fourteen and he'd been an intern with generations of old money behind him. "Have you thought about the consequences of this kind of social interaction?" he asked.

I frowned. Consequences?

"Touching peoples' glasses, taking their money. What if you get vibes about them? Stuff you don't want to know."

I knew what he was getting at. Truth was, I hadn't thought about that aspect of the job, although I had been counting on the somewhat erratic empathic ability I'd developed after the mugging to help me look into Walt Kaplan's death. I couldn't read everyone I encountered—Richard was a prime example. We were brothers—okay, only half-brothers—but he was a total blank to me, yet I could often read Brenda like an open book.

I met his gaze, didn't back down. "I guess I'll have to deal with it."

He nodded, still scrutinizing my face. "And what's the rest of it?"

"Rest of it?"

"Whole Nine Yards—isn't that where the bartender who was murdered last week worked?"

My half-filled coffee mug called for my attention. "Uh. Yeah. I think so."

"You know so."

"Okay, I'm taking his job."

"And…?"

Talk about relentless. "And the owner asked me to look into things. Nothing official. The guy was his cousin."

Richard's mug thunked onto the table. "Jeff, don't get involved."

"I'm not."

Richard's gaze hardened. "Yes, you are. The question is why?"

Brenda folded the newspaper, all her attention now focused on me, too.

How much of a shit did it make me to admit I wanted the dead man's job? And that I was willing to endure a certain amount of unpleasantness to get it probably said even more. It's just as well that Richard's MD wasn't in psychiatry, not that I was about to admit any of this to him.

"Okay, as you won't answer that question, then when do you start?"

"Today. Afternoon shift."

He raised an eyebrow.

"You'd better tell me if you'll be late for dinner—not that you eat enough to keep a sparrow alive," Brenda said.

"How long a shift will you work?" Richard asked.

"I didn't ask."

His other eyebrow went up. "How much will you make an hour?"

"I didn't—"

"You didn't ask," he said, glowering.

I got up from the table, cup in hand. "You want a warm-up?"

He shook his head. "I'm worried about you, Jeff. You're not ready for this."

I poured my coffee, my back stiffening in annoyance. "Is that a medical opinion?"

"Yes. You've made tremendous progress, but your recovery is by no means complete."

He was one to talk—Mr. Short-of-Breath. I wasn't about to argue with him though, as I felt responsible for him being that way. He'd been shot trying to protect me not ten weeks before. Walking up stairs or any distance was still a chore for him. I didn't want to cause him undo concern, and yet…

"*You're* about to start a new job," I said, more an accusation than a statement.

"It's only a volunteer position. It's not full time, and doesn't start for almost another month. By then I'll be fully recovered. Head injuries like yours don't heal on that kind of timeline."

Somehow I resisted the urge to say, "Oh yeah?" Instead I turned to Brenda. "What do you think?"

"As your friend or a nurse?"

"Take your pick." Why did I have to sound so damned defensive?

She sighed and reached for Richard's hand, her cocoa-brown skin a contrast to his still pasty complexion. "As a nurse, I agree with Richard."

He smirked at her, his mustache twitching.

"As your friend." She turned to face me. "You're driving me nuts—the two of you, because you're both going stir-crazy."

Richard's smile faded. He sat up straighter, removed his hand from hers.

Brenda pushed herself up from the table, and headed out of the kitchen. "You're going to do what you want anyway, so—get on with it."

I avoided Richard's accusing stare, added milk to my coffee and stirred it. Stir-crazy, huh? Too often, Brenda could read me, too. Still…

I faced my brother. "You want to come with me?"

Richard blinked. "To work?"

"No, to check out where the guy got stabbed."

"I thought you weren't getting involved in this?"

"I'm not. I'm just curious."

"And curiosity killed the cat."

I sipped my coffee. "I figure I've got at least eight lives left."

"Don't kid yourself, Jeff. You could've died from that mugging."

"And I could get hit by a bus going to the grocery store. Are you coming or not?"

Richard drained his cup, pushed back his chair and rose. "I'll come."

***

The vibrant green grass down the steep grade stood out in chunky tufts, belligerent in the wake of someone's weed whacker. It had probably been cropped a week before, but already looked long and lanky and ready to defy another swipe by a plastic whip cord. A six-foot remnant of yellow crime tape fluttered in the breeze. Twenty or thirty feet below and a hundred yards further on, Ellicott Creek rushed past.

Ignoring the "Danger—No Trespassing" signs, Richard craned his neck to gaze down the hill. "So where was the dead guy found?"

"I'm not sure." I glanced over my shoulder at the scarlet-painted barn of a building that hugged the embankment. As in years before, a huge stone wheel once again milled corn, wheat and rye, but was the end product more for show than commerce? Pallets of ground grains in sacks sealed in plastic were stacked on the mill's back porch. The north end of the building housed a little café and bakery. Could they really use that much flour?

"Tell me about the murdered man," Richard said.

I repeated what Tom had told me the night before.

"You get any impressions yet?"

"That depends on your definition of impressions. So far, not here. But I did flash onto something weird that relates to the dead guy last night at the bar. Probably because he spent so much time there. I don't know what it means." And I wasn't ready to talk about it.

Richard did not look pleased, but he didn't push. He understood what I'd said—that I was already caught up in the guy's death, and that something beyond my usual senses was going to feed me information about it until...well, corny as it sounds...until justice was done. One way or another.

Goat-footed, I tramped down the rocky slope, over flattened grass and weeds to where the crime tape flapped. As Tom said, there was nothing much to see. No blood marred the spot. The ground hadn't been dug up for evidence. Had Walt been killed elsewhere and just dumped here?

I closed my eyes and the flash of what I'd seen the night before came back to me. A sparkling—sequins?—woman's stiletto-heeled shoe. I tried to tap into that memory once again, opening myself up, but it was someone else's experience that assaulted me. *Walt's face, chalk white—his body drained of blood. Milky eyes open, staring up at the sky.*

Nausea erupted within me, doubling me over. I grabbed onto a sapling to keep from falling down the hill, retching, choking, until the inevitable. Then Richard was beside me, his hand on my shoulder until my stomach had finished expelling my breakfast.

"What the hell happened?" he demanded.

I coughed, gasping, trying to catch my breath. "Not me. I got caught in someone's reaction to seeing Walt. I dunno. Maybe some rookie cop's first time seeing a body."

"Good Lord," Richard muttered.

I wiped my mouth on the back of my hand. Poor Walt had been dumped here like so much garbage.

"Excuse me, but what are you doing here?"

We both turned. A tall, buxom blonde stood between the sacks of grain stacked on the porch. The morning sun highlighted the fine lines around her eyes, but the overall effect was not detrimental. Dressed in a denim skirt and peasant blouse, she was the epitome of Southwest fashion from her silver-and-turquoise squash-blossom necklace to her tooled leather boots.

"Just looking around," I said lamely, and staggered back up the hillock, with Richard following me.

"This is not public property. I'm the owner, and unless you're a mill customer, I'll have to ask you to leave."

"Cyn Taggert—is that you?" Richard asked.

The blonde squinted at him. "I'm sorry. Do I know you?"

"Richard Alpert. We were friends when you were at Nardin and I was at Canisus High."

The anger dissolved from her features and a mix of astonishment and delight lit her face. "Richard?" She lurched forward, capturing him in an awkward embrace.

I got another flash—so fast it almost didn't register: *Hands. Blood.*

She pulled back, the movement startling me, and examined Richard's face. "How many years has it been?"

He laughed. "Too many."

The two of them stood there, staring at one another, oblivious of what I'd just experienced. Then the woman gave a nervous laugh. "I'm Cynthia Lennox now. I was married for twenty years to Dennis. He passed away last fall."

"I'm so sorry," Richard murmured.

Her smile was wistful. "So am I."

I looked away, realizing my fingers were clenched so tight they'd gone white. Flexing them, I noticed half-moon indentations in my palm. That latest burst of insight had affected me more than the sparkling red shoe or the vision of Walt Kaplan's body.

The woman took Richard's hand. "What happened to you? Last I heard you were in medical school."

"A lot of years ago," Richard admitted, smiling. "I got my MD and moved to California for eighteen years. I'm back now."

I waited for him to say something like, "about to get married to the most marvelous woman in the universe," but he kept looking at this stranger with a vacant, sappy grin. Ex-girlfriend, I mused? So what. Why not tell her about Brenda?

I cleared my throat.

Richard seemed to surface from the past. "Cyn, this is my brother, Jeff Resnick."

"Brother?" she asked, puzzled.

Richard hadn't even known about me when he was in high school. "It's kind of a long story."

She didn't look interested in learning it. I was too far away to shake hands—not that I wanted to—so I nodded at her. She did likewise. No love lost there.

"Well, come on in," Cyn told Richard, gesturing toward the mill. "We've got the best coffee in Williamsville, and a wonderful apple strudel." She looked at him with eyes half focused on the past. I wondered if I should just slink back to the car and disappear. Then again, it had been someone from the mill who'd found Walt Kaplan, and I wanted to know about it. Uninvited, I trotted along behind them.

We followed Cyn up the stairs and into the mill's side entrance, stepping into the dim interior of what looked to be a storage barn. Crates and more pallets of grain and flour were stacked so that there was only a narrow path between this and a larger room with bright lights to the left: the bakery and storefront.

Cyn stopped dead ahead of us and like two of the Three Stooges, Richard and I bumped into one another. Richard's at least six inches taller than me, so it was difficult to see around him.

"Tigger," Cyn chided. A fat tabby leaped onto the stack of crates, giving a lusty yowl and looking self-satisfied. "Stay there," Cyn told us. "I'll take care of it."

Richard stared down at his shoes—no, just beyond them, at a gray, furry lump. Either a very large mouse or a small rat.

Cyn returned with a worn and stained gardener's glove on her right hand. She picked up the limp creature and inspected it. "Good work, Tigger." Cyn started off again, paused to take aim at a trash barrel with a black plastic bag folded over its rim, and tossed the body in. Two points!

Richard followed, his gaze straight ahead as he passed the barrel. I had a quick look inside and grimaced.

Cyn ditched the glove.

We entered the café, taking in the mingled aromas of fresh-ground coffees, vanilla, and baking that filled the upscale bakery's storefront. Only one of the white-painted bistro tables stood empty. At the rest, customers sat lingering over conversations with cappuccinos, lattes, and decadent pastries. Not a bad mid-morning weekday crowd. Had business been this good before the dead man had been found on the property?

Cyn sailed across the room to a door marked "Private," ushering us in. "Gene, bring us some coffee and strudel, will you?" she called over her shoulder.

"Sure thing, Cyn," said a thin, balding, enthusiastic young man behind the café's main counter.

"That's not necessary," Richard said.

"Nonsense. It's the least I can do for an old friend." Cyn closed the door behind her.

Like the storefront, the brightly lit office was immaculate. No stray papers marred the desktop or hung out of the four-drawer file cabinet in the corner. Unlike the country charm outside this small room, Southwest accents of hanging ristras and a stenciled border of coyotes were cheerful against pale turquoise walls. Behind the desk was a large-framed photograph of a younger, happier Cyn arm-in-arm with a sandy-haired man—the now deceased Dennis?—in front of a low adobe building with the legend "Santa Fe *Café au lait.*"

"Sit," Cyn urged and took her own seat.

We complied, taking the two upholstered office chairs before her antique wooden table of a desk.

Cyn folded her hands and leaned forward. "It's wonderful seeing you again, Richard, but what on Earth were you doing behind my café?"

"Curiosity," he said with a touch of embarrassment. "Murder isn't an everyday occurrence in Williamsville."

"Who found the dead man?" I asked.

Cyn turned hard eyes on me, her mouth tightening. "Our miller, Ted Hanson."

"Is he in today? Can I talk to him?"

"No." Her rebuke was adamant.

"Excuse me?" I pushed.

"No, Ted isn't here today. In fact, he's out of town on a buying trip."

"When will he be back?"

"In a few days. Why are you so interested?"

"Morbid curiosity," I said, echoing Richard's words. "Last night I was hired to take Walt Kaplan's job at a bar down the street."

She gaped at me, unprepared for honesty; sudden fear shadowed her eyes.

A sharp knock preceded the door opening. Gene held a loaded tray in one hand and bustled inside. He set cardboard cups before Richard and me, placing frosted rectangles of strudel on baker's tissue next to them. His smile was genuine. "Enjoy." He eased the door closed behind him.

The awkward silence lengthened.

Richard cleared his throat. "Do you ever see any of the old crowd, Cyn?"

Cyn seemed grateful for a change of subject. "Since I came back to the area nine months ago, I've only caught up with Cathy Makarchuk. She married Barry Garner. They have five children—can you believe it?"

Nothing on Earth is more boring than listening to old school chums reminisce. I reached for my coffee, eager to rid my mouth of the lingering sour taste of vomit, and my hand brushed the edge of the desk. The image of a smiling man burst upon my mind. Heart pounding, I snatched up my cup with a shaking hand and took a sloppy gulp.

At some time before his death, Walt Kaplan had sat on the edge of that desk.

Chapter Two

"Fill the beer cooler, and later we'll talk," Tom said, and slapped me on the back, nearly knocking me off my feet.

"Sure thing," I said and faked a smile.

He left me standing by the bar's back door, where a Molson truck had just made its weekly delivery. Thirty cases of beer sat stacked against the wall. I found a dolly behind the door, so at least I wouldn't have to kill myself dragging the beer into the cooler. Then again, I wondered how much stress my recently broken arm could take. I'd only been out of the brace about seven weeks.

The first five cases proved easy to lift. By the time I'd hauled the rest of them in I'd worked up a sweat and had rethought my ambition to work as a bartender. I much preferred cutting up fruit garnishes and washing glasses to actual physical labor.

Four construction workers sat at the bar nursing beers, picking at bowls of pretzels while they watched ESPN on the TV bolted to the wall. Since Tom didn't serve food, I wondered if liquid bread—aka beer—constituted their midday meal. Tom had already given me the cut-off lecture. Nobody left drunk from his establishment unless they had a designated driver. In the twenty years he'd owned the tavern, he'd never been sued and wanted to keep it that way.

I hadn't worked behind a bar in at least twelve years, but it all came back within minutes as I waited on my first few customers, rang up the sales, and collected my first paltry tips. No doubt about it, I wasn't going to get rich working here. Still, it felt good to be among the employed once again. For as long as it would last. Tom hadn't mentioned this being a permanent arrangement.

Luckily I wasn't picking up too many disquieting vibes, either. One of the guys was behind in his truck payments, sweating the repo man. Another hadn't been laid in three weeks and wondered if his old lady was boffing someone else. Just the usual errant signals I picked up on shopping carts, door handles and money. Inconvenient at times, but I'd learned to ignore most of it. I knew when to pay attention, too.

The lunchtime crowd had emptied out when Richard ambled through the side entrance. He'd never been to The Whole Nine Yards before, and I guess he wanted to see for himself what I'd gotten myself into.

He paused at the end of the bar, taking in the dark bead board that went halfway up the walls, the chair rail, and stucco above it decorated with sports posters and memorabilia. He took the first stool, rested his forearms on the bar. Dressed in a golf shirt and freshly ironed Dockers, he looked out of place in this working-class establishment.

I strolled down and halted before him. "What can I get you, sir?"

He looked up at me with no show of recognition. "Got any Canadian on tap?"

"Labatts."

He nodded.

I drew him a beer and set a fresh bowl of pretzels down in front of him. "What about those Bisons," he said, setting a ten spot on the bar.

I didn't follow minor-league baseball, but I guessed I'd have to while working in a sports bar. Bummer. "Uh, yeah. What about 'em?"

Richard's mustache quirked as he reached for his glass.

I rang up the sale and gave him his change. Tom was stooped over the other end of the bar, watching TV. I wandered over to him. "I've got some questions I wanted to ask about Walt."

Tom tore his gaze away from the tube. "Sure thing."

"You said he was a loner. No best friends?"

Tom shook his head, then looked thoughtful. "Well, maybe me. But we didn't talk all that much. I gave him the job because he'd been hurt working construction and couldn't go back to it. He got some kind of disability payments, which is why he only had to work here part-time."

"What kind of disability?"

"Bad hip. Had a limp. Sometimes he used a cane."

"What did he do with his free time?"

Tom shrugged. "He never really spoke about it."

I glanced over my shoulder. Richard was looking down the bar beyond us, gazing intently at the TV. He'd never shown a burning desire to watch waterskiing before and was no doubt eavesdropping.

I turned back to Tom. "Did Walt ever mention women or describe his ideal girl?"

"Not that I recall."

"He wasn't gay, was he?"

Tom straightened, his eyes widening. "No!"

"Just asking." Where did the red stiletto heel fit in? "Did he go to strip joints?"

"Not that I know of."

"Did he buy his sex?"

Tom squirmed. "I don't know. I don't think so. Walt was private. He didn't talk about stuff like that. But he listened when the other guys would talk. Why'd you ask such a personal question?"

"I didn't know Walt. Maybe nobody—even his family—really did."

Tom's brow wrinkled. Maybe he hadn't wanted to know.

"It would help if I could see where Walt lived. See *how* he lived."

"I got his keys from the cops. I'll give them to you later." Tom cleared his throat and glanced over his shoulder at the back room. "I've got some paperwork to take care of. Will you be okay out here alone for a while?"

I gazed at our only customer, Richard, and nodded.

Tom took off and I grabbed the damp rag by the sink. The bar didn't need wiping down, but I did it anyway, ending up back in front of Richard.

"How's the job going?" he asked.

"So far so good."

He nodded, but seemed to expect more of an answer. I didn't have one.

"I'm gonna check out Walt's apartment later. Wanna come?"

Richard drained the last of his beer. "Why not?" The words sounded bland, but the crinkle in his eyes and the set of his mouth betrayed his interest. Brenda was right. He'd been bored silly during his convalescence, but looking into Walt's murder wasn't a lark. Odds were we wouldn't be in danger this early in the game. I had no desire to put myself or anyone else in harm's way. But the last time I'd gotten caught up in the web of emotion surrounding a murder, it was Richard who'd nearly paid the ultimate price. Truth was, I wanted him to accompany me, and yet anxiety gnawed at my nerves. For all the insight I'd experienced while pursuing a murderer three months earlier, I'd never had a clue that Richard might be in danger. That he'd be so grievously injured.

I didn't like to revisit that guilt.

Pawing through Walt's possessions was another matter. We might not find anything that would give me answers. And if I did, well, I didn't have to share it with Richard.

"Want another?" I asked Richard, indicating his glass.

He stood. "I'm all set. Give me a call later and I'll meet you."

"Sure."

He headed for the door. Under his empty glass was a five-dollar tip.

***

The south side of Main Street near Eggert Road was already in shadow as Richard and I stood on the sidewalk looking up at the apartment windows over a dress boutique. The drapes were drawn. Good. I wasn't interested in attracting the attention of the neighbors. Not that it mattered. I had permission to be there. Still, poking around a dead man's possessions cranked up the creepiness factor a notch.

Steep, narrow stairs led up to the second floor.

"Did I hear your boss say the guy was disabled? Why didn't he find first-floor digs?"

I shrugged and pulled out the keys Tom had given me. Richard stooped to pick up newspapers that had accumulated. The shelf under a two-receptacle apartment mailbox overflowed with Walt's junk mail. He grabbed that, too, and we trooped up the stairs.

I picked out the key Tom said would open the door. It did. I stepped into the apartment's dark interior, groping for the light switch just inside the door. I flicked it and wan yellow light illuminated the entryway. Walt had been dead only five days, but already the place smelled of disuse. Still, the air felt heavy with Walt's presence. Not that I could take in the essence of his soul, but I could feel some residual part of what and who he was, and also the first tendrils of migraine stirring behind my eyes.

Richard thrust the mail at me and shoved his hands into his pants pockets, gazing around the cramped place. The cops hadn't made too big a mess, leading me to believe Walt kept his home meticulously clean. I sorted through the circulars, dumping them into the empty kitchen waste basket, then backtracked to open the entry's closet door and found winter coats and boots. Nothing very interesting.

Back in the tidy galley kitchen, the cabinets housed plain white Corelle dishes and Coke glasses from fast-food restaurant giveaways. In the closet pantry, cans were stacked in descending sizes, heavy on store-brand tomato soup and mac and cheese. I'm no gourmet, but when it came to dinner prep even I could do better than Walt.

I wasn't eager to touch everything, but already I understood a lot about Walt Kaplan, a man who listened and rarely gave much of himself to others. There was no sense of joy in his home. Nothing that mirrored the smile he had given someone in Cyn Lennox's office.

The spotless bathroom brandished much-washed, frayed brown towels on the racks by the sink and bathtub. I poked through the medicine cabinet and found mint mouthwash, toothpaste, dental floss and a prescription bottle of anisindione. "Rich?" He poked his head around the door and I handed it to him.

He read the label, frowned. "It's an anticoagulant. You might be more familiar with the commercial name, Coumadin."

"What do you think was wrong with Walt?"

Richard shrugged. "Blood thinners treat deep vein thrombosis, pulmonary embolus, arterial fibrillation—any number of things."

"So what's that mean?"

"Prevents strokes."

He might've said so. Richard scrutinized the label again. "Being stabbed while on this dose would've greatly speeded up his death."

The thought made me shudder.

Richard went back to the living room.

The bedroom door was ajar; the place most people stored their secrets. Not a wrinkle marred the fiberfill burgundy quilt that lay across the full-sized bed. Like the living room, no reading material littered the flat surfaces of the dresser or nightstand. No dust, either.

A dresser stowed underwear, socks, and golf shirts folded with expert precision, although the contents had been disturbed—probably by the cops. Suits, shirts and slacks hung in color-coordinated order stuffed the pokey little closet. A plastic shoe rack attached to the back of the door contained six pairs of Walt's shoes, polished to a glow. A stack of nine identical, nondescript shoeboxes sat huddled on the closet floor. No manufacturer's name graced the generic boxes. A couple of years' worth of Victoria's Secret catalogs sat beside them in a tidy pile. Pretty tame stuff. My gaze kept wandering to the stack of shoeboxes. I knelt and ran my right palm over the front of the boxes. It gravitated toward one in particular on the top left of the pile. I pulled it out to examine it.

The wide box was standard gray cardboard, nothing out of the ordinary, and no different than the others. I held it in my hands and the red sequined shoe flashed before my mind's eye once again, bringing a stab of pain with it. I ground my teeth and concentrated. This time, the view was from the back; pear shaped, cupped to accept a soft-skinned foot upon its tapered heel, the ankle strap looping to look like an overgrown, sparkling halo. No saint wore shoes like those. And why associate Walt's death with the shoe? It was gaudy, flashy—not at all Walt's style. I hadn't come across any sex toys—not even a box of condoms. I doubted he'd ever brought any of his playmates home.

And come to think of it, in my vision I only ever saw one shoe.

I lifted the lid. Empty, except for a couple of papers: A brochure of Holiday Valley, the ski resort south of Buffalo, and a scrap with four hand-written numbers: 4537. Pin number? Combination lock? Last four digits of a phone number? And I got the feeling that the collection was incomplete. Walt had hoped to add more things to it. His time had simply run out.

I replaced the cover and set the box behind me, grabbing the one that had been right next to it. The collection of items in this box was much more varied. Piece by piece, I withdrew an ordinary blue Bick pen, a plain white, soiled cocktail napkin with no embossed name of a bar printed on it or other clue as to its origin, an unsigned birthday card with a lipstick kiss. The last item was a small black velvet pillow with the name Veronica embroidered on it in Day-Glo pink thread. I picked it up by its pink-ribboned hanger, and was assaulted with the same image I'd seen when we met Cyn Lennox: *Hands. Bloodied.*

Startled, I dropped the pillow so fast, it went flying. Nerves jangled, I sat there for a few seconds waiting to recover. God, I hated that flashes of insight could catch me off guard like that—sour my stomach and make my muscles quiver. And I was glad Richard hadn't witnessed it.

I took a couple more breaths to calm down before retrieving the pillow, lifting it by its hanger with the pen and replacing both items in the box before setting it aside, too.

The idea of checking all the shoeboxes was not pleasant, but it had to be done. Methodically, I went through every one of them, making sure I handled each item. No insight, no creepy feelings. Each box held just as curious collections of oddball items that could have meaning only for Walt—and none of them with the emotional investment the first two had had. Had the shoes been gifts to his lady friends? Why had Walt kept the boxes? If the sparkly shoe I kept seeing was representative of the rest, they were not cheap.

I replaced the boring boxes, closed the closet door and picked up the two interesting ones, tucked them under my arm, and returned to the living room.

Richard sat at the desk, Walt's receipts and papers spread out before him on the blotter. He looked up, zeroing in on the boxes. "What's so special about those?"

"I'm not sure," I lied. "But I think I'll take them home with me. Find anything worthwhile?"

Richard scooped up the papers, replacing them in the manila folder. "All his bills and receipts are segregated into envelopes by year. You want the latest?"

"Sure. I'm most interested in credit card and phone bills."

"Looking for anything in particular?"

"Yeah, a clue to his sex life. I think his death may have hinged on that."

"Wouldn't be the first time." Richard selected a couple of envelopes from the lower left-hand drawer, pushed it shut and handed them to me. "This ought to hold you for a while. Are you about ready?"

"Yeah, let's go."

Richard followed me to the door. "Brenda's making shrimp scampi tonight."

"With garlic bread?"

"You got it."

I closed and locked the door behind us. Richard trundled down the stairs without a backward glance, but something tugged at my soul. I turned back to stare at the featureless steel door. *Find the truth,* something whispered inside my head.

Walt or my conscience?

I'd have to figure that out.

Chapter Three

Richard's after-dinner Drambuie sat on a Venetian tile coaster. He'd parked behind his grandfather's big mahogany desk, poring over yet another book. But this wasn't some dry, medical tome. Fuzzy black-and-white photographs checkerboarded the pages, with short paragraphs of text annotating each one. Brenda brushed past me in the doorway, clutching the latest Tess Gerritsen hardback. "Run for your life," she hissed. "He's parked back on Memory Lane again."

Amused, I watched her make a beeline for the stairs.

I cleared my throat and stepped forward. "Is that your high school yearbook?" I asked Richard.

He didn't bother to look up. "One of them."

I entered the room and rounded the desk to stand behind him. He tapped a faded color photo that had been used as a bookmark. "Here's Cyn Taggert—er, Lennox."

The now-buxom blonde had been a skinny brunette with timid eyes some thirty years previous. Hard to believe the little waif had grown into the hardened businesswoman I'd met earlier that day.

I hadn't told Richard about the flash of insight I'd experienced in Cyn Lennox's office. On its own, it meant nothing.

Maybe Walt had once applied for a job at the Old Red Mill. Perhaps he was an old or a new friend—someone Cyn had known Richard hadn't trucked with. The fact that Walt had been in the place, only yards from where his body had been found, wasn't proof of anything. Yet it did give me a starting point. Something I was pretty sure the Amherst Police didn't know.

I hadn't asked Cyn if she'd known Walt. The timing wasn't right. I needed to know more about the dead man before I went that route. And I was pretty sure I wouldn't hear the truth from Ms. Lennox anyway.

Once again Richard had a sappy look on his face, still studying Cyn's picture.

"I thought you went to an all-boys Catholic high school."

"Yeah, Canisus guys always hung out with the girls from Nardin."

"You enjoyed those years, didn't you?" My words came out like an accusation.

Richard didn't seem to notice. "Yes, I did."

Why shouldn't he sound satisfied? He hadn't been wrenched out of his freshman year at the three-quarter point from an inner city school and dumped across town with a bunch of snotty rich kids. He had fit in from day one. He hadn't been beaten to a pulp on his first day, either.

I moved around the front of the desk and sat in one of the leather wing chairs, surprised at the depth of my bitterness. I tried to let it go. "What if your friend Cyn knows more than she's telling about this murder?"

Richard looked up from the decades-old pages. "Cyn's a good person. I'm sure she's told the police everything she knows."

"You knew this woman over thirty years ago. You don't know who she is today."

"Yeah, but people don't change that much. Look at you."

"Me?"

"In some ways, you haven't changed at all from when you were fourteen."

Anger flared within me. I'd come a long way from that cowed boy who'd been forced to go live with strangers. I changed the subject. "Once I wire up the light over the dining room table, the apartment is finished. I guess we ought to think about calling movers to come and I'll be out of your hair on a daily basis."

He closed the yearbook, a smile raising the edges of his mustache. "You ready to leave the nest?"

"Moving sixteen feet across the driveway is hardly leaving the nest."

He shrugged.

The loft apartment over the three-car garage had been empty for at least twenty years before I got the brilliant idea to make the place my own. I'd intended to give it a good clean and move right in, but Richard wouldn't hear of it. The next thing you know he'd hired a contractor, put in a new heating and cooling system, all new wiring, had the hardwood floors sanded and sealed and the walls painted. All the planning had kept him occupied for a few hours a day while he recovered.

Brenda had entrusted her friend Maggie Brennan to help her decorate the place. I'd introduced the two women. At the time I thought I might have a shot at a relationship with the lovely Ms. B. That hadn't worked out, but I also hadn't given up on the idea, either. Gut feeling told me we'd be more than just acquaintances one day. I listened to my gut.

"Go ahead and arrange for movers whenever you want. It's on me," Richard said.

Yeah, like everything else these last few months.

He'd reopened the book, his attention back on the picture of young Cyn Taggert. Was it the memory of puppy love that made his smile so wistful? The present-day woman gave me bad vibes. I'd have to pursue that avenue of investigation.

And if Richard found out his long lost love had some deadly secret—how much would he blame me?

***

I punched the rheostat switch and bright white light flooded the apartment's empty dining area. I cranked it back to a tolerable level, grateful the pills I'd taken earlier had quelled the headache that had threatened.

My gaze traveled around the pleasant room. There was no reason not to call a bunch of movers for estimates first thing in the morning. And yet, I wasn't quite ready to move in and I wasn't sure why. The most painless route was to do the deed while Richard and Brenda were on their honeymoon.

Painless. What did bloody hands have to do with Walt's death? Okay, he'd bled to death. But I was pretty sure the image of the hands had nothing to do with his death. I'd had flashes of clairvoyance and they were different than seeing things from the past. The shoe was the past. The bloody hands were something yet to come. So who was Veronica and why was she in danger? Perhaps the next victim?

The phone rang, making me jump. Once, twice. I never pick up until at least the fourth ring, just to thwart telemarketers, who usually hang up after three. Besides, only Richard, Brenda, and the employment form I filled out for Tom at the bar had my new telephone number. I had only one sort-of friend in Buffalo, Sam Nielsen, now a reporter for the *Buffalo News*—and I hadn't even given him the two-week-old number.

I picked up the phone. "Hello?"

"Where do you get off involving Richard in another one of your dumb psychic schemes? Haven't you done enough to the poor man?"

I should've just hung up, but the voice was vaguely familiar. "Excuse me?"

"I said—"

"I heard what you said. Who is this?"

"Maggie. Maggie Brennan."

Ah, the lovely Ms. B. Only now I was on the fiery end of her Irish temper. Brenda must've given her the number.

"Did Brenda ask you to say something?"

"Well…no. She wouldn't. But I thought—"

"Yeah, well you thought wrong. Just butt out of my family business, will you?"

"No, I won't. Brenda and Richard are my friends. And in case it escaped your attention, you nearly got Richard killed at Easter."

"Hey, I was the target. Richard pushed me out of the way."

"Yeah, well it's still your fault."

A lump rose in my throat. I didn't need *her* to tell me that.

"If that's all you called for—I think it's time we ended this conversation."

Silence.

I counted to ten. "Was there something else you wanted to say?"

"I guess not." Did I detect reluctance in her voice?

When we first met, we'd connected almost immediately. That is, until we found a body in her ex-lover's condo. That had definitely put a damper on what seemed like the beginning of a meaningful relationship.

I decided to take a chance. "Do you want to go out with me sometime?"

More silence.

I counted to ten again.

"Maybe," Maggie answered at last, and again her tone was soft. "What did you have in mind?"

I remembered the Holiday Valley brochure in Walt's shoebox. "Just a ride in the country. A day trip."

"A magical mystery tour?" Aha! She was intrigued.

"Something like that."

Again silence.

This was like a replay from my high school days. My sweaty hand tightened around the receiver as I counted to ten one more time.

"Okay. When?"

I let out the breath I hadn't realized I'd been holding. "Saturday."

***

I never drove to the bakery up on Main Street. I'd walked there in snow, rain, and on starless nights to find Sophie Levin standing behind the plate glass door in her faded cotton house dress, maroon cardigan sweater, and silver hair tucked into a wispy bun at the base of her neck, ready to usher me into her backroom inner sanctum. That night was no different.

"In, in already," the elderly woman said, locking the door behind me. I followed her to the small card table she had set up beside a pallet of collapsed bakery boxes. She pointed to my usual seat, a metal folding chair, and settled her bulk on the one adjacent. The coffee was hot and my favorite macaroons, still warm from the oven, sat piled on a chipped white plate.

I set the plastic grocery bag with the shoeboxes on the table.

"Show and tell?" she asked, her brown eyes riveted on it.

I took the boxes out, shoved one of them closer to her. "I'll show and you tell me what you think."

She leaned on the wobbly table, clasping her hands before her and studied the box. "Hmm. Fancy shoes once lived in this box." Her voice, with its slight Polish accent, held reproach. She rested her fingers on the top of the other box. "Hmm. This one, too."

I sipped my coffee and nodded. I thought of Sophie as a kind of psychic mentor, although her inner radar was much different than mine. She saw auras—colors, she called them—and then she knew things. And it made me feel less of a freak to have a kindred spirit to confide in.

Sophie traced a finger along the first box top. "Not the kind of shoes a *nice* woman wears."

I tried not to smile. "That depends upon your definition of nice. But in this case, I think you're right."

She raised the lid, setting it aside. Her gaze fell on the contents and she frowned. "Hmm. Not too interesting." She selected the Holiday Valley brochure. She stared at it for a few moments, then ran her fingers along the long edge. "A good time was had."

"That was my impression, too. But that was all I got. Take a look at that little scrap and tell me what you think."

Sophie replaced the brochure. Her weary, red-rimmed eyes widened when she picked up the paper fragment. "Now this is more interesting."

Intrigued, I leaned forward.

She closed her eyes, concentrating. "Hmmm."

"What is it? What do you see?"

Sophie opened her eyes and frowned at me. "You aren't usually this impatient."

I backed off. "Sorry."

She rubbed the scrap between her forefinger and thumb, her head bobbing. "Yes. That's it."

"What?"

She reached over, grabbed my hand, pressing the fragment into my palm with her thumb. A negative image burst upon my mind; trees, a rural mailbox with the numbers 4537 glowing upon it. Then the pressure was gone and I found myself sitting there, open-mouthed, staring at Sophie's self-satisfied expression.

"Wow. How'd you do that?"

She flicked the paper from her thumb and it drifted back into the box. "It's a gift." Her smile faded. "But knowing it's a house number doesn't tell you where to find the house."

"It's obvious. It's in Holiday Valley."

She picked up a macaroon and inspected it. "Oh sure. If you know what street it's on."

I thought back to the image she'd shared with me. The fact that it had been a negative made it harder to discern details. A mailbox, glowing numbers. Maples and pines in the background, but nothing else to help me identify the location. And she had a point. "Can you tell me anything about this place?"

"More about the paper the numbers were written on."

I was all ears.

"The man who wrote it is dead." She shuddered. "He died violently."

I nodded.

Sophie concentrated. "He wasn't well."

I nodded again.

Her gaze strayed to the other box, then to me. "This one frightens you."

"I wouldn't say 'frightened.' More—" Okay, she was right. But it wasn't the box; just the damn little pillow inside it.

"Yes?" she prompted.

"Concerned."

"Mmm." She lifted the lid, peered inside and frowned. "Oh. Yes. Not nice."

We could fence around it all night. "How so?"

Her chin rose defiantly. "You tell me."

"That would taint your perception. Come on—give."

Her brow again furrowed with concentration. When she spoke, her voice was pensive—subdued. "Blood. Like a slaughterhouse."

Damn, I hadn't wanted to hear that. "Yeah. Walt Kaplan bled to death."

She shook her head. "What we see is not his blood."

My heart sank. She'd used the present tense. "I got that, too."

"What will you do about it?"

"What can I do?"

"Try to stop it from happening."

"Can I?"

She shrugged. "All you can do is try."

"What about fate? If it's supposed to happen—"

"If I had my life to live over, I would always try harder to do what was right. Always. It's too easy to turn away, to give up. I would be very disappointed in you if you took the easy way out."

Sophie had a knack for inducing guilt. I found I couldn't meet her gaze.

She tapped the other shoebox. I looked up to see her frown, her brow furrowing. "What about this fancy shoe?"

"I saw it, too," I said, grateful for the change of subject. "But I don't know what it means."

Sophie nibbled on her cookie, her expression thoughtful. "Feet."

"Huh?"

"The man who died had one of those feet things."

"Feet things?"

"You know—he was fascinated by toes."

Understanding dawned. "A foot fetish?"

"Yes!" She popped the rest of the cookie in her mouth, chewed, and swallowed, quite pleased with herself; then her expression soured. "Why would anyone want to suck on another person's smelly toes?"

"Ya got me."

Sophie shrugged, selected another macaroon and winked. "These are better."

Chapter Four

He was dead. Chest, clothes saturated with blood. A lifeless body stretched out on the cold, stone floor. No hope of revival. No hope at all.

Dead.

Forever gone.

Like everyone else I'd ever loved.

My father. I don't even really remember him. Not his face. Nothing.

My mother. The haggard-faced Madonna with a whiskey glass clutched in one hand, pleading for release from this life.

My wife—Shelley, her eyes glazed and vacant, lips smiling after a line of blow.

And now...

The image of the dead dissolved, replaced by a pair of masculine hands covered in blood. Palms away from me, rivulets of blood dripping down the wrists, snagged by a forest of dark forearm hairs—someone's life blood gone, as though in a slaughterhouse. Just like—

I jerked awake, sweating, muscles quivering—my heart pounding like the rhythm of a rap tune.

I rolled over onto my stomach, hugged my pillow. The scarlet numerals on my bedside clock read 4:09. I closed my eyes and tried to get my ragged breathing under control.

I didn't need a shrink to tell me the significance of the nightmare. It came to me a couple of times a week, only now it had a new ending. But the dream lied. Unlike my parents and ex-wife, Richard *hadn't* died.

Another reality was that Richard *could've* died because of me. He'd been willing to sacrifice himself to save me, and I wasn't sure if I was worthy of that. Worse, if I'd find the courage to do the same for him.

Those circuitous thoughts were unproductive. I had a new problem: the vision of the bloodied hands. What did it mean and how was I going to prevent seeing them in reality?

***

Warm, incandescent light washed over the kitchen table where I'd scattered the envelopes of financial information Richard had appropriated at Walt's apartment. The contents—heavy on receipts—indicated Walt had fallen into the trap of credit card debt. He'd maxed out four major cards, with finance charges far exceeding the monthly minimum, which he dutifully paid. Top creditors were Erie Professional Laundry, Sunoco Gas, a smattering of family restaurants, and Macy's. He also had a car loan with Bison Bank. His disability payments were direct-deposited to a checking account regularly drained by ATM withdrawals, and had an ending balance of forty-seven cents for the previous month.

I sipped my second cup of coffee. Disability payments would've saved me from my current deadbeat existence.

Richard had consulted an attorney about my filing a Social Security claim, but taking a job at the bar had probably killed my chances at ever seeing a check.

I pushed the thought aside as I shuffled through Walt's monthly credit card statements. Pay-per-view was a favorite with Walt, and I could guess the content of the movies he chose—not that they were listed. Was that the total extent of his sex life? Had his disability prevented him from performing with women, or was he shy about a scar or other infirmity? Revealing a colostomy bag or stoma would not be the highlight of a sexual encounter.

No shoe company was listed amongst his creditors. Walt didn't have a computer, so did he buy the footwear over the phone or via mail order? I glanced over the miniature checks printed at the bottom of his statement, but most of them were either for his regular bills or the local grocery chain.

Richard hadn't snagged a savings account statement or anything from a brokerage firm. How long had it been since Walt's settlement? If he'd been a union man it could've been hefty—minus the attorney's fee, of course. Even so, where had the money gone?

It was almost seven-thirty and I was about to pour my third cup when I heard footsteps in the hallway. Seconds later Brenda entered the kitchen, heading straight for the fridge. "Someone's got a date," she teased in a singsong cadence. She took out a pound of bacon and the egg carton, setting them on the counter.

"News travels fast." I doctored my cup and sat back down at the table, collected the papers and returned them to their Kraft envelopes.

Brenda retrieved a skillet from a cupboard, set it on the stove and lay the bacon strips across its bottom. She always made too much food, expecting me to tuck in when I just didn't have the appetite. When I moved across the driveway, it was possible cold cereal or coffee alone would fill the bill of fare twenty-four/seven.

I pulled out the coffeemaker's basket, dumping the grounds in the wastebasket before starting a new batch. "Are you and Maggie tracking each other's hourly movements these days?"

"She is my best friend here in Buffalo. Naturally she keeps me informed on what's going on in her life."

A little too well informed.

Richard entered the kitchen from the hallway. "So, you're taking a trip to Holiday Valley tomorrow."

Once upon a time nobody knew or cared when I came and went or what I did. Next I expected a headline in the *Buffalo News*.

Richard sat down at the table, his expression wistful. "I had some good times skiing there, back in the day."

I remembered those days, too. Not for skiing. I'd been stuck here in the house with the elder Alperts, one of whom despised me, while Richard would escape on his all-too-rare days off from the hospital.

Brenda turned the bacon. "Get the bread and the toaster out, will you, Jeffy."

"So, you're taking Maggie Brennan," Richard said.

I busied myself at the counter. "Uh, yeah." I glanced back at Richard, whose eyes had widened, though his face remained immobile.

"What's on tap for today? Are you working at the bar or on your case?'

Brenda cringed. "Don't call it a case."

I took out plates from the cupboard. "She's right. But maybe a little of both."

"Uh-huh."

"What are you guys doing? Making more wedding plans?"

"It's two weeks away, and as far as I know all I have to do is show up at City Hall in a suit."

"You'd better be prepared for more than just that," Brenda said.

Richard ignored her. It wasn't like they were planning a splashy affair. Just the two of them with me and Maggie as witnesses, then lunch at a swank restaurant before they caught a plane for Paris.

"Have you got enough money for your date?" Richard asked me.

My stomach tightened. "It's not a date. And yeah, I've got money." Of course I did. He'd peeled off a couple of twenties for me a few days before. I'd be taking the day trip with his gas in the car he bought me. I didn't feel good about any of that, but being practically destitute engenders humility. I intended to pay him back for everything now that I was working, but as the days passed, and the debt I owed him increased, I found it harder and harder to look him in the eye.

"I'm sure Richard would love to hang out with you today, Jeffy, but we've already planned our day." Hands on hips, Brenda aimed her pointed stare at Richard. "Or are you trying to get out of marrying me?"

Richard leaned back in his chair and frowned. "Did I miss something?"

"We're going to get the license."

"We have plenty of time."

Brenda stood rigid, her steely gaze arctic cold.

"It's good for sixty days," Richard continued, then cleared his throat and looked away. "Isn't anybody going to offer me a cup of coffee?"

Brenda shook her head in disgust and turned her attention back to the skillet. I took two more mugs from the cupboard, pouring coffee for both of them.

Truth was, I wished the four of us *were* going to Holiday Valley. Safety in numbers and all that crap. I had a feeling I was going to learn something that Richard either wouldn't want to know or wasn't likely to believe.

***

I had an hour to kill before reporting to the bar and figured I may as well work on the apartment. It didn't look or feel like home and the only way that was going to change was to unpack some of my stuff; the furniture would come later. None of the boxes had been labeled by the moving company Richard had employed to move my possessions from Manhattan to Buffalo, but I didn't need an itemized list. There are some perks to having acquired a sixth sense.

The kitchen seemed the best place to start, and I found the boxes of silverware and dishes with no problem. They'd sat in the garage for months, and who knew how clean the hands were that had packed them, so into the dishwasher they went.

As I sorted the knives, forks and spoons, putting them into separate sections of the silverware rack, I considered all I knew about Walt Kaplan and the circumstances of his death. Not much. There were shortcuts I could take to obtain more information, and the easiest was to contact my ex-schoolmate Sam Nielsen, a reporter for the *Buffalo News*. The problem was, he'd want to deal and I didn't yet have anything to offer him.

What the hell, I figured, and dumped in the dishwashing powder, shutting the door with my foot. I hit the start button then picked up the phone. It was answered on the first ring.

"Newsroom. Sam Nielsen."

"Hey, Sam, it's Jeff Resnick."

A long pause followed, then, cautiously he said, "Long time no hear from. Got any hot tips for me?"

"Don't play the slots at Batavia Downs."

His tone changed. "Okay, what do you need?"

"Have I ever called you for a favor?"

"No, but there's always a first time and this is it, right?"

The silence between us lengthened. I could hear other phones ringing in the newsroom, the chatter of a busy office.

"Is there a story for me in this?" Sam asked finally.

"Maybe. Eventually. Tell me what you know about Walt Kaplan's death. He was the bartender in Williamsville who—"

"I know, I know." Sam exhaled a long breath. "Look, I didn't write the piece."

"I know that. What's the office scuttlebutt? The articles only said stabbed multiple times and other wounds. How many is multiple?"

"Forty-six."

"Jeez. He must've really pissed somebody off. Any defense wounds on the hands or arms?"

"No."

"A stiletto, wasn't it?"

"Yeah. That wasn't reported in the media. The fact you know means you're looking into this, huh?" Sam knew about my…gift. So far he hadn't tried to exploit it—or me—much.

"Kind of. I took his job."

"And what does your intuition tell you about his death?"

"I'm not ready to talk about it yet."

"But you will sometime in the future."

"Possibly. What about those other wounds mentioned in the articles."

"Burns."

"What kind?"

"Hey, I told you this wasn't my story. But I'll tell you what, I'll keep my eyes open. If anything develops, I'll let you know. By the same token—if you find out anything, I'd better be the one you call."

"Guaranteed."

***

Like at most other bars, the Friday crowd at the Whole Nine Yards was larger and more exuberant than the regular weekday group. And they wanted to talk—about Walt.

I could tell Tom was uncomfortable recounting what he knew about the murder—several times during the day—but who could blame the customers for their curiosity. None of them had ever known a murder victim. I didn't contribute to the conversation, listening carefully in case Tom mentioned something I hadn't yet heard, but it seemed I knew more about Walt's death than even he did.

"To a great guy," said one T-shirted man in jeans and geeky-looking safety glasses. He raised his glass and a host of others raised theirs as well.

"I didn't know Walt," I said. "Tell me about him."

"Natty dresser. Always had a crease in his slacks."

"Great listener," another one of the guys piped up.

"Yeah, but he was also a walking encyclopedia of golf. Knew all the players for the last fifty years—and their stats. Could even tell you who won all the major tourneys and their scores."

"Did he play?" I asked Tom.

"Not that I know of."

I could see the appeal of the game to a man like Walt. Quiet, and for the most part, solitary. A player's greatest competition was himself.

I thought about the shoeboxes. I'd already determined I wasn't going to mention the red shoe to Tom, but the other one was fair game. "Did Walt ever have a girlfriend named Veronica?"

Discomfort flashed across Tom's features. He shook his head. "I don't think so." He looked around at the crowd. "Anybody need a refill?"

Okay, so he wasn't being straight with me. Eventually he'd have to. For the moment, I decided to let it slide.

The testimonials continued throughout the afternoon. Walt was a helluva guy. He didn't deserve what he got. Why hadn't the cops arrested someone? But in all the talk there was something missing: the essence of who Walt really was. He'd been part of the scenery around the bar. He didn't talk much, didn't make waves, and yet someone had been angry enough to stab him over and over again. Why hadn't he fought back, why hadn't he tried to protect himself?

And all he'd left behind for me to try to find his killer was the image of the damned red shoe.

Chapter Five

Maggie's little blue Hyundai pulled into Richard's driveway at precisely eight fifty-nine the next morning. "Right on time," she said as she got out of the car. She looked terrific in a sleeveless white blouse over light blue slacks with her red-polished toes poking out of a pair of white sandals. The outfit looked a bit cool for the mountains—or should I say tall hills—of Holiday Valley, but she grabbed a white sweater along with her purse before slamming the car door.

I opened the passenger door of my car and ushered her in, wondering if my next gig should be valet parking. Within moments, we were on our way.

The Thruway traffic was heavy, and I forced myself to concentrate on driving, not easy when Maggie, an emotional powder keg, sat a mere foot from me. The tension continued to build with each passing mile.

"Why Holiday Valley?" she blurted at last, looking at me askance.

I kept my eyes on the road, grateful the traffic had begun to thin. I kept my voice calm. "Just a hunch."

"I asked Brenda about this." She paused. I risked a look to see her lip had curled. "This psychic thing you think you have. She believes it."

"What about you?"

"I want to see it in action."

"Well don't count on it." I hoped she caught the annoyance in my voice. "It shows up when it wants to and comes with some pretty dreadful aftereffects." I glanced back at her. Her expression was still skeptical. That I could accept. If it hadn't happened to me, I'd have been skeptical, too.

"It's been years since I visited Ellicottville," she said. "As I recall, it's quite charming. Lots of cute little boutiques, restaurants, and bed and breakfasts."

"I've never been there."

"Then we're both in for a treat." Her lips turned up—a very pretty smile, and for the first time in three months, I felt the chill she'd been directing toward me warm. I smiled, too.

The rest of the journey passed with Maggie humming along with the songs on the radio. She seemed glad for a day out of harness. My internal pressure intensified as I considered my mission. I'd be looking for a mailbox among the thousands lining the roads of this winter vacationland. Of course, without snow they'd be a lot more visible. But I wasn't sure I'd recognize the right one even if I saw it.

I slowed the car as we entered the village. Maggie's eyes widened in delight as she took in the quaint little shops. I kept up with the rest of the traffic—a crawl. "Ooooh. Pretty," Maggie cooed, craning her neck. "Did you see that gorgeous landscape in that little gallery's window?"

I braked. "No, I'm driving."

"We keep passing parking spots. Aren't we going to stop?"

"I hadn't planned on it. At least not right away." I glanced at her.

Maggie's brows had narrowed. "Why not?"

"I came here to find something."

"What?"

"A mailbox."

"What's the big deal? Just go to the address."

"I don't know the address."

She turned her head to stare straight ahead. The big chill was back.

"Don't worry. I'll find it."

I got no reaction from Maggie. I was going to look like a real jerk if I didn't find the damn thing.

The charming storefronts diminished and I accelerated as we left the village behind us.

For the next hour we drove slowly up and down the hillsides, trying to peer through the trees and foliage to see the expensive homes. Mostly we saw mailboxes and long narrow drives posted with "No Trespassing" signs. But that was okay; I was looking for a specific address. I just didn't know what street it would be on.

Maggie kept sighing restlessly, but I was too preoccupied to give her much notice. Probably not the way to win her heart.

We drove up yet another steep road. The sequence of numbers on the mailboxes fell into line: 4517, 4527, 4537. "That's it!"

I jammed on the brakes. Maggie's seatbelt locked as she lurched forward. "Hey!"

Slamming the car into park, I yanked off my seatbelt and jumped out.

Another car slowed, its driver staring at me as I ran my fingers over the freshly painted numbers on the rather battered old mailbox. Less visible were the faded letters of a name, probably painted decades before: T-GG-RT.

Cynthia Lennox's maiden name was Taggert.

***

Being a Saturday, of course the town hall was closed. I wondered if Ellicottville listed their tax information online. If not, then I'd have to return to the area. Still, the return trip would be worth it if it gave me the answers I wanted.

Maggie's stomach gurgled, and not for the first time.

"How about lunch?" I asked.

"Finally," she muttered.

One slice of Quiche Lorraine and a side salad later and Maggie was a charming human being once again. I made a note to self: Never let the woman go hungry and I might just stay in her good graces.

We were the last of the quaint little bistro's midday crowd. Maggie sipped her tea, studying me over the cup's rim. "How did you know?"

I gave her a blank stare. "Know what?"

"Finding that mailbox made you very happy. But it means more to you than just some silly treasure hunt. Why? What's its significance?"

I shrugged, folding my napkin over the half liverwurst sandwich I hadn't been able to finish. "I'm not sure. Yet. I have some suspicions, but I don't have enough information to put it all together. I—"

The heat from her gaze was enough to scorch. Apart from my initial reaction upon finding the mailbox, I thought I'd done a pretty good job at hiding what finding it meant to me. "How did you know finding it made me happy?"

Maggie leaned back in her chair, her expression guarded.

The air between us seemed to shimmer.

My mouth went dry.

She knew.

She'd sensed what I'd felt.

"Have you ever had a psychic experience before?" I asked her.

Maggie looked even more uncomfortable. "No. *I* have not. But when I'm near you…I don't know how to explain it. You do something weird to me. It's awful and nice at the same time. I don't think I like you very much, but…maybe I'm attracted to you because of it."

"Thanks. I think."

Her cheeks colored. "I'm sorry. That didn't come out right. I'm afraid of you, and yet…oh, I don't know."

"Why did you agree to come out with me today? To test it?"

Her gaze wouldn't meet mine. "Maybe."

I reached over, took her hand. Her head jerked up and she gasped, her mouth dropping open. Her fingers felt fever hot against mine. She was afraid and yet fascinated. "What do you feel, Maggie?"

Her breaths were more like pants. "You."

I let go of her hand, remembering how my first experiences with this…whatever it was, had freaked me out. We'd briefly shared something similar once before—but I hadn't given it much thought. Obviously she had. I wasn't sure I liked it any better than she did. Then again, it was kind of a kick to know I connected with someone on more than just a physical level.

"What do we do about…this?" she asked, her voice sounding small.

"I don't know. What do you want to do?"

"I don't think I can answer that. At least not today." She gathered her purse and sweater. "Can we go home now?"

"Yeah." I signaled the waitress, who brought the check. I paid the bill and followed Maggie to the door.

Maggie didn't look at me during the long, quiet ride back to Buffalo. When I pulled up Richard's driveway, she mumbled a "thanks for the lunch" and got out of my car. I watched as her car pulled away.

She never looked back.

Chapter Six

My weekend didn't improve on Sunday. I awoke with the grumbling inside my head that always foretold a migraine. I took my medication and stayed in my darkened, quiet room until I absolutely had to get up to go to the bar for my shift.

Tom was on the phone when I got there—ten minutes late—and waved me to take over out front. Several customers were already perched on stools, watching the golf pre-match commentary on the bar's big-screen TV. I leaned against the backbar, massaging my temples, wondering if I could get away with wearing sunglasses in the darkened bar, and praying it would be a slow day.

No such luck. Six leather- and denim-clad bikers barreled through the side entrance, grabbing a table near the big front window. Boisterous and full of energy, their voices clawed at my already ragged nerves. I had to force myself to approach the screaming white glare of the window. "What can I get you guys?"

"A couple of pitchers of Coors," said the one closest to me, a grizzled, bearded guy with a faded blue bandana tied around his head. Even seated he looked twice my size. His tattoos and leathers were Harley Davidson all the way and he was celebrating, pure joy bombarding my senses like a tsunami. Birth of a grandson? I wasn't sure. But even pleasant emotions can overwhelm when they're directed with battering force. I turned abruptly to get away from the mental assault.

Filling the pitchers took an eternity; the smell of hops seemed overly strong for such a mainstream lager. I balanced them and six glasses on a tray and started for the table when my sneaker toe caught on the rubber mat behind the bar. Time shifted into slow motion and I watched, horror-struck, as the tray flew from my hands, the beer rising out of the pitchers like geysers. The glasses tumbled end over end and seemed to take a lot longer than me to hit the floor. The spectacular, shattering crash threatened to split my already aching skull. Thank God I shut my eyes as beer drenched me and glass shards peppered my face.

Except for the drone of the TV commentators, the bar had gone silent. I lay on the floor, dripping with blood or beer—I wasn't sure which—for what seemed like eons. Then the strongest arms in the world pulled me to my feet.

"Hey, man, are you okay?" The big biker leaned me against the bar, found a cloth and was gently mopping at my face. "Did you get glass in your eyes?"

I shook my head—a definite mistake. "I'm okay."

"What the hell?" Suddenly Tom stood behind the biker. "What happened?"

"I tripped."

"Good grief! It sounded like the end of the world. You okay?"

"Yeah, yeah." The biker pressed the cloth into my hand, and I mopped at my dripping arms and neck. "Sorry, Tom, I—"

"Don't worry about it. I'll take care of the customers. Go in back and grab a T-shirt, then get the mop and broom out, willya?"

"Sure thing." I gave the biker a grateful smile. "Thanks."

"No problem," he said and picked his way through the beer and glass to head back to his seat.

Avoiding the gazes of the other patrons, I slunk off in back and peeled off my shirt to hose myself off in the slop sink. I returned a few minutes later in one of the bar's giveaway shirts, mop and broom in hand. My hands were shaking as I cleaned up the mess. Tom had the bikers laughing once again. He, too, was in a celebratory mood that even the mess behind the bar hadn't doused.

Sheepishly, I took my place by the taps, feeling the eyes of several customers upon me. My smile was forced—probably a grimace. Tom was still engaged in conversation with the bikers, who had resumed their rowdy revelry. I turned my back to the customers and closed my eyes as waves and waves of emotions engulfed me. Joy from the bikers; misery—a gambling debt?—and worry; someone's wife was dangerously ill.

The pounding in my head intensified, leaving me nauseous and shaky. Someone nudged my elbow. I turned. Tom.

"Good news, Jeff. Your services are no longer required."

The pounding paused for half a second, then shifted into overdrive. Shit. I'd smashed some glassware and now he was firing me. My shock and disappointment must've registered: Tom laughed.

"I mean looking into Walt's death. The cops arrested someone last night. But you're welcome to stay on at the bar, if you want."

I swallowed with relief. Then the red shoe image slammed my mind's eye with the force of a jackhammer. "Tell me more about the arrest."

"Some homeless geek. Been hanging around Williamsville for the past couple of months. The dumb shit still had the murder weapon on him."

"A stiletto?"

Tom nodded, smug.

It didn't feel right. Not only was I still getting flashes of insight, they'd led me to the mailbox in Ellicottville and possibly property owned by Cyn Lennox. While I couldn't be sure without more information, my gut told me they had the wrong person. I pondered that thought for a second. Not man, not woman. Person. Yeah. I definitely needed more information.

Tom frowned. "You don't look so good."

I swallowed down the bile threatening to erupt. "Sorry, Tom. I want to keep the job here, but I don't think I can put in my hours today."

The eyes that met mine were not judgmental. "I knew when I hired you that you had health problems. I won't be a prick and make you stay when obviously you're not up to it. Can you get home by yourself? Want me to call your family?"

I shook my head and winced. "I can make it home."

"Don't be stupid." Tom placed a hand on my elbow, steered me to the back room and plunked me into a chair.

It was all I could do not to throw up on his carpet. I heard his voice, couldn't understand the words, then he was gone.

I covered my eyes and bent over, concentrated on breathing. In out, in out. I was not going to puke. An eternity later, a tap on my shoulder alerted me to buff-colored Dockers at my side. Richard. "Let's go home."

Too sick to be angry or even embarrassed—that would come later—I let him lead me out the bar's back door. All too soon I felt the sensation of acceleration. I was in the passenger seat of my car with Richard at the wheel, and no memory of how I got there.

"How'd—?"

"Brenda's driving my car back. What happened to your face?"

I rolled down the window, hot air blasting my eyes. "Long story." But I didn't offer it. I was too busy trying to quell the urge to purge my stomach. I leaned back against the upholstery, concentrated on breathing only. A million years later, Richard braked and I saw the shimmering outline of his house out the driver's side window beyond me. Richard got out, slammed the door with a deafening bang and seconds later hauled me out and was leading me up the steps and through the door. Half a minute later I was on my bed, head hanging over the edge. Richard grabbed my left hand, placed the wastebasket in it.

"Just in case," he said.

I closed my eyes and his footsteps faded away. Time stopped for a couple of decades. I wasn't truly asleep, but I wasn't awake, either. Caught in a limbo that threatened but refused to deliver blessed oblivion, my mind kept recycling thoughts and images of the sparkling red shoe, glistening, scarlet-drenched hands, and a blood-drained Walt, his vacant eyes forever focused on an empty eternity.

***

The sun had been up at least three hours when I cracked my eyes open the next morning. I wasn't sure how bad I felt—but I knew it was better than I'd been the day before. Before the thought of food or even coffee entered my mind, I needed to find out about the arrest Tom had told me about the day before.

I sat on the edge of my bed, phone in hand, and punched in a number I'd memorized months before.

"Newsroom. Sam Nielsen."

"The cops made an arrest?"

"Jeff? I was going to call you. You need a cell phone."

I closed my eyes against the onslaught of light leaking around the back window. "You can always reach me here. Besides, cell phones take money and I've only had a job for four days."

"Your brother's sitting on millions. He can't buy you one?"

Sam and I weren't close enough for me to get into that situation. "Just tell me what you know."

"Schizophrenic homeless guy. Name's Craig Buchanan. He had the murder weapon on him."

"A stiletto."

"You got it. But he didn't do it, right?"

"I don't think so."

"You got a line on who did?"

"Not yet. What else can you tell me?"

"Just the guy's next of kin. A sister in Cheektowaga—not far from you." Paper rustled, as he must've consulted his notes. "Cara Scott. I'll save you some time." He gave me her address. "The story's in today's edition. You can check it online now."

"I'll do that." He was being too helpful. What would he want in return?

I pushed some more. "The cops gave Kaplan's cousin his house keys. Did they say anything about his wallet or the missing ring?"

"Nothing on the wallet. The ring hasn't been hocked—at least not yet. I guess the keys were on the body, along with pocket change. You know, Jeff, we should work together on this."

The memory of Richard's blood-soaked trench coat was still too fresh for me to want to take up anyone's offer of help. As it was, had I put Maggie in danger by allowing her to come with me to Holiday Valley?

"I thought you said this wasn't your story."

"It wasn't. The guy who had it went on a cruise. The Caribbean in June, can you believe it? So what've you got?"

"Nothing I can talk about yet. Just some impressions that don't add up."

"Yet."

"Yeah. Yet."

"The two of us would make a helluva team," he tried again. "I don't have to name my sources, you know."

"I know. But I don't have anything concrete to give you yet."

"Yeah, well keep me in mind. I'll be talking to you, Jeff." The receiver clicked in my ear.

***

I wasn't ready to talk to Craig Buchanan's next of kin. Instead, I called Tom to apologize, but he blew me off and told me not to bother to come in that day as he'd already asked Dave the other bartender to step in, but I'd better show up the next day. Fair enough. I was just grateful I still had a job.

After showering, I inspected the small cuts on my face, which were no worse than razor nicks. But the patches of redness were not attractive. So what. It's not like I'd be going on a date with Maggie—or anyone else—any time soon.

The thought of food didn't turn my stomach, so I downed my medication with a chaser of Cheerios and two cups of coffee, then appropriated Richard's computer to read Sam's article. It didn't tell me much more than I already knew. Next up I tried to find a web site with information on the Cattaraugus County tax base to track down the owner of the house at 4537 Alpine Road. If it was there, I couldn't find it.

Sophie was convinced Walt had a foot fetish and Google gave me an assortment of URLs to try. Each was set up like any standard porn site. Lots of shots of hot lesbians licking toes, naked bi chicks sucking toes, contorted women sucking their own toes. Walt didn't have a computer. Did he buy the magazines with skinny, scantily clad or naked chicks on the cover, tongues hanging out seductively and masturbate to his heart's delight? And if he did, where did he hide them?

Footsteps approached from the hall and Richard wandered into his study. "You must be feeling better this morning." I turned to see him do a classic double take as he focused in on the image on his nineteen-inch monitor. "What are you doing with my computer?"

I leaned back in his big leather chair and swung around to face him, struggling not to grin. "Checking out foot fetish web sites. Wanna look?"

"No, thank you. Is there a reason for this sudden interest in feet?"

"Walt Kaplan. It seems like it might've been his Achilles heel, if you'll pardon the pun."

Richard shoved his hands into the pockets of his slacks. "Oh-kay. I suppose you know they've made an arrest."

"Yeah, but they've got the wrong guy."

Richard scowled. "And you're going to keep pursuing this."

"They've got the wrong guy," I repeated, enunciating clearly.

"That really isn't your concern. Did your boss ask you to keep looking into it?"

I let out a sigh and got up from his chair. "He wants to believe the cops have solved the crime. I haven't told him everything I've found out yet. When I do—"

"He may still tell you to give it up. Will you?"

I didn't answer.

"Jeff."

"I don't know."

Richard frowned. "What do you get out of it? You've already got the man's job. Does it give you a vicarious thrill to play investigator?"

I exhaled a breath and chose my words carefully. "It used to be my job."

"And it isn't anymore. Maybe it's time you accepted the fact you have limitations. If nothing else, yesterday should've proved that to you."

Anger and shame burned through me as I pushed past him. "Thanks for the use of the computer."

"You're welcome."

I tramped through the house with a single thought: escape. The next thing I knew, I was in my car and driving north toward Main Street with no clue as to where I was going. I pulled over and switched off the ignition. Since the mugging, I was prone to anger outbursts. The quack back in New York had warned me about it. But had it really been necessary for Richard to rub my nose in the fact that I wasn't yet capable of holding a full-time job?

Memories of decades-old hurts surfaced. Our first Christmas together, when Richard canceled plans we'd made to spend the day together just so he could suck up to a surgeon he never ended up working with. The times his family's chauffeur showed up at school to cheer me on when he was too busy working to make it himself.

I thought I'd let it all go, but there it was rubbing my ego raw once again.

Playing investigator, huh?

Well screw him! If nothing else, I'd find Walt Kaplan's murderer and bring the bastard to justice just to shove it up Richard's ass once and for all. And I had a place to start, too. Sam's story had mentioned a witness. I started the car and headed for Main Street.

***

The Sweet Tooth Chocolate Shoppe was devoid of customers, but the silver-haired, well-rounded proprietress greeted me with enthusiasm even before the bell over the door had stopped jangling.

"Welcome! I'm Sue. Let me know if I can be of any help," she offered from behind the glass counter.

The rich, fudgy scent of chocolate was heavy in the air. The day before it would've sent me to the curb to purge my gut. I could handle it now. I'm not a candy freak, but the aroma took me back to something good from my childhood, though the exact memory had been lost thanks to a baseball bat slamming into my skull three months earlier.

I gazed into the multi-shelf display case at the mountains of bonbons and truffles, milk, dark and white chocolate, creams and caramels—the presentation alone was worth the exorbitant price per pound. I took a deep breath, exhaling loudly. "It smells so good in here, I'm not sure what I should get."

"Are you looking for a gift?"

"For a special lady." Brenda wasn't likely to turn down chocolate. It would cost me at least a pound's worth to get the information I wanted—but in the long run, a cheap price to pay. "I'll take a pound—your choice."

"You can't go wrong with our ultimate selection."

"Let's go for it."

I watched as she brought out a flattened box with embossed gold script proclaiming the shop's name. She twisted it into shape and slipped in a piece of baker's tissue before selecting a number of chocolate covered morsels from the mounded glass plates until she'd filled the box.

"I take it this is your first visit," she said, securing the lid.

"I read about you in the *Buffalo News*. That story about the homeless man they arrested for murder."

She shook her head, her welcoming smile fading. "I didn't think they'd quote me."

"It sounded like you knew the guy."

"He Dumpster-dived in all the area merchants' trash. I suppose that's the only food he got. I felt a little sorry for him." Her expression soured further. "But the smell."

"Smell?"

"A combination of body odor, pee and—" She shuddered.

"He never changed clothes?"

"Not in the four or five months he hung around the neighborhood."

"Was he arrested in those clothes?"

"Of course."

And I'd bet there wasn't a drop of Walt Kaplan's blood on any of them. "Do you remember what they looked like?"

"I saw him nearly every day," she said, taking my purchase over to the cash register. "Grubby jeans, a stained tan sweater, and one of those long, black duster coats. Even when the weather warmed up, he still wore it." She lowered her voice. "It probably came in handy for shoplifting."

Sue rang up the sale and I extracted all the tip money from my wallet. "You've got a great shop here. I'm sure I'll be back again."

"Thanks. Have a nice day now."

Back in my car, I wrote down Sue's description of the suspect's clothing. Maybe Sam and I could work together on this. He had a pipeline to the cops, and I wanted to keep a low profile. I reset my trip odometer and headed back to the Old Red Mill. It clocked in at six-tenths of a mile when I parked by a motorcycle in the lane off the main drag. Buchanan had probably tramped up and down Main Street in search of food and a dry place to sleep.

I got out and walked around to the side of the mill. The fresh red paint and white trim lent the place a cheerful atmosphere. That Walt Kaplan's body had been found on the property didn't detract from its ambiance.

The grass still hadn't been cut, but the crime scene tape was missing. Probably Cyn Lennox had wanted to remove any evidence of Walt's death. Already the parking spaces in front of the mill weren't as full as they'd been when Richard and I had visited four days earlier.

I made my way down the incline to the spot where I believed Walt's body had lain, closed my eyes, breathing deeply, and tried to soak up something, anything. Something niggled at the edges of my mind. I crouched down and laid a hand on the grass. An image of the red shoe exploded in my mind. Shit! Other than finding the box it had been purchased in, the shoe didn't mean anything to me. But it had to Walt. It must've been pretty damned important to him for the memory of it to linger even after he'd died.

"Are you back again?"

I straightened and turned to find an irritated Cyn Lennox standing, hands on hips, on the mill's back porch. "Good morning."

"What are you doing here?"

I feigned innocence. "Nothing."

"Then why are you here?"

"I told you. Morbid curiosity."

"Which should have been satisfied on your last visit. Look, Richard's my friend; you're not. And I'd appreciate it if you'd stop hanging around my property."

"I was hoping to speak to your miller. Has he returned from his trip?"

"Yes," she grudgingly admitted. "But why should I let you talk to him?"

"Because we live in a free country, and presumably he and you have nothing to hide."

Her eyes widened, her cheeks going red. It was either a hot flash or I'd just made an enemy.

"Get out of here."

Yup, she'd definitely never be my friend now.

"I'm sure you heard they made an arrest."

"Yeah. Which means you should give up your Sherlock Holmes routine and just go home."

"I don't think they arrested the right man. Or should I say woman?"

Fury boiled beneath her seemingly in-control facade. "You keep talking and I'll have one helluva fine lawsuit against you."

"Wishful thinking," I bluffed. "We both know you haven't told the police everything you know about Walt Kaplan's murder."

"What I did or didn't tell them is none of your damn business. Get off my property—NOW—or I'm calling the cops."

I waved a hand in submission. "Sure, but we'll talk again. I guarantee it."

"Not if I can help it."

There was no point in annoying her further. I walked back to my car, feeling the heat of her stare on my back with every step. Confronting her hadn't given me any new information, but it had confirmed what my gut kept telling me: however convoluted, Cyn Lennox had some involvement in Walt Kaplan's death—as either a participant or a witness. Only time would tell which.

In the meantime, I'd made an enemy. Not a smart move if she'd had a hand in Walt's death. But I didn't feel threatened. Not yet at least.

***

Since I didn't have to be anywhere else that day, I figured I'd look up Craig Buchanan's sister. Cara Scott's white colonial stood in stark contrast from every other house on the street in Buffalo's Cheektowaga suburb. Forest green paint on the trim was its only decoration. No trees, shrubs, or flowers adorned the yard, but the grass was freshly cut and there wasn't a stray blade on the driveway. The woman who answered my knock looked just as severe, with her dark brown hair scraped back into a ponytail and no makeup. Her navy slacks and sleeveless white shirt were crisp with a just-ironed look to them.

"Cara Scott? My name's Jeff Resnick. Can I ask you a few questions?"

"I don't have any more comments for the press," she said, about to slam the door in my face.

"I'm not from the press. I'm a friend of the murdered man." Okay, not a friend. But I had his interests at heart.

She avoided my eyes. "I'm sorry. I—"

"Can we talk for a few moments?"

Cara sighed, her weary face seeming to age five years in five seconds. She stepped out onto the concrete porch. "I'm sorry," she repeated, her lips going thin. "I've spent most of my life apologizing for Craig, but that's all I can offer you."

"I'm not so sure. You see, I don't think Craig killed Walt Kaplan."

Her head snapped up and she gazed at me with suspicion. "The police wouldn't have arrested him if they weren't sure. What makes you think he didn't do it?"

I had nothing concrete. "Just a hunch."

"This'll sound cruel, but getting caught for this murder is probably the best thing that could've happened to Craig. He'll be in a place where he can be cared for—he'll be off the streets."

"And he won't be your problem anymore," I guessed.

She crossed her arms across her chest. "I'd be lying if I didn't agree. You have no idea of the hell Craig has put my family through. My father left us when Craig was seven. My mother bailed him out of one mess after another. He drove her to bankruptcy and finally suicide because she couldn't take it any longer. He disrupts my life—my kids' lives. It would be easier on us and society in general if the cops locked him up and threw away the key."

"But what if he's innocent?"

"Don't be absurd. They found the knife on him."

"He might've come across it picking through Dumpsters."

Her level glare was as cold and uninviting as her sterile house and yard.

"He's your brother," I tried again, thinking about Richard and what, in a short time, he'd come to mean to me.

"Excuse me, Mr. Resnick, but I really don't have time for this."

She slammed the door in my face.

"Enjoy your freedom, Mrs. Scott."

As I climbed back behind the wheel of my car, I couldn't help but think that arresting Craig Buchanan solved everyone's problem. Tom was satisfied someone, anyone, had been arrested for Walt Kaplin's murder; the police were happy to close the books; and Cara Scott was finally free of her space cadet brother.

The problem remained—he didn't do it. And there was still a murderer hanging around lovely, picturesque Williamsville.

Chapter Seven

Evening shadows filled the backyard as I worked at emptying my third bag of mulch, carefully nestling a blanket of fragrant cedar fragments around my begonias. The smell of damp earth reminded me that Walt Kaplan had been committed to the ground less than a week before, and that maybe I was the only one who cared if his killer was caught. I left a message on Sam's voice mail, asking him to find out about bloodstains on Buchanan's clothes; now to wait and see if he followed up on it.

Brenda approached me from the house. I hadn't seen her all day, but had left the box of candy on the kitchen counter with a note. She paused about five feet away and gazed down the east border, which had taken me more than an hour to weed, then focused on the clump of flowers in front of me. She'd wanted a garden and Richard had given me *carte blanche* to make it happen. I'd staggered the pink and white begonias with darker vincas. After years of neglect, the perennials were in sad shape. In the back of my mind I had a plan for how I wanted to bring the garden back to its former grandeur over the next couple of years, but it would take careful planning.

"Such industry. I can't believe what you've accomplished in this yard in such a short time. Wherever did you garden in Manhattan?"

I looked over my shoulder at her. "I didn't."

"Then how do you know so much about it?"

I scattered a handful of mulch around a pink-veined coleus. "For years I saved for a house in Jersey. Shelley and me and a picket fence, and maybe a pack of kids. I read up on gardening. Figured it might make a good hobby."

"Has it?"

"It's only been three weeks, but…yeah. I like it—it's calming. Plants don't give off weird vibes like people do."

"And they don't say things to upset people, either."

Brenda hated it when Richard and I had disagreements, and this was her chance to play peacemaker. She watched as I dumped the rest of the bag, trailing its contents over a six-foot area. "Why didn't you come in for supper?"

"I wasn't hungry."

"There's leftovers if you want something later."

I didn't meet her gaze. "Thanks."

"Richard doesn't understand," she said. "He thinks you should just ignore those funny feelings and the insight you get. I know you can't."

I leaned back on my heels and looked up at her, saw the depth of concern in her dark eyes.

"He's worried about leaving you alone for two weeks when we go on our honeymoon," she continued. "After yesterday—"

"Oh come on. It's only the second time in three months it happened. I'll get a handle on it eventually. But

I don't need him holding my hand for the rest of my life, either."

"I know. I trust you to make the decisions you need to. When we're here, we're your backup. I just hope you'll take care of yourself while we're gone. Promise me."

I exhaled. It wasn't exactly admitting defeat to say what she wanted to hear, but it felt like it. "Okay. I promise."

She patted my shoulder, her genuine concern and caring washing over me like a warm, pleasant breeze. "Thank you. And thanks for the chocolates. They're really decadent."

"You're welcome."

A cardinal scolded us from the silver maple next door. Brenda had something else on her mind. I can always pick up on her anxiety.

"You want to ask about Maggie, right?"

"I think she'd like to talk to you," she said.

"And you're playing go-between?"

"Sort of."

Brenda waited while I finished spreading the mulch, and then offered a hand to pull me to my feet. "Ugh. How can you stand dirt under your fingernails?"

I shrugged. "I don't like gardening gloves. They get in the way."

"Then I hope your tetanus shot is up-to-date."

She was stalling.

I grabbed the empty plastic bags and headed for the garage. Brenda trotted along behind me. "Are you going to call her?"

"I don't know." I shoved the bags into the garbage tote and glanced at my watch: Seven-thirty. Maybe I'd call her.

Maybe I wouldn't. "I'm going up to the apartment to empty more boxes. Want to help?"

Brenda frowned. "If I do, you won't call her."

She was probably right.

"Okay, I'll think about it."

She nodded. "Then I won't nag you anymore tonight."

"Does that mean tomorrow's fair game?"

She smiled. "Always."

***

I was beginning to really like what would be my new digs. It was actually double the size of my Manhattan apartment, and every time I entered the space I felt at peace. I knew I could live here and be happy, and yet…it wasn't quite home. The elusive piece of the puzzle was still missing. Maybe once I had all the furniture in place it would feel complete. Still, I wasn't in a hurry to move in.

The only things to sit on were the new stools at the breakfast bar. So far I hadn't needed any more. I plunked down and found my gaze traveling to the telephone. I'd been waiting months for the opportunity to call Maggie, but I hesitated. Timing could be everything, and I didn't want to rush into anything. Then again, if I made her wait too long, would she lose interest?

The trip to Ellicottville had piqued her curiosity about me. Maybe she thought experiencing someone else's emotions could be kinky.

Hmm. I hadn't considered that aspect of my so-called *gift*.

I shook the thought away. I'd begun moving some of the stuff from my room in the big house over; among them were Walt's shoeboxes and the envelope of his financial papers. I'd examined the box with the Holiday Valley brochure from every angle and done everything but wear the damn thing. The absurdity of that thought made me laugh. Then I figured what the hell, dropped the box on the floor and kicked off my grass-stained right sneaker. I stuck my foot in the empty box with no expectations. Instantly, the vision slammed into my consciousness with the greatest clarity yet. *Bare, red-painted toenails slipped into the sparkling shoe, guided by a man's rough hands. With exaggerated care he buckled the thin red strap around the ankle. The toes wiggled in what seemed like delight while the man's hands traveled up to caress the shapely calf.*

When I kicked the box off my foot, the vision winked out. I exhaled a breath and flexed my own toes. Would these dreamscapes eventually escalate into soft- or hard-core porn? That could be interesting, but I didn't really want to experience that aspect of Walt's personality.

And how did Walt's foot fetish relate to his death?

My hands were still shaking as I resumed my seat and put on my shoe. The creep factor was back in full force. A beer would be just the thing to eradicate it. Too bad I hadn't put anything, let alone a six-pack, into the new fridge.

To distract myself, I spread Walt's financial papers across the breakfast bar, sorting through them to find the checking account statement. I'd glanced at the miniature replica checks before and hadn't noticed anything out of the ordinary. This time I studied them more carefully, wishing I knew in which of my unpacked boxes I'd find a magnifying glass. I went through all the checks and this time one did stand out: Amherst Self Storage.

Well, well, well. And just what could Walt be storing? Tom hadn't asked me to return Walt's keys, and I hadn't surrendered them. The problem was, how many storage units did this place have, and how would I find Walt's? Could I trust my insight to lead me to the right one?

There was only one way to find out.

***

The night air was cool for late June, and I shivered as I crossed the driveway for my car. I got in, started the engine and was backing out when I saw Richard silhouetted by the lamplight shining down on his side steps.

He jogged over as I braked, tapped on my window. "Where are you going?"

I rolled down the window. "Out."

"Where?"

Anger flared through me. "Why don't you jump in and find out."

Incredibly, he walked around to the passenger side and got in. I watched in awe as he fastened his seatbelt. "Go," he said and gestured with his hand.

I backed out of the driveway. "What's Brenda going to say when she finds you've gone?"

"Oh. Yeah." He maneuvered around the seatbelt, took out his cell phone and called her. "I'm going out with Jeff. Be back in an hour—" He looked at me.

I nodded.

"Yeah, an hour. Bye." He pocketed the phone and glared at me. "Where are we going?"

"Amherst Self Storage on Transit Road. Walt Kaplan rented a unit there."

"How do you know?"

"From the check statement you copped the other day. I looked the place up in the phone book."

"And what do you hope to find in there?"

"I'm just hoping to find it."

Richard rolled his eyes. "I should've told Brenda two hours."

I concentrated on my driving. "Oh ye of little faith." It would've been nice if I'd felt as confident as I sounded.

After that, the conversation ceased. I risked a couple of glances at Richard and he was just as studiously ignoring me. My earlier conversation with Brenda kept recycling through my mind. Finally, I couldn't stand the quiet. "Ya know, I was quite capable of taking care of myself before I came back to Buffalo. I still am."

"Yeah," Richard agreed, his voice full of scorn, "and Santa comes down my chimney on Christmas Eve. Want to sell me a bridge in Brooklyn, too?"

My hands tightened on the wheel. Choking the life out of him would only land me in jail for way too many years.

The gates of Amherst Self Storage were still open when I pulled in and parked. As we got out of the car, a string bean of a kid, no older than twenty, opened the door on what looked like a concrete pseudo guard tower. "We're closing in half an hour."

I waved him off and turned away. Richard followed.

The place was divided with inside and outside accommodations. The outside units had roll-up doors, but I got the feeling Walt had opted for something inside, with better climate control. I yanked open the plate glass commercial door and headed up the well-lit corridor.

"So?" Richard taunted, his voice echoing as he struggled to keep up with me.

"Okay—so I don't know where we're going. Just keep walking."

"Why I let myself get involved—" he grumbled.

I shot him a look over my shoulder. "Hey, I didn't ask you to come."

His glare intensified. "Do the words 'why don't you jump in' ring a bell?"

I kept walking, clasping Walt's keys in my hand, hoping they'd act as a divining rod to lead me to his storage unit. Funny thing is, they kind of did. The farther I walked along the corridor, the warmer they seemed to grow in my hand.

I slowed my pace and started paying attention to the unit numbers. I stopped before the one marked 4537: the same number on the mailbox in Holiday Valley. A coincidence? The mailbox had said—well, almost—Taggert. It had to have some connection with Cyn Lennox. Only now I wasn't sure if I trusted that piece of insight.

A brass padlock secured the aluminum hasp. I held the key ring in my left hand, sorting them until I came to the smallest one. I slipped it into the lock and it turned.

"Jesus, you amaze me," Richard murmured behind me.

I removed the lock, pulling the hasp open, then clasped the door handle, trying to pull it open. Something was jammed behind it. I yanked harder, but it still wouldn't give. "Dammit."

"Let me do it," Richard said, stepping forward, his condescending tone grating on my nerves.

I held him back. "You're just along for the ride, remember."

He looked like he wanted to haul off and hit me, but he did back off.

Grabbing the handle, I yanked it with all my might and the door jerked forward. A cascade of cardboard cartons came tumbling out. The next thing I knew, I'd hit the floor—pinned, the wind knocked out of me.

"Jeff!" Richard hollered, scrambling to extricate me.

I couldn't answer—there was no air in my lungs. I couldn't move at all.

Gasping and puffing, Richard pushed the heavy boxes off me and I rolled onto my side, knees drawn up to my chest, struggling just to breathe.

Richard was panting as hard as I was. "Are you okay?"

I nodded, but the truth was I didn't know. It felt like I'd broken a couple of ribs. Richard must've had the same thought. Next thing I knew, he had my shirt up and was palpating my chest, sending me into new spasms of agony.

"Doesn't feel like anything's out of place—but I'll bet it hurts."

"Eleven years of medical training and that's what you come up with?"

He yanked my shirt back down before collapsing next to me on the concrete floor, leaning against the opposite storage lockers. "Talk about the walking wounded. What a pair we make."

"Speak for yourself," I managed. "I don't think I'll ever get up again."

I caught sight of a security camera protruding from the ceiling nearby, but if the kid up front was monitoring the corridor, he hadn't raised an alarm or ventured out to help us. We sat there for a couple of minutes, trying to catch our breath before Richard helped me into a sitting position.

"You gonna be all right?" he asked.

"Yeah. Let's see what nearly killed me." I crawled over to the closest box. Walt had securely taped it. Using his keys, I worked at the tape until I'd slit it, and pulled open the carton.

Richard peered inside. "Porn?" he moaned.

Scores of copies of magazines with covers similar to the ones listed on the foot fetish web sites were stacked in the box, none of them newer than five years old. Had he moved on from magazines to…something else? "That's why his apartment was so clean," I said. "He kept his collection here. I wonder if he had other storage units?"

"There's got to be more than just magazines. Open another box."

I did. More out-of-date magazines. I pushed it aside. A lighter box contained foot-fetish videos. Another box held old financial records. Nothing very interesting. I tried one last carton. "Hey, look at this." I pulled out a heavy, metal professional shoe sizer. Also inside the box were more of the generic shoeboxes like I'd found in Walt's apartment. Each also had an odd collection of paper and souvenirs. I checked them all but their contents weren't as remarkable as the one with the Veronica pillow. One had a hand-written receipt: Received: $237.54 for custom shoes, dated three years before. "Whoa, this is what I've been looking for."

Richard looked over the faded slip of paper. "How can it help? It doesn't tell you where he bought them."

But it was as though the paper was vibrating against the skin of my fingers. "I hope I get an inkling when I get home and pull out the phone book."

"Closing in five minutes," came a voice from a speaker embedded in the ceiling. I put the receipt in my wallet.

"How are we going to get all this crap back in the storage space in only five minutes?" Richard groused.

"We could take some of it with us."

"I don't want this stuff at my house."

"Just until I can dump it."

"You're not dumping it in my garbage."

He glared at me. If looks could kill and all that shit...

Between the two of us, we managed to wedge all but the carton of shoeboxes back inside the unit and slam the door just as the lights winked out. I replaced the padlock and struggled to lift the bulky box. Not that it was heavy, but every part of me hurt.

Out of breath again, we sounded like a couple of asthmatics as we started back down the corridor. Yellow safety lights kept us from groping our way to the exit.

String bean was waiting for us outside the door, keys in hand to lock up. "I warned you we were closing." He turned his back on us and we headed for the car.

Richard watched as I maneuvered the box into the back seat and slammed the door. He was pale, his skin looking eerily white under the lot's mercury vapor lamps, and we were both sweating in the cool night air. Richard groaned as he settled himself into the passenger seat. Gingerly, I climbed behind the steering wheel and chanced a look at myself in the rearview mirror; my own face was chalky. Walking wounded sounded about right.

"Wanna go somewhere for a drink or something?" I asked Richard, wincing as I buckled the seatbelt around me.

"Just take me home."

I started the engine. "You didn't *have* to come."

"If I hadn't, you'd have been suffocated by those boxes."

He was right about that, not that I'd give him satisfaction by agreeing.

"This is the second time in two days I've had to pull your ass out of the fire. What the hell are you going to do for two weeks when I'm gone?"

"Give me a break. I got along fine for eighteen years without you. You think I can't make it for fourteen days?"

"No, I don't."

The light ahead turned yellow and I jammed on the brakes. Only Richard's seatbelt kept him from sailing through the windshield.

He glared at me. "It doesn't make sense."

"It's called inertia. I put my foot on the brake—you keep going."

"No, that Walt had all this stuff in storage, but there wasn't a trace of it in his place."

"What do you mean?"

"Well, from what I remember from abnormal psych, people with fetishes like their trigger objects near them. That kind of personality just can't turn it off, either."

"Do you think someone cleaned out the apartment before we got there?"

"I'm betting it was your boss. Are you sure he really wants this thing solved?"

No. I wasn't.

The light changed and I pressed the accelerator. I hadn't thought to look in the Dumpster behind Walt's place when we'd been there days before.

The rest of the drive back to the house was a replay of the drive out—silent. But despite a little lingering animosity, we were at least speaking to one another again.

I parked in front of the garage. Richard got out and shuffled toward the house. "You coming?" he called over his shoulder.

"I'm going upstairs. Be over in a while."

I left the carton in the back seat, too pooped to deal with it, and trudged up the stairs to the apartment. Easing myself onto a stool, I stretched to grab my brand new telephone book. Big mistake, as it set off more twinges of misery along my ribs. I squeezed my eyes shut and counted to ten. This was already getting old.

There were six listings under SHOES—CUSTOM MADE. All but one of them were generic and boring; only Broadway Theatrics sounded flashy enough to have made the sparkling high-heeled beauty in my visions.

I punched in the phone number. It rang three times before a recorded male voice spoke: "You've reached Broadway Theatrics. We're open by appointment only. Leave a message at the sound of the tone and we'll get back to you." Beep!

No point in leaving one now. I hung up, noting the address before closing the phone book. Maybe I'd just drive over there tomorrow after my stint at the bar. The more I thought about it, the more I warmed to the idea.

The clock on the microwave read nine twenty-five and I wondered if it was too late to call Maggie.

Probably. And what was I going to say to her anyway? "Hi, you're hot and I want you as much as you want me."

Yeah, that would go over well.

Then I figured what the hell—I'd already risked death once tonight; nothing else could faze me—and grabbed the phone, punching in the number I'd memorized three months before.

It rang twice before Maggie picked up. "Hello?"

"It's Jeff."

"Oh." She sounded startled—or maybe disappointed.

"I can call back another time."

"No, now is fine. Uh, hi."

"Hi." Now what? *I'd* called *her*. Say something you idiot!

"Are you okay? You sound funny."

"I tangled with some boxes."

"Oh yeah. Brenda said you'd be unpacking tonight. Listen, did you find out who owned that property outside of Ellicottville?"

"I haven't had a chance to go back yet."

"Well, I have a cousin whose husband works for the Cattaraugus County Highway Department, and his sister works for the Ellicottville Town Clerk, and he—"

"Whoa—slow down. I can't keep track of all those people."

She laughed. "You don't have to. Bottom line—I found out who owns the house and where the tax bill is sent."

For a moment I was speechless. "Cynthia Lennox?"

"How did you know? Oh yeah," she said and laughed again, "I forgot. You're psychic."

"Never use the 'p' word in front of me," I chided her.

"Want the address?"

"Definitely." I jotted it down. Cyn lived somewhere in the northern part of Amherst. "How can I ever repay you for this?"

"That's not necessary. Although…maybe we could go out again sometime. Maybe another magical mystery tour."

My heart rate picked up. "I'd like that. A lot."

"Yeah, me too."

So ask her out already, ya dumb ass!

"Well, thanks for calling. Bye."

"Maggie, wait—" But the connection was already broken.

I hung up the phone.

That didn't exactly go as planned, but at least she wasn't pissed at me anymore. I glanced at the address I'd just written down. At least now I knew for certain that Cyn Lennox had a connection to Walt Kaplan.

Now to prove it.

Chapter Eight

It had taken twenty minutes under a hot shower to ease the aches that twisted my poor bruised body the next morning. It was after ten by the time I staggered into the kitchen, with no Richard or Brenda in sight. She'd left a note, however: "We're off to look at wedding corsages. See you for supper." Then she'd drawn a little heart and signed it with a B.

Corsages? Poor Richard. He wasn't even married and already he was pussy whipped.

I knocked back a couple of aspirins and hoped they'd take out the rest of the soreness. Primed with that and a couple of cups of coffee, I headed off to work.

Off to work. I liked the sound of that—especially after being unemployed for more than eight months. The Whole Nine Yards was beginning to feel as much like home as my new apartment. And after only six days I even knew a couple of the regulars by name. But I wasn't feeling optimistic as I entered the bar. It was time for Tom and me to discuss what I'd discovered about Walt's murder.

The place was empty except for Tom at the bar cutting fruit garnishes. He'd end up tossing more than half of it at the end of the day since beer was his biggest seller, but he liked to have it ready—just in case.

He looked up from the cutting board. "Hey, Jeff. What's new?"

I came around to the back side of the bar and tied an apron around my waist. "Depends on the subject. For me, nothing. But I wanted to tell you what I've learned about Walt."

Tom straightened, ever so slightly, his jaw tightening. "So talk."

I took a fortifying breath before starting. "Tom, I don't think the cops arrested the right person."

Tom snorted a laugh and put the knife aside. "Come on, they found the murder weapon on him."

"That doesn't mean he used it. Where'd he get it? Witnesses say Buchanan was a Dumpster-diver. He might've found it anywhere. And what's his motivation for killing Walt?"

"Maybe it was a mugging."

"Walt was stabbed forty-six times. That says big-time anger. He had no defensive wounds. He might've been unconscious when it happened. It's also possible Walt knew his killer. Where would he have encountered Craig Buchanan?"

"Jeez, I don't know. Anywhere around town. Walt lived in the area."

"From what I gather, Buchanan never made it up as far as Eggert Road, and Walt didn't hang around Williamsville."

Tom frowned, his conviction faltering.

"What happened to Walt's settlement?"

He grunted. "It's long gone. The lawyers got the biggest chunk and Walt blew the rest on a big red Caddy and a year of high living. After it was gone, he moved into that dump of an apartment. It was only monthly disability payments and the money he made here that kept him going."

"What happened to the Caddy?"

"He traded up every few years, although I don't know how he managed to pay for it."

"Do you have the car?"

Tom hesitated. "Uh, no."

"I didn't see it at his apartment. You might want to report it as missing."

"Aw, shit." He slapped the bar with his open palm.

"Tell me Walt didn't keep the title in the glove box."

Tom's shoulders slumped. "I don't know, but I wouldn't be surprised."

I leaned back against the bar. "I doubt Walt's killer would be driving it—too conspicuous. It could've been dumped or maybe even sold, if only for junk value. That would make it harder to find, but not impossible. The cops can trace it with the VIN number."

"If we can find that."

"The DMV will have it. It's tied to the registration and title." I wondered how much more Tom could take. But I needed answers. The question was, would he give them?

"I found some stuff in Walt's apartment that led me to check out a vacation home in Ellicottville. Did he ever mention going there?"

Tom shook his head.

"It looks like the owner of that house also owns the property where Walt was found. Do you know a Cynthia Lennox?"

He shook his head, his expression hardening. "Did you tell the cops any of this?"

"I don't have enough evidence yet."

"What do you need to get it—and get this over with?"

"Time. And maybe a little luck."

"You will keep looking into this, won't you?" The words were right, but the conviction was missing. I couldn't dismiss my gut feeling that he knew much more than he'd shared with me.

"Of course," I answered. As Brenda said, I really didn't have a choice. I knew the flashes of insight would continue until I got to the bottom of this—case, situation—whatever it was.

"You didn't by any chance go through Walt's apartment before I got there, did you?"

His eyes flashed, his cheeks going pink. "What do you mean?"

"Just that it seemed awfully neat, considering the cops had already been there and all."

Tom shook his head and looked ten years older when he picked up the knife to finish his dissection of a lime. He didn't ask me any more questions and he obviously wasn't ready to hear what my next lines of inquiry would be.

At least not yet.

***

It was almost four-twenty when I pulled up to the little cinderblock building on Colvin Boulevard. Broadway Theatrics was a flashy name for such a dumpy locale. I almost didn't find the place because it was tucked behind a derelict gas station. A forlorn and battered blue Lumina sat near the entrance. No windows graced the front of the building, and its unattractive and peeling brown paint made it look like it had survived a war.

I got out of my car and wondered if I really wanted to venture inside. I pressed the grimy button of a doorbell and waited for thirty seconds before trying again. And again. I was about to give up when the door was wrenched open by a stooped man with long white hair, captured in a ponytail at the back of his neck. He couldn't have been more than fifty, but looked older because of his posture. His face hadn't seen a razor in at least a week. "You want something?" he growled.

"Women's shoes. Red stiletto heels. Lots of sparkles."

His eyes lit up, his spine straightening. He looked me over, shrugged, and held open the door. "Come on in."

Broadway Theatrics was a good name for what I found inside the shabby little building. Theatre props—a golden-haired angel in white with a ten-foot wingspan was suspended from the ceiling. Hand-carved marionettes, the expressions on their painted faces macabre and menacing, glared at me from pegs on the wall. Shelving units stood in parallel rows, neatly stacked with shoe and other boxes. Bolts of metallic purple and red fabrics rested on a makeshift service counter, its old-fashioned register painted a Day-Glo shade of pink.

"The workroom's back here. Follow me," the proprietor said.

I did.

The back room was even more magical than the first. Original drawings and paintings decorated the walls. Flashy costumes on hangers hung on racks, while shoes-in-progress littered a worktable.

The owner pulled an oblong box off a shelf and set it on the table. Lifting the lid, he pawed through the hundreds of photographs inside before selecting one. He tossed it to me. "Those the shoes you mean?"

I glanced down at the picture in my hand. The shoes were exactly the same as the one in my visions. "Yeah. How'd you know?"

He shrugged, a smile tugging his lips. "I have a sixth sense when it comes to shoes."

A shiver ran up my spine, and it wasn't from the air conditioning. "Do you remember who you made them for?"

"It's on the back."

I turned the photo over. A typed sticker listed the date, two years before, the price, and the customer: Andrea Foxworth. Damn. I'd been hoping it would say Cynthia Lennox. "You know this woman?" I asked.

"Sure, she's the wardrobe mistress for the Backstreet Players—a theatre group here in town. I made them for some show they were doing. Integral to the plot or something. I've actually made two pairs of them. Another customer came in a few months back and requested something similar. I showed him that picture and he asked me to make another pair."

"Do you have a photo of them?"

"I didn't bother, since I already had this one."

"You remember the other customer's name?"

"Sure. Walt Kaplan. He's a regular customer. He likes to give his lady friends mementos of their friendship. I must've made a couple pairs of shoes for him every year for almost a decade."

"Did you know he was murdered?"

"Walt? God, no. What happened?"

I explained.

The older guy looked genuinely upset. "I get so wrapped up here, sometimes I don't read the paper or watch TV for weeks at a time. Poor Walt."

"Did you know him well?"

"Just as a customer. He loved women's shoes—and was very knowledgeable on the subject. Sometimes he'd bring me in a picture he'd seen in a magazine and want me to copy it. I told him he'd be better off buying knock-offs on the Internet, but he wanted original, hand-crafted shoes—and he was willing to pay for them."

I indicated the photo. "Were these the last shoes you made for Walt?"

He nodded. "He picked them up a couple of weeks ago."

"Do you remember exactly when?"

He thought about it, exhaled a breath. "First of the month maybe. He usually paid me after he got his disability checks."

I studied the picture. As an amateur photographer myself, I recognized a damned fine shot. This was professional quality work. "Can I borrow this?"

He shook his head. "It's my only record."

"Can I get a copy?"

"I wouldn't know where the negative is. I take digital shots nowadays."

I held the photo out. "You did this? It's great."

"Thanks."

"Have you got a scanner? I'll give you a five to copy it."

He laughed. "That I can do. I think I even have some photo paper around here somewhere."

Ten minutes later I left the shop with my copy of the picture and the address for where I'd find Andrea Foxworth. She might be another dead end, but there was no way to find out until I spoke to her.

Bottom line: I was making progress.

But I had another stop to make and would've risked a speeding ticket to get back to Williamsville if it weren't for all the damned red lights and stop signs at every friggin' intersection. Still, I pulled up to a vacant parking space near the mill at 5:04 p.m.

The mill officially closed at five, and I wondered how long it would take for the employees to leave. I kept watch on the building's front entrance as the minutes dragged by. So far I'd only seen Cyn and the counter guy, Gene. By process of elimination—and if there weren't any other employees—the only other employee should be Ted Hanson, the miller. And I hoped he wouldn't be accompanied by Cyn when he left—otherwise I'd have to try again on another day. That or follow him home. I didn't want to do that and be accused of stalking the guy, which I was sure Cyn would do.

The minutes ticked by and my car began to feel like a sauna. I couldn't decide what was worse, stake out duty in the winter or the summer. One constant—it was always a bore.

The counter man was the first to leave at 5:22. He paused just outside the main door, checking out the street, caught sight of me and charged ahead. Cyn must've warned him I might lay in wait for the miller.

He stopped only feet from my car. "What're you doing here?"

"Sitting in my car. What's it to you?"

"Cyn told me to watch out for a runty guy who'd try and harass us."

Runty? I was at least two inches taller than this jerk.

"You've been warned to stay away from the mill," he continued.

"I was warned not to trespass. I'm not on mill property."

"Yeah, well—well—"

Articulate, he wasn't.

"We'll just see about this." He did an about-face and headed back for the mill. Less than a minute later, Cyn Lennox came flying out of the building and down the stairs, reminding me of a charging rhino as she made a beeline for my car. I got out, ready to face her.

"What're you doing here?" she demanded, fists clenched, face pink with anger.

"I want to talk to Ted Hanson."

"This is harassment."

"For whom? I'm not on your property. You came to speak to me—I didn't seek you out."

She pursed her lips, looking ready to implode.

"But as long as you're here, I wouldn't mind asking you a few more questions. Like do you have a pair of red, sparkling stiletto high heels?"

Anger turned to shock as her mouth dropped open, and it could've been fear that shadowed her eyes. "Get out of here."

She turned and stalked back to the mill. Another man had joined Gene on the little front porch. I leaned against the driver's door of my car and watched as the three of them conferred for a couple of minutes. Cyn kept gesturing, her arms waving in anger while the newcomer tried to reason with her. Eventually she threw her hands up in the air and reentered the mill. The man descended the stairs and started toward me.

"Are you Ted Hanson?" I asked when he got within earshot.

"Yeah."

"My name's Jeff Resnick." I offered my hand. He ignored it, which was just as well. I sensed a bubble of animosity surrounding him and wasn't eager to embrace it.

"Cyn says you want to talk to me."

"You found Walt Kaplan's body."

"Yeah, and I've already told the police everything I know."

"They didn't share it with me."

"What's your interest?"

"I work for Walt's cousin. He asked me to look into it."

"What are you, some kind of investigator?"

Not anymore, I could've told him. I lied. "Yeah."

Hanson looked skeptical. "Do you have a license?"

"I'm not a private investigator. Insurance."

"Oh." His hostility instantly backed off. As a businessman, he understood liability. "What do you want to know?"

"Just what you saw."

He shrugged. "I had an order of rye flour that was supposed to go out the next day and I came out to the porch to check how many sacks I had. At first I thought it was a bag of trash on the hillside. I looked again and saw it was a person."

"Did you think he was dead?"

"No. I figured he was a drunk or something. The Hawk's Nest," he jerked a thumb over his shoulder to the restaurant across the way, "has a bar. A couple of years ago someone fell down the hill beside the mill and broke his neck."

I glanced at the pile of rubble at the side of the road. "Why doesn't somebody put a fence around it?"

"They demolished an old building earlier this year. There was a construction fence. I don't know what happened to it. Kids probably tore it down."

"So you found Walt," I prompted.

He shuddered. "Yeah."

"The body was on its back, looking up at the sky," I said, describing what I'd already seen in a vision.

"Yeah. No blood that I could see, but he was this awful blue-white color."

"No blood on the clothes?"

Hanson shook his head. "Not that I saw."

"That's strange. The medical examiner said he was stabbed forty-six times."

"Really?" The news seemed to trouble Hanson. "He was wearing a dark red shirt, dark pants, and shoes. I suppose there might've been stains, but…not for that many wounds, and there was no blood around him on the ground. That would mean someone had to clean him up and dress him after they killed him."

"Yeah," I agreed. "Then somebody dumped him here. There had to be a reason they chose this place. Had you ever seen Walt around here?"

Hanson shook his head. "I'm not a part of the retail operation. Cyn and Gene deal with the customers on a one-to-one basis. They have a baker, Dana Watkins, but she's usually gone before I get here in the morning."

"You have a phone number for her?"

"No, and Cyn would just be pissed if I gave it to you anyway."

"I hear you, man." I relaxed against my car once again. "Cyn called you a miller, but I noticed most of the stuff in the warehouse has already been ground."

"That's my product. They use what I mill and I sell the rest to boutique bakeries throughout the northeast. The coffee shop is just the icing on the cake. The real money is and always has been the mill."

"That wasn't the impression I got from Cyn."

"She doesn't own the mill. It's been in my family for over a hundred years. If she tells people she owns the business—well, it's kind of true. The coffee shop is her baby—but she just leases space from me. Cyn's very good at what she does. She's only been in business here about six months and is already turning a profit. And she's helped me find new markets for my flour. She's hoping to sweet talk me into selling her the place, but that'll never happen."

"She's got money, then?"

"She and her late husband owned a chain of coffee shops in the Southwest. She sold them when he died and came back to Buffalo. I guess she's got family here, which is why she returned."

With a home in Amherst and a vacation home in Holiday Valley, yeah, that sounded like money. I'd have to check out the address Maggie had given me to get an idea of how much Cyn was worth.

And why would someone with that kind of dough be caught dead wearing a pair of sparkling red hooker shoes?

Hanson shot a look back at the mill. "She's probably having a fit because we've talked so long. Please don't come around anymore. There's nothing to see. The guy's dead and the cops have already made an arrest. It's over."

"Thanks for your time."

"No problem."

I offered him my hand, and this time he took it, and I tuned into him. He'd been straight with me. Now all he wanted was a beer, his recliner, and the Mets game on the tube.

Hanson headed back for the mill and I got in my car and turned the key in the ignition. The steering wheel was hot to the touch as I maneuvered onto the street and turned the corner for Main Street. Talking to Hanson had definitely been worth it. And I now had the name of the mill's baker. If she left before he got there, she had to start work before dawn. She probably opened the place, which meant I'd have to be out here first thing in the morning if I wanted to catch her.

The red light at the corner took forever. I glanced down at the photo on my passenger seat. Was there any point in trying to chase down Andrea Foxworth this evening? Brenda was expecting me for supper, and I had the feeling I had better show up. But I also wasn't sure of the reception I was likely to receive.

Still, I steered for home. With every mile, uncertainty tightened my gut.

Chapter Nine

I arrived back home just after six to find Maggie's little car parked in my usual spot in the driveway. Curious. I pulled along beside it. The feeling of unease intensified as I entered the house through the back door and headed for the kitchen, where I found Richard, Brenda, and Maggie sitting at the table having a drink; wine for the ladies and Richard's usual scotch sat on a coaster in front of him.

"There you are," Brenda said with a decided maternal lilt. "I was beginning to think you'd fallen into a black hole."

"Hi," Maggie said and blinked, her eyelashes looking longer than I remembered. She looked pretty in a pink sleeveless sweater and matching slacks. Business casual never looked so good.

"I invited Maggie to stay for supper," Brenda said.

I chanced a glance at Richard, who raised his eyebrows and his glass in salute.

Set up!

I flashed a smile, wondering if it looked forced. "Boy, I could use a beer." I stepped across the kitchen to the fridge, pulled out a bottle of Labatts, cracked the cap and took a fortifying swig.

"Tough day?" Maggie asked.

"Long." I leaned against the counter, suddenly feeling very tired. "It's been a while since I worked, and I had some extracurricular stuff tacked on at the end."

"Oh?" Brenda asked.

"Yeah." I wasn't about to go into detail about where I'd been or who I'd talked to. Instead, I took another long pull on my beer.

Brenda and Maggie were on different frequencies, but the feelings they transmitted were pretty much the same: smothering.

I took a couple of deep breaths, which made my ribs scream in protest, worsening the tightness in my chest. Brenda wanted Maggie to take care of me—presumably while she and Richard were on their honeymoon—while Maggie's hunger for sexual release loomed like a dark gray cloud.

"Is it hot in here?" I asked and took another gulp of beer.

Richard swirled the ice in his glass. "Not that I noticed."

My breaths were coming short and fast, and the throbbing had already started behind my eyes. I had to get away from Brenda and Maggie before I went through a painful repeat of two days before.

"You grilling tonight?" I asked Richard.

"Yeah."

"Maybe we should get it going?" I hoped Maggie wouldn't detect the desperation in my voice.

Richard shot a look at Brenda. "Sure," she said, resigned, and rose from the table.

Maggie's lips pursed, but she said nothing as Brenda retrieved a plastic-wrapped plate of steaks from the fridge. She grabbed a long-handled fork from the counter and passed them to Richard. "Don't burn mine," she said, but her humor sounded strained.

"They'll be perfect." Richard retrieved his glass and made for the door. I gave Maggie a smile and a wave, but I was so close on Richard's heel I nearly stepped on him.

The screen door slammed on my back and Richard turned on me. "What the hell is wrong with you?"

I was nearly hyperventilating and collapsed in a sit on the back steps with a jolt that reawakened all my other aches and pains. Hunched over, I set my beer down and covered my eyes, not sure if I was about to puke in the geraniums. "I thought I was gonna die in there."

Richard's pique instantly turned to concern. "What's wrong?"

I hauled in a few good breaths, my head still muddled, my stomach still threatening to erupt. "That kitchen was like a tornado of emotion. Between the two of them I felt like I was about to be squashed."

Richard studied me with his physician eyes—and yet there was puzzlement behind them as well. "I don't get it. I thought you liked Maggie."

"I do. But she wants…" Christ, she was practically vibrating with desire, not that I was going to tell him. "I'm not sure what she wants. And Brenda, she's definitely in matchmaker mode."

"Tell me about it."

I rubbed my eyes, grateful the anxiety was starting to ebb.

Richard juggled his glass and the plate of steaks, grasped my left arm under the bicep and pulled me to my feet. "Come on. Get past it."

Easy for him to say.

I shuffled after him back to the deck and the gas grill. He lit it and shifted the steaks onto the rack. He seemed preoccupied. I dropped down on the top step and held my beer between my hands, trying to absorb the chill into myself, accepting it as a balm for my ragged psyche.

"When are you going to tell me what's going on with you?" Richard said at last.

I squinted up at him. "What?"

"You're chasing around, talking to all sorts of people. Kaplan's death is connected to custom-made shoes, but you haven't told me even half of it. Why?"

I took another couple of breaths, stalling for time. Should I level with him—tell him how I was scared to death that the next time he helped me out I might get him killed—or lie with some cock-and-bull story, especially since I suspected his former girlfriend of murder?

"I haven't put enough of it together yet."

"Maybe I could help."

Yeah, and this time would someone come after him with a knife or a claw hammer or a 2001 Buick, and again I wouldn't see it coming or be able to protect him?

"I need to think about it some more."

Richard poked at the steaks with the fork. "I'm praying you wrap this up before we head for Europe, or that I can talk you out of pursuing it. Brenda will be heartbroken if we have to cancel our flight."

"What are you talking about?"

"I can't leave you here to figure this out alone. If I hadn't pushed you out of the way back in March—" He stopped himself.

He was talking about the gunshot that nearly killed him. "Don't go there, Rich. It was my fault you got hurt. If I hadn't gotten you involved—"

"So this time you want to go it alone—no backup—and get killed?"

Pain seared through my head as I flashed again on the dripping, bloody hands. "That isn't going to happen."

"You dig too deep and whoever killed Walt Kaplan is going to come after you."

"It won't go that far. I won't let it."

"Yeah, like you have any control over other people and how they react." He snatched up his glass, slopped scotch on the deck. "Why don't you just let the police handle it?"

"Because they arrested the wrong person."

"Just because you have some kind of insight doesn't mean you have all the answers."

"I never claimed to. Look, why are you so angry?"

"Because, goddamnit, I don't want to lose you." He forked a steak with unnecessary force and flipped it. It sizzled as it hit the grill. "The thing is, you like all this intrigue. You revel in it."

"I do not. Tom asked me to look into Walt's death. The insight kicked in and now I'm trapped. It'll keep happening—"

"Until it stops," he finished.

"Yeah."

He turned the steaks again. They weren't ever going to cook at this rate. "Will you be able to eat dinner?" It sounded like an accusation.

"No. I can't be around those women with what they're feeling."

"Maggie will be disappointed."

"For months she wouldn't give me the time of day. Now suddenly I'm a hot commodity."

Richard eyed me, his anger dissolving as his mustache quirked upward. "In more ways than one, apparently."

I glared at him, but that jibe was what was needed to soothe his ire.

"Please ask Brenda to back off. I can't take being double-teamed. If anything's going to happen between Maggie and me, it has to develop naturally."

He nodded, poking at the steaks once more. "Are you sure you can't make an effort to sit through dinner?"

I closed my eyes to assess how I felt: marginal. "No. Will you make my apologies?"

"Yeah. Are you going up to the apartment for a while?"

"No. Think I'll hit the rack." I had somewhere to be in the middle of the night, and I wanted to feel, if not rested, at least better than marginal.

***

I wrapped my arms tighter around my chest and winced. Thirty-two hours down and my ribs still hurt, and though I was cold, at way-too-much a gallon I didn't want to waste gas by running the engine for the heater. Besides, cold I stayed awake; warm, I'd probably fall asleep. I hadn't wanted to miss Dana Watkins, so I'd been parked a short distance from the mill since three a.m., cursing myself for not stopping for coffee first. And why hadn't I worn a heavier jacket?

Headlights broke the darkness and a car pulled up in front of the mill's front door. Seconds later, a figure exited the car. I yanked open my car door and made to follow. "Dana Watkins?"

The person at the door turned. A flashlight's beam caught me straight in the eyes. "Hey." I held an arm up to block the light.

"I've got a gun," the woman warned, "And I'm not afraid to use it."

I tried to peek around my fingers. "I hope you've got a permit."

"A permit?"

"Yeah. I wouldn't want to be shot illegally."

The light dipped. "Are you that Resnick guy?" She sounded annoyed.

"Would you rather I be a robber?"

No answer.

"Look, I only want to ask you a few questions."

"Cyn told me not to talk to you."

"It's a free country—you can talk to anybody you want." I still couldn't see behind the ice white light.

"Let's see some ID, buddy."

I reached behind me.

"Ah-ah-ah!" she warned.

"It's in my pocket." I turned my back to her and slowly retrieved my wallet, took out my driver's license, and handed it to her.

She scrutinized the photo and winced. "Oh! Bad hair day."

"I wasn't at my best," I admitted. My head had been partially shaved at the hospital after I was mugged. The picture was taken three weeks later.

She kept looking at the photo and back at me. "Well, I guess it looks a little like you." She handed it back and I put it away.

"Come on in," she said and turned for the door.

I had to blink until I could make out her silhouette on the little porch. I stumbled up the stairs. She had keys, not a gun, in her other hand, and used the flashlight to find the keyhole. "Cyn said you'd probably ambush me when I left work. I wasn't expecting anyone to be here now."

"I didn't want to run into Cyn. She doesn't seem to like me."

Dana reached inside and flipped a light switch. "And why should I?"

"I'm a nice person." She stepped inside, and rounded on me. "Once you get to know me."

"Uh-huh."

I shrugged. She did an about face and crossed the overly bright café and made for the espresso machine. Maybe I'd get offered a cup. "Gotta get this thing going first thing," she said. "That way it builds a good head of steam so I can have one before I leave."

That would be hours away. Scratch one free espresso.

She breezed through white swinging doors and flicked on the lights. I followed her into the kitchen where she tossed her purse on a counter to the left. Her next stop was the professional coffeemaker on the back wall. "Want some?"

"You bet. This is a bit earlier than I usually get up."

She dumped beans into a grinder before retrieving water from the triple sink's faucet, and filled the reservoir.

With the coffee brewing, she fired up the ovens before heading for the industrial sized fridge, where she extracted trays of what looked like bread dough, croissants, and cinnamon rolls. Next she scrubbed her hands like a surgeon before donning gloves to work with the food. She worked with such efficiency that I was mesmerized.

"You've been here almost five minutes and haven't asked one question. Are you a bakery spy or something, trying to steal my pastry secrets?"

I laughed. "Sorry. I don't even like the stuff, but it's fascinating to watch." I cleared my throat. "I assume you never saw the dead guy."

She shook her head. "Only after Ted called the police. I suppose he was there when I came in early that morning." She shuddered. "But like I told the cops, I didn't see anything or anybody. No familiar cars—no strange ones either. Coffee's ready. Pour me a large black and get whatever you want out of the fridge. Sugar's on the counter if you need it."

"Would Cyn approve?"

"Of course not. Why do you think I invited you in?"

A smile creased my lips. I might just get some good gossip out of Dana.

I poured the steaming coffee and doctored mine before setting hers on the counter beside her. She grabbed it with flour-dusted fingers and took a huge gulp. I wondered about the state of her esophagus as I sipped mine more carefully.

"I take it you and Cyn don't get along all that well."

"That's not true," she said, spreading apple filling over the bottom of a dough-filled pan. "We just don't see eye to eye on certain aspects of the business. Like her staying out of my kitchen. She hired me to bake, but she thinks she's got to have her sticky fingers in everything."

"So delegation isn't her specialty?"

"Control freak might be a more accurate term. My first day here I churned out half a dozen strudels, three dozen scones, two dozen cinnamon buns, and a couple dozen doughnuts. Since then she's expected that on a daily basis—and then some. Don't get me started about the biscotti fiasco back in March."

I smiled as she obviously wanted me to. "Ted Hanson said Cyn's already making a profit on the café."

Dana shook her head. "Nah, it's the outside orders that put us in the black. But people first try our pastries as customers in the café, then make special orders. We're a little too successful for a three-person operation. I've been trying to get Cyn to hire me help, but she's resisting. Gene helps out now in the afternoons. He's the one who got all this dough ready for me. He comes in around eight and gets the café set up, too. Restocking bags, taking phone orders, and polishing the display cases. We should be paying someone for that, too."

"How does Cyn get so much work out of Gene?"

"He's her nephew. I think she promised him a percentage of the profits. He works too hard for just a straight salary."

So, nepotism was alive and well at the Old Red Mill. "Is his last name Taggert?"

"No, Higgins. I think he's her younger sister's kid."

"You and Cyn aren't related, are you?"

Dana looked up from her work, her eyes ablaze. "Hell no!"

"Do the two of you ever socialize?"

"Cyn rub elbows with the hired help? Please." She gulped more coffee.

"So you wouldn't know if she ever lets her hair down."

"Cyn? I can't imagine. Then again, I sometimes think she's a frustrated actress."

"How so?"

Dana folded the dough over the filling, sealed the ends and cut steam holes, then went to work on another. "Those costumes she wears. She's been a cowgirl for weeks now. I guess she wore that stuff out West, but it looks kind of silly here in Williamsville, don't you think?"

"Oh, I dunno. They do call this the Niagara Frontier."

Dana laughed, from deep down in her belly. "No wonder Cyn hates you. You've got a sense of humor."

I'd rarely been accused of that. "What other kinds of costumes does she wear?"

"Accessories mostly. Shawls, lots of rhinestones, big earrings. And she usually manages to carry it off."

"Do think she'd ever stoop to red-sequined stiletto heels?"

Dana looked thoughtful. "Maybe." Then she giggled.

"What?"

"I'm trying to imagine her in heels, pasties and a G-string. *That* would be too funny."

Dana finished with the strudel, popped them in the oven, and began working on the cinnamon buns.

"Tell me more about Gene," I said.

"I get the feeling he's the son Cyn never had. He worked for her in Santa Fe, too."

"Did he want to come back east?"

She shrugged. "I guess. He's here. I really don't know much about him. Our conversations usually revolve around orders and supplies. He seems nice enough. And very protective of Cyn."

I remembered him scoping out the street the afternoon before. "So I noticed. What do you know about Cyn's place up in Holiday Valley?"

Dana frowned. "I didn't know she had one. She never talks to me about personal stuff—like, 'How was your weekend, Dana?' It's more, 'Can you come in early tomorrow to fill the Henderson order?'" This last she whined.

"Why do you stay?"

Dana laughed. "Because I love it. I love the work; I love the place—and I don't mind working with Gene. I only have to put up with Cyn for half an hour every day before I'm outta here. If I get some help, I could be happy working here for years." She smiled at me and I hoped I gave her one of equal wattage. But as I looked around the spotless kitchen, the racks of product and the shining equipment, I knew the place would soon be closed and Dana would be baking elsewhere.

That at least cheered me. Dana would go on, find work somewhere else and be happy doing it.

The future didn't look so bright for Cyn and Gene. I only wished my insight gave me more hints as to what that would be.

***

I made it home before six a.m. Brenda and Richard were still in bed and I figured there was no reason to even let them know I'd been out. I crashed for a few more hours sleep and found my way back to the kitchen and the aroma of fresh-brewed coffee at a little after ten.

No one was in sight, but a flower arrangement bright with pink carnations and white daisies sat on the kitchen table. I stopped cold. Had I missed Brenda's birthday? No—that was in the fall. A glance at the wall calendar told me nothing had been penciled in on this day. So was there an occasion I wasn't aware of, or had the flowers arrived from one of Brenda's cross-country friends in advance of the wedding? Maybe the corsage florist they'd visited days before was desperate for business and....

I abandoned the thought, grabbed a mug from the cabinet and poured myself some coffee. Footsteps echoed in the hall—too heavy for Brenda—and Richard entered the kitchen.

"Finally up, I see."

I blew on my coffee to cool it. "I gotta be at the bar by eleven."

He nodded and parked his ass against the counter. "Your car got moved since last evening."

Gee, and I thought he wouldn't notice. "Uh, yeah."

Richard crossed his arms over his chest, waiting.

"I got up way too early. Figured I'd go out for a cup of coffee."

"We didn't run out."

"Uh, yeah. But I guess I felt kind of restless."

"Uh-huh.

"Yeah." I sipped my coffee and then changed the subject, hoisting my cup toward the flowers on the table. "Pretty. Did they make Brenda happy?"

"Well, they might've—if they'd been for her. It's your name on the card."

I almost spewed my coffee. "My name?"

Richard nodded toward the vase. "Check it out."

I crossed the kitchen in four steps, set my mug down on the table with a thunk, and tore open the envelope.

Sorry to overwhelm you last night. Let's try again...this time on your timetable. Maggie.

I blew out a long breath.

"From anyone we know?" Richard asked with mock innocence.

"Yeah." I handed him the card. He scrutinized it before passing it back.

"No one's ever sent *me* flowers."

"It's a first for me, too."

"What're you going to do about it?"

"I don't know. Say 'thank you' like my Mama done taught me. Then, I don't know."

"You do like her."

I thought about Maggie's all-too-elusive smile. "Yeah, I do."

"Then what's the problem?"

Should I tell him that in thirty-five years no one had ever pursued me? That "overwhelmed" was more than an apt description of how I now felt? Sure, I'd been married. I'd had sex with a bunch of women. But sharing what I felt had never entered the equation before. That Maggie could read me, too, was more than a little terrifying. I wasn't sure I could deal with it.

Richard still waited for an answer.

"Fear of failure," I bluffed.

He nodded, then shook his head in what seemed like amusement. "You and Brenda are so much alike."

"What?"

"You're so afraid to just trust what's offered to you."

Man, he just didn't know—couldn't understand—what it was Maggie was after; what I was afraid to give.

I grabbed my coffee mug, walked over to the sink and dumped the contents, then put the mug into the dishwasher. "I gotta go to work." I looked over at my brother, found his expression smug. "See ya."

"See ya," he echoed, and I scuttled out the door.

Chapter Ten

I was getting used to the routine at the bar, picking up the ins and outs of Tom's business and even enjoying being around people again. The regulars weren't used to a bartender with loads of personality, so I filled Walt's absence with surprising ease. And I was learning to better shield myself from the onslaught of others' emotions.

Almost. It was still a drain being bombarded with sensations, but I found distance was a good buffer. If someone at one end of the bar was depressed, I took to hanging around the other. Mundane tasks like washing glasses also helped keep me from absorbing others' emotional baggage.

It was after two when I looked up from polishing the brass taps to see a familiar face studying me from the last stool on the end: my ex-schoolmate, Sam Nielsen. I hadn't changed much over the years, but Sam's head of once-thick dark hair was long gone, and I didn't think I'd ever get used to seeing his chrome dome.

I walked down to the end of the bar. "What can I get you?"

"A beer."

"Any preference?"

"Canadian."

"Draft or bottle?"

"Bottle."

I grabbed a Molson and a clean glass, and set it in front of him.

"Have you got time to talk?" he asked.

A couple of guys were nursing beers at a table in front, watching the tube. Tom held court at the other end of the bar with one of his cronies. Nobody seemed in dire need of my services. "Sure. How'd you find me?"

"Hey, I *am* an investigative reporter." He poured half the beer into his glass. "I called your brother. Have you got anything to tell me about Kaplan's murder?"

"Shut up," I whispered, and jerked a thumb toward Tom. "The owner was his cousin."

Sam glanced down at Tom, then shrugged. "Sorry. You got anything?"

"Questions. I understand the body was cleaned up and re-dressed after death."

"Yeah. Sloppy job, too. I saw the police photos. Shirt buttons were mismatched, no underwear—no socks, and the pants were zipped, but not buttoned."

"And no bloodstains on anything."

"Surprisingly little, plus the usual bodily secretions. Contrary to what you see on TV, it's way too soon for a lab report."

That, I knew. "You got my message about Buchanan's clothes. Any blood on them?"

"No. I asked my contact at the Amherst PD about it and he wasn't interested in pursuing it, either. He figures Buchanan and Kaplan weren't clothed when the murder happened. Either that or Buchanan ditched the clothes he'd been wearing at the time of the murder."

"He only had one set."

"You can't prove it."

"Why'd he re-dress Kaplan?"

"Maybe some kind of ritual?"

"That's bullshit."

"That's politics. They've arrested someone. They don't want to see their case go down the tube." Sam sipped his beer. He accepted the situation. I couldn't.

He eyed me. "I gave you everything I had. It's time to return the favor."

My spine stiffened. "I'm still putting the pieces together."

"That's what you said two days ago. Come on, give."

I looked down the bar at Tom. I hadn't even confided to him all that I knew—or suspected. But I'd have to toss Sam a bone, if only to keep him feeding me what he knew. I leaned closer, lowered my voice. "I keep seeing a custom-made woman's shoe."

Sam waited for more. When I said nothing, he frowned. "That's it?"

"I've tracked down the maker. He made two pairs, one for Kaplan, another for someone else. I got a line on who ordered the originals. I'm going to look into that later today."

His frown turned to disgust. "Talk about bullshit. What the hell's that got to do with his murder?"

A quick glance down the bar showed me Tom had heard Sam. "Pipe down, willya?"

Sam poured the rest of his beer and took a gulp. "You think whoever wore those shoes killed Kaplan?"

"Maybe. But those two pairs of shoes are tied in somehow."

Sam's gaze bore into mine. A grin slowly curled his lips. "You've got a suspect."

I straightened, looked away.

"Come on, spill it, Jeff."

I shook my head. "Not until I have more than a suspicion."

"Who is she?"

I folded my arms across my chest and leaned against the backbar.

Sam picked up his glass and drank, never taking his eyes off me.

"Jeff?" Tom pointed to the two guys at the table out front.

I headed back for the taps, poured another two beers and delivered them to the customers. By the time I got back to the bar, Sam had finished his drink. "Am I going to have to hunt you down again for my next update?"

"I'll call you when I know something."

His expression said, "Yeah, right," and he stood, reaching for his wallet.

I put out a hand to stop him. "It's on me."

He nodded and headed for the exit. At the door he turned, pointing a finger at me. "Call me."

I'd call. But not until I was certain. And right then I still had a lot more questions than answers.

***

I hate to admit when I'm wrong, but Richard may have been right about my not being ready to return to work. I was dead on my feet by the time my shift ended at four p.m. And yet, Sam's visit had reignited my curiosity about what had happened to the first pair of red-sequined heels.

I found the home of the Backstreet Players, an old grocery store reconfigured with a stage, near the edge of Buffalo's theatre district, but had to park a block away at a ramp garage. The elevator was broken, so I had to hoof it down three flights of stairs. The humidity was high with ninety-degree temps. I wasn't looking forward to duplicating my footsteps on the way back.

Though I'd called Andrea Foxworth beforehand, she hadn't warned me I'd find the box office dark and all the entrances around the building locked. Someone finally heard me banging on one of the doors at the back of the building, and opened it. "I'm looking for Andrea Foxworth."

A burly guy in jeans and a grubby white T-shirt looked me over. "She expecting you?"

"Yeah."

He shrugged. "Okay." And let me in.

So much for security.

The dim backstage area, plastered with "No Smoking" signs, was full of people. In contrast with outside, the air felt dry and chilled. Voices yelled across one another as stocky men wheeled scenery around the stage and banks of lighting were adjusted overhead. Grubby pointed toward a set of stairs going down. "She should be down there—in wardrobe."

"Thanks."

The temperature dropped another couple of degrees as I descended the stairs into the bowels of the building. A double door marked "Wardrobe" stood ajar and I sidled inside to find several women poised over commercial sewing machines. Dressmakers' dummies stood in full regalia—uniforms and period dresses. The marquee had said "HMS Pinafore." An older, harried-looking woman with gray-streaked brown hair, shouted into a cell phone. A baggy, full-front apron, not unlike what Sophie always wore, covered her street clothes, while an unlit cigarette dangled from her lips.

"You were supposed to deliver them by five o'clock today. It is now," she glanced at a wall clock, "four-thirty-seven and I expect to see those wigs here within the next twenty-three minutes or I will haunt you in this life and into the next!" She pulled the phone from her ear, stabbed a finger on the off button, then looked up to glare at me. "Who are you and what are you doing down here? Security!" she bellowed toward the door.

"Andrea Foxworth? I'm Jeff Resnick. I called a couple of hours ago."

She exhaled a couple of exasperated breaths, yanked the full-size cigarette from her lips and tucked it behind her ear. "Sorry. I forgot you were coming." She turned her back on me and marched over to one of the women sewing. "Are those alterations going to be finished any time soon?"

"Chill out, Andrea," the woman said without looking up from her work. "We'll get everything done."

Andrea whirled, and for a moment I thought she might explode—at me. "I don't have a lot of time. We're doing a dress rehearsal tonight and I have a million things to accomplish before then."

"Just five minutes. Please."

She reached up, rubbed the cigarette with her thumb and forefinger, then sniffed them. "I just quit and I'm a little strung out. We'll have to talk while I work."

The second time in one day.

I followed her to a lumpy-looking, faded upholstered chair where she plunked down, snatched up a dress from a table beside it, and started ripping the seams apart.

I figured I'd better talk fast. "I understand you ordered a pair of custom shoes from Broadway Theatrics about two years ago."

"Dear boy, I order lots of custom shoes from Broadway Theatrics."

"I have a picture." I pulled the photo from my shirt's breast pocket, noting the goose bumps dotting my arm as I handed her the picture.

She gazed at it for a second and the smile that appeared took five years off her face. "Ah, the tramp shoes."

"The what?"

"That's what the actress who wore them called them. Said she felt like a fifty-dollar hooker in them."

"Do you know what happened to them?"

"Sure. They were auctioned off with a lot of other costumes and props at our big fundraiser back in the winter. It was in all the papers."

"Damn. That probably means you have no idea who bought them."

"You got that, although the auction company gave me a list of the buyers and the final lots. That way next year I can pair up the items that sold best and inform our target market. I can't let you look at it, though. It lists addresses and I'm not giving out that kind of information to just anyone who walks in off the street."

"I don't blame you. But if I gave you a name could you confirm this person participated in the auction?"

She thought about it for a few moments. "Mmm...I don't think so. It just wouldn't be right."

I looked around to make sure none of the other ladies was paying attention to me. "Are you sure I can't change your mind?" I showed her the edge of a twenty-dollar bill I'd put in my pocket—just in case.

Andrea hesitated, leaned to her left to look around me. "Well, I guess that would be okay. I mean, if you already know the person. But what if the name isn't on the list?"

"I'd still expect to compensate you for your trouble," I whispered.

With a lot more poise than she'd shown just moments before, Andrea set aside the garment, got up from her chair and crossed the room to a file cabinet. She pulled out a ledger, thumbing through it until she came to a particular page. "Who are you looking for?"

"Cynthia Lennox, of Amherst."

Andrea flipped ahead and ran her finger down the list. "Lot ninety-six: red tramp shoes, vampy dress, feather boa, and jaunty hat. Paid two hundred and thirty-five bucks for it." She closed the book and held out her hand. "Very nice meeting you, Mr. Resnick."

Palming the bill, we shook on it. "Likewise."

I escorted myself back up to the stage area, which felt positively balmy after the icebox below, and aimed for the first door with an exit sign above it. The bright sunshine nearly seared my retinas after the backstage gloom, but this time I welcomed the heat as I squinted my way back to the garage.

So, Cyn Lennox had purchased the original pair of shoes. But what did that have to do with the pair Walt ordered? How had he seen them? Perhaps in the closet of her vacation home in Holiday Valley? Or had he replaced shoes that she'd ruined? I hadn't thought to ask the shoemaker if the shoes had been the same size. Would he even remember, as he hadn't bothered to document the second pair of shoes?

And how did all this relate to Walt Kaplan's murder?

I needed something more—some other piece of the puzzle before I'd be able to put everything together. I needed to grill Sam for additional information, and I needed a picture of Cyn to show around the bar. Maybe one of The Whole Nine Yard's customers would recognize her. It didn't seem likely, and yet I had a feeling a picture was exactly what I needed to move forward in my investigation.

"*Don't call it an investigation,*" I could almost hear Richard rant.

Yeah, and I also needed his camera, computer, and printer to do the deed. And I had to take a halfway decent picture of Cyn without her knowledge.

Oh yeah—this was going to be so easy.

Not!

First things first, I told myself. Get the camera; worry about the rest later.

Already sweating, I reached the ramp garage, following a man and woman in office attire, briefcases in hand, their suit jackets draped over their arms. Good looking and cheerful after a hard day's work, they looked like they just stepped out of a Lord and Taylor ad. The three of us entered the stairwell.

Damn broken elevators. Damn stinking muggy weather. A vein in my temple throbbed by the time I made it to the second level, where the woman peeled off with a wave to her colleague. The guy picked up his pace, leaving me shaking with fatigue by the time I trudged up the last few steps.

My car was at the end of the aisle, a million miles away. The guy had already unlocked his car, had ditched the briefcase and was setting his folded jacket over the top of the passenger seat as I plodded past.

The roar of an engine reverberated off the concrete and a motorcycle rounded the corner, going far too fast. I froze, like a deer in headlights, as the bike rushed toward me.

"Look out!" the office worker shouted.

The rider's black faceplate reflected the dull glow of the overhead fluorescent lamps.

A jerk at my neck pulled me off balance. I landed on my ass, rolling into the wheel well of a car, my nose scraping rubber.

"Are you okay? What an asshole!"

I'm not the asshole, I felt like shouting, then realized he'd meant the biker, not me.

He helped me to my feet and steadied me. "Are you okay?" he asked again.

"Yeah." I dusted off my jeans, realized he must've grabbed me by the back of the shirt and pulled me to safety. "Thanks, man."

He studied my face, was probably about my age, and looked as shook up as I felt. "Do you need help getting to your car or something?"

It was adrenaline that had me shaking now. "I'm fine. Thanks again."

I felt his gaze on my back as I headed for my car. Okay, was the biker just some idiot having fun, or had I pissed someone off?

I preferred to think the former, but I suspected the latter.

* * *

Brenda was setting the table as I entered the kitchen. She turned to give me an ambivalent stare. "Are you actually going to grace us with your presence tonight?"

I glanced at the table. "Well, there are three plates, so I sort of thought I might. And I might even eat something, too." I crossed to the fridge and took out a beer and cracked the cap.

Driving for twenty minutes in my air-conditioned car had had a calming effect on me. I had no intention of mentioning my little adventure.

I took a tentative sniff of the aroma permeating the kitchen. "Roast chicken—on a Wednesday?"

"Is there a better day?"

"When I was a kid, roast chicken was reserved for Thanksgiving and Christmas."

Brenda straightened the tablecloth. "My mother made it every Sunday—winter, spring, summer and fall. But this came from the Deli Department at Wegmans."

I leaned against the counter and took a long pull of my beer.

Brenda scrutinized my face. "You look tired. You're not pushing yourself too hard, are you?"

If she only knew. "Isn't that what I need to do to find my limits?"

She seemed preoccupied as she turned away to fold the paper napkins into miniature bishop's miters, setting them on the plates; a nice touch. Then again, Brenda always managed to add simple joys to everyday life.

"Are *you* okay?" I asked.

"Sure. It's Richard who's bummed. He's making himself crazy over you."

"Me?"

"He's bored. Right now, you're his only diversion. If something's going on with you, couldn't you share it with him?" Her voice was nonchalant and she didn't bother to look at me. Meanwhile, all my muscles tightened.

I'd been over my little adventure again and again in the last half hour. What had I actually seen in the seconds from the time the bike turned the corner to me landing on the concrete floor? A black motorcycle—manufacturer unknown; a biker clad in black leather and a black helmet. I hadn't even thought to report it. I couldn't give a better description and I'd bet the guy who also witnessed it couldn't either. I might just be paranoid.

I might.

I tilted my bottle back for another swallow. "Nothing's going on with me."

Brenda eyed me for a long moment. "If you say so."

She knew how to challenge me, but I wasn't going to bite—not this time. And yet I felt an unreasonable anger toward my closest of kin. Okay, I was a member of Richard's household, but I still deserved my privacy. I'd lost a lot since the mugging; my health, at least half my possessions, and a hell of a lot of my dignity. I didn't feel the need to consult with him on everything I did or experienced. Especially with what I'd recently experienced.

I didn't need to hear "I told you so."

Footsteps foretold Richard's arrival. He paused at the doorway. It didn't take a psychic to feel the tension in that kitchen. "Supper almost ready?" he asked Brenda, like I'd turned into the invisible man.

"Almost."

He crossed to the cabinet next to me, withdrew the Famous Grouse bottle, then grabbed a whiskey glass. "Ice."

"It's in the freezer," I said.

"Yes." He half-filled the glass with ice, then poured his scotch. He leaned against the counter, his elbow brushing mine, and sipped his drink. "Tough day at the salt mine?"

"Just peachy."

He nodded.

I knew what he was up to, invading my personal space, but I wasn't going to be the first to move. I fixed my gaze on nothing, tipped my beer back and took another swig.

Brenda shook her head and charged forward, pushing us away from the sink. "I need to get the vegetables going—so outta my way."

We retreated to our regular seats facing one another at the table.

Richard stared at me.

I stared back.

"I need to borrow your camera."

"What for?"

"To take a picture."

"Of what?"

"Possibly a suspect."

"Who?"

"I don't want to talk about that right now."

"Why not? Do you think Brenda or I will go blabbing about it to someone?"

"No, I don't. I just…don't want to talk about it. Can I borrow your camera or not?"

Richard took another sip of his drink and shrugged. "I guess. When?"

"Tomorrow."

"Fine."

"Thanks."

Brenda whirled. "Will you two just stop it! I'm sick of it. You're behaving like a couple of spoiled brats."

Richard turned his gaze to me, all wide-eyed innocence. "Do you know what she's talking about?"

I shook my head. "Nope."

"Neither do I."

Fists clenched at her side, Brenda exhaled a breath, her irritation palpable. "Men!"

Chapter Eleven

There are distinct pleasures to being filthy rich—which Richard most certainly was. His top-of-the-line Nikon could probably be found at any newspaper around the country, and it was just what I needed to get candids of Cyn on her way into work. The problem was finding an inconspicuous place to take them from.

I spent an enjoyable evening reading the entire manual and playing with the camera. Not that I hadn't fooled with it before. Photography had long been a hobby of mine, and I still planned to set up a black-and-white darkroom in my new apartment. I loved digital, but there was something about good old-fashioned silver halide that kept me hankering for my old single lens reflex.

By the time I turned out the light, I felt comfortable using the camera. Richard and I hadn't sniped at one another while we went over the downloading procedure on his computer, either. Even Brenda's ire had cooled when I presented her with a minutes-old shot of her most-charming smile.

Dana, the mill's baker, had said Cyn usually strolled in around nine. I wasn't going to take a chance of missing her, so at eight-thirty I'd already parked my car two blocks away on Main Street and hoofed it down the side street to case out a hiding place.

The sun was already blazing and I was grateful to duck into the shadow of a Dumpster near the Hawk's Nest restaurant. Sweat beaded along my temples as I considered Cyn's reasons for legal action should she see me: harassment, stalking. If she was friendly with the restaurant's owner she might even get me picked up for trespassing. And who was I going to show the photo to anyway? The whole idea was beginning to seem absurd when Cyn's black Mercedes with New Mexico plates parked across the way.

I really was out of practice doing this kind of work. My hands were shaking and I had to steady the camera against the Dumpster to take the shots. Bing, bing, bing. She never suspected a thing. I waited for her to get inside the mill before I dared move out of the shadows. Still, I couldn't wait to see the pictures and punched them up. They looked pretty good on the camera's tiny screen. Only an enlargement would tell me how good.

"Hey!" A skinny, T-shirt-and-jeans-clad kid stood on the deck at the back of the restaurant, an unlit cigarette in his hand, staring down at me. "What the fuck you doin' down there?"

Shielding the camera, I took off, jogging west, away from the mill and the guy's heated shouts. Cold sweat poured off me as I circled round to the front of the building, easing into a brisk walk—not looking left or right—until I got to my car. I jumped in and burned rubber, hightailing it out of there.

The bar didn't open for another two hours, so I had plenty of time to go home and download the shots, but reconsidered. I wasn't yet ready to let Richard know my suspicions about his former friend and instead made for a professional photo shop.

Two of the shots weren't up to my usual standard, but then Cyn wasn't nearly as photogenic as Brenda—or maybe it was just because I didn't like her that the thought occurred to me. The third picture was good enough to show around.

I could've gone home, returned Richard's camera, and still had plenty of time to get back to the bar before opening. Instead, I purged the camera of the morning's pictures, packed it in the trunk, and headed straight for work.

I wasn't ready to face Richard's inevitable questions.

Tom was already at the bar when I got there, nearly forty-five minutes early. "Don't you ever sleep?" I asked as I tied an apron around my waist.

"Ya never sleep when you run a business like this," he said, looking over his reading glasses from behind the desk in his office.

I withdrew Cyn's photo from the envelope I'd brought in with me. "Have you ever seen this woman before?"

Tom studied the picture, and then shook his head.

"She didn't show up at Walt's funeral?"

Tom looked annoyed. "There were five of us there. I think I would've noticed."

I took the picture back. "It's the woman I told you about—Cynthia Lennox."

He studied my face. "You think she had something to do with Walt's death?"

"I don't know. I know he was in her place of business sometime before he died. I just don't know why."

Tom's eyes narrowed. "Where'd you learn that?"

I turned away, unwilling to look him in the eye. "Around."

The Molson truck had made its weekly stop and another thirty cases of beer awaited me. Loading the cooler had to be the worst part of the job. I hauled out the dolly and loaded it with beer. Before I had a chance to move it, though, Tom emerged from his office and headed into the men's room with a squirt bottle of Lysol and a roll of paper towels. It was then I decided I'd rather load the cooler.

Our first customer showed up at 11:02. Construction hadn't been kind to the orange-shirted worker with a heavily lined face, a halo of salt-and-pepper hair, and a five o'clock shadow, who took the stool closest to the taps. He rested his arms on the bar, looking up at the blank TV.

"It's too damned quiet in here," he bellowed across the dead-silent room. I found the remote, switched on the set and cranked up the sound two clicks.

"What'll you have?"

The older guy stared up at me. "Who the hell are you?"

I turned from the beer taps to face him. He had to be on the high end of fifty. His voice sounded like gravel—the cigarette pack folded into the upturned sleeve of his T-shirt gave away the reason for that. He didn't seem angry, more… depressed. I cut him some slack.

"Name's Jeff. Tom hired me last week. What can I get you?"

He hunkered down on the barstool. "A Molson and a shot."

I poured him the beer and gave him a shot of well whiskey. He lifted the shot glass in salute. "To poor Walt. He didn't deserve to go like that."

I watched him down it in a single gulp, then slam the glass onto the bar top. I reached under the bar to grab a bowl of pretzels and plunked them in front of the old guy to grease the wheels of conversation. "I never met Walt. What was he like?"

"A good guy." He nodded, staring off into space, sadness making his mouth droop.

I forced myself to be patient.

The man took a sip of his beer, set it down and stared into its foamy head. "We worked together for over twenty years with Belfry Construction before he got hurt." He shook his head. "Damn shame."

I waited for him to continue.

"Cable snapped on one of the cranes. Crushed him under a slab of concrete." The old guy shuddered and took another gulp of beer. "He never really was the same after that. Hell, who would be?"

"Yeah," I agreed lamely, and thought of the mugging that had forever changed me.

"Walt didn't have a lotta friends, ya know. Not real ones. Maybe just me." Then he laughed. "And a course his fancy women." He laughed again, a greasy, smarmy kind of giggle.

"Sorry?"

The old guy leaned closer, lowered his voice. "He liked to buy 'em pretty things. God knows why. They didn't do anything for him, if you know what I mean."

"No, I—"

"Can I get some service?" came a voice from the other end of the bar. I looked away from the old geezer. An overweight man whose sour expression conveyed his outlook on life sat at the far barstool. He punched the bar with a clenched fist. "Gimme a Bud light."

"Excuse me," I told the geezer and poured sourpuss his beer. He gave me a five and I rang up the sale, handing him the change, which he promptly pocketed. By the time I turned back, the old geezer had gone. A five and two ones sat under his glass.

Damn. I hadn't even had a chance to show him Cyn's picture, let alone ask him about Veronica.

Fancy women. That accounted for the sequined shoe. And that Walt got nothing in return from these women bore out my theory that he might've visited strip clubs. Still, it didn't feel right.

I picked up the geezer's glass, hoping he'd left behind some of his aura. No such luck. Like Richard, he didn't leave a trace I could tap into, and I had a feeling he wouldn't return to the bar now that his friend was gone.

But where the hell would I find Walt's fancy women? There was only one person I could ask.

Sourpuss was on his second beer and a couple of the regulars had arrived by the time Tom emerged from his office. Neither of us had done the fruit garnishes and he took a lemon and a lime from the little fridge under the bar and started cutting.

It was time to risk it all. I sidled closer. "Tom, what do you know about Walt's fancy women?"

Tom's head snapped up, his mouth dropped open, and his eyes went wide. He grabbed me by the arm and dragged me out of sourpuss's earshot. "Who the hell told you about that?" He licked his lips nervously and glanced over my shoulder, giving the regulars a once-over.

"Tom, you had to know once you asked me to look into Walt's death that I'd discover his secrets."

"Nobody knew about that stuff. *Nobody.*"

"An old work buddy of his did—he was in a little while ago and mentioned it. So who were these women? Strippers?"

"Not exactly. He only told me about it once. I didn't want to hear, so he never mentioned it again."

"Hear what?"

Tom ducked his head, whispered: "Drag queens."

This time it was my mouth that dropped open. How had my insight missed that little nugget?

"After his accident, Walt couldn't—he wasn't able to…" Tom sighed, groping for an explanation. "He couldn't do 'it' anymore. And I'm not sure he really missed it. He was never what you'd call a ladies' man. I think he was afraid of them. But he liked sexy stuff. And he told me he thought the drag queens were more…I dunno, more feminine than the kinds of women he was used to meeting. On the weekends he'd go to some place downtown—around Pearl Street. Just to watch, he said. But that can't have anything to do with his death."

"Tom, it could have *everything* to do with his death," I said, thinking about the damned red-sequined high heel and the evil little pillow emblazoned "Veronica."

Tom shook his head, definitely in denial.

"There's more," I said. "Walt rented a storage unit on Transit Road. I checked it out the other night and it's full of porn—specifically, foot-fetish stuff."

Tom's head sagged. He looked like he wanted to puke. "I don't want you digging into this anymore, Jeff. Please, just drop it."

"I can't. The cops arrested the wrong person for his murder."

"So? What's that to you?"

"It means an innocent man will probably go to jail for the rest of his life."

"The guy's crazy. He's a career criminal. He's—"

"That still leaves the person who killed Walt running around loose, and free to kill again. Do you want that on your conscience? Because I sure don't."

Tom sighed, guilt and despair twisting his features. "No, I guess I don't either. But if this stuff about Walt becomes public, it'll kill my aunt. Damn it, Jeff, she's eighty-seven. I don't want her to know how low her son sank."

"It's bound to come out. But she doesn't have to know you were ever involved."

He held out his hands. "I'm not. I'm out of this as of right now."

Exactly what I'd expected. Now to voice my bigger fear. "Do you want me out of here, too?"

Tom let out a shuddering breath. "If I thought it would keep you from poking around in this whole mess, I'd shitcan you right now." He wiped a trembling hand over his mouth. "You're a damn good bartender, much better than Walt ever was, and the guys seem to like you. But don't talk about Walt to the customers. Not now—not ever. In this bar, Walt's memory is respected. You got that?"

"Got it."

Tom nailed me with a glare. "Okay. But let's not talk about this anymore. No matter what you find out."

I didn't answer because I couldn't promise I wouldn't need more information from him later.

"You girls about done with your chitchat?" I looked over my shoulder at sourpuss who held up his almost-empty glass.

Tom turned away. I straightened, hardened my features, and faced the jerk. "That was a Bud light, right?"

"Damn straight."

Sourpuss picked up the glass, raised it in salute, tipped it back and took a big gulp.

And may you never lose someone you care about to murder, I wished him. Because whatever else I'd find out about Walt Kaplan, I had a feeling the worst was yet to come. Tom didn't hate me now; how would he feel when whatever else there was to discover came to light?

Chapter Twelve

Upon my return to Buffalo, I hadn't been in any shape to investigate the local nightlife, so I knew nothing about it and even less about its drag clubs. The phone book was the first stop in my quest for knowledge. Nothing under bars. Taverns took up an entire page, and nightclubs a mere five inches of type. None of them had display ads. So much for the phone book. Next stop, the Internet.

Since arriving home, I'd successfully avoided Richard, and even found his computer unoccupied. I slipped into the big leather chair in his study and powered up the machine. I needed my own computer, but that wouldn't happen until I got my finances back under control. My palms were damp as I logged onto the Internet, fighting the urge to keep looking over my shoulder for Big Brother.

A Google search later, I had a list of URLs for Buffalo gay bars and drag shows. I clicked on the first one: Club Monticello. White type on a black background gave way to color pictures of the featured acts. Queen Camilla, Libby Lips, Tammy Ten Toes—that sounded like a possibility for Walt—and a trio billed as the Divine Divas. No Veronica.

I clicked on one of the pictures and a bio and several other professional photographs appeared. Tammy Ten Toes, a buxom pseudo-wench, wore a silver lamé cat suit, one hip thrust forward toward the camera, with her best foot forward—encased in a glittering silver platform heel, her silver-painted toenails sparkling.

Walt had been titillated by this kind of stuff; I wasn't. Instead, my thoughts wandered back to Maggie, and the fact that it had been a long time since I got laid.

"Now what are you up to?"

I jerked in the chair—my heart racing. Richard appeared behind me, looking surly.

"Do I have to ask your permission every time I want to look something up online?"

"No," he said, but his expression said otherwise.

It was taking all my self-control to hold onto my temper. "Thank you." I turned back to the monitor and clicked on the "Home" button, then on "Show Times." The image changed, the club's schedule filling the screen. Club Monticello was billed as the "Biggest, Best Gay Bar in Buffalo," but the drag shows were listed only for Friday, Saturday and Sunday evenings.

Richard leaned in close enough that I could feel his breath on the back of my neck. "First foot fetishes, now drag shows? What's next, kiddy porn?"

Slowly, I swiveled the chair around to face him. "I'm going to pretend you didn't say that."

He backed off a step. "You know what I mean."

I kept my mouth shut, afraid of saying something I might always regret. I turned back to the monitor, shut down the connection and turned off the computer. Pushing back the chair, I got up and headed for the door. Richard moved to block me.

"I got a call from Cyn Lennox this afternoon. A worker at the Hawk's Nest saw you taking photos of her. What the hell is going on? Don't tell me *she's* your suspect."

"Fine. I won't." I moved to push past him but he blocked me again.

"You can't be serious. She didn't even know Walt Kaplan."

"Did she tell you that?"

He had no answer.

"Walt was in her office just days before he died."

"How do you know?"

"How do you think?"

Richard gritted his teeth in annoyance. "You got that the day we visited her?"

I nodded.

"Why didn't you say something then?"

"What for, and get you angry—like you are now? No one wants to hear an old friend might be a murderer."

"'Might be,'" he repeated. "Does that mean you're not sure?"

"You're damn right I'm not sure. And I don't like going around telling my suspicions to people when I don't have the facts to back them up."

That mollified him, but only for a moment. "She said she'd file charges if you show up again."

"I don't need to go back there anymore. I have what I need to keep going."

"Her picture?"

I nodded.

He shook his head. "I'm asking you, Jeff, please drop this."

"Why, because your friend's got something to hide and doesn't want the truth to come out? Even if she didn't do it, she knows something about Walt's death and isn't telling."

"Then what is it you think you know besides Kaplan was in her office?"

I clamped my lips together and looked away.

"Could it be you haven't got anything *but* a hunch?"

"I've got more. Lots more."

"Then why don't you share it with the cops?"

"I told you, I'm not ready yet."

"Then why don't you tell me?" He waited for an answer. "No, you don't want to talk to me, either. You've hardly said a word to me in days. What's going on?"

The frustration in his voice only cranked up my feelings of guilt. Yet I refused to meet his gaze.

"I thought you counted me as not only your brother, but your friend. Lately you're cutting me out. Why? It can't be just because of Cyn."

The fatigue I'd been denying for days finally caught up with me, and I knew I wasn't in any shape for a battle. "I don't mean to, it's just that—" I shut my eyes and exhaled, wishing I could be somewhere—anywhere—else. When I opened them again, Richard was still staring at me, disappointment shadowing his eyes.

"Look, Rich, you don't approve of what I do, be it getting a job or looking into Walt Kaplan's death, or even how I'm handling this situation with Maggie Brennan. I can't do a damn thing right in your eyes."

"Don't give me that shit. If you can't be honest with me, at least be honest with yourself."

His words stung, but he was right. I wasn't telling the truth. I wasn't capable of telling him what I really felt. I trusted Richard more than anyone else on this Earth and still I couldn't level with him.

Richard was the first to look away. He crossed the room to the dry bar across the way and poured himself a neat scotch. I stood in the doorway, unable to move.

He took a sip and didn't look back. "Go on, take off. It's what you do best."

My memory flashed back to the day, eighteen years before, when he'd driven me to the airport. Without his knowledge, I'd enlisted in the Army. When, bags packed and needing a ride, I finally told him, two hours before my flight, he'd been hurt and angry. Really, really angry. By the time we stood together in the airport's departure lounge, he'd come to reluctant acceptance.

"Thanks for…" After nearly four unhappy years in the Alpert residence, I wasn't sure what. "Everything," I'd mumbled.

I'd been shocked when he'd grabbed me in a fierce hug. "I love you, kid," he'd managed to croak in my ear.

I didn't hug him back. I'd been embarrassed beyond words.

When he let go, I'd clutched my carry-on and bolted for the jetway. Yet at the last second, I'd turned back to see tears in his eyes. Guilt made me give him a perfunctory wave before I charged ahead to escape what had become for me a very painful exit.

I didn't see Richard again for six years, and even then hadn't been able to let go of the bitterness.

Richard's back was still to me. He raised his glass to drink again and, true to form, I fled for the safety of my room, feeling just as stupid and unworthy as I had all those years ago.

***

I rang the buzzer and waited. Except for the dim light within, the bakery was dark…as usual. Then, a bulky silhouette blotted out a portion of light.

Sophie ambled forward and unlocked the heavy plate glass door, her face creased with worry. "You don't look happy."

"I'm not."

She ushered me inside, closed and locked the door. "So come in and tell all."

I shuffled along behind her. "Nothing much to tell."

We sat down at the wobbly card table. Tonight, oblivious of the outside temperature, she had hot chocolate steaming in mugs with hairline cracks crazing them.

"It's this murder, isn't it?" she asked. I nodded. "Things aren't going fast enough for you, eh?"

I took a sip of my cocoa and shrugged. "The police arrested the wrong man."

"What else?"

Again I shrugged. "Did you ever connect with someone who knew what you were thinking, feeling?"

"Your Maggie?"

"She's not exactly mine. But she says she can feel what I feel. I guess she's never done that with anyone else."

"Mmm."

"Is that a yes or a no?"

Sophie tilted her head to one side, considering. "I wish I could say yes. Sometimes these gifts we have isolate us from others. We both know how frightening it can be to know things we'd rather not know. Is Maggie afraid?"

"She's freaked. So am I."

Sophie leaned back in her chair and folded her hands over her ample stomach. "This murder—Maggie—that's not really why you came here tonight."

I met her gaze. "I guess not."

"Tell me."

She was right. I had come there to talk about something else, only now I wasn't sure I could.

She reached across the little table and patted my hand. "Guilt is a terrible thing to live with. I know about it firsthand."

I stared down at the circle of tiny bubbles rimming my cocoa.

"When Richard got shot, I actually prayed to God, 'Don't let him die.' I thought that would be enough. I thought everything would be all right if he made it and was okay. But I can't get away from the fact it's my fault he almost died, and makes me one helluva shit as a brother."

Sophie frowned. "That's not true. You love him and you need each other. And who's filling your head with this nonsense, anyway?"

Maggie. Myself. "Nobody important."

"Then why do you listen?" she scolded. "Does your brother blame you?"

"No. He worries about me like, like—" I laughed. "An old yenta."

Sophie reared back as though offended. "I'm not a yenta, but I do worry about you. I worry about all my," she hesitated, "friends."

I couldn't help but smile. "And you're not old, either."

"Oh, you lie so well." She grinned and reached across to pat my hand again. Then her smile faded and it was her turn to inspect the depths of her mug. "Your brother has reason to worry. Like what happened to you yesterday."

My head jerked up. Sophie's expression was reproachful.

"Do you think that was deliberate?" I didn't have to clarify what I meant. She already knew what had happened to me in the ramp garage.

"You need to be careful. More careful than you've been."

"That only proves me right. Getting Richard involved would only endanger him."

"You *need* him. And maybe somebody else will need him, too."

"What do you mean?"

"Drink your cocoa," she ordered, and took a sip of her own.

"What is it you aren't telling me?"

"I don't know the whys of everything, either. I just know." She leaned closer. "There's a reason you two were brought back together after so many years. It's best not to tempt fate by staying apart."

I sipped my hot chocolate, its warmth spreading through me, making me sweat. Sophie's logic didn't make a whole helluva lot of sense to me, but in only the short time

I'd known her, I'd learned to trust her advice. Still…"What if something happens to Rich again and it's my fault?"

"Didn't you tell me he pushed you out of the way of that bullet?"

My hands tightened around my mug. "Yes, but—"

"Then how was it your fault?"

"Because the killer came after me."

"Would *you* rather be dead?"

Sometimes—like right then—I wasn't sure about the answer to that question.

"I don't want anyone's death—particularly Richard's—on my conscience."

Sophie scowled, sat back in her chair and exhaled through her nose. "Didn't you hear what I told you just now?"

"Yeah—and didn't you hear what I told you?"

Sophie grabbed her mug of cocoa, chugged it, and smacked it down on the table. She pushed back her chair and stood. "It's time for you to go."

I stayed put.

"Come on, I need my beauty sleep," she said and grasped my arm, pulling me up.

Her abrupt dismissal annoyed me, but I wasn't going to be obstinate about it. Then again, she probably thought I *was* being obstinate.

I followed her to the front of the shop. "Am I going to be welcome next time I come?"

Sophie stopped abruptly and I nearly fell over her. She stared up at me, looking at once puzzled and distressed. "Why wouldn't you be welcome?"

"Oh, I dunno—the fact you're kicking me out right now."

"I told you. I need my beauty sleep." She grasped my shoulders, pulled me down and gave my cheek a wet kiss. "Next time I'll make *placek*. You'll feel better about things by then."

"Okay."

She patted my back before leading me to the door. I passed through it and she locked it behind me. I crossed the parking lot and paused, turned back to wave but Sophie had already retreated.

You won't solve this without him, she'd said.

I could take that two ways, I thought as I made my way to the corner to cross at the light. Either I just gave up and let the visions of a red stiletto high heel torture me for the rest of my life, or I caved in and put my brother's life at risk by letting him help me solve Walt Kaplan's murder.

I wasn't sure which was the worse form of purgatory.

***

Sleep didn't want to come to me. Tired as I was, there were too many thoughts, too many scenarios swirling around in my brain. In the early days of my marriage to Shelley, I'd often lie awake in the middle of the night. Sometimes during the torment of sleeplessness Shelley would wake and we'd make love. Those way-too-early couplings were the sweetest memories of our time together. We were in sync back then. Somehow she always seemed to sense when I needed her most, and she'd be there for me. That was, of course, before cocaine became her lover of choice.

I rolled over onto my side and tried to blank out my thoughts, but an image of Maggie flashed across my mind's eye. She seemed to want me, and God knows I'd wanted her from the first time I'd met her. And yet...I didn't want our first time together to be cheap or tawdry.

I closed my eyes and once again saw her sitting at Richard's kitchen table days before, her lashes long and the hunger in her eyes reaching out for me. I couldn't handle it then, but right about now...

A myriad of sensations swept through me and I allowed myself to enjoy them, letting it build inside me until—

My eyes snapped open, every muscle in my body tensing as I made a grab for the bedside phone. "Maggie?"

"Jeff?" She sounded startled. "It didn't even ring."

I exhaled and rolled onto my back. "I didn't want it to wake Richard and Brenda."

"You knew it was me?"

"Yeah."

She was quiet for a few moments. "I was lying awake and had this irresistible urge to call you. I didn't even think that I might wake Brenda and Richard. Oh, God, what if you hadn't picked up? I would've looked like such an idiot."

"But I did pick up."

"Yes." Her voice relaxed, and I could envision her smile. "You did."

"I meant to thank you for the flowers. They were very pretty."

"I hope they didn't make you feel uncomfortable. Brenda said you liked flowers. She showed me your garden. You've done a beautiful job."

"Thanks."

I closed my eyes, concentrated until I could hear Maggie's soft breaths against the receiver. I was content to lie there and just listen, but eventually she broke the quiet.

"How long are we going to wait?"

I wanted to laugh. In my own mind, we'd already—"Are you in a hurry?"

"I…might be. It's been a long time since I even wanted—Since I…" Her words trailed off.

I remembered what she'd told me months before. A husband who'd preferred men to Maggie, and had been too chickenshit to admit it to her until they'd been married eight years. She knew my tale of marital woe, too. I thought we'd get together back then, but the timing hadn't been right.

"What are you doing tomorrow?" I asked.

"Working."

"All day?"

"What did you have in mind?"

A stupid grin creased my lips. "You ever hear of afternoon delight?"

She hesitated. "Your place or mine?"

"I haven't got a place…yet."

"Then mine it is."

"I get out of work at four."

"I could get out a bit early. Do you know where I live?"

"No, but I bet I could find you."

"I bet you could." Still, she gave me the address. I didn't bother to write it down. I wasn't likely to forget it.

"Then I guess I'll see you tomorrow."

"Tomorrow it is."

Long seconds turned into a minute, then two before Maggie finally hung up the phone.

Minutes later I drifted off to sleep, and dreamed of Maggie Brennan.

Chapter Thirteen

My second Friday at the bar was pretty much a repeat of the week before, except this time the customers had accepted Walt's departure from this world and the talk was back to sports.

I'm not the world's biggest sports nut. I can hold my own in conversations about basketball and football, but baseball and golf leave me yawning. I didn't want to dwell on my upcoming evening with Maggie, either, so I had a lot of time to think about Walt's death and what I did and didn't know about it.

If I hadn't been working, I might've accomplished more with my half-assed investigation. Like taking a look at Cyn Lennox's home, not that it would tell me anything more about her. I realized I knew virtually nothing about little workaholic Eugene Higgins other than he was Cyn's nephew. And how was I going to find out anything about him? I could tail him after we both got out of work, but I wasn't sure I had the stamina that a stakeout would require.

It bugged me that Walt hadn't fought against his attacker. Could he have been unconscious at the time? The newspaper reports hadn't mentioned any kind of head injury. Had he been drugged or even drunk? How long would it take for the crime lab to come back with a blood and tissue workup? They'd already closed the books on Walt's murder and weren't likely to prosecute Buchanan for months, so what was the hurry anyway—at least from the cops' or prosecutor's perspective?

Walt had been re-dressed and dumped behind the mill. If Cyn had been involved in his death, it would be pure stupidity to dump the body behind her place of work, and Cyn didn't strike me as brainless. And yet, the flash of insight I'd had of Walt in her office was really the only evidence I had against her—pretty insubstantial at best. The two pairs of shoes were somehow connected…but how? It couldn't have been a coincidence that Cyn owned the shoes Walt had copied. For one thing, I didn't believe in coincidences despite the fact Cyn's vacation home's address and the storage locker number had been the same.

I could go back to Walt's apartment and soak myself in whatever was left of him, but I didn't think that would yield any results, either.

A dull pounding in my skull told me I needed to take a break from this train of thought—especially if I wanted to be in any shape to socialize later in the day. But suddenly something else occurred to me. That flash of insight I'd experienced in Cyn's office hadn't been from Walt's perspective. Someone had been looking at him, had experienced seeing Walt's smile of pleasure. I tried to refocus on the image but it wouldn't come. I'd been so obnoxious that there was no way Cyn was ever going to let me back in to soak up any leftover vibes, and I could kick myself for not thinking of it when I'd gone back to the mill to talk to Dana Watkins.

Had I been picking up on Cyn? Would she be attracted to an introverted loner who could no longer perform sexually? Or had she and Walt been casual acquaintances who shared a love of women's footwear?

Maybe if I could touch Cyn, I'd know, but that wasn't going to happen, either.

"Give it up!"

Startled by this piece of advice, I glanced up to see one of the customers shaking his fist at the TV.

"God, what a bunch of losers," he groused.

Give it up. Yeah, I ought to, at least for the day. The prospect of an evening with Maggie was far more appealing than beating myself over the head with circuitous arguments and half-baked theories.

I wanted to do something nice for Maggie, something she wouldn't expect. Flowers or candy seemed too clichéd. Something unexpected—but something that showed her a facet of my personality she might not have considered. A glance around the bar didn't fill me with creative ideas. Then again…

***

At four fifty-three, I pulled into the driveway of Maggie's rather average looking duplex in Clarence. She stood behind the screen door in a white tank top, pink shorts, and flip-flops, waiting for me. No sexy dress, no heels—looking the antithesis of tawdry.

"You're here," she said with pleasure.

"I am."

"Come in." Maggie opened the screen door and immediately a dog planted its nose in my crotch. "Holly!" Maggie admonished and pulled her golden retriever back by its collar. "I'm sorry. Dogs like to—"

"I know," I cut her off, and offered the dog my hand as an alternative. She sniffed my fingers and I must've passed muster for she licked them enthusiastically.

Maggie eyed the brown grocery bag in my other hand. "You didn't have to bring anything."

"It's not much. Just an icebreaker. That is, if you've got ice. I need to borrow your fridge, or maybe freezer, too."

"Sure. Come on into the kitchen."

I followed her up the stairs to the second floor apartment. If I was unimpressed with the outside of her home, the inside changed my mind. Contemporary leather furniture stressed comfort. Signed lithographs lined the walls—the ambiance peaceful and laid-back with a southwestern flair. For an absurd moment I wondered if I should introduce her to Cyn.

Maggie led me into the cozy kitchen with its butter yellow walls and frosted-glass-fronted cabinets. She leaned against the white Formica counter. "It's all yours," she said with a sweep of her hand.

I set the grocery sack on the counter. "So, what do you like to drink?"

"I'm strictly a gin-and-tonic kind of girl. At least when it's hot out. Winters, I revert to whiskey sours."

I thought as much. "It's the taste of juniper that attracts you in summer."

She shrugged. "I guess."

"Then let me make you a surprise. But first I've got to wash my hands. Dog saliva and a good drink don't go together." Maggie laughed and pointed toward the sink.

She watched as I withdrew a bottle of Beefeaters gin, a pint of Perry's French Vanilla ice cream, and a liter of club soda from the grocery bag. "I need ice, a tall glass, a shot glass, and an ice cream scoop."

Maggie gave me what I needed before hauling out the remains of what was once a seven-pound bag of ice. She radiated pure delight as I added ice, measured the gin, plopped in a scoop of ice cream, and topped it with club soda. I gave it a quick stir before pushing the fizzing glass toward her.

Maggie's expression was enigmatic as she picked up the glass and took a tentative sip. Then her eyes widened and a smile lit up her face. "Wow, you are a good bartender."

I wish I could've taken credit for the drink. "It's called a silver stallion."

"It tastes like magic." She took another sip. "Is this your way of lowering my inhibitions?"

"Do I really need to?"

She looked away, blushing. "I guess not. Are you having one?"

"I'll take a beer, if you've got one."

She crossed to the fridge and came up with a bottle of Labatt Blue. "Want a glass?"

"It's not necessary." I cracked the cap and held it out for a toast. "*Na Zdrowie!*"

Maggie's glass touched the bottle. "Cheers."

We watched each other drink, then Maggie said, "Let's go sit down."

She put the ice cream and ice in the freezer before leading me back to the living room. Her second-floor apartment was as hot as Hades, but a fan pointed at the couch recirculated the air. We sank into the sofa's depths, and Holly stood before Maggie, looking expectant.

"You had your dinner," Maggie said, but Holly didn't seem interested in our drinks. She maneuvered herself between the coffee table and us, sitting down so that her warm body pressed against my right leg. I petted her head and she turned her dark brown eyes on me. I didn't know dogs could smile.

Maggie set her drink down. "Holly, it's too hot for that. Go lie down." The dog obediently got up, trotted across the room to a plaid cushion and settled herself on it, perching her head on her crossed front legs, letting out a loud, doggy sigh.

I wiped my sweating beer bottle against my equally damp forehead. "Hot in here."

"You, or the air?" Maggie asked, her eyes glinting.

"Both."

She picked up her drink again, sipped it, not meeting my gaze. "My bedroom is air-conditioned."

I raised an eyebrow. "Do tell."

She flashed a glance my way. "I'm not usually this forward. It's just—"

I set my beer down, clasped her moist palm. A current passed between us. Her gasp was more surprise than pleasure—that came a few seconds later.

"Oh wow," she muttered, her breaths coming fast and shallow. Mine had picked up, too. We looked at one another for a moment, then I pulled her to me and kissed her. She returned it with equal vigor, the hunger I'd sensed days before building inside her.

"First kiss," she whispered, eyes wide with growing anticipation.

Despite the heat, a delightful shiver of longing ran through her—through me. Dizziness and desire whirled through me—a rush like I'd never known. She leaned in to kiss me again. "It's more comfortable in the bedroom," she breathed.

"I'm all for comfort."

She pulled me up from the couch, led me toward the back of the apartment. As she reached for the door handle, I stopped. She looked up at me, puzzled. I drew her close, nuzzled my nose against her ear. "Don't tell Brenda everything," I whispered. "Let's save this for just us."

She kissed me again and opened the door.

I didn't go home that night.

Chapter Fourteen

I sat at Maggie's kitchen table, the newspaper spread before me, nursing my second cup of coffee when her phone rang the next morning. "You wanna get that?" she called from the other room.

I pushed away from the table and grabbed the kitchen extension. "Maggie's house."

"Jeff?" It was Sam.

"How the hell did you find me this time?"

"I asked—"

"Yeah, yeah, my brother."

"Maggie's house, huh? Sounds like you got lucky. How'd you like to bat a thousand?"

"How so?"

"I'm going to interview a contact this morning. Thought you might want to tag along."

"What's in it for you if I do?"

"I dunno. Maybe you could play human lie detector for me. Tell me if this guy's hosing me."

"You don't trust your own instincts?"

"Of course I do, but I figure it can't hurt for you to tag along. You might get something he doesn't want to share with me—if you know what I mean."

"Just who are we going to talk to?" I asked.

"A cop wannabe. Jailer in the county lockup. He called and asked if someone wanted the inside scoop on Craig Buchanan. I told him I'd meet him since I can't get to Buchanan myself. You know they won't let a reporter talk to a suspect until after a trial. Think we might sway the pool of jurors."

"I did know that. But shouldn't Buchanan have been transferred to the county psych unit by now?"

"Apparently he talked to this guy before they shipped him out."

"Any reason why he waited so long to contact you?"

"No one else bit. He's got a bit of a reputation. You'll see what I mean when you meet him."

"Did you tell your contact you were bringing a psychic along?"

"You're a fellow reporter. A stringer."

"Gee, suddenly I feel empowered. When?"

"An hour. I'll meet you at your brother's house?"

"You got it."

***

Maggie had made other plans for later in the morning, so we said a quick good-bye, sealed it with a kiss and a vague agreement to meet again sometime soon.

She'd radiated happiness when I left her.

So did I.

I lay low when I returned home. I snuck in the back—went straight to my own room, showered, shaved, changed, and was standing in the driveway when Sam's SUV pulled in.

I never saw Richard or Brenda, and heaved a sigh of relief at not having to explain why I hadn't called to let them know I wouldn't be home the night before.

"Where are we going?" I asked Sam when I jumped into his car and buckled my seatbelt.

"To Starbucks. I hope you like coffee."

As Sam backed the car down the drive, a big black motorcycle blasted down the street, heading south. "Hey, catch up with that guy, will you?"

"What for?"

"Just do it."

Sam tromped on it, tires spinning, his Lincoln Navigator earning its reputation as a kick-ass vehicle. "What's going on?" he asked again as we roared down the quiet street.

"I got a hunch about that bike."

By the time we reached the Y where LeBrun Road runs into Saratoga, there was no sign of the biker. "Now what?" Sam asked.

I shook my head, exasperated. "We head out for Starbucks."

Sam took the right fork; that would take us back to Main Street. "What was that all about?"

"Somebody on a big black bike tried to run me down the other day. I guess I'm just paranoid."

"Or smart to be careful."

We turned right on Main and I explained what had happened, making light of it. I was glad when Sam went into his grand inquisitor act, asking me about Maggie in as many ways as he could possibly phrase one question. I resisted his attempts to wheedle information from me until we ended up on Transit Road and ordered our preferences. Sam paid—no doubt on an expense account—and we sat down at one of the tables. Some kind of new age music played in the background. Nice. Mellow. Very Saturday morningish.

"How are we supposed to know this guy?" I asked.

"He said he'd be wearing a Bills cap."

I looked around the joint. Two of the other four male patrons were Buffalo Bills fans. "Should we raise a flag or something?"

Sam scowled. "Shut up and drink your coffee."

I sipped my coffee.

"Oh, and when he gets here, make sure you shake his hand."

Sam hadn't been kidding when he said he'd wanted a human lie detector. He'd be damned disappointed if I couldn't sense a thing about the guy.

I drank my coffee. In fact, I'd drained my cup and was about to start twiddling my thumbs when an acne-scarred bozo in a Bills cap, T-shirt, and team red-and-blue striped sweatpants entered the front door. I swear Sam actually cringed.

"My crap-o-meter just flew into the red zone," I muttered to Sam.

"Don't rub it in." He stood, braved a smile, and waved the guy over. "His name's Mike," Sam said under his breath.

Mike swaggered over with the confidence of a high school jock who'd just made the big game's winning touchdown. But high school had been at least two decades ago, as evidenced by the beer gut expanding his sweats. Mike's confidence wavered as he saw me at the table. "Who's this guy?" he demanded. "I can't afford to lose my job because of this, you know."

"You won't lose your job," Sam assured him. "I keep my sources confidential. This is my colleague, Ernie Pyle."

I rose from my seat, offered my hand. Mike shook it and I was immediately toasted with a blast of what I can only describe as nonexistent hot air. At least fifty percent of what he was about to say was sure to be pure horseshit—just what I was sure Sam already suspected.

We all sat down.

"So what've you got to tell me?" Sam asked.

"You wanted to know about Craig Buchanan, the guy they got for murder in Williamsville."

Sam nodded.

Mike crossed his arms over his puffed out chest. "He's certifiable. Gonna plead insanity."

Sam gave me the fish eye, struggled for composure, and asked, "How does Buchanan feel about that?"

Mike shrugged. "Aren't you gonna buy me coffee or something? I at least deserve a coffee for what I'm about to reveal."

Who did this guy think he was, David Copperfield?

"How do you take it?" Sam asked, sounding bored.

Mike ordered the most expensive brew on the menu board, taking great delight in his first sip. Then he settled back in his chair, ready to regale us with his tale. He didn't seem to notice our lack of real interest.

"Buchanan," Sam prompted.

"They dragged him in on a Saturday night. Poor creep stank to high heaven. We hosed him off and threw him in a cell 'til they could get a psychiatric evaluation."

"And after that?"

"'The shrinks were gonna put him on meds to calm him down."

This could take all day. "What did Buchanan say about the murder?" I asked.

"He don't know if he did it or not. Says he found the knife in a Dumpster. It's a pretty thing. Silver sparkles in the handle."

I took in a sharp breath as an image flashed in my mind. *A smooth, manicured hand—firecracker red nail-polished fingers—holding the stiletto knife. Gently waving it in front of a sparkling silver high-heeled foot. Lightly tracing the blade along the ankle and up the shapely calf.*

Was this the same person who'd worn the red stiletto heels or someone else?

I wasn't sure.

Tuning back to the present, I found two pairs of eyes staring at me.

"Go on," Sam said, diverting attention back to Mike.

"Buchanan said he used the knife to kill rats. He'd build a fire in the parking lot behind the Burger King and roast 'em then eat 'em."

The horseshit had now begun. I tuned out and pondered the significance of the new vision. I'd seen the murder weapon. Big deal. It didn't bring me any clearer understanding of what had happened to Walt. My certainty about a number of things wavered; was I seeing the knife and the shoes from perhaps the killer's perspective, not Walt's, Cyn's, or somebody else's?

I needed to thin out my list of possible suspects. To do that, I needed to touch Cyn, or if not her, something of hers, something personal, to see if I could home in on the same aura—perspective—whatever. The only handy thing that came to mind was her car. She left it parked outside the mill seven days a week, so I would have access to the body, but I wasn't sure that would be good enough. I'd need to touch the seats or the steering wheel.

Damn, I should've checked out her house. If she parked outside, I'd have a better shot of breaking into the car under cover of darkness than in broad daylight in a commercial area where people came and went all day.

"Hey, Ernie. Ern," Sam called.

My head jerked up. I'd forgotten my pseudonym. "Yeah?"

"You got any more questions for Mike?"

"No."

Sam stood and offered Mike his hand. "Give me a call when you have another hot tip."

"You bet. And thanks for the coffee."

Mike swaggered away from the table and Sam reclaimed his seat. "Well that wasn't worth the price of admission."

"Tell me about it."

"But you got something. You always zone out like that when it happens?"

I ignored the question. "I saw the knife. Whether it was used to kill rats, I can't say." I wasn't ready to tell him about the other visions. "I need to break into a car without destroying anything. You know where I can lay my hands on one of those plastic things cops and tow truck guys use to open locked doors?"

"Breaking and entering. What do you hope to gain?"

"Knowledge."

Sam looked thoughtful. "I might be able to get my hands on one. But they don't work in every car, you know.

If it doesn't, are you willing to smash a window and commit a misdemeanor?"

"I don't know. I'm not that desperate yet."

"Okay. I'll look into it. What's your next move?"

I didn't want to tell him, and that was unfair because he'd included me on what was for him a waste-of-time interview. "Do you want to come with me when I look into that car?"

"Not if you're going be destroying private property. But I'll bail you out if you get caught. That is, if you're willing to share what you learn."

"I'm willing—but on my terms."

He leaned closer, lowered his voice. "I'm giving you a lot more rope than I'd give any other source."

"Why's that?"

"You have your hunches, I have mine. And one day we're going to break a big story. Much bigger than this Kaplan murder. I'm willing to be patient."

For someone used to getting weird vibes and insight out of nowhere, his words sent an unexpected and frightening chill through me.

"Meanwhile," Sam continued. "I'm working on getting Kaplan's autopsy photos. You want a look?"

I shook my head. "I saw him dead, and I'll probably see him dead again—in a lot more detail than I'll want. That's enough for me."

Sam looked intrigued, but luckily didn't push it. He grabbed our empty cups. "Let's get outta here. I've got other things to do today that have nothing to do with murder."

***

Fifteen minutes later, Sam dropped me off at the base of Richard's driveway. I gave him a quick wave before I turned to head up the drive. I didn't see any cars except my own, but then Richard and Brenda usually parked in the garage. I hoped they were off playing golf, as I didn't want to run into them. Okay, I didn't want to run into Richard.

I headed straight for my car, had the keys in my hand, when I heard my name called: Richard, coming at me from the backyard.

Slowly I turned and tried not to look annoyed. I couldn't say the same for him.

"Where are you off to now?" he demanded.

I couldn't tell him the mill, he'd already warned me not to go near the place. "Out."

"You just came back."

"And now I'm going out again."

"Where?"

"To the drugstore," I lied. "I'm running out of shaving cream. You need anything?"

"You didn't call last night. We were worried."

"You knew where I was. Otherwise you wouldn't have told Sam where to find me."

"Yeah, but—"

"Rich, you didn't keep tabs on me this close when I was a teenager. Why the sudden interest?"

"It's not me," he lied. "It's Brenda. You know how she is—how she worries."

"Uh-huh." I opened the driver's door, a burst of hot air assaulting me. "You didn't answer my question. Do you want anything from the drugstore?"

He shook his head. "Are you gonna be home for supper?

"Probably. If not, I'll let you know."

"Good."

I got in my car, unrolled the window and buckled up before starting the engine. "See ya."

Richard moved aside as I backed down the driveway. He walked to the center of the drive and watched me take off down the road.

I hated this crap. I hated the tension between us. Maybe moving into the apartment over the garage was a big mistake. Maybe I needed to cut ties. But I couldn't. My job paid shit and in less than a week Richard had had to bail my ass out of trouble—twice, as he had already pointed out.

Sophie was right. I needed him. And not just for what he did for me monetarily. He'd helped me solve the banker's murder. Without him, I couldn't have done it. And, if I was honest with myself, I needed him because he was my brother and we'd wasted a lot of years—years we'd never get back.

I'd been so lost in thought I didn't realize I'd driven to the mill on autopilot. The lunchtime crowd hadn't yet piqued, but there were enough cars parked outside to hide mine further up the street. I grabbed a baseball cap from the back seat of my car and found my sunglasses in the glove box. Not much of a disguise, but all I had.

I felt conspicuous as I walked along the sidewalk and over to Cyn's car. As expected, it was locked with all the windows rolled up. I clasped the driver's door handle and closed my eyes. The sensations that traveled through me were vague, meaningless shadows of emotions I couldn't quite grasp. Was Cyn the same person who'd worn the sparkling silver high heels, played with the silver-sparkled knife that had taken Walt Kaplan's life? Dammit, I just wasn't sure.

The mill's door opened and a young couple stepped out onto the small front porch. I did an about-face and started back for my car. It would take a baseball bat to smash Cyn's driver's side window. My skull had been fractured by a baseball bat. I didn't want to sink to wielding one to get what I wanted. But I needed to get into that car, and if the lock opener wouldn't work, I'd have to seriously consider visiting the closest sporting goods store and buying a bat.

Unless...

Richard and Cyn had been friends. What kind of influence could he still have over her?

No, that wasn't an option. And convincing him Cyn might be capable of murder would probably be impossible. I'd have to continue on my own and hope that later I could make it up to Richard.

And what about the next time I got insight on a murder, because I had a feeling this wouldn't be the last time it would happen.

I got in my car, slammed the door, and clasped the steering wheel until my knuckles went white. Giving in to this psychic shit felt like embracing the dark side, and I sometimes wondered if surrendering to it would condemn my soul to eternal damnation. I wasn't a churchgoer, wasn't even sure I believed in a higher power, but going after the scum of the earth that committed murder had to be a one-way ticket to salvation. Didn't it?

The more experienced I became at it, the less sure I was.

Chapter Fifteen

Dinner that night proved awkward. Richard spoke in clipped sentences and seemed to have a stick up his ass. Brenda made innocuous small talk while I pushed peas around my plate until I felt I could gracefully escape their company. That still gave me way too long to wait until the midnight hour. I took a nap, first setting my alarm for ten fifty-nine p.m.

I wasn't used to staying up 'til all hours of the night anymore. Richard and Brenda weren't early-to-bedders, but they rarely stayed up past the eleven o'clock news, either. As a temporary member of their household, I'd adopted the same routine—in fact, often pooping out long before they did. So just the thought of waiting until after 11 p.m. to head out for an evening had me yawning.

Sneaking out without them seeing me was another matter. Then again, in the evenings the two of them tended to live in Richard's study before heading up to bed. The driveway was on the other side of the house. I just had to hope they didn't look out the window when I took off. To make sure, I didn't turn on my headlights until I was at least three houses down the well-lit block.

I had to wait eons for the light at Main Street to go green. The heat had backed off and I rolled down my window, hoping for a cool breeze. The light changed and I turned left, heading for the city.

Buffalo may be the second-largest city in the state, but the travel time was far shorter than traversing the same territory in Manhattan. Yet like the Big Apple, you could also count on every damn traffic light going red as you approached.

An old Stones tune came on and I cranked up the radio, glancing in my rearview mirror. Some damn fool behind me had his lights off.

Maybe I should've asked Maggie to come with me, then perhaps afterward she might've invited me back to her place for another night of pleasure. But then I really didn't want to involve her in any of this for the same reason I hadn't shared any of what I knew about Walt's death with Richard.

You need him.

The idiot without headlights was still behind me. The main drag from Amherst to downtown was nearly ten miles long, and it wasn't unusual for cars to travel in a pack.

The Stones gave way to Stevie Nicks and I felt like I was listening to the radio of my youth. Sometimes music had been the only high point of those shitty days. I pushed the thought away and noticed the jerk was still behind me. He or she was probably the same kind of driver who left their turn signal on for endless miles on a straightaway.

I paused for a red light and took note of the business addresses. Club Monticello couldn't be too much farther ahead and I wondered how far afield I'd have to go to find a parking space. Too far, it turned out. I had to walk two blocks before I stood in front of the nightclub.

Club Monticello looked to be the hottest spot in the neighborhood, with ribbons of Day-Glo neon and colorful posters of the featured acts decorating the front facade. Smokers of both genders—and those in between—loitered the sidewalk out front, polluting the air while the thumping bass of canned music vibrated through us all. My internal batteries seemed to be recharging as I read the Coming Attractions poster. Then suddenly Richard strode up and was at my side.

My temper flared as I turned on him. "What the hell are you doing here?"

His eyes were blazing. "What do you think?"

"You followed me?"

"Of course. And I almost lost you at least a dozen times."

Understanding dawned. "You were the jerk on Main Street without headlights."

"I didn't want you to recognize my car."

"Brenda's car."

"Yeah," he admitted. He wasn't about to drive the Lincoln into unknown territory on a whim. "Now what the hell are you doing here?"

"Trying to find a lead in Walt Kaplan's death."

Richard glanced at the flashing neon sign. "At a drag show?"

"Hey, it was his preference—not mine." Sophie's words came back to me. *You won't solve this without him.* My apprehension soared even as my anger at seeing him dissolved.

I cleared my throat. "Now that you're here, you may as well come in with me."

"You just want people to think I'm your date so they won't hit on you."

I hadn't thought of that, but now that he mentioned it, it sounded like a good idea. "Come on."

We paid the cover and entered the dark nightclub which, as expected, was crowded and hopping. A part of me had been reluctant to dive into a place with so many people—fearful the mix of emotional pandemonium might overload my circuits—but instead of chaos, the overlapping emotions seemed to cancel themselves out. I felt like I was protected in a bubble of nothingness, and was determined to revel in it. We'd just missed the first show, and it would be another twenty minutes before the second.

"Let's get a drink," I told Richard. We threaded our way away from the theater and to the bar through the crowd of dancers. Club Monticello was not only a gay bar, but billed as the best dance club in Buffalo, welcoming gays, lesbians, and straights. We saw men with men, women with women and, true to their advertisement, a smattering of hetero couples. We also got bumped and jostled more than either of us would've liked. I ordered a couple of beers and Richard paid, receiving a wink from the heavily mascaraed male bartender. I had to laugh as he left a tip on the bar and quickly turned away.

I let myself move with the rhythm of the music and happily soaked in everything that was happening around me, eavesdropping on conversations. The drag queens—the amateurs and pros—seemed to be referred to as "girls," no matter what their chromosome structure. And damned if the happy gyrating people around me didn't all look just fine.

Meanwhile, Richard looked like he'd be more comfortable in a straitjacket. "Now what?" he yelled over the din of music and other people shouting to be heard.

"Don't get pissed, but I'm here to show Cyn's picture around. I want to ask the club personnel if they've seen her before."

"What makes you think she'd come to a place like this?"

"She had the same pair of shoes Walt had made."

"What shoes?"

I realized he was in the dark about everything I'd been investigating. "I'll fill you in later."

I turned back to the bar, and elbowed my way in, waiting until the bartender took a breather between customers. I pulled out Cyn's picture, shoving it under his nose. "Have you ever seen this woman?"

He took the photo, squinting at it between the flashing lights overhead. "Yow—that's one ugly bitch. Never seen her here. But then she's kind of on the old side."

"You're positive? She wears sparkly red stiletto heels. Maybe a red dress and boa?"

"Come on, man, you're describing half the queens in here—not to mention the straights playing dress-up."

I thanked him and sucked on my beer until it was gone. Then I went into automaton mode, flashing Cyn's picture at anyone who had two seconds to focus on it.

"Oy, God, he oughta get a closer shave," said what I guessed to be a woman at the bar.

"Not my type," said a guy in a red velvet Bolero vest, his hairy chest heaving from exuberant dancing.

"Just another wannabe," said a guy in a bad blonde wig and a baggy blue dress.

"Wanna dance?" a voice beside me asked.

I turned to find next to me a sweating, shirtless male of indeterminate age bouncing to the music. Linking arms with Richard, I answered, "Sorry, I'm already spoken for."

Richard yanked his arm away and looked ready to commit murder.

I spent another twenty minutes flashing Cyn's picture to the patrons, but no one claimed to know her. Richard followed me to the closest exit. "That was a complete waste of time," he said.

"I'm not ready to give up yet. There're other, smaller clubs. And come to think of it, I probably should've started at one of those. Walt was a loner. He'd probably go for less flash and less notoriety."

Richard glanced at his watch, his mouth drooping. "The clubs are open until four. Do you intend to hang around until then?"

I didn't think I could. "Most of them have Sunday shows. Maybe I'll come back tomorrow." I met his gaze. "Are you game?"

He shrugged. "Maybe."

Liar. I had a feeling if I let him, Richard would have himself surgically attached to me, at least until Walt's murder was solved—and/or his vacation plane took off.

We walked out of the club into the clear, dark night. The thumping music faded as we walked farther away. Six motorcycles were parked on the street near the club, none of them looking flashy, and it was hard to make out any distinguishing characteristics in the dim light.

You're being paranoid, something in me taunted. And no doubt would be every time I saw a motorcycle until Walt Kaplan's killer was found.

I put it out of my head. The evening hadn't been a total loss. Richard and I were back on an even keel. It felt good. It felt right.

Until something bad happened. But I wasn't prepared to think about it just then.

***

I got up early the next morning, went out for bagels and Danish, then made an extra big pot of coffee. If we were going to have a serious talk, caffeine would be a necessity.

When they finally showed up, I dragged Richard and Brenda out to the deck for breakfast alfresco. The cool morning air and bright sunshine were such a contrast to Club Monticello's gaudy interior that our adventure the night before almost seemed like a surreal dream.

Richard plastered his bagel with cream cheese as I told him about the visions of the sparkling shoes—both red and silver—the knife, and Walt. He didn't react when I told him my suspicions about Cyn, either. I'd already decided not to mention what happened at the ramp garage. It had no bearing on anything I was investigating. At least I wanted to believe that.

"There is something else." It must've been the tone of my voice that caused both Richard and Brenda to look up from their plates.

"This is the bad part," Brenda muttered.

"It could be. I see these…hands. They're covered in blood."

Richard leaned forward. "Whose blood?"

"That's what I don't know. And as far as I know, that blood is still circulating inside somebody. Only I don't know for how much longer. I got the vision the day we went to the mill and met Cyn, then again later when I touched something I found in Walt's closet: a little pillow that says 'Veronica.'"

"So find Veronica."

"Easier said than done."

"How much detail do you see with these hands?" Richard asked.

"Not much."

He nodded, leaned back in his chair. "So right now it's a dead end."

"Yeah, but it won't be for long." I poured a coffee warm-up from the insulated carafe.

"Let's get back to Buchanan," Richard said. "I can see why you don't think he makes a viable suspect. But your evidence against Cyn is pretty damned flimsy."

"That's why I need to keep showing her photo around. I know she's got something to do with this whole mess, I just don't know what. That's where you can help."

That stirred a response. "You can't ask me to implicate an old friend."

"I'm not. I'm asking you to distract her while I touch something that belongs to her. I was thinking her car's steering wheel. If I don't get anything from it, I'll know she's not the source of these visions. It would clear her."

"In your mind, at least."

"Yeah."

Brenda had been silent during all this. "What do you think?" I asked her.

She sighed. "Except when it comes to your own health, I trust your judgment."

"Thank you. I think."

She pushed back her chair, picked up her dish and silverware, and put them back on the serving tray. "But how do you expect Richard to get her away from her car, and then to leave it unlocked?"

"Well, he could invite her here."

Brenda flopped back into her chair and for a second I thought she might lose her balance and fall off. "What makes you think I want to meet one of his old girlfriends?"

"Basic curiosity. Besides, she's at least thirteen years older than you—and she looks it."

That appeased her—a bit. "Be that as it may, what's his excuse for inviting her?"

"I don't know. Drinks. Show her your old yearbooks. Bore her with a talk on skin diseases of the Ecuadorian rain forest."

"Ecuador has no rain forest," Richard piped up.

"Then choose another country. Or you can use me as an excuse. You want to apologize for my oafish behavior—"

"Yeah, while you jump in her car and soak up her residual aura. Then I'm no better than you."

"Thanks."

"You know what I mean." Richard shook his head. "I don't know. I still don't like the idea. It's like entrapment."

"How? I can't prove anything without solid evidence, but at least I'll know for sure if I should continue to annoy her."

"Yeah, you're like a pit bull. Once you get your teeth into something, you don't let go."

I couldn't argue with that.

"But," he continued, "you're trying to get her thrown in jail."

"Only if she's guilty. If she's not…I've eliminated her from suspicion and I try something else."

"Couldn't you try something else first?"

"I have no other starting point."

"Then what happens if you eliminate her?"

"I don't know. Maybe I'll get some other insight from touching her car that will direct me somewhere else."

Richard drained his cup. "I still don't like it, but I'll go along with you, because I happen to think you *will* have to look elsewhere for Kaplan's murderer."

"All well and fine," Brenda said. "That is, if you can lure her here and she doesn't lock her car."

"Yeah."

Richard stared at his empty cup. "Why the change of heart?"

"What?"

His gaze shifted to meet mine. "Why did you decide to let me help? Just because you want to get to Cyn?"

I wasn't ready for this question, but I guess I knew he'd eventually ask it. "It's against my better judgment. But…" He didn't know about Sophie. I'd tried to tell him about her, had even taken him to her bakery once, but the owner said she didn't live there. I couldn't tell Richard that a figment of my imagination had told me I needed him to help me solve Walt's death. It was all too complicated.

Then again, maybe it was time for truth.

"I need you, Rich."

For a second he looked puzzled, then the barest hint of a pleased smile appeared beneath his mustache. "Oh. Okay."

Chapter Sixteen

Richard was blessed with something I'll never have: charm. I don't know what he said, but Cyn Lennox agreed to come by after the mill closed later that afternoon. Richard had to promise her that I wouldn't be around, and we'd jockeyed Brenda's car out of the garage and put mine in to reinforce the deception.

The plan was for them to lure Cyn to the other side of the house so she wouldn't see me when I violated the sanctity of her Mercedes.

At 5:47, Cyn pulled up Richard's driveway. The loft apartment's living room window was the perfect vantage point. I stood to the right side, peeking around the drape as she stepped out of her car. I couldn't see the driver's side door and didn't know if she'd left the window down or the car unlocked. All this could be for nothing. I watched as she stepped out of the car, once again dressed in western garb. A cowgirl, Dana Watkins had called her. Well, not quite; her denim jumper was embroidered with multicolored flowers, and again she wore the silver-and-turquoise squash-blossom necklace, reminding me of what Monticello's bartender had said about straights playing dress-up.

Cyn glanced around the drive, craned her neck to see into the backyard—probably looking for me. I moved back a step. No way did I want to scare her off.

The phone rang.

I looked back toward it, imploring it to silence, but it rang again and again.

Another peek out the window and I saw Cyn was at Richard's back door, knocking.

Ring! Ring!

Thank God she couldn't hear it.

The back door opened. Cyn stepped inside.

Ring! Ring!

I charged across the room, snatched the receiver. "What?"

"Jeff?" Maggie.

"Oh, hi."

"Everything okay?" she asked, sounding uncertain.

"Sorry about the greeting. It's just—I'm kind of in the middle of something. Can I call you back?"

"Well, not really. I'm supposed to be at my parents' for dinner in ten minutes, and they live all the way out in Lackawanna, and I don't like to use my cell phone when I'm driving."

Good old letter-of-the-law Maggie.

"When I didn't hear from you yesterday or today, I wondered…I mean, I just thought—"

The clock ticked overhead. "I had a wonderful time Friday night. When can we see each other again?" Talk about pushing.

"Oh. Well, when are you free?"

"Every night this week." Speed it up, I need to get outside, I wanted to bellow.

"Well, maybe we could talk about it later tonight. Make some plans."

"I may be going out tonight. With Richard."

"You're not getting him involved in this murder thing again are you?" The disapproval in her voice came through loud and clear.

"Richard's a big boy. He can take care of himself."

Dead silence. This was not the way I wanted the conversation to go.

"What time do you think you'll be home later? I could call you—"

"That's okay," Maggie said. "Maybe we'll talk some other time."

"Maggie, wait—"

Clunk!

The receiver felt sweaty in my hand as I jammed it back into its cradle. For a moment, all I could do was stand there, seething. If we were destined to be together, and I honestly felt we were, then why the hell was it so fucking hard?

The window beckoned. I crossed the room and looked down on the empty car, then at my watch. Cyn had been inside less than five minutes. Surely Richard would have enticed her into the living room by now. Something inside me said Cyn wasn't going to stay long and I needed to get out there and in her car.

I trotted down the stairs and opened the door, not letting it bang shut. This felt weird—sneaking around our own driveway. Why couldn't Cyn have backed up so I wouldn't be seen from the kitchen window? Yeah, didn't everybody back into driveways when coming for casual visits?

The driver's window was rolled up tight, like the others, but the handle lifted under my fingers. The door opened and I slipped inside, pulled the door closed but not quite shut, and sank into German leather-clad comfort. The air inside was still cool from the air conditioning, but uneasiness threaded through me. I was getting something, but it wasn't the same connection I had with the red shoe.

I leaned back in the leather seat, my hands poised at four and eight o'clock, closed my eyes, and clutched Cyn's steering wheel.

An absurd thought flashed through my mind: Jacob Marley. Yeah, Marley's ghost, forever encumbered in death by fathoms of chains and cash boxes. Cyn's life revolved around her spreadsheets and the numbers on them. Cash flow, income, expenses. Money, money, money. And when she'd last held that steering wheel she'd been worried sick. But that didn't make sense. Ted Hanson said her café was already in the black.

I shook those thoughts away. That wasn't what I'd wanted to get. I wanted to tap into what Dana had called Cyn's theatrical side. I tried another position on the steering wheel. The image of the red shoes blasted my mind. Plural. I'd never seen more than the one when I homed into what I perceived as Walt's psyche. And though they were the same style, these shoes weren't perfect—they'd seen some wear: scuffed, with sparkles missing. These were the shoes made for Andrea Foxworth, the ones Cyn had bought at auction. She'd danced with joy in them—and joy had not been abundant since the death of her beloved Dennis. She'd danced slow, and fast, with multiple partners. In those shoes she'd felt sexy, beautiful. She'd had *fun*.

I moved my hands up to ten and two o'clock on the steering wheel. Shards of music—too brief to comprehend... disco mostly—wound through my gray matter like a dozen radios playing simultaneously, much too much to assimilate. My fingers tightened and the sensation of joy swooped over me like a sirocco; wind, speed and the thrill of danger.

I repositioned my fingers to nine and three on the wheel. A horrible weight pressed against my soul. Something so terribly wrong—horribly bloody—could never be righted.

Walt's death?

I clasped harder, hoping for clarity, but I wasn't sure Cyn had actually seen Walt in death—seen his blood splashed on tiled walls—in a bathtub?

True? Real? Nothing was set in concrete. It was nothing I could grab onto—truly understand.

One and seven on the wheel brought something different: Gene. A powerful pull to protect him. She loved him like nothing else in her life. But that, too, had been tainted. Her love for him was black and blue and the startling crimson of fresh-spilled blood.

Sorting through the plethora of thoughts and feelings that bombarded me, one thing was certain; Cyn had not killed Walt. Just the thought of his death had horrified her. I couldn't quite grasp what she knew or how she was involved, but instinct still told me that she knew or suspected something terrible about Walt's death and it had done much more than unsettle her. She was in deep denial about something. I couldn't comprehend what, but whatever it was had shaken apart this sometime party girl's world.

Nausea pulled at my insides as I tried to sort through the building maelstrom, but I couldn't seem to pick up any one emotion and stay with it. Like slogging through Jell-O, I kept getting bogged down and losing track of what it was I was tuning into. My hands fell limp to my lap, lay there for eons—lead weights too heavy to ever lift.

The dashboard's dark displays eventually drew my attention. How long had I been sitting there staring at nothing? A glance at my watch told me at least twenty minutes.

Had I suffered a seizure? One of the quacks I'd consulted during the past few months had warned I might have one—or more—at some time in the future. Head injuries weren't predictable. There was so much medical science didn't know about the brain…and probably never would.

I managed to pull open the latch, slunk out of the car and shoved the door with my hip to make it catch. I shuffled away from the Mercedes, ducked into the side door to shamble up the apartment stairs. Less than thirty seconds later, I was back behind the drape, panting, and counting. Ten, twenty, thirty—

At forty-seven seconds, Cyn stepped out of Richard's back entrance. She paused on the steps, speaking to my brother. The afternoon shadows were already starting to lengthen.

Ten, twenty, thirty—

Cyn turned, took the last step and headed for her car. Richard came out on his step.

Cyn opened the driver's door, ducked to enter, then paused.

Could she smell the stench of the fear I'd experienced—relived—in the cockpit of her Mercedes?

She straightened, staring down at her pretty little car, her brow furrowed. Then she tilted her head to look up to the apartment, her face pale, eyes shadowed. I jumped back, pressed myself against the wall, my heart thumping, my breaths coming so fast I was in danger of hyperventilating.

I closed my eyes and started counting again until I heard the car door slam, and seconds later the sound of an engine. I waited until I couldn't hear it anymore before peeking out the window. Richard stood in the driveway. He waved me down.

By then I had my breathing almost under control and trotted down the stairs. Richard's back was to me as I rounded the corner of the garage, his arms crossed over his chest, looking down the empty driveway.

"Well?" I asked.

He turned, his eyes troubled, and I wasn't sure if I was in for a scolding or a lecture—or both. "That's one unhappy lady."

"Go on," I urged.

Richard closed his eyes briefly and shook his head. "I need a scotch." He turned and headed into the house, with me at his heels.

The screen door slammed behind me and I followed him through the pantry and into the kitchen.

"You could've moved a little faster," Brenda scolded me from her seat at the table. We both watched as Richard opened the cabinet where they kept their kitchen liquor. "That woman wouldn't leave the room. You have no idea how nerve wracking it was to try to keep her attention from straying to the window while you were out in her car."

"I thought you were going to entertain her in the living room."

"What took you so long?" Richard asked, getting out a glass. "You sat there for the longest time."

I swallowed, afraid to tell him what I experienced—what might have happened. "I kinda got mesmerized."

"And?" Richard demanded.

Looking him in the eye wasn't easy. "She didn't kill Walt."

He let out a ragged breath, his shoulders slumping. "I told you so. But knowing that still doesn't make me feel any better about luring her over here. You want something, Brenda?"

"Wine. Pour it into one of the really big glasses."

Richard had a right to his feelings. And that he'd believed in me enough to risk what he thought of as betraying a friend said even more.

"Well, what went on?" I asked. "Cyn looked upset when she left."

Richard reached for one of the balloon stem glasses. "I don't know. Something to do with her business. She had an argument with one of her employees."

"Since she only has two, and one of them works mornings, that leaves her nephew, Gene." I had to swallow, didn't want to betray what I already knew—suspected—really had no clue about. "Did she say what the problem was?"

"No." Richard opened the fridge, retrieved the previously opened bottle of wine, yanked out the cork, and poured it for Brenda, then handed her the glass.

I tried another tack. "You looked upset when you came out of the house. Why?"

"You try keeping someone captive for half an hour when they'd rather be elsewhere. I had visions of her yanking out her cell phone and calling the cops on you. And you sat there and sat there and sat there." He poured his scotch—didn't even bother with ice. "She asked about you, too."

"Yeah?"

"She wanted to know why you were so damned nosy. She inferred that your harassment was behind her rift with Gene."

"How?"

"She didn't say. *I* didn't know what to say." Richard downed another healthy swig.

"Sorry."

I watched him take another swallow. He hadn't offered me a drink. But then, I wasn't sure I wanted one. I needed a clear head to figure out my next move. And then there was Maggie—a sweet diversion from what we'd all just gone through.

"I got a call from Maggie just as Cyn arrived. She's pissed at me again."

"Why?"

"If I could figure out how women think, I'd sell the secret and be rich."

"Oh, I'm sure I'll hear all about it," Brenda said and swirled the wine in her glass.

Of that I had no doubt.

"So what's your next move?" Richard asked.

"I also got the feeling Cyn was upset about something and she was in denial about it. Someone was talking to Walt in her office. If it wasn't her—"

"You think it was her nephew?"

"It makes more sense, really, especially as she seems paranoid I'm going to find out what went on with her and Walt and Gene. Maybe Gene's a drag queen, and maybe he befriended Walt. I don't have a picture of him to flash around, and what good would it do if the people at the clubs only knew him in his female persona?"

"Do you think you'd recognize him dressed as a woman?"

"I don't know, what with makeup, a wig, and jewelry. If you see some of these before and after pictures, sometimes it's hard to tell. I've been in Gene's presence twice, and he didn't give off strong vibes, so it's not like I could just tune into him like I can with someone like…" *Maggie.* "Like I can with others."

They'd both noticed my hesitation. Neither of them commented.

Don't think about her, I urged myself. My mind raced to grasp onto something—anything else. "I need a picture of Walt to flash around," I murmured, wondering if Tom had one back at the bar. Then again, I hadn't noticed one—not even a grab shot tacked behind the bar with a bunch of other photographs. "I think I'll go back to Walt's apartment. You wanna come?"

Richard looked up. "I'll sit this one out." He took another swallow of his drink. "Brenda, how about a steak dinner? Are you up for going out?"

"Any time I don't have to cook is cause for celebration. But I'll drive," she said, putting down her untouched wine and getting up from the table. "I think I'll go drag a comb through my hair first. Be right back."

I watched her head down the hall for the stairs, and waited until she was out of earshot before speaking again.

"You'll hear all about it later tonight. Maggie's pissed because she thinks helping me look into Walt's murder will get you killed."

Richard poured himself a bit more scotch. "She's got it wrong. It's only me that's keeping you alive."

It felt like he'd punched me in the gut. Was that what Sophie meant when she said he had cause to worry about me—and that I needed him?

I wasn't sure I wanted to know.

Chapter Seventeen

The last time I'd been to Walt's apartment, I hadn't noticed if the air conditioning was on—or even if the place had air conditioning. Entering the dark apartment gave me a chill that had nothing to do with the ambient temperature. I turned on the light and paused in the doorway. Nothing looked different, but it felt like someone had been there. Not Tom. Someone else—and that person had gotten in with a key.

I did an abrupt about-face and looked around the dimly lit landing. Two sconces, with what could only have been twenty-watt bulbs, faced one another, giving only enough light for the tenants to find a keyhole. I ran my hand across the lintel and found dust, as well as a dull brass key. Okay, so who knew Walt kept an extra? Had he locked himself out one time too many and used it himself, or did his friends know about it?

I pressed the key into my palm. Bam! The bloodied hands were back. But damn it, whose hands were they?

Replacing the key, I reentered the apartment, again picking up the feeling that someone had been there in the last day or so. I stood for a long time, studying the apartment. Maybe I'd found it so tidy on my previous visit because there really wasn't much in it. The walls and flat surfaces were devoid of homey touches. It was a place to eat a nondescript meal, watch a little TV, and hit the rack. The focal point of the apartment was the desk.

Made of cheap pine, the student's desk had been painted glossy black and lacked the nicks and dings usually associated with such a piece of furniture. I pulled out the chair and sat down, then turned on the goose-necked lamp. A blotter of faux leather covered most of the surface, and on it were a stapler, a mug filled with pens and pencil stubs, and a cork-bottomed coaster. Had Walt sat here with a beer or a cup of coffee to write out his bills?

It had been a tactical error for me to let Richard go through Walt's papers instead of doing it myself. Not that he probably missed much—but he wouldn't feel a psychic vibe during an earthquake.

Pulling open the center drawer revealed more pencils, pens, a legal pad, rubber bands, and Scotch tape. Just the usual junk. The contents of the other drawers were more interesting. Bold block letters labeled files as tax receipts, insurance papers, and one marked "Will." I ran a hand over the files and papers. Someone had rifled through them after Richard. Looking for... something they hadn't found. What that was, I had no clue.

The will wasn't that interesting. Walt had left everything to Tom. He probably thought he'd outlive his widowed, elderly mother.

I folded the document and laid it on the desk. I'd give it to Tom tomorrow. Yet I wondered why Tom hadn't gone looking for it himself, especially as he'd already been through the apartment, presumably right after the cops. Then again, he hadn't been back to clear out the place, either.

My gaze focused on the blank wall in front of me. Something didn't add up. Tom flat out told me he didn't want to know what else I'd find, and made it clear he was revolted by his cousin's lifestyle. Yet he wanted Walt's memory kept intact. Or was it just a matter of family pride? As far as I knew, Tom had never married, either. Was he worried his customers might think he and Walt were lovers? It was only when I'd shamed him that he'd told me to go ahead and keep looking into Walt's death.

The will bothered me, too. Why cut the old lady out? Did she know about, or at least suspect what Walt's sexual preference was? Tom said it would kill her if the truth came out, so yeah, she probably did. Were she and Walt estranged because of it? I wasn't sure Tom would answer me if I asked.

I pawed through the rest of the documents. As Richard had said, the receipts were grouped by year in envelopes. I did a perfunctory check, but nothing looked to be of interest. It still bothered me that he appeared to have no real assets. Could he have had a safety deposit box somewhere that even Tom didn't know about?

The next drawer contained more file folders of uninteresting receipts and held six or seven envelopes of photos. The first couple were old family shots. Birthdays, dinners, other social occasions. A much younger Tom wore a green, cone-shaped, sparkling Happy New Year hat, and toasted the camera. Happier times.

Two newer envelopes had recently been disturbed. I fished through them, all the same subject matter: Walt, usually dressed in dark slacks and sports shirts, looking shy, posing with a cadre of drag queens. Single shots, group shots, and none of these pseudo-women were the same caliber as I'd seen at Club Monticello the night before. From cheesy wigs and gaudy blouses, to holes in their fishnet stockings, Walt's "fancy women" were losers, pathetic souls who hadn't been able to cut it in the straight world, and didn't look like they were doing much better in their chosen haven. The background décor was just as seedy. I'd have to hit the less popular bars tonight to see if I recognized any of them.

Shuffling through the pictures also gave me a sense that Walt's alliances with his so-called fancy women were short lived. Tom had said that Walt wasn't gay, but was that something Walt was likely to reveal to his straight-laced cousin? I pressed a photo of Walt and one of his fancy ladies against my forehead and a stab of pain lanced through my skull, revulsion flooding through me. Walt's accident had left him impotent, but that hadn't been the end of his sex life.

Shoving the pictures back in the envelope, I pushed it away from me, wishing I could get that image—and the accompanying sensations—out of my thoughts.

Anxiety forced me to my feet to pace the room, to walk off the tension and work up the courage to pick up the last envelope. I hadn't thought of myself as a homophobe before this. Then again, accepting someone's lifestyle on an intellectual level and inadvertently experiencing it were two different things. I thought of Maggie and the way our bodies had melded together a couple of days before—how right it felt—and welcomed the returning calm.

I felt okay by the time I'd shuffled through the next set of photos. Same kind of stuff—the background decorations changed from New Year's to Valentine's to St. Paddy's day. I turned the photos over. By the date on the back, they must've been processed just days before Walt's death. I hadn't seen any sign of a camera or a smart phone when poking around before and wondered if old-fashioned Walt had managed to find a disposable one. I counted the prints: twenty-four. Next I withdrew the negatives. The strips were in four- or five-frame segments. One of them had been lopped off, its slanted edge different from the uniform cuts on the others.

So that was at least one thing Walt's visitor had come to retrieve.

Or did I have that wrong? First the cops had gone through the apartment, then Tom. They had to have seen whatever foot-fetish stuff he had on hand. Tom had later eradicated it. But if the cops had seen these photos they would have done more investigating into Walt's background and wouldn't have been so eager to pin the murder on Buchanan.

So why would someone come in and plant the photos? Being dead, Walt had no use for them. His family wouldn't want them. Why not just trash them?

The rest of the desk's contents were of no consequence and I eased the drawer shut. But I took the planted envelope of photographs, along with Walt's will, and locked up behind me. I wouldn't be returning.

***

At ten p.m., Lambrusco's, a gay bar two blocks from Main Street, wasn't half as crowded or as flashy as Club Monticello. The cover charge was half the price and even the smokers on the sidewalk had a tired, used-up look to them.

Richard's steak dinner had revived his spirits and I was glad to have him along. We surveyed the poorly lit barroom and the sparsely populated tables. The patrons were also older than at their biggest competitor's. The canned disco music wasn't cranked up as loud as at Club Monticello, so we didn't have to shout at one another either.

"Do you think they wash the glasses here?" Richard muttered in my ear.

"Ask for a bottled beer."

The bartender was not overworked and stood watching an overweight couple jiggling out on the dance floor. I ordered a couple of bottles of Canadian to placate Richard, and we commandeered two stools at the bar.

"First time here?" the bartender asked. His name tag read "Kevin."

I nodded.

"Slumming?" he asked.

Richard eyed me, then tipped back his beer.

"Is it that obvious?" I asked.

Kevin shrugged. "We don't often get newcomers. And tonight probably isn't a good night to be here."

I wrapped my right hand around my beer bottle and soaked up feelings of unease the bartender had imparted. My gaze went back to Kevin, but he wouldn't look me in the eye. I leaned closer to Richard. "Uh…I don't want to alarm you, but something's going to go down. And pretty soon."

"What do you want me to do?"

"Drink up."

He raised his bottle and took a swallow.

I turned my attention back to Kevin. "Are you pretty familiar with the regulars?"

He nodded. "Know most of them on a first-name basis. At least, the names they give me."

I took out Cyn's picture and one of Walt with one of his fancy women and placed them on the bar. "Ever see any of these people?"

Kevin squinted at the photos in the bad light. He tapped one. "That's Walt and Veronica. She was one of our featured acts back in the winter. 'Fraid she's moved on to bigger and better venues." He tapped Cyn's picture. "This one came in a few times with some queen I don't know. Drinks Cosmopolitans."

"Do you usually get straight women her age come in here looking for a place to hang and not have to worry about assholes trying to jump their bones?"

He shook his head. "This ain't Club Monticello where they encourage that kind of thing. She didn't fit in and—" he paused, sizing up Richard and me. "You don't, either."

I swallowed some more beer. "What do you know about Walt?"

"Nice guy. Shy. Made friends with lots of the girls."

"By girls you mean drag queens?"

Kevin shrugged and glanced at his watch.

"Have you seen Walt lately?"

He shook his head. "Not for a couple of weeks."

"Did he leave with anyone special the last time you saw him?"

"I wasn't his babysitter." Kevin looked at his watch again. "You ought to drink up."

Richard, who had only been half-listening, tipped back his beer.

The uneasiness in my gut intensified. "We gotta get outta here," I said, pushing off my stool.

"What's the hurry?" Richard asked, proffering his half-drunk beer.

A commotion at the entrance made us look up. Kevin ducked behind the bar. I grabbed Richard's elbow, hauling him off his stool. "Let's get the hell out of here!"

Six or seven menacing biker-wannabes blocked the main entrance, pounding their studded, leather-gloved fists. Bikers—like the one who'd tried to run me down in the ramp garage. As one they charged forward, overturning tables, sending pitchers and glasses flying, and delivering what sounded like Indian war cries.

For a moment, the shocked patrons stood stock still, unbelieving as the Bee Gees wailed "Stayin' Alive." Then, like frightened birds, they scattered, heading for the sides of the room and the emergency exits. I tried to hustle Richard out, but his feet seemed glued to the floor.

One of the customers tripped and the bullyboys converged, their booted feet finding a target.

"Hey!" Richard was off.

I stumbled after him. "Rich, no!"

Richard charged into the melee. He was at least as tall if not taller than the bullies, but didn't have their bulk.

Fists flew, catching Richard off guard as he stooped to help the guy on the floor.

Someone grabbed the back of my shirt, hauled me off balance, and tossed me against the bar. The ribs that had barely stopped hurting screamed in protest and I sank to the floor, winded.

Richard was in the middle of the fight now, arms pumping as he took out one, then another of the bullies, looking like something out of a cartoon.

Long seconds passed and still I couldn't breathe—couldn't join in the fray.

Richard ducked one punch, but caught another that sent him reeling.

The main lights flashed on and suddenly the place was swarming with cops.

The bikers evaporated in the chaos.

My diaphragm finally relaxed enough for me to take in short, painful breaths.

One of the cops grabbed Richard, hauling him to his feet. "Hey!"

The cop shoved him against the bar and handcuffed him.

Using a barstool, I hauled myself up, realizing none of the bikers had singled me out.

"Are you in on this?" The cop snarled at me.

Kevin was back. "No, he and this guy," he pointed at Richard, "tried to help out."

The cop glowered at Richard. "What were you doing fighting?"

"I was trying to save some guy from being kicked. Then they went after me."

"Oh." Still, the cop didn't hurry to release Richard's bracelets.

"It's a hate crime," Kevin said. "Bikers picking on innocent gay people."

My insides seethed. "Bullshit. Officer, this guy," I jerked a thumb at Kevin, "warned us we'd better leave. He kept looking at his watch. He knew these bikers were coming to disrupt the bar."

The cop's sharp gaze was riveted on the bartender. "Go on," he told me.

"Could be a scam—break up the place and insurance pays for a quick facelift. Or maybe it's been just a little too quiet lately. A little notoriety might bring in curiosity seekers who'd spend money. And by the way, are there any motorcycles outside?" The cop didn't answer, but I'd bet a week's tips there weren't.

Still wrapped over the bar, Richard craned his neck to speak to the officer. "You guys got here awful fast. When did the call come through?"

Kevin kept quiet, his expression defiant.

The officer's glower could've blistered paint. He stormed off to confer with the other cops. Kevin glared daggers at me and slunk down the bar.

"Are you okay?" Richard asked.

I hitched in a breath and pressed a hand to my side. "I'm back to square one with the ribs. How 'bout you?"

"I'm fine." He struggled to straighten and I gave him a hand. There was something different about him. Something that had been missing from his eyes since the shooting three months before.

"My God, you enjoyed it."

Richard didn't bother to try and hide his delight. "Great, wasn't it?"

I noted the growing red puffiness under his left eye. "Brenda's gonna kill us."

Chapter Eighteen

The phone rang way too early. I blinked awake, grabbed it, hoping it hadn't already awakened Richard and Brenda. "What?"

"Jeff?"

Long, aching seconds passed before the voice registered. "Sam?"

"What's this about you and your brother being involved in a brawl at a gay bar last night?"

I closed my eyes and cringed.

"Hello?" Sam tried.

Squinting at my clock made me wince: 6:59 a.m. "How the hell did you hear about that?"

"Hey, I'm on top of everything that happens in this city."

"It was a setup, and don't you goddamn quote me. In fact, bury our names, willya?"

"My, we're a bit testy this morning. Did you get that setup angle from one of your…uh, pieces of insight?"

"It didn't take a genius to figure it out." I gave him the Cliff Notes version of our adventures the night before.

"I've got Kaplan's autopsy report, as well as photos. They're pretty gruesome."

"What about those electrical burns?"

"The poor guy was tortured before he was stabbed. Had a couple of fingernails ripped off, as well."

I grimaced. "Nasty."

"Looks like he was sodomized, but there was also scarring, so it wasn't like this was the first time. You did know that, right?"

"Yeah, yeah." Okay, I hadn't until the night before, but he didn't have to know that. "And the cops still think it was Buchanan?"

"Not necessarily. The detective in charge wants to make further inquiries, but his superiors figure they've got an arrest and aren't pushing. It'll depend on what the DA says. They've scheduled a meeting for next week."

"Next week?" This whole situation would come to a head well before that.

"Where you going next with this?" Sam asked.

"My original suspect fizzled. But I might have a line on someone else. I'll keep you posted."

"You do that."

***

The mouse under Richard's eye was puffy and purple. Add a beard to his mustache, give him a bandana and a gold earring, and he would've looked like a pirate. Brenda hadn't exactly forgiven me for Richard's new look—muttering something about ruined wedding pictures—but she made me a hard-boiled egg and toast for breakfast and served it without dumping it in my lap.

"So what're we doing today?" Richard asked, setting aside the sports section.

I swallowed a mouthful of toast. "I'm working. Then later...I don't know. All I've got is a flash of insight from

Cyn's office. I know she didn't kill Walt, and it wasn't Dana Watkins, the baker, or Ted Hanson, the miller, either. That only leaves Gene Higgins. I don't have a starting place for him. He comes up clean on a Google search. No address. He's not in the phone book—probably only has a cell. I was thinking of tailing him for a couple of days."

"That's *all* you have," Brenda interrupted, shoving her engagement-ringed finger under Richard's nose. "A couple of days. We're getting married on Friday. No ifs, ands, or buts."

Richard saluted her. "Yes, ma'am, but we'll have a much better time in Paris if we aren't worrying about Jeff." He turned back to me, sounding like an excited kid. "We can use Brenda's car. They already know yours."

"Cyn saw Brenda's car on Saturday. It's your car or nothing."

That didn't please him, but he didn't protest either. "Why don't you see if you can get off work early?" he said.

"Because Gene doesn't leave the mill until at least five-thirty. And, besides, if I'm ever going to pay you back the gazillion dollars you've spent taking care of me these past few months, I need all the hours I can get."

Richard opened his mouth to speak, but I cut him off.

"You're welcome to come play with me later if you really want." I got up to leave. "I'll be back home about four-thirty."

***

Tom was vacuuming as I entered the empty bar, which meant he hadn't gotten to it the night before. I'd probably get to mop the floor—oh, the thrill of steady employment.

Tom saw me, waved a hello and continued his work. I tied an apron around my waist and grabbed a stool to wait for him to finish. Eventually he hit the off-switch, unplugged the cord, and started reeling it in.

"You must like it here. You come in early most days," he said.

"I gotta be somewhere. Have you got a few minutes?"

"A few." I handed him the envelope with Walt's will.

Tom took a seat at the nearest table, pulled reading glasses out of his shirt's breast pocket and quickly scanned the paper, then let out a breath. "He left me everything?"

"That surprises you?"

He frowned, his gaze dipping back to the document. "I guess not. Besides his mother, I was his only other close relative. Not that we were ever really close. And what's he left me, a pile of bills?"

"Why didn't he mention his mother in the will?"

Tom sighed. "They didn't exactly get along. That branch of the family has a lot of money and although he was an only child, Walt was definitely a black sheep. He could've gone into the family business, but he opted not to. You've heard of Ben Kaplan Jewelers, haven't you?"

"Whoa—only their commercials every five minutes on the radio and TV. They've got to be the biggest jewelry retailer in the city. So why did Walt go into construction?"

He shrugged. "He probably thought it would make him look…I dunno, more manly. He couldn't have been any good at it. He hated to get dirty. I think he was relieved when he got to quit after his accident."

"Does your aunt still own the business?"

"Yeah, but Walt's cousin Rachel runs it these days. She's good at it, too. I wouldn't doubt my aunt leaves the whole thing to her."

I tapped the document still in his hand. "You're also listed as Walt's executor. That means you've got to settle his estate. By law you're supposed to get things started within ten days of a death."

"Man, I don't have the time for that. And after what you've told me, I don't want to know what Walt had in that apartment or storage unit."

"The apartment is already pretty clean, as you know." He didn't deny he'd already been through it, and I went on. "I found some pictures you wouldn't want to see, but I'll wait to dispose of them. Eventually the police might want them. In the meantime, you could call in an estate liquidator to get rid of everything else. If you leave the stuff at the storage place, eventually they'll either sell or dump it, although as executor of Walt's estate they might haul you into small claims court for back rent." I handed him Walt's keys. "You really should go through the storage unit, just in case there's something of value."

Tom nodded. "Walt was a pain in the ass in life, and is proving to be an even bigger one in death."

"I know you said you didn't want to know what else I've found out, but—"

He exhaled a long breath. "It was one of his fancy women killed him, right?"

"I think so."

"It's gonna come out," he groused, shaking his head. "It's all gonna be made public and…" He didn't finish the sentence. I wasn't quite sure if he was angry at me or just the situation. His gaze met mine. "Do you know who?"

"Maybe. But I don't know as we'll ever be able to prove it."

Tom was silent for a long moment, staring at the floor—or maybe he didn't see it at all. Finally he looked up at me. "Back off, Jeff. I don't want you to get hurt."

"You sound like my brother."

"I'm glad someone looks out for you. I should have looked out more for Walt. If I had—"

"From what I've learned about Walt, he didn't want a lot of people in his life. That he found something of value in his transient friendships with his ladies…well, maybe that's all he needed."

Tom didn't look convinced. He folded the will and stood, then walked back to his office without looking back.

I'd finished swabbing the floor and was about to dump the bucket of dirty water when Tom finally emerged. "I'm thinking about adding happy hour food on the weekends. What do you think?"

"More important, what does the health department think?" I asked, accepting his change of subject.

"Yeah, I'd have to look into that. There's debate as to whether it encourages customers or just invites freeloaders. Do you have any experience with that?"

We talked about my former bartending job, and had moved onto sports when the first customers came in. No more talk of Walt. Until I could prove who'd killed him, I decided to keep it that way.

***

The two o'clock doldrums had hit and there were only a couple of Tom's cronies nursing beers in front of the tube when Brenda strode into The Whole Nine Yards. "Can I help you?" Tom asked, in his most surprised and subdued voice. It wasn't often a woman walked into the bar. It was almost unheard of for a black woman to do so.

"Sure," Brenda said, sliding onto a barstool. "I'll have a Coke."

"I'll take care of the lady," I told Tom. "She's a friend of mine."

Tom raised an eyebrow, gave Brenda a nod, and headed back down the bar to chat with his friends. Their eyes had been on Brenda, too, but Tom distracted them.

"Looks like I gave them something to talk about for the rest of the day," Brenda said.

I half-filled a glass with ice, and squirted the soda from the well trigger. "Here you are, ma'am." Brenda reached for her purse, but I stopped her. "It's on the house. What brings you to this part of town?"

"I didn't come to spy, if that's what you think." She took in the bar's décor: artfully suspended hockey sticks, baseball bats and other sports equipment. "Not a bad little place. But it was actually that little candy store where you got the chocolates that drew me out here. They were just the best, and I kind of ran out."

"Kind of ran out?"

"Okay, I pigged out on them and they're gone and I craved some more. Is that a crime?"

"No, I'm glad you liked them."

"Yes, well, I haven't made it there yet. On my way, I thought I'd take a look at Cyn Lennox's little café at the mill.

You and Richard have spoken so much about it, and *her*. Not that I was going to go inside and actually check it out. I mean, the time we spent with her yesterday was just too awkward. But when I got there, there was a big hand-written closed sign on the door."

All my nerves went on red alert. "What?"

Brenda lifted her glass. "I thought you'd be interested, since you and Richard were planning to play Starsky and Hutch tonight—not that you bear the least resemblance to Ben Stiller. And you can't follow Cyn's nephew around if he isn't there."

"Did the sign say anything like, closed for repairs—or sickness, anything like that?"

She shook her head and took a sip of her drink. "No emergency telephone number, no nothing."

My mind was racing. Cyn had been upset when she'd come to Richard's house the afternoon before. She'd had an argument with Gene, and now her café was closed—just the vibe I'd gotten while talking to Dana Watkins.

"What do you think it means?" Brenda asked.

"Nothing good."

She nodded. "Where will you start now?"

"With the telephone book." I looked up. "Tom, a phone book?"

"In my office."

A minute later, I'd retrieved the telephone book. I'd already checked for Gene with no results. This time I looked for Dana Watkins. More than a column of numbers were listed under Watkins, and as luck would have it, one of them simply said D. Watkins. I grabbed the wall phone and dialed. Unfortunately, D. Watkins stood for David Watkins, not Dana. I'd have to try them all, and there was always the chance her number was unlisted—or that she only had a cell phone.

I slammed the phone back on the receiver.

"No luck, huh?" Brenda asked.

I shook my head.

Brenda took another sip of her Coke, her gaze wandering to the still-open phone book. "I'm not doing anything this afternoon. If you want, I could call all those numbers and see if I can find your Dana. Would that help?"

"Oh, Brenda, that would be worth a million bucks to me."

"On the contrary, it's very selfish of me. Richard and I are not going to leave on this honeymoon if you're still looking into that man's murder. The quicker you nail the sucker, the easier we'll all sleep."

I could've kissed her.

She rose from her seat. "But before I do that, I really have to go to that candy store. I'll see you at home." With a wave of her hand, she was out the door.

Before I put the phone book away, I looked up Cyn Lennox. Nothing listed in Amherst—just like nothing for Eugene Higgins. Then again, why would there be? She'd returned to Buffalo after it had been printed. Directory assistance was no help either; the number was unlisted.

I spent the next two hours doing any busy work I could think of while I pondered my next move. To find Gene, I'd have to find Cyn. I had a feeling she'd gone to ground, but I'd have to check out her house anyway. The actual mill wasn't part of the café. If Ted Hanson was on the premises, he might have an idea of where Cyn had gone. But even if he did, he might not tell me.

Tracking Cyn would be difficult, but not impossible. The problem was, according to Sophie's timetable I was running out of time. Brenda and Richard's plane tickets were for Friday. And then there was the vision of the bloody hands. Time may have already run out for someone. Cyn? Gene? Veronica?

I caught up with Tom before I left, pulled him aside so the customers wouldn't hear. "I might need some time off in the next couple of days. The stuff I'm looking into has taken a turn I hadn't expected, and—"

Tom raised a hand, cut me off. "We've already been over this; I don't want to know about it." He exhaled a ragged breath, exasperated. "It's my fault. I should've never talked to you about Walt. I only thought…maybe, him being a nobody, the cops wouldn't care about finding his killer. And then they made the arrest…."

I remained silent, felt my fingernails dig into my palms as I waited for him to fire me.

He nodded toward the door. "Go on. Just call if you're not coming in."

I swallowed, my mouth dry. Cutting me this kind of slack would cost Tom; he'd either lose money if he had to open later, or he'd exhaust himself doing both our jobs.

"Thanks."

Chapter Nineteen

Brenda hadn't yet found Dana Watkins, having another ten or twelve numbers left to call. But she had packed a picnic dinner for Richard and me to eat should we need to go on stakeout duty. "I'm going on my damn honeymoon, and nothing is going to stop me," she'd said as she pushed us out the door with our life-sustaining supplies. Richard wasn't as thrilled. The value some people place on their car's leather upholstery is simply unnatural.

We hadn't even made it to Main Street when I'd investigated the large paper grocery sack and assured him Brenda had packed plenty of napkins, and a half-used tin of saddle soap—just in case.

Our first stop was The Old Red Mill. A metallic purple motorcycle was parked in front. The bike in the ramp garage had definitely been black. Still…

As Brenda described, a hand-written sign was tacked to the café's front door. The lights were off; already the place looked abandoned.

Richard and I circled the building, found a door on the far side, and rang the buzzer until Ted appeared at the door. "You again," he muttered in greeting, his expression sour.

"I'm looking for Cyn Lennox."

"She isn't here, and I doubt she'll be back. She told me you were bad news."

"How am I responsible for her troubles?"

Hanson dragged a hand through his graying hair. "Sorry. It's just…since I found that guy dead on the hill, I had a feeling my life was going to change—that I'd be looking for a new tenant for the café."

"What was Cyn's excuse for closing?" Richard asked.

"She was so upset she was babbling when she called me last night. All I got was that she'd fired her nephew, and she had orders for restaurants that needed filling. I asked her about hiring someone else, but she said she couldn't talk anymore and hung up. The sign was up when I got here this morning."

"Did Dana come in today?"

Hanson shook his head. "I went in and had a look around the café. The office is a disaster. Cyn must've come in and cleared out what she could. Baking supplies and equipment were also missing."

"Did Cyn tell you why she fired Gene?"

"No, she isn't talking to me at all. I don't understand it. She thought the world of him. What could he have done to make her so angry?"

I had a suspicion. And I had another suspicion: that Ted and Cyn were—or had been—lovers.

I offered Hanson my hand and we shook.

The floodgates opened and I was bombarded with images and sensations. One in particular he enjoyed, though might never happen again: Cyn, on the back of his motorcycle, her arms wrapped around him.

Ted took back his hand.

"Thanks," I managed.

He nodded, then went back inside and closed the door.

We started back for the car. "Well?" Richard asked.

"Cyn and Ted have been more than just landlord and tenant."

Richard raised an eyebrow, said nothing.

"He's worried about her—and probably with cause."

Richard's cell phone rang. He answered it, then handed it to me.

"Get a pencil," Brenda said, her voice sounding tinny on the little phone. "I've got Dana's address. Wouldn't you know it was the next to last name on the list?"

I had a pen and jotted it down.

It was a toss-up if we went north to Cyn's house or south to locate Dana. I was pretty sure we wouldn't find Cyn home, but I had to check it out. So north we went, battling the last of the commuter traffic.

As anticipated, the drive was empty and no one answered when I knocked on the condo's door.

"She's not home," came a quavering voice. Sitting on a white plastic chair on the front porch of the next condo was an elderly woman in a green-plaid cotton housedress, with worn, what had once been pink, fluffy slippers on her feet.

I descended the steps and joined the old woman. "Do you know when she'll be back?"

She shook her head, her tight white curls never moving. "Not soon. She had suitcases."

"Last night?"

"About ten o'clock. She didn't even turn on the porch light when she loaded the car. And when she drove away, her headlights were off. I thought to myself, 'that is strange.'"

"Yes, it is," I agreed. "Has anyone else been around asking for her?"

"Just a nice young man in a silver car."

"Kind of thin, short, and balding?"

"Yes. Reminded me of my husband Charles when we were first married, oh, sixty years ago now."

"When did the young man stop by?"

"Oh, several times today. You just missed him about ten minutes ago."

Damn. But at least Gene didn't know where Cyn was, either. That meant she was probably safe.

"Thanks for your help," I told the old woman and went back to Richard's car.

"So?" he asked as I slammed the door shut. I gave him a recap. "Do you want to hang around in case Gene comes back?"

"There's no guarantee he will. We'd better go see Dana. That is, if she'll give me an audience."

Richard started the car.

Dana Watkins lived in a typical, older middle-class housing tract in Cheektowaga. Rows of purple petunias bordered the sidewalk up to the front door of the neat little brick bungalow. Richard and I got out of the car and headed up the path. Dana's car was parked in the driveway, and there were lights on inside the house, but no one answered our knock.

Richard followed me around the side of the house to the back, where a central air conditioner hummed. I stretched to peer through a kitchen window. Dana was hard at work, kneading dough on a 1950s chrome-and-Formica table. I tapped on the window. She looked up, annoyed.

"Can we talk?" I yelled, probably loud enough for her neighbors to hear.

"Go away," she mouthed. "I'm busy," and went back to her kneading.

I tapped on the window again. No reaction. I kept tapping. Thirty seconds. One minute. Finally she stomped to the back door, yanked it open. "Will you stop bothering me!"

"I need to talk to you. We're pals, remember?"

"You are not my pal."

"I was last Wednesday."

Impatience shadowed her eyes. "I have a lot of work to do. And you're keeping me from it."

"Then tell me where to find Cyn or, better yet, Gene."

Anxiety tightened her lips into a thin line. She breathed through her nose, her breaths coming in short snorts. "I suppose if I asked you to leave you'd ignore me and just keep bugging me."

"A man has died and the police have arrested the wrong person for the crime. I'm working on behalf of the murdered man's family to find out the truth."

She scowled. "Well, you might've put it that way earlier. Oh…come in."

I climbed the three concrete steps with Richard right behind me. The aroma of breads, cakes and cookies filled Dana's kitchen, which was overrun with flour sacks, spices, and cans and jars of other ingredients. The oven timer counted down thirteen minutes and six seconds. The table and sideboard in the dining room beyond were stacked with boxes and racks of baked goods. Dana was already back to work at her kitchen table.

And there was something else in the room. An aura I recognized and it didn't belong to Dana.

"You're filling Cyn's orders?" I asked.

"It's a great opportunity for me."

"Why did Cyn close the café?" Richard asked.

Dana looked up, for the first time noticing Richard. "This is my brother. He's also a friend of Cyn's," I said.

She didn't believe me. "Look, all I know is she said she was shutting down. I don't know any more."

"This doesn't look like a licensed kitchen," Richard said conversationally.

Dana's head snapped up, her eyes blazing.

"I'm a physician. I've got friends who work for the health department. I wonder what they'd say if they knew about your little operation."

Dana's grip on her pile of dough tightened. "I've got a line on a commercial kitchen. I just need to find the financing." The words were fine, it was the quaver in her voice that belied her conviction.

"That won't help if you're shut down," Richard added.

Dana bit her lip, turned back to the dough on the table. "I don't know why Cyn closed the café. The two of us could've handled the business for a couple of days or weeks. She was in such a snit—"

"Why'd she fire Gene?"

Dana paused in her work, but didn't look up. "I don't know."

She was a terrible liar.

"Cyn called me about seven o'clock last night and told me she was shutting down the business. By the time I got there, she'd already cleaned out most of her office. I asked her about the orders, but she said she didn't care. She told me if I wanted to take them on, I could. She even gave me the supplies to do it, too."

"That seems overly generous of her."

Dana merely shrugged.

"Cyn's neighbor said she saw Cyn leave with suitcases last night. Did she tell you where she was going?"

Dana shook her head. "Just away."

"You said she cleaned out her office. Does that mean her financial records?" I asked.

"I guess."

"Could Gene have been embezzling from her?"

"Gene and I weren't really friends, but we did work well together. I won't believe he could do that to Cyn."

"I don't suppose you know where Gene lives?" Richard asked.

She shook her head. "Just that he had an apartment on Hertel Avenue or just off it."

"That's a lot of territory," I said. "What's he drive?"

"A silver Alero."

"New York plates?"

She nodded.

I reached back and took out my wallet, withdrew one of my old calling cards with Richard's phone number written on the back and handed it to her. "I don't know where your loyalties lie, but I honestly want to help Cyn. If you hear from her, please consider calling me."

She scrutinized the card, said nothing.

"I'd like to talk to Gene, too. If he's threatening Cyn, she really should go to the police. This isn't something she should try to handle on her own."

Dana stood in the doorway and watched us until we turned the corner for the front yard.

"Well?" Richard asked.

"That was a nice piece of blackmail you pulled back there."

"I like to feel useful. Did you believe anything she said?"

"Most of it. She may or may not be there now, but Cyn's been in that house. I can't blame Dana for not saying more. She's scared."

We got back in Richard's car. "So what's next? We pull stakeout duty here and wait for Cyn?"

I shook my head. "Dana would only warn her away. Our best bet is to find Walt's fancy lady, Veronica. She might know Gene, or might be able to point us in the right direction."

"And how do we find her? More gay bars?"

"The bartender at Lambrusco's said she'd moved up. We might have to try all of them."

"Didn't you say most of the bars only have drag shows on weekends?"

"That doesn't mean we can't flash her picture around."

The dashboard clock said 7:12 p.m. "Most bars don't even start to fill up until at least ten," Richard said.

"Most popular bars," I clarified. To my knowledge, The Whole Nine Yards had never filled up.

"We may as well go home to wait," he said, and turned the key in the ignition.

Three hours.

"Some of those drag queens had their own Web sites. You think maybe this Veronica does?" Richard asked.

"It wouldn't hurt to do a search."

Three long hours.

Bloodied hands. A rivulet of scarlet cascading down a wrist...

Whose hands? Whose damn blood? And was it already too late to save him or her?

***

Thunderclouds threatened the sky to the west. Nightfall looked imminent instead of two hours away. Richard pulled his car up the driveway, parked the car in his garage. The humidity had almost doubled since we'd left Dana's house some twenty minutes before. A storm hadn't been predicted, but the weather along Lake Erie changes fast.

Richard hit the button on the remote above the visor and the garage door obligingly closed. "We don't have to take my car tonight, do we?"

"No, it can rain on mine or Brenda's."

We got out of the Lincoln, went out through the side door and headed for the house. Brenda was waiting for us in the kitchen. "I've got a message for you."

"Me?" Richard asked.

"No, Jeffy. Dana Watkins called."

"That was fast," Richard muttered.

"She said Gene Higgins lives on Norwalk Avenue, off Hertel. Here." She handed me a slip of paper with the full address.

"Why didn't she just tell us when we were there?" Richard asked.

"My guess is she had to wait until Cyn wasn't listening."

"Cyn was there?"

"I had a feeling she was close by. I'll bet her car was in Dana's garage. I should've looked."

"Why wouldn't Dana want Cyn to know she gave us the address?"

"The bigger question is why doesn't Cyn want us talking to Gene? Especially if she's so angry with him—angry enough to close her business?"

Richard looked thoughtful.

"I guess this means you're going out again." Brenda said.

"I guess."

"What about looking up Veronica on the Internet?" Richard asked.

"Yeah, let's do that first." So off we went to the study.

Brenda accompanied us, plunking down on the leather couch and picking up her novel. We spent at least an hour jumping back and forth between the Buffalo gay bar web sites looking for Veronica. If she had moved on to bigger and better things, she hadn't shown up on anyone's radar.

The sky outside had darkened. Brenda got up to turn on another lamp. Thunder rumbled, and the phone rang. She picked up the extension. Richard clicked back to Google, typed in another keyword.

"Who is this?" Brenda asked, annoyed.

Richard and I looked up.

Brenda held out the phone, covering the mouthpiece. "It's for you, Jeffy. Sounds like a nutcase. Got one of those voice disguisers working."

I got up from my chair. More thunder reverberated overhead as I took the phone. "Jeff Resnick here."

"You will cease poking your nose into other people's business," said the slow, electronically altered voice.

"And if I don't?"

"I could have killed you in that ramp garage."

My spine stiffened, my hand growing tight around the receiver.

"I won't be so generous next time."

The connection broke.

Lightning flashed out the window.

I hit the phone's rest buttons, then punched *69.

"That number is out of range," came the prerecorded voice. Whoever it was had probably called from a cell phone.

Thunder boomed and I replaced the receiver.

"What was that all about?" Richard asked.

I exhaled through my nose. "A nutcase," I said, echoing Brenda's assessment.

"Did that person threaten you?" she asked.

"Sort of. Just that—" The image of Richard lying on the cold stone floor, shot, blood soaking his London Fog raincoat, came back to me. "That I'd be sorry if I didn't mind my business." Lightning flashed again. "You'd better log off before the storm fries your hard drive." As though to reinforce my words, thunder crashed overhead.

Richard turned back to his monitor, logged off, and shut down the computer. "Are you worried?" he asked, swiveling his chair to face me.

"I'd be a fool not to be concerned, all things considered. But worried?" You bet. "No."

"Where does someone get one of those voice-altering devices?" Brenda asked.

"At the mall. Radio Shack sells them. Or the Internet. Anybody can buy one."

Neither of them looked too worried and I was glad I hadn't mentioned the incident at the parking garage. "Are you about ready?" I asked Richard.

"Yeah." He got up, kissed Brenda good-bye, and we headed for the back door.

We crossed the drive and made it to the garage just seconds before the rain hit, coming down in drenching sheets of liquid silver. For a long minute or two Richard and I stood under the eaves looking out at the house with the curtain of rain before us. I can't read Richard at all, but a weird kind of electricity crackled between us. He kept looking out at the rain pouring down and his smile grew wider and wider.

"What's with you?" I asked. "You're happy."

"It's my last couple of days of freedom and I want to enjoy it."

"Freedom? For years you've nagged Brenda to marry you. Are you having second thoughts?"

"Not at all. But getting married means commitment and responsibilities, and—"

"Being a real grown up?"

His smile dimmed. "Yeah, but it's also the first time in months that I've felt good."

I envied him that. I didn't like to dwell on it, but the fact I might never fully recover from the mugging, and might even develop new symptoms, like seizures, was a constant shadow hanging over me. And now the threat from that phone call loomed over me as well.

"You've got to get over it, Jeff. What happened, happened. It's over. Move on."

I stared at the rain dancing on the driveway. Was he talking about the shooting that nearly killed him, or me being mugged? It didn't matter. And I didn't want him to know how much that weird electronic voice had freaked me.

"I'm working on it."

"Good." His smile returned. Then he hauled off and punched me, hard, on the arm.

For a long second I stood there, stunned, then I punched him back with equal force.

He rubbed his bicep, grinning. "Come on," he said. "Let's go!"

***

A torrent of rain did nothing to improve the gray, peeling exterior of the house where Gene Higgins lived. As luck would have it, a parking space was open right out front—just like what always happens on a TV drama. Richard did a superb job of parallel parking and we sat there gazing at the drab building.

"Ugly, isn't it?" Richard said.

"Butt ugly." Most of the houses were either duplexes or had been divided into apartments, which meant off-street parking was at a premium. I scanned the road for a silver Alero, but didn't see one.

"Do you think it's worth knocking on the door?" Richard asked.

"Nah. But as long as we're here."

Richard glanced over his shoulder to the back seat. "I think Brenda's got an umbrella back there."

"You won't melt."

"I've already got a black eye. Do I need to catch cold four days before I leave on my honeymoon?"

"Wuss."

"Idiot."

He might be right. "Come on."

Leafy maple trees sheltered the car and sidewalk, so we weren't actually soaked as we made a run for the cover of the duplex's porch. At the sound of our footsteps, the muffled sound of a dog barking came from within the house. A plastic strip labeled "Higgins" was attached to the second-floor apartment's mailbox. I pressed the doorbell. Some part of me was hoping to tap into the vision I'd seen with the red sparkling shoe, the polished nails, and the stiletto. I didn't. Then again, how many people actually push their own doorbell?

The dog continued to bark.

"Is he here?" Richard asked.

I clasped the door handle, closed my eyes and concentrated. I expected the vision of the red shoe to burst upon my mind, but nothing happened. I opened my eyes and stared at the door's chipped white paint. I jiggled the handle; it was locked. "I figured I'd get something, feel something familiar, and I'm not getting anything."

Richard shifted from foot to foot.

The door to the other apartment opened, and the wild yapping got louder. A short, white-haired woman in dark slacks and pink polyester tunic stood behind the screen door. "What do you want?" she snapped.

Richard faced her, had to shout to be heard. "We're looking for Gene Higgins."

The old lady homed in on his black eye and scowled. "He's not home."

"He's usually here weeknights, though, isn't he?" I asked.

"Is that any of your business?"

We'd get nowhere with her. I took out my wallet, another calling card, and my pen. I jotted a note on the back and wedged it between the doorframe and screen. Gene might miss it if I just shoved it under the door.

"I'd appreciate it if you wouldn't remove the card. Mr. Higgins needs to talk to me."

A brown-and-white terrier mix jumped up and down at her side. "Are you some kind of repo guy?"

"I'm a friend of his aunt's. She's gone missing. He'll want to talk to me about it."

She looked skeptical, but my mostly true explanation would probably keep her from ripping the card to shreds the minute we took off.

I took the steps two at a time. Richard murmured a "good evening" and was right on my heels.

Once back inside the car, Richard grasped the steering wheel and looked out through the foggy windshield. "We forgot the bag with the food in it."

"Damn. It's still in your car."

"Where to now?"

"Do you want to get something to eat, right?"

"It'll help kill time until we can hit the gay bars."

"You say that with such enthusiasm."

He ignored the comment. "If you didn't get anything on Gene just now, whose vibes have you been tuning into? Veronica's?"

"It's a possibility. But Gene is definitely involved. What if Veronica killed Walt? Dumping his body by the mill could have been done to implicate Gene."

"Only the cops didn't bite?"

"Exactly."

"What if Veronica has skipped town?"

"I don't think so."

"Gut instinct?"

"I trust it."

Richard started the car and switched on the front and rear defrosters to take care of the windshields. "Have you got a motive?"

"Not yet." The old lady continued to watch us from her door, her yappy dog still bobbing up and down like a yo-yo. She'd probably wait up for Gene just to tell him about us, which was okay with me—if it made him call. I had a feeling that right now he was sweating. Cyn must have pieced things together and wanted to distance herself from her nephew—even if it meant closing her café. But what was it that Gene feared if Veronica was Walt's killer?

And what if we found Veronica? I wasn't sure what I'd do.

Richard pulled away from the curb and headed for Hertel Avenue. He was enjoying the chase. I wish I could say the same. The closer we got to resolution, the more my insides squirmed. It wasn't going to be a happy conclusion—of that I was sure. Something inside me—and the damned vision of the bloody hands—told me it would be awful and messy and…somebody was going to die.

I just hoped to God it wasn't going to be Richard.

Chapter Twenty

BoysTown was probably the next-to-best gay hotspot in Buffalo after Club Monticello. Loud disco music boiled from within and gyrating, shirtless men in tight jeans hopped around the dance floor in—what else—gay abandon.

"God, they look happy," Richard shouted in my ear.

"Of course they're happy. They're—"

"Gay!" he finished. "I need a beer." He headed straight for the bar and ordered for us. I fished out Walt's and Veronica's, as well as Cyn's, pictures. We sucked back our brewskies and I asked everyone within listening distance if they'd ever seen any of the people in the pictures.

No. No. And—no!

I asked the bartender which was the next club below them.

Fifteen minutes later, Richard and I had moved the car two blocks and we headed for Club QBN—Queer Boys Network—and had ordered another round of beers. More disco music, more sweating, shirtless guys boogying down.

I shoved the pictures under every available nose. No, no one had ever seen Walt. Veronica looked familiar, but nobody would stake his or her life on it. Sparkly red stiletto heels? Why darling, every girl in here has at least one pair!

Next down the line was Daddy's Place. A little less noisy, a little less boisterous, and still no one knew Walt. Veronica, however, was a known entity, although no one had seen her in at least a week—maybe two.

Closer, but no cigar.

Richard wasn't looking quite so cocky. "What the hell do we do if we find her?"

Good question. Confrontation was out—especially in such a crowded venue. She could deny she even knew Walt—except for all the picture evidence, and even then she could say Walt had been a patron and it was just good PR to pose with the clients. Then again, the bartender at Lambrusco's could verify she and Walt had at least been acquainted. That is, if he could be trusted to swear by it.

That Veronica was familiar was one thing. Where she lived, no one knew. No one knew the name on her/his driver's license. Wigs and makeup and fancy dress were great concealers of the truth. In a feel-good place like a bar, who knew or who cared what people did in their regular lives—what their day jobs entailed and/or how they made their daily bread?

I hefted my third bottle of beer and found I couldn't take another sip, setting it back down. Richard, however, sat facing the dance floor, elbows on the bar, enjoying the spectacle. "I haven't been bar hopping since my college days," he said, his head nodding in time with yet another Bee Gees favorite.

"Why don't you get out there and dance?" I suggested.

"If Brenda was here, I might. Then again, this isn't my kind of dancing. I'm better cheek-to-cheek."

"Any time, sailor," said a skinny guy with a black tank top and painted-on white pants.

I snagged the guy's shirt strap. "Hey, have you ever see this queen?" I shoved Veronica's picture under his nose.

God knows how he focused in such bad light, but his eyes lit up. "Veronica! Oh, she's a sweetheart. Yeah, I've seen her. Every weekend over at Big Brother's. She's moving up in the world. Another year or so, and she'll be the toast of the town."

"And where do we find Big Brother's?" Richard asked.

"Over on Pearl. But not until the Wednesday night show. She does a mean Brittany Spears. Doesn't quite have the nose for it—but hey, you can't have everything." He danced by us and dissolved into the crowd.

"Two days?" Richard almost whined.

I glanced at my watch. "Technically, it's one day and twenty-two hours. And I thought you were enjoying yourself?"

"Sure, as a change of pace. But I wouldn't want to do this on a regular basis."

"We ought to go over there and ask, just to make sure. But I won't go flashing Veronica's picture again. That could scare her off. As it is, if someone I've already shown it to mentions it to her, she'll probably leave town in a hurry."

So off we went to our fourth bar that night.

Big Brother's was smaller than I anticipated; intimate was how it was advertised out front. Sure enough, a poster-sized color photograph of Miss Veronica Lakes in a white, baby-doll dress, blond wig, and pouting lips greeted us. Her co-stars, Margarita Ville and Sandy Waters, only rated eight-by-ten black-and-white photos.

"I don't think she looks like Brittany," I told Richard.

"I couldn't pick Brittany out of a lineup," he admitted.

"God, you're an old fart." He followed me inside, where we made sure that yes, Miss Lakes would be appearing on Wednesday. Did we want to make reservations?

We headed out the door. A glance at my watch told me it was after one. The sidewalk was still wet, but the storm and the lingering rain had passed, breaking the hot spell. Richard yawned as we walked toward the car. "I'll drive," I said, and unlocked the passenger side door for him, then moved to the driver's side.

Richard fastened his seat belt, crossed his arms over his chest, and settled back in his seat. "Home, James, and don't spare the horses."

I pulled away from the curb and headed back for Main Street. Richard was asleep before we got there.

I braked for a red light, one of those crazy ones with the strobing bar of white in the middle. Bloodied hands flashed before my eyes. I tightened my grip on the steering wheel. Not now, not when I'm driving.

Bloodied hands. Rivulets of scarlet cascading down the wrists, soaking into a forest of dark hair past the wrists. No jewelry, no nail polish.

Slowly the hands turned, palms out to face me. Strong, masculine hands.

So much blood!

Honk!

The vision winked out. I jammed my foot on the accelerator and the car lurched forward. Richard didn't stir.

I was glad to have the wheel to hang on to—it kept my hands from shaking. I wouldn't have to worry about some crazy coming after Richard if I crashed the car and killed us both. But the vision didn't replay. I drove like an old lady, made it home and parked the car in the garage before giving up my death grip. I sat there, listening to the engine make tinking noises for at least a minute before I could move. The garage door opener's light would go off in another minute. I gave Richard a poke to wake him.

"We're home."

He took in a deep breath and straightened. "I wasn't asleep."

"Sure," I said and opened my door. Richard did likewise.

We got out of there and I closed and locked the garage's side door before the light winked out. Brenda had left the outside lights on and I sorted through my keys to open the back door. Richard bumped into me. "God, I'm tired."

I opened the door. "Go to bed."

He saluted me and stepped over the threshold. "Yes, sir."

Stepping up behind him, I pushed him in the direction of the kitchen. "Good night."

Eyes closed, I stood in the silent pantry, listened until his footsteps faded, and realized I was too wired to sleep. What I needed was a walk. A nice long walk to calm my nerves.

I headed back out the door, paused to lock up, and started down the driveway.

* * *

"You're late tonight," Sophie told me as she ushered me inside the bakery, then locked the door behind me.

"I was out."

"Investigating?"

"Sort of."

She scuffed ahead of me in her worn slippers. Tonight it was tea. The cups were set out with a little white pitcher of milk and a plate of fresh-sliced *placek*—just as she'd promised days before.

"Sit, sit," she urged, taking her own seat.

I sat.

She poured milk into my cup, then added the strong, dark tea from an old brown pottery pot. "See, no need for a spoon," she told me, proud of her cleverness. She pushed the plate closer and I took a slice, setting it on the napkin she'd provided. It was still warm.

"How do you always know when to have things ready for me? I didn't even know I was coming here until I started walking."

She shrugged, then leaned forward, her eyes worried. "You have a lot on your mind."

"Yeah," I admitted, and broke a crumbly corner off my cake. "I got one of those flashes of insight when I was behind the wheel of the car. I don't know if it was that or the vision that freaked me more." I stuffed the morsel in my mouth, savoring its sweet, buttery—comforting—taste.

"The bloody hands," she said.

"Yeah."

Sophie nibbled on her own piece of *placek*. "I don't know what to tell you. Only that…you have to do what you feel is right. That's not always easy."

"Tell me about it." I wasn't sure how to tell her—how to phrase—what I was feeling. "The vision was much stronger tonight, telling me that whatever happens will come pretty damn quick. And when it does—I'm worried I won't react in time to do what's right, what'll save lives, or time, or—anything! Dammit, I'm scared to death whatever I do is going to cost someone's life."

"Your brother?" She shook her head. "Now you're being paranoid."

"Can you guarantee it won't happen?"

"Nobody can. But, to ease your mind—I see things ahead for your brother."

"Good things?" I asked, thinking about Brenda, their wedding, and the future.

She shrugged. "Eh...things."

Things?

Like living as a veg in a nursing home?

Crippled?

Maimed?

Okay, so maybe I *was* being paranoid. And then there was the incident in the parking garage. Should I ask her if I had a future? She hadn't volunteered the information.

Sophie sipped her tea and avoided looking at me. I sipped mine and did the same.

Finally, Sophie pushed back her empty mug. "You have someplace else to go."

"Yeah."

"If you can, come and see me on Saturday," she said, rising from her chair, her expression solemn.

Saturday. That meant whatever happened, this whole convoluted mess would be over with by then. Then again: *If you can*. Maybe I wouldn't be able to. Her words had given me no peace.

But she was right; I did have somewhere else to go.

***

I did a sweep around Norwalk Avenue, didn't find Gene Higgins's silver Alero, and so cruised the surrounding dark streets. Sure enough, two blocks over the little car sat parked under a dripping maple. Thanks to alternate street parking, Gene was going to have to move the car by eight o'clock or risk a ticket. So I had a decision to make. Stick with the car, or stake out his apartment until he emerged. If he emerged.

I circled back to Norwalk and found a space with a clear view of the house. By parking so far away, Gene had obviously tried to make me—or someone else—think he wasn't home.

Talk radio bored me, and I could find nothing but loser love songs, hip-hop or gangsta rap on every other station. I snapped off the radio and hunkered down in my seat, my gaze fixed on the homely gray house. Green numerals on the digital clock gave me the bad news. I'd been awake twenty hours, and fatigue had settled in with a vengeance. Now I not only had to hope I wouldn't fall asleep, but that some cop wouldn't find me and roust me.

I had to be out of my friggin' mind. Gene was probably nestled in his warm, comfortable bed and here I was cold, cramped, sleep-deprived, and verging on misery. I didn't have a clue what I was going to say to him if I caught up with him. Should I tell him about the sparkling red shoe? Ask him about Veronica?

A car rolled past, its red taillights glowing. Already the sky to the east was beginning to brighten.

An hour after that, I was sure my mind teetered on the verge of imminent brain death from lack of sleep and absolute boredom.

I'd been staring at the house so long, it took a good ten seconds for me to realize someone had come out of the door to the upstairs apartment and had descended the steps to the street. A shot of adrenaline rushed through me as I stumbled out of the car—slamming the door and running across the street.

"Gene! Gene Higgins!"

Gene stopped dead, his head hanging. He didn't move as I jogged to catch up with him.

"What do you want?"

"Tell me about Walt Kaplan. How you knew him. Why his body was found on the hill by the mill."

He took a step away and I grabbed him by the shoulder. The image of the bloody hands burst upon my mind and I let go as though scalded.

Gene whirled on me and caught me with a fist to the gut. I fell flat on my ass on the still-damp sidewalk, doubled over onto my side, gasping for air.

Gene crouched beside me. "Jeez, man, I'm sorry!"

I looked up into his panicked face.

"I never hit anybody before."

Anybody in a position to hit back, I'd bet.

Crawling onto my knees, I struggled to catch my breath as I inched toward the curb and a parked car to haul myself up. Gene hovered over me, babbling apologies, but I couldn't focus on the words.

Once upright, I found I couldn't stand straight, and hunched over, hands clutching my knees, my ass plastered to the water-beaded Sebring's fender to keep from falling over.

"You're not going to sue me, are you?" Gene asked anxiously.

I looked up at him, my breaths finally coming easier. "You answer my questions and I might not call my attorney the minute I get home."

"I don't know anything. Ted found the guy dead by the building. End of story. Besides, the cops already arrested someone. Case closed."

"Their case against the homeless guy will fall apart as soon as the DNA evidence comes back from the lab. Walt had backdoor sex before he died. They'll have a new angle to investigate and how long do you think it'll be before they start asking you questions?"

Gene said nothing.

Time to bluff. "How did you end up with Walt's pictures, and why did you take them back to his apartment? Uh, all but one. The last negative on the roll had been snipped—your picture. Did Walt tell you about the key over the door?"

"You've got no proof."

"When the cops go back to Walt's apartment, they'll find your fingerprints. Walt was a bit of a pack rat. Did you know he kept shoeboxes filled with stuff to remind him of his past liaisons? And who knows what other keepsakes he kept from his time with you at the house in Holiday Valley."

"Holy Christ," Gene wailed and smashed his fist against the roof of the car, leaving a noticeable dimple.

I stayed rock still, hoping like hell he wouldn't hit me again.

"Where are they? Do you have them?"

"I gave them to a reporter at the *Buffalo News*," I lied. "I disappear from his radar and he goes straight to the cops with it and my suspicions." Well, it sounded good.

"Shit!" This time Gene punched his right thigh.

"Pipe down," I warned. "You want your neighbors calling the cops? Then again, it would make it easy for me to file a police report for assault."

Gene squeezed his eyes shut, about to cry.

"Look, why don't we go get some coffee and talk?"

"I can't—If it gets out—My parents—Cyn will kill me."

"It's only a question of time before everything comes out. Either you cooperate and spill what you know or the cops are going to try to nail you for everything, and life without parole can be pretty damned boring."

Arms hanging limply at his sides, Gene stood in the middle of the sidewalk, his lower lip trembling, looking at least ten years younger.

With some effort, I managed to straighten, my insides taking their time to settle back into their rightful places. "Coffee," I repeated. Gene nodded. I gestured toward my car. "Come on."

He followed me like a docile lamb and got into the passenger side.

The drive to Dunkin' Donuts was silent. I stopped at the drive-up menu, gave our order, and proceeded to the window. A perky blonde teenager held out her hand for the money, made change, and handed me the cups in less than thirty seconds. I handed Gene his before pulling over to an empty parking space on the far side of the building.

As though on autopilot, Gene removed the cap from his cup and blew on it to cool it. I took a sip. It burned my mouth and I thought of Dana Watkins and her asbestos esophagus.

"You want to start at the beginning?" I prompted.

Gene's gaze seemed to be focused on the door handle. "It started off as fun. Cyn wanted to cut loose. Dennis was a great guy, but he had no soul for adventure. When he died, Cyn mourned him but was ready for new hobbies, new friends, and an escapade or two. I took her to one of the gay bars on drag night and we had a ball. We kept going back, but we liked the smaller clubs best. Less people. More fun."

"She accepted that you were gay?"

He nodded miserably. "Cyn has always been there for me. She's more like a sister than an aunt. If my father finds out, he'll disown me."

"How long have you been—" God, this sounded stupid. "—dressing up?"

"Since I moved out of my parents' house. But I never went out in drag. Never had the nerve until Cyn dared me. She bought some costumes at a charity auction a few months ago. She gave me the dress as a joke."

"But you didn't take it as a joke?" I guessed.

He wouldn't look at me, but nodded. "She helped me build an outfit."

"But she kept the shoes."

His head bobbed again. "They didn't fit me."

"And then you met Walt." It was all falling together in my head. "He admired Cyn's shoes, then later, once the two of you got better acquainted, he surprised you with a pair to go with your red dress."

Gene said nothing.

"How does Veronica fit into this?"

"She and Walt broke up before I came along. See, Walt used to brag about money. He dressed nice and always flashed a big wad of cash at the clubs—paid for lots of drinks.

Veronica insinuated herself into his life. She kept hounding him for money so he dumped her."

"But she wouldn't let go. She was angry he took up with you."

His head sank to his chest. "Yeah."

"Did she know Walt's family owns the Kaplan Jewelry stores?"

"Everybody did. Course, Walt didn't let on that he had virtually nothing to do with them anymore."

"Then how did you know?"

"I told you; we were friends. We spent a lot of time talking."

"At the clubs?"

"Sometimes. Sometimes we just went out for dinner. Walt and I weren't...I mean, I like older guys, but we only did it a couple of times. It wasn't like we were—"

"But you were with him hours before he died.

"We had dinner at Eckl's in Orchard Park that night."

"I know the place. And afterward?"

Gene was silent, wouldn't look at me.

"After the sex, what happened?" I tried again.

"Walt dropped me off at my apartment. He said he was going home. Veronica must have tracked him down and killed him. I figure she dumped him by the mill to implicate me."

That wasn't all. "Did you find him?"

"Veronica called me." Gene closed his eyes, let out a shaky breath. "I don't even know how she got my cell number. She said they'd argued—about me. She said she'd dumped Walt by the mill. She made it sound like he was hurt—but alive."

It had been Gene's revulsion I'd experienced when I'd first visited the mill. "Why didn't you call 911?"

"Walt was my friend. He'd never come out to his family. I wasn't going to do it for him. So I rushed right over there and—"

"Found him dead."

Gene nodded miserably. "She'd dumped him all right—naked. I wasn't about to let him be found that way. But he was a lot bigger than me. I knew I'd never get him up the hill on my own so I put his clothes back on him. I hated to leave him there, but what else could I do?"

"Why didn't you call the cops?" I pressed.

"I was scared. I still am. Of her."

"Have you heard from Veronica since?"

Again he nodded. "She's left threatening messages on my voice mail. Someone broke a window in my apartment. I think Veronica tried to get in. My landlady heard a noise and let her dog out. Since then, I've had a new lock installed and have tried to watch my back."

"What about Cyn?"

"She was furious when Walt turned up dead. Like it was a stain on *her* character." He turned anguished eyes toward me. "I told her about Veronica's call, how she blamed me for her and Walt breaking up. How she wanted the ring."

That grabbed my attention. "You've got Walt's ring?"

Gene dug into his collar and pulled out a chain from around his neck. A sparkling, man's diamond ring flashed. The stone was easily three or more carets. "How—when—did you get it?"

"Walt didn't want Veronica to get her hands on it. He said he didn't have a safety deposit box and asked me to take it for safekeeping. It was only supposed to be for a couple of days. She killed him that night."

Had Walt finally told Veronica he was broke? I could imagine someone with an obsessive personality being angry and determined enough to try to seize Walt's only real asset. She must have tortured him until he told her what happened to the ring.

"Anyway," Gene continued, "Cyn and I talked about it and decided to keep quiet. Cyn was ecstatic when that homeless guy was arrested. But you kept poking around and she got paranoid. We argued on Sunday afternoon. She went berserk after she visited your brother. She was afraid she'd be accused of being an accessory to the crime. She wouldn't listen to me—to reason. She left town. At first I thought she'd gone to Holiday Valley, but I went out there and she hasn't been around. I don't know where she is."

And I wasn't going to tell him. Yet, I believed him. He wasn't a killer, and he wasn't a drag queen. He was just a boy in a dress on Saturday nights.

Gene held his coffee under his chin, but didn't seem willing or able to drink it. The hands holding onto the cup were small and soft, the nails short. They weren't the bloodied, masculine hands I'd been seeing for almost two weeks. Yet, when I'd touched him, the vision had exploded across my mind.

A chill ran through me. It was Gene's blood on those glistening hands.

Like a slaughterhouse, Sophie had said.

"Why did Veronica think Walt had money?"

"He drove that big Caddy. She never saw where he lived—how he lived. See, at first Walt was a sucker for her.

He wanted to impress her. He told her that after his accident he received a million-dollar settlement."

"But he didn't."

"Nah, more like a hundred grand."

"He must've eventually told her the truth."

"He did. She didn't believe him. She's…one scary person."

"How did you and Walt become friends?"

He laughed. "Golf. He told me one day we'd play a round. It never happened." His mouth sagged. "Never will now."

Walt hadn't had many people in his life that cared about him. Hell, I'm not even sure Tom really gave a damn about him. But wimpy little Gene did. And now he was just as vulnerable as Walt had been.

"I'm sorry you lost your friend."

Gene looked over at me, his eyes bright. "Thanks."

"You're not safe here in Buffalo."

His gaze intensified, fear tightening his lips. He'd seen firsthand Veronica's handiwork.

"Does Veronica know about the Holiday Valley house?"

He shook his head.

"It might be a good idea for you to go stay there for a few days. Do you have clothes there?"

"Yeah."

"Good. Because I don't think you should go back to your apartment. I won't say I'm great at reconnaissance, but I can usually pick up a tail. I'll drop you off at your car and follow you out to the Thruway to make sure Veronica isn't staking you out. You stay put out there until at least Saturday. After that—"

After that he'd either be dead or alive, but the truth would be out.

"What do you say?"

He sighed and recapped his coffee. "Okay."

Chapter Twenty-One

It was almost nine-thirty when, feeling punch drunk, I staggered into Richard's kitchen. He and Brenda were at the table, finishing breakfast, and neither of them looked happy.

"Where the hell have you been?" Richard demanded. "Didn't you think we'd be worried sick? Your car's gone, your bed hasn't been slept in."

"That'll teach me to make the damn thing every morning," I said and collapsed into a chair.

"Did you sleep at all?" Brenda asked.

"Not since yesterday."

"Do you want something to eat?"

"Toast, please."

She got up to make me some.

"Well?" Richard asked. His eye wasn't so black this morning; it had turned a bit green with yellow edges—it was healing nicely.

Resting my elbow on the table, I leaned my cheek into my palm and tried to keep my eyes open. "I went back to Norwalk Street and found Gene Higgins."

"And?"

"He says Veronica admitted to him that she killed Walt and dumped him behind the mill. The poor kid's scared shitless."

"With cause, I'd say."

"He's going to hide out at Cyn's house in Holiday Valley for a few days, but I don't for a minute think he's safe."

"Why not?" Brenda asked.

I sat up straighter and cleared my throat. "That vision of bloody hands I keep getting—it's Gene's blood I see."

The toast popped up. Brenda put it on a plate and handed it to me. "I don't see how you can eat it dry like that."

"I like it that way."

"Do want some milk with that?"

I nodded.

"What makes you think it's Gene's blood?" Richard asked.

"I touched him and bang! There was the vision. What I don't get are the hands themselves. They're definitely strong, masculine hands. And so far nobody involved in this murder has hands like that."

Brenda placed a short glass of milk in front of me. "I could warm it up," she offered.

"No, thanks."

"What'll you do next?" Richard asked.

I chewed and swallowed some toast. "Crash for a few hours."

"Oh, good," Brenda said, "because the zipper broke on one of the suitcases and I want to see if we can get another one."

"You don't need me for that." Richard said.

"It's your suitcase," she deadpanned.

End of that discussion.

I gulped down the milk, grabbed my second piece of toast and pushed myself up from the table. "If I'm not up by one, give me a yell, willya?"

"Will do," Richard said, resigned.

I threaded my way through the pantry to my room off the back hall. I needed to call Tom, tell him I wouldn't be in before I could allow myself the luxury of sleep. And later in the day, I'd have to turn my efforts to figuring out how to protect Gene and corner Veronica.

And I didn't have a clue how to accomplish either.

***

Instead of Richard, it was the telephone that woke me. It rang four times and I grabbed it before voice mail picked up. "What?"

"Do you always answer the phone that way?" Maggie asked.

My grip on the receiver slackened. "When I'm yanked from a deep sleep, yeah."

"It's almost one o'clock. What are you doing in bed at this time of day? Are you sick?"

Eyes closed, I asked myself the same question. Maybe. Subtle rumblings behind my eyes told me I'd better take my meds when I got up, in hopes of staving off one of my all-too-frequent skull pounders.

"I don't know where Brenda is. Do you want to leave a message?"

"Well...actually, I wanted to talk to you."

That statement warranted the opening of one eye. "Oh?"

"I...kind of wanted to apologize to you."

The other eye opened. "What for?"

"Apparently it's none of my business if you risk your brother's life."

"Who told you that?"

"Richard."

I blinked.

"He called me earlier this morning and very politely told me to mind my own business."

"And what did you say?"

"I apologized."

I rolled onto my back and stared at the ceiling. "Does this mean the two of us can move forward?"

"I'm not sure what it means."

"Neither do I, but it might be fun to find out. What are you doing on Friday?"

She laughed. "I'm the maid of honor at a wedding."

"What a coincidence. I'm the best man. I meant after that."

"I took the whole day off from work."

"Me, too."

"Then maybe we could spend the rest of the day together."

"How about the evening, too?" I suggested.

"Maybe."

"That sounds nice."

"Yeah, it sounds nice to me, too." Did I detect the hint of a smile in her voice? "Okay," she said at last. "I guess I'll see you Friday."

"For sure."

The phone clicked in my ear and I hung up the receiver. My grin of anticipation waned. Now if we all lived until Friday, we might just have a happily ever after.

***

The first time my bony ass had ever settled in an Adirondack chair had been on a trip to Vermont with Shelley. We'd stayed at a quaint country inn, sucked in clean mountain air and decided that rural vistas could entice us away from the city. That is, until Shelley realized that cell towers and kosher delis weren't available on demand.

The sun had already maneuvered around ninety percent of the deck when I'd gone to sit outside to soak in its rays on Brenda's new lawn furniture. She'd won that battle, but still hadn't convinced Richard that a hot tub was a necessity.

Sitting back, my face tilted toward the sky, legs outstretched before me, arms limp on the long flat rests, I lazed, inviting sleep to come. And maybe I even dozed for a few minutes before something cold thwacked beside my hand.

"Don't spill it," Richard chided.

My eyes jerked open, my fingers closing around a frosted glass. A lemon wedge floated amongst a cluster of ice cubes. I took a sip. Unsweetened iced tea—just the way I liked it.

Richard had taken one of the other rustic chairs and sipped his drink.

"Where's Brenda?" I asked.

"Ironing and packing for the trip. She's making it a ritual, taking pictures and everything. It's unnatural."

No, it was Brenda's way of coping with what Richard and I were doing. She was worried, with reason, after what had happened to Richard less than three months before. Yet she loved him enough not to be clingy.

I leaned back in my chair, the sun warming my face. "Shelley was the same way the first six months we were married," I said, lamely. It was later that everything soured. That the mere thought of her made me angry. That she lied and cheated on me and stole all our assets to feed her drug habit.

I put her out of my mind and wondered if Richard realized just how lucky he was to have Brenda.

"What's on your mind?" I asked, changing the subject.

"Airplane tickets for Friday night."

This wasn't a conversation I wanted to have. I took another sip of tea, waited for him to continue.

"We have to wrap up this investigation of yours. Fast."

"I don't know where to find Veronica until tomorrow night."

"It's time you told the police what you know."

All the muscles in my body tensed. "I haven't got a shred of tangible evidence."

"You've got pictures of Walt and Veronica together. You've got Gene Higgins's testimony." Richard had adopted his patient, comforting, reasonable physician's voice, which tended to piss me off.

"It's not enough."

Richard set down his glass and crossed his arms over his chest, his expression dour. "To use an old cliché, I'm caught between a rock and a hard place. You and Brenda."

"No you're not. Brenda's your future. I'm only a small part of your past, and damn lucky to still have a place in your life. You can't let whatever's going on with me influence the big decisions in your life."

"That's a crock, and you know it. If I needed a kidney tomorrow, you'd be there for me—just like I'd be there for you."

I shook my head. "It's a question of priorities. It's—" Useless to argue with him, my better judgment screamed.

There were alternatives. I could call Sam, tell him everything I knew and let him run with it. But that wouldn't stop the visions, the nagging feeling I'd picked up at Walt's apartment that told me to find the truth.

Sophie had more or less told me everything would be over by Saturday, but that was a day too late for Richard's timetable.

I picked up my glass but found I couldn't take another swallow. I set it beside me on the deck. "Look, give me two days. If I don't have everything wrapped up by Thursday night, I'll share what I know with someone. Either Sam Nielsen at the newspaper or the Amherst police. Will that satisfy you?"

He took a few moments to mull over what I'd said. "I don't like it. But I guess I understand where you're coming from, and I suppose I'll have to accept it. What do we do next?"

I let out a breath. "Hang out tonight at Big Brother's and see if Veronica shows up. She might socialize there as well as perform. But it could mean a long night."

"Hey, I'm up for it."

After pulling an all-nighter and with only three hours of sleep, I wasn't sure I was.

Chapter Twenty-Two

After supper I spent two hours pulling weeds, which proved to be a satisfactory way of working off aggression—tension—I wasn't sure exactly what emotion prickled through me. My bushel basket was full by the time I finished and the garden looked beautiful. If I didn't get around to mulching, I'd have to do it again in another week, but the thought didn't bother me. It gave me a goal—a reason to live. The garden also represented order, and that's exactly what I craved.

The sun had set by the time I wandered into Richard's study. Brenda sat under the glow of a genuine Tiffany lamp, a yellow pad on her lap, refining her final packing list while Richard pored over the latest issue of the *New England Journal of Medicine*—still boning up for the new job, I supposed.

"Are you about ready to head out?"

Richard set his reading aside. "Sure thing."

Brenda looked up. "If you come back early, bring some wings, will you?"

Richard paused to give her a kiss good-bye. She grabbed his hand—hung on for long seconds, but didn't say anything.

He gave her a reassuring smile, kissed her fingers, and pulled away, and we headed for the door.

Richard drove and the ride across town was a silent one.

"You seem preoccupied," Richard said.

"I am. You want to wrap this up and I've got a feeling..." I had a feeling, all right. Only I wasn't sure what it was. Uneasy covered a lot of territory. I was almost afraid to close my eyes because I knew the vision of those damn bloody hands could swoop down over me at any time. I was going to see those hands in reality in the not-too-distant future and dreaded it. Blood in that volume meant death and I was probably going to be an unwilling witness to Gene Higgins's death.

My paranoia shifted into overdrive. "When we get there, you wouldn't want to just wait in the car, would you?"

"Why?" Richard asked.

He had no clue how...well, dead he'd looked lying on the floor with a bullet wound to the chest. How I never wanted that to happen again. How thinking about Gene's probable death was scaring me shitless.

I looked out the passenger side window. "I just wondered."

"Why don't you tell me everything you know about those bloody hands," he said.

"I've told you everything."

"I don't think so. You've seen hands. Can you focus in on what's around them? What else do you see?"

I wasn't sure I could conjure the vision on command. I closed my eyes—concentrated. I felt the car slow...for a red light? I heard the radio as background noise. Squeezing my eyes shut tighter still didn't bring up the vision. No, it would show up when I *didn't* want it to.

"I can't get it."

"Next time it hits, pay more attention to the periphery. It might give you a clue as to where you need to be."

Where I needed to be. He'd accepted the inevitable, too. Only he was banking on it happening before Friday.

So was I.

***

Big Brother's wasn't as kinetic as the other gay bars we'd visited. A glittering silver disco ball revolved overhead, but it was a ballad—Ella Fitzgerald?—playing in the background, while a few couples, males only, clung to one another on the small dance floor. The stage up front was unlit, the folds of its heavy curtains melting into the darkness. Flickering oil lamps glowed on each bistro table, illuminating the faces of the few patrons. Either we were too early or the place was dead on a Tuesday night.

I spotted Veronica right away, sitting at the far side of the horseshoe-shaped bar, a nearly full martini glass sat before her as she swayed dreamily to the music.

"This is where we part company," I told Richard.

"Not on your life."

"Look, I don't want to argue about this."

"Then don't," he said, and stalked across the room, taking the empty stool on Veronica's right. He signaled the bartender, then gave his order.

I couldn't let some other joker grab the seat on her left, so I hurried over to take it.

The bartender handed Richard a bottle of Labatt Blue and a glass. He paid for it and received his change, laying down a couple of bills and shoving them forward.

The bartender wandered up before me. "Get you anything?"

"Bottle of Molson."

He nodded, handed me my order in record time. "Three fifty."

I shoved a five toward him, waved him to keep the change. Veronica hadn't opened her eyes, hadn't noticed her new neighbors.

Richard leaned forward, around her, and gave me an imploring look.

I cleared my throat. "Miss Veronica?"

Veronica turned her head in my direction. "Yes?"

Her startling blue eyes surprised me—reminding me of my mother's, of Richard's. I offered my hand. "My name is Jeff Resnick. I'm a friend of Tom Link's."

"Sorry, I don't know anyone by that name." Her voice was higher and softer than I anticipated.

"No, but I believe you knew his cousin: Walt Kaplan."

Her spine stiffened and her gaze traveled from my offered hand to my face. "I'm afraid I don't. You must have me mixed up with someone else."

I pulled back my hand and withdrew a picture of her and Walt from my pocket, placed it on the bar, shoved it in front of her. "Did you know this man?"

Veronica feigned indifference. "I don't think so."

She'd missed that my question was asked in the past tense.

"This is you in the picture, isn't it?"

She smiled. "Sure. Although it couldn't have been one of my better days."

"So you knew him?"

"I have my picture taken with lots of the customers." She picked up her drink and took a small sip.

I studied her long fingers; the nails looked phony—removable, but there was strength in the hand that held the stemmed glass. Long sleeves covered her arms. No way to see if the hair on her forearms was thick and black. "Let me refresh your memory. His name was Walt Kaplan. He was found dead two weeks ago behind the Old Red Mill in Williamsville."

"The poor man. Heart attack?"

"Stabbed. Forty-six times."

Veronica simpered. "Oh dear."

"So you didn't know him?"

"Not that I remember."

"That's funny. I have quite a collection of pictures of the two of you together."

She pouted. "I find that hard to believe."

"Believe it."

"Just what are you getting at, mister?"

"I've been wondering who might find these photographs of particular interest."

"I can't imagine."

"Perhaps the police. Especially since Mr. Kaplan's death wasn't an accident."

"So you say." Veronica picked up her sequined clutch purse and slid off her barstool. "Excuse me, but I'm meeting someone." She took a step away from the bar, then turned back, snagged her drink and, hips swaying, sashayed off in her black high heels.

Richard eyed me. "That didn't do much except tip her off that you're interested in her. Is this where we start watching our backs twenty-four/seven?"

"I asked you to back off."

"Yeah, like that's an option." He downed a mouthful of beer.

"I wish she'd left her drink. Who knows what I might've gotten from touching that glass."

"Excuse me," said a low, soft voice from behind us. "But I couldn't help but overhear parts of your conversation with Miss Veronica."

I looked behind me to see what appeared to be quite a beautiful black woman in a form-fitting, chartreuse sequined gown with a plunging neckline, blonde wig and sparkling silver heels. "And you are?" I asked.

She offered her hand. "Margarita Ville." Her voice held just the hint of a Southern lilt.

I took her fingers in mine and gave a gentle squeeze. She simpered coyly, batting her false eyelashes. Under her serene veneer lurked a panther ready to spring. "Won't you join us?" I asked.

"Why, thank you." She settled herself on the stool next to Richard, smiled sweetly at him, smoothing down her hair, her gaze lingering on the remnants of his black eye, raising her eyebrow in approval before turning back to me.

I signaled the bartender, and gestured toward Margarita. "The usual?" he asked.

She nodded. A minute later, he presented her with what had to be her signature drink: a margarita. She took a dainty sip, setting the glass back down on the cocktail napkin. "Now I know this will sound utterly catty of me," she told me, confidentially, "but Miss Veronica Lakes' life is totally based on a lie—including most of what she just told you."

"Oh?" I asked.

"Well, it can be said that all the 'girls' here have based their lives on a lie. We are, after all, not women. But Lord don't we look and act more like ladies than half the gals you've ever met?"

"Uh…yes." I didn't know what else to say. "What can you tell me about Veronica?"

Margarita tossed her synthetic mane. "A person of good repute does not accept monies from gentlemen she beds."

"Does she turn regular tricks?"

Margarita shook her head. "Veronica doesn't go in for that. Like me, she's an artiste, not a prostitute. That said, she does hook her gentleman friends for the long haul. She has a goal."

"Which is?" Richard asked.

Margarita dabbed a finger on her tongue and pressed it against the salt on the rim of her glass—then licked it. "Miss Veronica needs several hundred thousand dollars to pay for gender reassignment surgery. I believe she plans to go to one of those former eastern bloc countries."

"Why doesn't she have the surgery here?" Richard asked.

"One must pass a number of psychological examinations. The requirements aren't quite so strict elsewhere."

"She wouldn't pass?" Richard asked.

"I am definitely not an expert on the subject—but apparently I am not the only one who believes that Miss Veronica has more than just one screw loose."

"It doesn't sound like you approve of sex-change operations," I said.

"Look, dear, beneath all the sham, you're still who you were born. I may look like an enticing, beautiful woman—" She paused, gave me a pointed, expectant look.

"Oh, you are," I agreed.

"But the fact is, that under the makeup, wigs and beautiful clothes—" She smoothed her hands over her hourglass figure. "I'm still just a gay man in drag. And most days, that's pretty damn all right—despite what my father may have told me to the contrary."

Richard gripped his beer bottle, taking a healthy swallow before leaning back in his seat.

"And Miss Veronica?" I prompted.

"Amputating her penis and adding silicone breasts won't make her any more a woman than you are. I mean—let's face it, chromosomes don't lie, no matter what the outside package looks like."

I couldn't contradict her there.

"So Veronica wants a sugar daddy to pay for her surgery?"

She sipped her drink. "Daddies," Margarita emphasized. "She takes them for all they're worth. Eventually they get tired of her. I mean—she's not the brightest bulb on the Christmas tree."

I withdrew the photo of Walt and Veronica from my pocket. "Have you ever seen this guy?"

Margarita scrutinized the photo. "That would be Mr. Walt. Ever such a nice man. Kept a select few of us entertained with tall tales of money and excess. It's a pity he was always attracted to trash."

"He had other 'friends' besides Veronica?" Richard asked.

Margarita nodded, tucking a blonde lock behind her multipierced ear. "Those friendships were rather transitory. But Miss Veronica—well, she has very sharp claws and an attraction to fat wallets. Once she hooks a Sugar Daddy, she squeezes the life out of him."

Squeezes, or stabs?

"Did you know Walt Kaplan was stabbed to death?" I asked.

Margarita blinked several times, her gaze riveted on mine. "I do believe I read that in the paper."

"Do you think Veronica was capable of—?" I let the sentence hang.

"I wouldn't want to accuse anybody of anything," Margarita said, watching herself in the mirror on the backbar, batting at the curls around her face. "But it's common knowledge that Miss Veronica is quite handy with a knife. She always carries one. One never knows how violent a gentleman caller may become. Some of the girls feel they need to be prepared with hardware. I do not happen to be one with that mindset."

"Let me guess. You're well acquainted with the martial arts?" The way she spoke was positively contagious.

Margarita smiled. "Just something I picked up along the way." She sipped her drink, her gaze straying once again to the mirror in front of her.

"Veronica thought Walt had a lot of money?"

"Mr. Walt was very generous to those he liked. He was part of the Kaplan Jewelry empire, you know. I always admired that diamond ring he wore on his right hand. A gift from his father, if I'm not mistaken." Margarita raised a heavily penciled eyebrow. "I wonder if it went missing.

Miss Veronica seems to have come into some money of late."

Since Gene had the ring, it was more likely Veronica had sold Walt's car.

"If someone wanted to contact Miss Veronica at her home, where would they find her?" I asked.

"One would merely have to look in the phone book. The name would be M. Bessler." She spelled it for me, then gave a little shudder. "The M stands for Myron."

"Any idea how Myron makes a living?"

"By day he stands behind a counter and hands out keys for rent-a-cars—not much brain power required. By night Veronica has delusions of being a diva." She rolled her eyes. Richard's mustache twitched over a smile.

Margarita gathered her purse and carefully eased off her barstool. I stood as well. "It's been very nice speaking with you, gentlemen. I do hope you'll come back tomorrow to see my show." She offered me her hand.

I figured what the hell, and brushed my lips against her fingers. "Thank you."

Margarita took one more appraising glance at herself in the mirror and turned. "Until we meet again." She gave us a little wave and wandered off into the darkness.

"My weren't we gallant?" Richard commented.

I climbed back onto my stool. "There's something about the way she talks. It rubs off." My gaze flickered across the mirror behind the backbar, looking for Veronica. That I didn't see her didn't mean she hadn't been watching during our conversation with Margarita. She could have changed clothes, and personas, and I probably wouldn't recognize her—him.

Richard drained the last of his beer. "You get anything else out of her?"

"Margarita had an ulterior motive for ratting on Veronica. Until this week, *she* was the headliner. With Veronica out of the picture—"

Richard eyed our surroundings with disdain. "Talk about a big fish in a small pond. What's our next move?"

"Sleep on it. I don't know about you, but I'm tired. Maybe tomorrow I'll come up with an idea."

I pushed back my stool and stood again, taking in the bar and its patrons. Still no sign of Veronica.

I followed Richard out and we walked back to the car. I kept looking over my shoulder, but the darkness swallowed details. Anyone could have watched us leave, could have followed.

We got in the car and Richard started it, then pulled away from the curb. I nearly broke my neck straining to see if anyone had pulled out behind us. If they did, I didn't see their headlights—and didn't hear the roar of a motorcycle. All the way home I kept checking the side mirror, kept looking over my shoulder. Richard noticed, but didn't say anything. He parked the car in the garage, and we walked in silence into the house.

"See you in the morning," Richard said, and headed out of the kitchen and into the hall for the stairs.

I locked up and waited for his footfalls to disappear. Richard had been right. Now that Veronica knew I was onto her I'd have to watch my back, and Richard's, twenty-four/seven.

I slipped off my shoes and retraced his steps, diverting to the darkened living room. Peering through the leaded windows, I surveyed the quiet street in front of the house. No sign of a car or a motorcycle. No sign of movement. No sign of anything.

Veronica was out there somewhere, and within days she'd attempt, and probably succeed in killing Gene Higgins.

Find the truth.

I'd found it. Now to figure out how to use it.

Chapter Twenty-Three

It took hours for me to fall asleep. I woke up late the next morning feeling marginal again. I wasn't sure if it was because of an impending migraine or the growing uneasiness inside me. Time was running out and I had no idea how to nail Walt Kaplan's killer.

I let my new routine rule; I took my meds with a cup of coffee, ate a bowl of cereal, and headed off for work.

"We missed you," Tom called when I came in the back door. The bags under his eyes told me he'd probably had to man the bar alone the day before.

"Did Dave work last night?" I asked.

"Nope."

That was cause for a major guilt trip, especially since I'd spent the day either in bed or dozing.

"I'm assuming you've made some progress?" Tom asked. He didn't have to specify what he meant.

"I'm getting close."

He didn't ask any more questions.

I usually liked the daily tasks necessary to gear up for the day's customers, but not that day. The words *find the truth* kept eating into my brain, along with a new refrain: *cover your ass.* Covering my ass meant talking to someone about Walt's death. My first choice wasn't the Amherst Police.

The lunch crowd was just beginning to leave when Sam Nielsen strolled into the bar. Again, he sat down at the farthest stool from the taps, setting a steno notepad down in front of him as he waited for me to finish up with a customer. I grabbed a beer from the cooler, cracked it open, and snagged a clean glass before heading down to see him.

"You ought to serve sandwiches," he said as he focused on our one remaining customer. "It might be a boon for business."

I handed him the beer. "It's on the back burner. Thanks for stopping in."

"So who's your murderer?"

"A drag queen named Veronica Lakes."

Sam raised an eyebrow, then poured his beer. "Oh he, or she, of the custom-made shoes?"

"Not exactly. But that's what got me started on her trail."

Sam sipped his beer and listened, occasionally making a note but not interrupting, for the next ten minutes as I gave him an abbreviated version of what I'd been pursuing for the previous two weeks.

"And your plan now?" he asked at last.

"I don't know. Something's going to break soon. But until Gene makes up his mind to tell the cops what he knows, he's in real danger from Veronica. She's going to have to do something to protect herself, and it's gonna happen before Saturday."

"Another one of your insights?"

I nodded.

"What do you want me to do?"

"One of the other drag queens said Veronica had squeezed her other sugar daddies. Can you find out if any other gay men have been stabbed to death?"

"The answer's no. There were two other homicides of gay men in the past three years, but neither fit this MO, both solved. One was a robbery gone wrong, the other was a domestic dispute."

"Then the good news is our murderer isn't a serial killer. But where does that leave us?"

"I'll do some digging on your drag queen. Past history, arrests, the usual. I'll also dangle a carrot in front of my source at Amherst PD to see what kind of reception I get." He got up from his stool. "I'll give you a call this evening to let you know what I've found out. Maybe we should go together to see Veronica's show tonight."

Excellent. Then I wouldn't have to involve Richard. He could stay home, nice and safe.

"Thanks." Again Sam reached for his wallet but I waved him off. "On the house."

Sam smiled. "You're never going to get yourself a cell phone if you keep buying drinks for the general public."

"Get out of here and start your digging."

He gave me a salute as he exited through the bar's side entrance.

Time dragged for the rest of the afternoon, while the tension within me mounted. I poured beer, washed glasses, and tried not to think about Gene sitting alone up at the Holiday Valley house, and how easy it would be for Veronica to pick him off if she found out he was staying there.

It was almost three and I'd been polishing the taps with such vigor they glowed, when Tom called to me. "Phone."

Tossing aside the rag, I dipped into Tom's office and picked up the phone on his desk. "Jeff here."

"It's Richard. I just heard from a frantic Cyn. She said she got a call from a man saying Gene had been in an accident and was critical. She wanted me to meet her over at the ECMC Emergency Room. I tried to tell her Gene was in Holiday Valley, but she hung up on me. I called Dana Watkins, and she said Cyn had just flown out the door."

The vision of the bloody hands exploded across my mind.

He continued. "I asked how Cyn had found out about Gene's so-called accident. Dana said the call came in on the café's voice mail, which Cyn had had forwarded to her cell phone."

"When did Cyn leave?"

"Less than five minutes ago. Dana said she tried to tell Cyn the call could be phony, but Cyn said she couldn't take the chance it wasn't."

This was happening much too fast.

"Look, I've got to go. I hope I can get to Cyn before Veronica does."

"I want to talk to Dana, then I'll meet you there."

"See ya." Richard hung up the phone.

I borrowed Tom's phone book once again and called Dana's number. "Cyn?" she answered, breathless.

"No, it's Jeff Resnick. Tell me what happened."

She did, in an amazingly calm voice, despite the evident worry within it. "And then she jumped on Black Beauty and was outta here," Dana finished.

"Black Beauty?" I asked.

"Her motorcycle."

It all made sense. Cyn hadn't wanted me to prove Craig Buchanan didn't kill Walt. That would mean the cops would start asking harder questions—questions she didn't want answered, about Walt's lifestyle, about his relationship with Gene. Maybe she hadn't believed Gene was innocent, but she didn't want to see him go to jail. She'd followed me to the Backstreet Playhouse, and maybe other places, and called me with the voice-altering device. She'd managed to crank up my paranoia, but not high enough to stop me.

"I thought Cyn was angry with Gene. That she wanted nothing more to do with him."

"You don't abandon your child when he's in trouble," Dana said.

"Child? I thought he was her nephew."

Dana sighed. "We've had a lot of time to talk in the past two days—we may have even become friends. Gene is Cyn's biological son. He doesn't even know it. But that's the reason she's always been so close to him. Cyn wasn't up to being a single parent. Her sister adopted him because she couldn't have children of her own."

My mind was racing. "I'm meeting Richard at the hospital. Will you be at this number later?"

"Yes, and please call. I'm afraid for both of them."

I said good-bye and hung up.

"Tom!"

Tom, who'd apparently been eavesdropping, poked his head around the office door as I was untying the apron at my waist. "Something's come up. I have to go."

"Does this have anything to do with Walt's killer?"

"Yes."

He didn't hesitate. "Go."

*　*　*

The light ahead turned red and I braked. Even in heavy traffic, Richard's house was only minutes from the hospital, much less at this time of day. He'd get there in plenty of time to intercept Cyn, who had at least a twenty-minute ride from Cheektowaga. Rich *would* make it there on time.

Oh yeah? If I believed that, then why did I feel so antsy?

The vision of the bloody hands assaulted me once again. I squeezed my eyes shut. When I opened them again, the light went green. I hit the gas.

The should-haves started circulating through my brain. I should have contacted Sam sooner, I should have insisted Gene go to the cops.

The light at Eggert turned red. Goddamn the timing on these things.

I hung a left at Bailey Avenue, nearly sheering off the bumper of a Volkswagen Jetta, and stepped on the gas. I ran the first couple of lights, but got caught in traffic and had to wait. At this rate, I'd get to ECMC after—

Bloody hands, glistening—rivulets of scarlet cascading—

Yeah, yeah, yeah. The same old scene was getting tedious.

I gunned it, weaving around cars, SUVs, and minivans, their horns blasting me from every direction.

I didn't bother with the hospital's parking lot, pulling right up to the Emergency entrance. Richard was there, waiting for me, and hopped right in the passenger side of my car. "She's gone. Head for the Thruway."

My wheels spun on the asphalt. "Tell me."

"I flashed my ID and told the receptionist Gene was my patient, that I'd been told he'd been taken to the ER. She said Cyn had been there only minutes before looking for him, but told her no one by that name had been admitted. A tall, skinhead approached Cyn, spoke to her in low tones, and then they left together."

"What makes you think they're going to the Holiday Valley house?"

"Thank god for smokers. They had a brief conversation outside the door, one of the nurses heard Cyn say Holiday Valley. Then they walked to the parking lot, got in a car, and drove away."

"Wow, you're getting good at this investigation stuff."

"It must be your influence. Can't you go any faster?"

I was already breaking the speed limit, but I pressed harder on the accelerator, giving myself another five mph and hoped like hell the Amherst cops were all on a donut break.

"So how much of a lead do you think they've got?" I asked.

"No more than five minutes."

"Did your smoker mention Cyn's emotional state?"

"She said Cyn seemed to go willingly."

"Sure, if I had a knife sticking in my ribs—and that's Veronica's, or Myron's favorite weapon—I might appear to cooperate, too. Did your smoker say who was driving?"

"I didn't think to ask."

"I'll bet it was Cyn. If she's smart, she'll crash the car, but who knows what cock-and-bull story Veronica told her. And by the way, Dana Watkins told me Gene is Cyn's biological son—*not* her nephew. She had the unfortunate timing to have her baby out of wedlock and her sister adopted the boy."

"That ups the ante," Richard said.

"She might have been angry with him on Sunday, but now she's on a quest to save him. Cyn probably doesn't even know that Myron is Veronica."

We hit the Thruway ramp and headed south.

"It'll take at least an hour to get there," Richard grumbled. "Have you got a map?"

"Glove box."

He hit the button, pulled out a New York state map, and then spent far too long unfolding and refolding it to the right section. "You know where this house is, right?"

"Yup."

Richard kept staring at the map. "How weird is this? I hadn't seen Cyn for thirty years, and now I'm rushing to try to save her life."

"That's pretty weird," I said. Then again, since I'd been smacked in the head with a baseball bat, a big portion of my life had gone majorly weird.

Richard set the map on his lap and looked at his watch. "What are we going to do when we get there? We can't just drive up the driveway and yell 'Surprise!'"

"No shit. I figure we'll park on the street and go in on foot."

"And do what? Threaten Veronica with a stick?"

"Have you got your cell phone?" I asked.

"No, dammit. That lets out calling the cops. Unless we find a pay phone—which are few and far between these days."

"Cyn's house isn't in Ellicottville. It's up in the hills; there probably never were any pay phones nearby, and cell coverage is probably spotty, too. And anyway, what would we say? We think someone *may* be plotting murder at this location—meet us there. And what if we find Cyn, Gene, and Veronica sitting around the pool drinking gin and tonics and chowing on nachos?"

"You're full of answers," Richard groused.

My fingers gripped harder on the steering wheel. "Gene did give me the phone number at the house, but he told me he had caller ID and unless he knew the number—"

"Surely he'd answer a call from Cyn."

"I doubt Veronica would let her tip him off."

Richard kept consulting his watch, while only the air conditioner's fan and road noise filled the car for the next ten minutes.

I took the cut off for Route 219 and the traffic around us petered out. The expressway ran for another ten or fifteen miles before narrowing to a two-lane highway. Forty minutes down, another twenty to thirty more to get to Cyn's vacation home. Despite the car's cool interior, my palms were sweating. Richard was still fiddling with his watch. "Damn. The band just broke."

"Well if you hadn't been playing with it for the last half hour."

Richard pocketed the watch.

The "Welcome to Ellicottville" sign flashed by on our right. With no bypass, we were forced to go through the middle of town, stopped by traffic lights and pedestrians. Richard's fists kept clenching and unclenching. "Come on," he murmured at the longest red light in western New York.

Green. Go!

The village grew smaller in my rearview mirror. I pulled off the main drag and onto one of the side roads, leading up into the hills.

"This is where a plan would be helpful," I said.

"I haven't come up with anything. You?"

I shook my head. "Then it's on foot to reconnoiter. And after that—we wing it."

"Winging it sounds like it could be dangerous. And I don't know about you, but I'm not wearing my Superman underwear."

And bullets hadn't bounced off his trench coat back in March, either.

I hit the brakes and the car skidded to a halt. "Get out."

"What?"

"You heard me, I said get out. You're not coming with me."

"Don't start that shit again." He crossed his arms over his chest. "You can't make me. I'm bigger than you."

Brenda was right. Sometimes we did act like a couple of overgrown kids.

"You're wasting time," Richard said. "And unless you want Cyn's and Gene's deaths on your conscience, I suggest you get your foot off the goddamn brake and move this car."

We glared at each other for maybe ten seconds before I looked away and hit the accelerator.

Chapter Twenty-Four

Only one car sat in the middle of Cyn's vacation home's driveway, and it wasn't Gene's. Richard and I peered at it through a thicket. No other sign of habitation. Nice and quiet. Idyllic.

Too damned isolated.

"Okay, now what?" Richard asked.

I certainly wasn't going to risk his life. "I go in."

"And do what?"

"See if I can diffuse the situation. Veronica can't stab all of us at once."

"And what if she has a gun? Let me tell you from personal experience, getting shot hurts. A lot."

"Thanks for the news flash. Look, you're my ace in the hole. Someone's got to go for help if the situation warrants it."

"And how am I supposed to know when and if to do that? I'm not the one who's psychic."

Okay. Thinking rationally was and wasn't going to do it. Sophie told me to come see her on Saturday night—*if I could*. That wasn't an automatic death sentence. If I trusted her—and I did—that meant there was a possibility I'd survive. She saw a future for Richard. Maybe not a great one, and I didn't want to think about what that meant, but she saw a future for him. The missing elements of the equation were Cyn and Gene. Her clairvoyance hadn't included them.

I turned to Richard. "My gut tells me at least one of us is going to come out of this alive, but I don't know about Cyn and Gene."

"One of us? And who might that be?"

I hesitated. If I said him, he'd probably make some stupid, grandstand move that would blow Sophie's predictions about his future straight to hell. "I don't know for sure," I lied. "If we walk away, we're okay. If we storm the joint—we might both live. Living isn't the same as thriving, or happily ever after. You almost met your maker already this year. What do you think?"

Richard let out a breath. "Jesus, you couldn't give me something easy to contemplate?" He wiped a hand across his mustache, his expression grave. "The way I see it, Veronica's got two hostages. She's killed at least one person. I trust your gut. If we can save only one of them—we've got to try." He nodded, reaffirming it. "Yeah. One is better than none."

"What if it isn't Cyn?"

"From what you've said, Veronica is angry at Gene for replacing him—her—in Walt's affection. She'll go after him before Cyn."

"I don't want either of them to get hurt—"

"Do you think I do? A physician's first responsibility is to do no harm."

"I thought that was the witches' credo."

"Hypocrites came before Wicca."

"Says you."

"We're wasting time."

I wanted to believe Sophie. I wanted to believe with all my heart. But what if she was wrong?

I didn't have time to worry about it.

I studied Richard's worried blue eyes. "Okay. I'll go to the door. Knock. If it's open, I'll go in."

"If it's not?"

"I'll smash the window. If nothing else, that'll get Veronica's attention."

Richard cast around, found a rock the size of an Idaho spud on the ground, and handed it to me. "Here. Use this instead of your fist. If you get the chance, use it against Veronica, too."

I took it from him and hefted it. Smashed against a skull, it could do considerable damage. Yeah, like the baseball bat had done to me. I gulped, unsure if I could inflict that kind of damage on anyone else. Then again, if it meant my survival...

I met his gaze. "Whatever happened to do no harm?"

Richard shrugged, the barest hint of a smile on his lips. "You've got the rock. Not me."

I turned back to look at the house, took a couple of big gulps of air. Yeah—I could do this—and stood, pushing aside the branches.

I walked into the clearing that was the front yard, slowly making my way, as though a landmine might explode under my feet.

Nearer, nearer to the closed front door.

In less than two days Richard would marry Brenda. Maggie and I would stand up for them, then spend the rest of the day—and possibly the night—together.

I hoped.

I was within five feet of the door when it cracked open. My hand with the rock snaked around behind me as I backed up a few steps.

"What do you want?" asked a male voice I didn't recognize.

"Myron?"

The door opened wider. A swollen-eyed Cyn, her face streaked with tears, stood rigidly in front of the skinhead the hospital receptionist had described, the long barrel of a shotgun pressed against her jaw. "Help," she squeaked.

"Myron, you don't want to do this."

"Wanna bet? Seems to me I don't have a whole helluva lot to lose." He laughed, smug. The voice was and wasn't Veronica. Lower, rougher.

"You're looking at twenty-five years to life for Walt Kaplan's death."

"So what's a few more years on the sentence? I could probably have a whole lot of fun in jail. Think of all the fine, rough sex that could come my way? It might just be the answer to all my prayers."

"No operation. No more dresses. No more shoes, wigs, makeup—fun."

"Please help me," Cyn sobbed.

I gulped air. "Where's Gene?" I asked, sounding a lot braver than I felt.

"He's here. He's just—" Myron laughed. "A little tied up."

I stood only ten or twelve feet from the door. If he swung the shotgun down, he could very easily take me out. Had he ever used a gun before? Had he—?

Cyn slumped, catching Myron off guard. She rammed an elbow into his stomach.

Myron let out a painful oomph, fell back inside and landed on his backside.

Cyn stumbled down the steps. I dropped the rock and grabbed her hand, pulling her with me as I ran for the bushes.

No gunshot followed.

The front door slammed.

The yard was hauntingly silent.

Richard captured Cyn in a rough embrace and she started to cry in earnest.

"Where's Gene?" I demanded.

Cyn pulled away and wiped at her eyes. "He's...Veronica tied him up. He was kicking Gene, over and over again. I tried to stop him and he hit me."

Gently, Richard pulled the hair away from her face to reveal a bright red mark that would be a bruise before nightfall. "That was a pretty brave thing you just did."

"Cowardly you mean," she snapped. "I left Gene in there to die!"

Richard turned to me. "Why didn't he fire at you?"

"That might alert the neighbors, who might call the cops." I turned my attention back to Cyn. "Where's your cell phone?"

"In his car. But it's locked. He's got the keys."

"Damn!" Still, getting Cyn out of the house and away from Myron was one less life to worry about saving.

Richard's imploring stare cut through me.

"I've got to get in that house."

"*We've* got to," he corrected.

"No! You stay here with Cyn. In fact, get the hell out of here—both of you. Go to the neighbors. Call for help."

"Not until you promise to wait right here."

Placate him, placate him! "Okay. Yeah. I'll wait here. Go!"

"If you're lying to me—"

I pushed his shoulder. "Go!"

Richard grabbed Cyn's hand and pulled her through the trees, back toward my car.

I watched until they were out of sight, then turned my attention back to the silent house. Staying put was the smart thing to do. But knowing we were out here meant that Myron was going to have to do something. He knew we knew he'd killed Walt. He'd held Cyn hostage. That she got away didn't mean he couldn't be charged for it. If he made a break for the car—

The drapes in the leftmost front window moved. Still clutching the gun, Myron peered out, looking for us. He scanned the hedges and stared long and hard before the curtain fell again.

I waited, panic growing within me. Was it my own or Gene's? My connection to him had never been strong, but I couldn't ignore the feeling. I stood, feeling like magnetic north had made a sudden shift south and I was being pulled toward the house.

Closer.

Closer.

My heart pounded so loud and hard as I approached the front steps that I thought cardiac arrest was imminent.

My trembling fingers clasped the aluminum door handle and pulled the screen door open. Relief flooded through me as I entered the empty entryway and wasn't blown to pieces.

"Myron?" I tried calling, but only a croak came out.

No answer.

I moved a few tentative steps forward, peering into what looked like the living room.

No one.

A grand, wide oak stairway in the center of the foyer led to the second floor. To my far left a set of opened French doors led into a tidy library-office filled with wall to ceiling bookshelves. A large rectangular, intricately woven Persian rug in hues of red and gold covered the floor.

My ears strained, but no sounds broke the stillness, save for the call of a crow somewhere outside.

I took another step forward. The hardwood floor creaked beneath my sneakered foot.

I froze.

Sweat trickled down the back of my neck.

Bypassing the library, I crept along a long hallway that opened into a dining room. A door at the end was propped open with a wedge. I tiptoed up and hesitated before darting into what turned out to be an orderly kitchen. The components of a chef salad graced the dark granite counter, with a large clear glass bowl half filled with lettuce.

No sign of Gene or Myron.

I tiptoed across the slate floor, tried the back door, found it double locked. They hadn't escaped out the back. That meant they had to be upstairs.

Creeping back down the hall, my heart nearly stopped when I heard a noise in the foyer.

With my back pressed against the wall, I edged closer to the source of the sound. The doorway was only two feet from me when I saw a figure standing in the open. Weak with relief, I had to lean against the doorframe for support.

Richard.

"How did you ever become a doctor when you can't goddamn follow directions?" I grated.

"Look who's talking."

I pressed a finger to my lips to silence him.

He pointed down the hall where I'd just come.

I shook my head.

He indicated the floor above us. I nodded.

Cyn? I mouthed.

At the next-door neighbors'. Now what?

I jerked my thumb toward the ceiling.

He shook his head emphatically. *Let's wait for the cops.*

The cops' arrival might push Myron to pull the trigger. And if it didn't, how long would it be before they could pull in a hostage negotiator and a SWAT team from Buffalo?

Richard's anxious gaze implored me to think this through rationally. He was right. Why *should* we give Myron another two hostages?

Okay, I mouthed.

Richard turned and was reaching for the screen door's handle when we heard scuffling overhead and the muffled sound of yelling.

Then a gunshot.

Without thinking, I dashed across the foyer for the stairs, with Richard right behind me. My heart raced as I hit the landing and saw Myron standing in a doorway with an arm around Gene's shoulder, the shotgun jammed under his chin. A hole had been blasted in the ceiling above them, and powdered plasterboard clouded the air.

"Back off!" Myron shouted.

I raised my empty hands in surrender, took a step down, and ran into Richard.

Gene's legs were bound at the ankles, his hands tied behind his back; his wide eyes were nearly black with fear.

A panty hose gag tied around his mouth kept him from screaming.

"You don't want to do this," I told Myron and heard Richard swallow behind me.

"Oh yeah?" He jerked the gun's barrel, shoving Gene's head back farther. Panicked, strangled whimpers escaped the gag.

Richard backed down two steps, with me following suit, hands still held out in submission.

"That's it. Nice and easy and nobody gets hurt," Myron said, and laughed.

Richard retreated another couple of steps.

Gene's cries weren't clear enough to understand, but the look in his eyes pleaded, *Don't leave me!*

Myron stepped back, pulling Gene along with him farther down the hall until we could no longer see them. A door slammed shut.

"Now what?" Richard breathed.

"Unless he intends to jump, there's nowhere he can go."

The sounds of a struggle broke the quiet. I closed my eyes, my stomach turning as the vision of the bloody hands flashed through my mind.

Then came the gunshot—and then a second one.

I bounded up the four or five steps, thundered down the hallway and kicked open the door.

Two bodies lay on the floor. Blood and globs of flesh peppered the pale pink walls of what looked like a little girl's bedroom. I turned away and closed my eyes. *Dear Jesus, not again.*

Shelley had been killed execution style, though she'd been cleaned up before I saw her that last time. I'd seen another body with a bullet through the brain that had taken off the top of the skull.

The shotgun blast had obliterated most of Myron's head.

Richard pushed past me, paused, taking in the scene—his breaths ragged.

I held a hand up to block my peripheral vision, and could just make out Richard pulling a blood spattered chenille spread from the bed, tossing it over Myron's body before he knelt beside Gene.

My hand sank another inch. I could see Gene beyond Richard, took in what was left of his face—bloody, hanging flesh, the white of bone and a few shattered teeth.

"Holy Christ," Richard muttered and sank back on his heels. "He's still alive."

"Oh, God, no!" I turned away and quickly stepped into the hall.

"Jeff, get some towels from the bathroom. And call 911!"

I escaped and ran down the hall. The linen closet held neatly folded towels and washcloths. I yanked them all off the shelf and barreled back to the bedroom, tossing them at Richard. He balled up several washcloths and tried to staunch the bleeding.

My chest was heaving, the smell of blood was thick and sickening. I tried not to look, but like a rubbernecker at a car crash, my eyes were drawn to my brother.

To the glistening, scarlet blood that covered his hands.

The fear inside me twisted into downright horror.

"Holy Christ, Rich, you don't have gloves!"

Richard didn't bother to look up. "Did you call 911?"

"Rich, what if he's HIV positive?"

"Goddamn it! Call 911!" he shouted.

My feet foundered under me and I staggered away from the stench of death, found a phone in the next bedroom, and punched in the numbers.

"I'm calling to report an attempted murder-suicide. He blew half his head off with a shotgun—the other guy's still alive."

Who was the person speaking so calmly? It couldn't have been me. Shock was catching up with me. My legs felt rubbery. I sank onto the edge of the bed. The phone grew heavy. I wasn't sure I could hold it up for long.

I'm pretty sure I gave the address, told them a doctor was attempting first aid. I don't remember much else about that conversation.

Over and over again, the vision of Richard's bloody hands kept replaying in my head.

Gene was gay—was he possibly HIV positive?

You don't know that! You don't know that! my mind screamed.

Exposure to HIV days before Richard was to marry was just not fucking fair. And once again it was All. My. Goddamn. Fault.

By dragging him into this, I'd risked Richard's life again. Contracting a fatal disease was not as quick a death, but surely was as lethal as a gunshot.

"Sir? Sir?" the voice on the telephone implored.

"Can you give me a hand back here," Richard hollered.

The tinny-sounding voice kept calling me, but I dropped the receiver as the sound of running footsteps came from the stairwell. I dipped into the hall in time to capture a breathless Cyn. "What happened? What happened?" she cried, frantic to escape me.

"Myron's dead—but Gene's been badly hurt."

Her struggles intensified.

"Believe me—you don't want to see him right now."

More footsteps pounded up the stairs. Cops, firemen, and EMTs. The house had suddenly exploded with people. I pulled Cyn into the bedroom, where the voice on the phone still bleated.

"Oh god," one of the cops wailed from down the hall.

Cyn sagged in my arms, her wrenching sobs robbing her of any strength she might've had left. I pulled her close, this woman who had directed her hatred at me for the past two weeks, had threatened me, and I let her cry, her tears soaking into my shirt.

She faced the death of a loved one.

I wondered if I was in the same position.

Chapter Twenty-Five

The water ran hot. Steam curled into the air, vapor clinging to the cabinet mirror overhead. I watched as the last of the rusty water went down the drain, unable to take my eyes off the soapy brush in Richard's right hand. He worked at his fingernails, scrubbing, scrubbing, adding more soap, scouring hands that were already lobster red.

A uniformed cop stood in the hall outside the bathroom, watching, listening to us. We hadn't yet given a statement. They didn't want us talking about what we'd seen, comparing notes—contaminating each other's potential testimony. I didn't give a shit about their procedures. I had more important matters on my mind.

I cleared my throat, afraid to voice the fear that had been torturing me for the past twenty-seven—and longest—minutes of my life. "They can test Gene's blood. You could probably know tomorrow if he's HIV positive. Right?"

Richard avoided my gaze. "It's not as clear-cut as you might think."

"What does that mean for you?"

"It means I'll have to get tested for the next six months to see if I develop antibodies."

"And then?"

"And then we'll know."

He sounded so goddamned calm.

"But...you're supposed to start a new job at the clinic in a few weeks."

"They'll restrict me to noninvasive procedures."

"You were going to get married day after tomorrow."

He looked up sharply at me. "If Brenda still wants me—I *will* get married."

"Yeah, but, now—"

"Brenda and I are medical professionals. Risk of infection is something we and every other doctor, nurse, and EMT deals with every day. Granted, this isn't something I would've wanted to happen, but I wasn't going to stand by and just let Gene die."

"Oh, come on. He hasn't got a chance."

"Yeah, and where did you get your medical degree?" He turned his attention back to the brush in his hands.

I settled my weight against the wall, grateful the bathroom wasn't closet-sized. Richard squirted on more soap, began working on his other hand again.

"What about your honeymoon?"

"What about it?"

"The whole idea of a honeymoon is to—"

"Brenda and I have been together seven years. Besides, there's more to intimacy than just intercourse." His words had an edge, but I guessed they were directed more at the situation than at me.

The din of voices continued down the hall. Thanks to Richard's actions, the EMTs had been able to stabilize Gene and he'd been whisked away in an ambulance that would meet a Mercy Flight helicopter once they got clear of the hills. He was on his way to a trauma facility in Buffalo where he'd either live or die. And if he lived, his disfigurement would probably make him wish he'd died.

Some future.

We might never know if Myron meant to take himself out or if Gene's struggles to get away had caused Myron to pull the trigger. Myron…Veronica…was going to miss her opening night at Big Brother's. Margarita Ville would have to step into the star's limelight. Somehow I didn't think she'd mind. Life at the drag club would go on, just as it had gone on at The Whole Nine Yards without Walt.

Some epitaph.

Richard set the nail brush aside and turned off the water. I straightened and handed him a clean towel from the chrome wall rack. "I'm sorry."

He wiped his hands. "What for?"

"They were your hands I kept seeing. I didn't know that. I could've warned you. I could've—"

Richard grimaced. "You're not going to start with that guilt crap again, are you?"

I winced at the rebuke. "Well, I kinda thought I might."

"Give it a rest." He tossed the towel into the sink. "One of these days you're going to learn that shit happens. Today it happened for Veronica and it happened for Gene. But guess what, of the three of us, I'm the only one walking out the door and I'm damned grateful for it. I'm going to celebrate. I'm going home, kiss my fiancée, and in two days I'm going to get married. Then I'm going to Paris, drink the best-damned champagne, and have the time of my life. And when I get back home, I'll start my new job and a new phase in my life. Just like you did."

"Me?"

"Hey, you could've just given up after you lost your job, had your head smashed in, and lost almost everything you had. But you didn't. And you know why? Because despite all the garbage in our pasts, we survived. We're alike. We're brothers."

Yeah. We were.

***

Jeff Resnick's curiosity is piqued when he sees a sign advertising psychic readings. At first he's sure the medium is a fake, but then his funny feelings lead him to suspect that a murder has taken place in the dilapidated house where Madam Zahara holds her readings. Just who died and how? And why is Jeff compelled to look for bodies buried in the medium's yard?

When the Spirit Moves You

I'd passed the hulking, ramshackle house every few days for the last three months on my way home from my girlfriend Maggie Brennan's house. The yard hadn't seen the services of a lawnmower or weed whacker in quite some time. But it was the glowing pink-and-green neon sign that seemed to call to me: PSYCHIC $10.

Since I got whacked on the head with a Reggie Jackson baseball bat last winter, I can sometimes sense people's emotions. And sometimes I know stuff about them, and it's usually not good. I don't consider myself a psychic. No way. In fact, I've come to view that as a dirty word. But being mugged by a couple of teenage thugs changed me. Slammed my brains into my thick skull—mooshed them up a bit—and…now I'm not the same as I was before. Not the same at all.

It was all still pretty new to me, and I wasn't sure I always trusted the feelings—insight—that came to me. I mean, I did—and I didn't want to.

But that day I had an extra ten-dollar bill in my wallet and I decided—why not test it? If the person advertising such a trait was for real, I might find a kindred spirit. If not—okay, when you're broke, ten bucks is a lot of money, but I had a roof over my head, a part-time job and, thanks to the generosity of my older half brother, I was nowhere near starving. Maybe it was the neon that seduced me on that hot August afternoon when I found myself pulling into the gravel drive.

The sign on the lawn said "For Entertainment Only," but I was pretty sure the gullible would expect something more than that. And why was I so intrigued anyway? My friend Sophie Levin was like me. The old Polish lady didn't like the word psychic either. She read auras—or as she put it, she "saw colors" and then *knew* things.

I looked through the car's passenger-side window at what once might have been a lovely home. Hard times had fallen on the old two-story house. Was it supposed to be a poor man's Tara? The Corinthian columns that held up the porch roof were rotted at the base. Flaked paint chips the size of oatmeal cookies hung from the weathered clapboards. A rusty Buick LeSabre with current plates sat parked at the side of the house. Apparently psychic-for-hire was not a particularly lucrative proposition.

I got out of my car, my footsteps crunching on the gravel as I made my way to the porch steps. They creaked under my feet. Were they rotted enough to collapse or should I trust them to hold my weight?

They held.

The porch floorboards groaned under me as I shifted my weight and raised my hand to knock on the old screen door. A woman's voice called out. "I've been waiting for you. What took you so long?"

The words were disconcerting. I'd only decided to drop in on a whim. Or maybe that was part of her shtick.

I opened the wooden screen door and stepped inside. The interior didn't look much better than the exterior, but at least it was neat and tidy. A broad staircase wound up to the second floor. Only a few of its balusters were missing. The entry's floor was in desperate need of sanding and refinishing, and some of the old oak was warped and a large portion of it was discolored from water. A glance at the stained ceiling told me where the problem had originated. Probably from a bathroom.

"In here," the female voice called again.

I crossed the entryway to a side parlor and shuddered. Something in that room was not right. From her position behind a small square table, the woman could see straight through the window should any customers pull up the drive and approach the steps.

The room had little charm. The cracked and chipped brick hearth was in as sad a shape as the mantle, which had once been painted white. Instead of a fire, seven or eight white vanilla-scented pillar candles of different heights glowed in the old fireplace, and appeared to be the only source of heat or light in the gloomy room.

Two sheet-covered side chairs flanked the mantle, but instead of shabby chic, they just looked shabby—as did the faded wallpaper which, like the ceiling in the entryway, had its share of water stains around the windows. A tall, newish cabinet held up the wall behind me. No doubt a TV was stashed behind the closed doors. I'd bet the days were long and the customers few and far between, and soap operas and game shows helped to the pass the hours.

"Please, sit," she invited, and waved a hand at the worn upholstered chair before her.

I did as asked and, apart from feeling foolish, a growing disquiet seemed to radiate through me. I tried to shake it off and concentrated on the woman before me.

Talk about adopting a stereotype. The table was covered in a couple of layers of jewel-toned tablecloths and what looked like a lacy white shawl draped on top. A massive crystal ball sat in the middle of the table, and in front of the woman was a neatly stacked deck of worn Tarot cards.

I looked up into the woman's piercing blue eyes. She must have been in her early fifties, overweight, with a lined face and jet-black, shoulder-length wavy hair held back from her left ear by a rhinestone dragonfly clip. Seated behind the table like that, I could only see that she had on a white blouse with a black shawl drawn over her shoulders. But I suspected her outfit included a long dark skirt hidden beneath the table. Despite the candles, the pong of cigarette smoke still hung in the air. A trace of white on the edge of the table told me she'd hastily ditched her ashtray—probably onto her lap.

"I ask that my clients pay in advance, if you wouldn't mind."

"Sure." I grabbed the wallet from my left back pocket, withdrew the ten-dollar bill and offered it to her. She grabbed the money and stowed it under the table.

"Now, how can I help you, Mister—?"

Help me?

"Resnick. Jeffrey Resnick," I supplied.

Her eyes flashed and seemed to give me a quick once-over—evaluating me, and perhaps my stupidity factor.

"I saw your sign and wondered what you could tell me about…things."

That sounded lame, but I really didn't know what I expected. Probably just to find out what kind of cock-n-bull story she'd hand me. I get vibes from people, and so far the only vibe I got from this lady was that she had just robbed me of ten bucks.

"I can contact the spirit world in a number of ways. Via the crystal, the Tarot, or through my animal guide. How would you like me to proceed, Mr. Resnick?"

Animal guide? Cat? Horse? Rhinoceros? "I have no preference."

She nodded, moved the cards to one side, and pulled the crystal ball toward her. Leaning forward, she held her hands inches over the glass orb and gazed into it, her blue eyes going wide, her whole act looking kind of hokey to me. The ball's short gold-tone base was peeling on the side closest to me, not unlike the paint and wallpaper around us.

"I see you've fallen on hard times," she said, still gazing into the ball. She was one to talk. And did she have the gift of clairvoyance or had she deduced that by the wreck I'd parked outside her window, and the fact my shoes needed a shine?

"Go on," I urged her.

"You have not been well."

Another brilliant deduction. After the mugging that had almost killed me five months before, I'd lost weight and had never gained it back. I wasn't exactly gaunt, but I could have used another five or ten pounds to help me stand upright on a blustery day.

"What else do you see?" I asked.

She seemed to be puzzling over the crystal for an awfully long time and I was getting antsy. This wasn't much of a show for ten bucks.

It was then I noticed movement over her shoulder and in the darkest corner of the room. I squinted. I hadn't imagined it. A forty-something white man stood there. He had brown hair and a really bad haircut, dressed in dark slacks and a plaid flannel shirt. Funny thing was, I hadn't seen or heard him enter the room.

The feeling of disquiet grew within me.

I was about to ask the woman who the guy was, but he held up his right hand and pressed his index finger to his lips as though to shush me.

I sat back in my chair and frowned. I hadn't expected an expanded audience at this little performance.

"I'm curious about this house. Have you lived here long?" I asked the woman.

She waved a hand in the air as though batting away a pesky insect. "That has no bearing on your future—or your past," she said with the slightest bit of an edge to her tone. "I see trouble ahead for you."

"What kind of trouble?"

"With the police."

Oh yeah? "A traffic ticket?"

She shook her head. "Something much more serious."

As I'd already helped track down two killers in the short time I'd been back in Buffalo, I found her observation oddly disturbing. I'd figured she was a blatant fraud. Now I wasn't so sure.

I looked back to the corner of the room but the guy in the plaid shirt was gone.

How? He hadn't made a sound and I swear he never walked past the fortuneteller's table to escape the room.

Where the hell had he gone?

***

Thanks to my stop for psychic entertainment, I was late getting home for dinner that night. I live in the apartment over the garage on my brother's property, and I often join him and his wife for meals at their house, although house was a bit of a misnomer. Mansion wasn't quite right, either, but came pretty close. At any rate, it was a comfortable arrangement.

That night my sister-in-law, Brenda, had roasted a chicken, and had included all the fixings. Whipped potatoes, homemade sage-and-onion stuffing, peas, salad, and a bowl of jellied cranberry sauce, along with a plate mounded with grocery store dinner rolls.

"Are we doing a trial run for Thanksgiving?" I asked, taking in the table laden with food—a heavy meal for such a warm weekday evening.

"I thought it would be nice to have a hearty dinner for once. Help yourself to a beer and sit down," she said.

I grabbed a bottle of Labatt Blue from the fridge and took my usual seat at the table.

"So, what's new with you?" my older, half-brother Richard Alpert asked as he helped himself to a dinner roll.

I passed the butter. "I stopped off on the way home to visit the psychic on Route 5."

"What did you do that for?" he asked, annoyed, and hacked off a gob of butter, spreading it across his roll.

"Entertainment value only—although she didn't put on much of an act for ten bucks."

"What did she tell you? I assume it was a woman psychic," Brenda said, sounding much more interested.

I nodded and helped myself to one of the chicken thighs, a scoop of potatoes, and some peas. "She was a walking—or rather sitting—stereotype of the trade. And she didn't say much. Just that I'd fallen on hard times and had been ill."

"It doesn't take a psychic to deduce that," Richard said reasonably.

Amen. I decided not to mention her threat about trouble with the cops. Richard worries like an old lady about such things.

"Are you going to go again? Can I come along?" Brenda asked eagerly.

"You're *not* going," Richard said.

"You can't tell me where I can and can't go," Brenda countered defiantly.

"You're right. But I strongly suggest you *don't* go. It would be a waste of time and money. Pass the potatoes, please."

I handed him the bowl. "I am going back, and no you can't come, Brenda. There was something sinister about that place."

"Then why would you want to go back?" Richard asked and chased a couple of peas around his dinner plate.

"I've got a feeling something bad happened there."

He looked at me with disapproval. "All the more reason for you to stay away."

"What kind of bad?" Brenda asked eagerly. She reads mysteries—loves them, in fact.

"Violence. Maybe…a murder. I'm not sure."

Her expression soured and she turned her gaze back to her husband. "You're right, Richard—I don't think I want to go anymore. And you shouldn't either," Brenda cautioned me. "We all know that nothing good ever comes from your vibes."

That wasn't true. Matt Sumner's killer would have escaped justice if I hadn't looked into his death. Same with the person who murdered Walt Kaplan. Of course, it was Richard, not me, who'd paid dearly during both those encounters. I would go this little adventure on my own.

"You've hardly touched your dinner," Brenda chided me. "It's getting cold."

Thinking about that house, that woman, and the disappearing man made me lose what little appetite I'd had.

***

That night—and the next—my dreams were haunted by the chubby medium and the silent man from the eerie house on Route 5. Indistinct images of those two people and that creepy house played and replayed through my sleeping hours. Her speaking nonsense, and him saying nothing but listening to everything.

When disturbing stuff bothered me, I knew the only place I could go to and talk about it with someone who really understood was in a little bakery on Main Street. It was kind of like Brigadoon. Sometimes it was there—and sometimes it wasn't. Well, the bakery was always there—but the person I sought wasn't always available.

It was nearly three o'clock in the morning and Main Street was empty as I jaywalked toward the bakery. Sure enough, the light was on in the back of the shop. I didn't even have to ring the bell. A silhouette tottered toward the door and my octogenarian friend Sophie opened the door to let me in. "You're late," she said in greeting, and offered her cheek for a kiss.

"Sorry. I wasn't sure I was coming."

"You always say that," she grumbled and turned to return to the back room. She moved stiffly, as though in pain.

"Are you okay?" I asked, concerned.

"It's this stinking humidity…it always cranks up my arthritis," she complained.

As usual, the bakery smelled incredibly good. The mingled aromas of bread, cookies, and cakes filled the air. Also as usual, Sophie had set the small Formica table with chipped plates. She'd placed large sugar cookies on a bigger plate in the center of the table.

I took my customary seat as Sophie checked the progress of the kettle on the hotplate that sat on a shelf over the sink. I'd warned her time and time again that it was a dangerous arrangement, but she always blew me off. For such a smart woman, she had a blind spot when it came to her personal safety.

"So what brings you here tonight?" she asked.

"Have you ever seen a ghost?"

Sophie picked up the kettle and paused before turning to face me. She'd make me tea, hot chocolate, or instant coffee—depending on the weather. Tonight it was instant coffee. The stuff tasted like shit—not that I'd tell her that.

"I think I have…but…I really can't be sure," she admitted, and poured the hot water into mugs. She set the mugs down on the table, took her seat, and then pushed the powered creamer toward me. "What makes you think *you've* seen a ghost."

"I didn't say I had."

She leveled a stony glare at me. "You didn't say you hadn't, either."

I told her about my visit to the Route 5 medium. With every sentence her expression grew more sour.

"That was a waste of your time *and* money," she muttered. "These people are all fakes."

"You're not a fake."

"And neither are you. But we don't go around advertising our gifts and trying to make money from desperate people, either."

"Well, it seemed like I needed to go there. And now I feel like I need to go back."

She shook her head. "Nothing but trouble can come from this."

"Trouble for whom?" I asked.

"You—in the short run."

"And someone else for the long run?"

She shrugged. "So, tell me about this so-called ghost."

"There's not much to tell. I don't even know if he *is* a ghost. It's just…the place gives off weird vibes and this guy suddenly showed up and then just as quickly disappeared."

"Could you see right through him?" she asked.

It was my turn to shake my head.

"He looked solid?" she persisted.

I nodded.

"In movies, ghosts always look transparent."

"That's movies. We're talking real life."

"Not if he's dead," Sophie pointed out. She reached for a cookie, placed it on her plate, and then broke it in half, nibbling on one of the pieces. "Are you afraid of meeting a ghost?"

I'd seen some pretty weird stuff since I'd been bonked on the head with a baseball bat and became...different. "I don't think I'm afraid as much as...worried."

"Why?"

"What if this guy is depending on me to discover what happened to him?"

"Is that what you hope to accomplish by going back to see this fraud of a fortuneteller? Figuring out why he died?"

"That's just it. I'm not sure. But if this guy died because someone helped him to the afterlife or...whatever... shouldn't somebody try to help him move on?"

"Has he asked you for help?"

I shook my head. "He hasn't said a word."

"Then how do you know he even needs help?"

I grabbed a cookie from the plate, broke it into about six pieces and shoved one of them into my mouth, chewing fast. It tasted pretty good, but I didn't care. I was wondering why I cared about some dead guy I'd never known in life.

But for some reason I *did* care. Shouldn't that be enough?

I voiced the question.

Sophie shrugged. "I guess if somebody did me in, I'd hope that somebody cared enough to find out why. But why does it always have to be *you*?"

"Maybe nobody else knows the guy is dead."

Sophie sipped her coffee, and then picked up the other half of her cookie. "Then I guess you'd better do something to find that out."

***

And so it was two days after my first visit that I returned to the decrepit old house, which looked no better on my second visit than it had on my first. The weather had deteriorated and a gentle rain had been falling for most of the day. When I knocked at the old screen door I could see a number of plastic pails and bowls had been placed in strategic places around the entryway to catch drips. Still, it suddenly occurred to me that maybe the dark stains on the floor might not be due to a leaky bathroom after all.

"I knew you'd be back," called the woman fortune-teller from within. I then realized that I hadn't thought to ask her name the last time I'd been there, and she hadn't introduced herself, either. "Come in," she encouraged.

Sure she was friendly. She knew if I walked through the door she would be able to order a small cheese-and-pepperoni pizza for dinner. If she'd already had one other customer that day, she could upgrade to a medium with enough leftover for lunch the next day and give the delivery guy a tip, too.

"Sit down, Mr. Resnick," she said, waving a hand to encourage me to take the seat opposite her. Today she wore a sleeveless blue shell top, but the black shawl was still draped over her shoulders—no doubt for effect. The oppressive humidity in that room wasn't improved by the presence of a large white oscillating fan that moved listlessly from left to right.

I sat down and, without a word, she held out her hand to receive her fee upfront. I counted out ten one dollar bills. I'd had good tips that day while tending bar at the Whole Nine Yards—a job I'd held for a little over two months.

"And why have you returned so soon?" the woman asked.

"What you told me the other day intrigued me," I lied. "I wanted to know more."

It had been the right thing to say. The corners of her mouth quirked into a smile. She reached for her crystal ball and pulled it closer.

Again movement in the shadows drew my attention. Once again the guy with the bad haircut stood in the corner, wearing the same plaid shirt—a garment much too heavy for such a hot, humid day—and I swear he hadn't been there when I'd entered the room. He smiled, waggled his eyebrows a la Groucho Marx and gave me a four-fingered wave with his right hand. He looked pretty substantial to me.

I turned my attention back to the woman. "I'm sorry, but I don't know your name."

"You may call me Madam Zahara."

Madam Zahara? O-kay.

"Madam Zahara, do you live here alone?"

She hesitated before answering. "Most of the time. My son comes and goes. He's a long-distance truck driver. He'll probably return tonight."

Had she added the last to warn me off should I be some kind of robber or rapist?

If she was in her fifties, her son was probably in his twenties or thirties. The guy in the corner had to be at least forty. He turned to look out the nearest window to the weed-strewn yard beyond. I got the feeling that before I headed for home I should probably take a walk around that yard. For some reason I wasn't quite sure I understood, I was *supposed* to look around that yard before I headed home. And I had a feeling I might find something I would definitely not like finding.

Once again Madam Zahara held her hands over her crystal ball as she gazed within its depths. "Ahh, today I see—"

"Death?" I supplied.

Her brow wrinkled and she frowned. "No. Why would you say that?" she asked, sounding frightened.

"Because there's a darkness that hovers over this house. Surely you've felt it."

Her blue eyes widened in suspicion. "Why do you say that?"

My gaze traveled up to the ceiling and ran back to the stained floor in the entryway. I had originally assumed the wood had been marred by dripping water over a long period of time. But now I thought I knew better. That knowledge made the humidity suddenly seem ten times as oppressive.

"You told me on Tuesday that an encounter with the police would be in my future. I think you were right."

"Is there something *you're* guilty of that *you've* been hiding?" she asked with a bit of a smirk.

"Not me. I think it's you."

She sat back, taking umbrage. "I don't know what you mean."

"Don't you?" I asked, unsure why I'd taken the offensive.

"No," she said quite firmly.

I heaved a heavy sigh and looked back at the guy who stood silent in the darkened corner of the room. He nodded and then raised a hand to make a slashing motion across his throat.

"How long have you lived here?" I asked.

"Ten years. And why the hell would you care?" She was definitely on the defensive. "Look, I think you'd better leave." She pushed the stack of ones back toward me, but I shook my head.

"I have a feeling you're going to need them. In fact, I think you're going to need a lot more than ten dollars to hire someone to tackle your defense."

"What are you talking about?" she demanded.

"The shallow grave out in the side yard. There's a body buried there—or what's left of a body. The big stain in the entryway isn't from water damage. It's blood."

She rose to stand, much shorter than she'd appeared sitting behind the table. "I think you'd better leave. Now."

"I agree. But if you don't call the cops about this, I will."

For a moment—just a moment—*I* was suddenly afraid. I'd made a baseless accusation. I had nothing more than a gut feeling to go with and she had called my bluff. Momentarily. But then a gush of remorse and sorrow threatened to engulf me. It wasn't my own…it belonged to her.

"Call the police," I said. "This has been a heavy burden on your soul for a long time."

Her lower lip trembled for a few seconds before she burst into tears.

"I think I should go now," I said and rose from my seat. "But I'm not going very far—and if I don't see a police cruiser park in your drive within the next half hour, I'm going to call them and that would complicate my life. You don't *want* to complicate my life," I told her in a tone I'd never used when talking with a woman.

Suddenly her fear shifted from whatever she'd done to whatever she thought I might be capable of doing. It wasn't a pleasant state of mind for me to accept.

She took a ragged breath and pulled a clunky old cell phone from her skirt pocket and hit three buttons—911. She lifted the phone to her ear and cleared her throat. "I'd like to report a murder."

I looked across to the corner of the room. The man who stood there smiled, lifted his right hand to give me a thumbs up, and then slowly dissolved into thin air.

***

True to my word, I'd pulled out of her driveway and drove a quarter of a mile down the road to turn around. Then I'd doubled back and parked in the used car lot directly across the road from the creepy old house to wait for the police cruiser to arrive.

I waited and waited. After more than an hour it was apparent that no cop car *would* arrive. She'd stiffed me. She'd pressed the correct buttons on her phone, said the words I'd expected her to say, and scammed me good. And obviously my best Clint Eastwood threat had not been believed for—sure enough—it was a pizza deliveryman who arrived, not a cop.

I started my car, pulled out of the dealership, and headed for home.

Once there, I hit the button on the remote, the garage door opened, and I parked my car. Before I could close the door and head upstairs to my own place, I saw Brenda hanging out the back door of the big house, waving me to come over and join them for dinner. Since I'd guzzled the last of my twelve-pack and had nothing but a blue box of mac and cheese in the cupboard, I figured why not?

"You're late again," Brenda accused as I entered their kitchen. This time she was cooking pasta. A bag of frozen shrimp sat on the counter, accompanied by a small dish of freshly chopped garlic. Scampi was on the menu that night.

"You went back to that psychic, didn't you?" Richard accused from his seat at the kitchen table.

I sat down opposite him. "Guilty as charged."

He shook his head and took a sip of the scotch and soda that had been sitting before him.

"Want a beer?" Brenda offered me.

I shook my head. "I think something stronger might be called for."

She sighed, but stepped over to the cabinet that held the kitchen liquor, hauling out a bottle of Makers Mark. She poured me a couple of fingers worth, tossed in some ice and soda, and handed it to me. Ahh—that hit the spot.

"And?" Richard prompted.

"The so-called psychic is hiding something. I'm pretty sure there's a body buried in the yard."

"Oh, God," Richard groused and downed what was left in his glass with one gulp.

"I was going to search the yard before I left, but the bitch called my bluff. I'd told her to call the cops and she produced a cell phone and pretended to do it. Only they never showed."

"So what happens next?" Richard asked.

"Like I said, I think there's a body buried in the yard. No one's going to believe me unless I can come up with some kind of proof.

"I don't like the sound of this," Richard said, and why would he? Thanks to my escapades he'd been shot, and now had the death threat of HIV hanging over his head.

"Don't worry," I said. "I'm not asking you to come with me—in fact, I don't *want* you to come. But if I can bring back some kind of evidence that you can identify as being human—say a bone—maybe you could go with me to the Clarence Police Department when I report it."

"Do you honestly think I'm going to let you go digging for evidence alone?" Richard asked.

"Why are either of you even *considering* going to that house?" Brenda cried.

I gave her what I hoped was a patient look. "Brenda, if a murder has taken place, then justice *needs* to be served." Geeze, I sounded like some kind of sanctimonious asshole right off a TV drama.

"And why is it always *you* that needs to be the catalyst for justice? Why can't somebody else play Superman?" Now she sounded like Sophie.

"No red cape and blue tights?" I suggested.

She glared at me.

"What made you suspicious of this woman in the first place?"

"I got weird vibes going into that house. When I asked her about it, she blew me off."

Richard frowned and shook the ice in his glass, as though hoping Brenda would take the hint and make him another drink. She didn't. Finally he got up and poured his own Scotch. "Okay, say the woman killed that guy. What are the odds she'll be armed if you show up?" he asked as he slopped Lagavulin over ice.

"I wouldn't put it past her. The entry was stained with what looked like a lot of blood."

"You two are not seriously thinking of going out there tonight to investigate, are you?" Brenda asked.

"She knows I know something," I pointed out. "She knows she's got to hide the evidence."

"And what if she's digging up the evidence when you arrive?" Brenda insisted.

"That would be the perfect time to call the cops and have *them* catch her in the act."

"And if she doesn't dig up the evidence?" she demanded.

"Then *we* can call the cops." I paused. Hadn't I already decided Richard shouldn't participate, and yet here I was including him in my plans. "It's a win-win situation."

Brenda shook her head. "Oh, no-no-no. Things never work out that neatly."

"Maybe, maybe not. But we've got to give it a try," Richard agreed.

"No, you don't. Call the police!"

"But I've got no tangible proof. They don't treat gut feelings as real evidence."

The pasta threatened to boil over and Brenda turned to tend to it.

I sipped my bourbon and looked at my physician brother. He already had a potential death threat hanging over his head, thanks to being exposed to a bloodied, high-risk patient and no latex protection between his hands and the dying man. Still, there was no denying the longing in his eyes, begging to be involved—to feel alive—especially at a time when he might be looking at his own mortality.

I wanted to protect my brother, but could I deny him the chance to *live* at a time when he wasn't sure what his future might bring?

"What's the plan?" Richard asked.

Brenda glared at him, but I sensed that she understood that it was up to Richard to decide his own fate.

"For now, we assess the situation. There's no reason we have to hurry on this." And yet as soon as I said that I knew that time was running out for finding the remains…and that guy in the plaid shirt. I was sure it was him buried in a shallow grave alongside the house. Had I really seen a ghost? Had whatever was left of the man been hanging around the place in hopes that someone would uncover his fate—find him—and finally see that he was properly laid to rest? Had Madam Zahara killed him or had her seldom-home son done the deed? And what was the dead man's relationship with the two of them? Lover? Husband? Father? Hapless mark?

Richard raised his glass, gazing at the amber liquid within it. "There's no time like the present. Let's have dinner and then go find your evidence," he said to me. He lowered his glass, took a sip, and then shifted his gaze toward Brenda. "You could come with us."

She shook her head. "Not on your life. I'll be here, keeping the home fires burning. And if you aren't home at a reasonable hour, I'll call the cops and report you as missing persons."

"You're overreacting," I told her.

"Oh yeah? We'll see," she said, glowering at me.

Since Brenda was a kindred spirit, and I meant that literally—she had a limited sixth sense about such things—I took her warning seriously and wished to God I hadn't mentioned anything about this mess to them. Richard felt some kind of misplaced guilt about my teenaged years spent in his home, and the lack of understanding and concern his grandparents felt on my behalf. In retrospect, I didn't blame them. I reminded them of our mother, a woman they'd disapproved of—despised, actually. That they'd allowed me to live in their home after our mother's death, and for the better part of four years, had to gall them. They had loved Richard enough to put up with me.

No one had loved *me*.

I shook my head to dislodge all the crap from so long ago, but somehow it always seemed to come back to haunt me at the worst moments.

Brenda got up and put a big skillet on the stove before she took a stick of butter out of the fridge to sauté the shrimp. She'd make sure her troops were well fed before they marched off to…battle? No, we weren't looking for a fight. But what we found might be a casualty of a domestic war. I was pretty sure if we dug in just the right spot, we'd find bones—and maybe the remnants of a plaid flannel shirt.

I drained my Makers Mark and got up to make another. I had a feeling I'd better fortify myself. What lay ahead could be pretty gruesome. Or was I being overly melodramatic? After all, I had no evidence—nothing but a gut feeling to go by. Still, gut feelings had served me well in the recent past.

I poured that fine bourbon and took a sip. This would be my last drink before we hit the road, but I had a feeling that bottle might run dry upon our return.

***

The clouds had dissipated, but thanks to Buffalo's light-polluted sky, no stars broke through the artificial haze. Richard had had a glass or two of wine with his scampi, so I elected to drive us to the psychic's neighborhood.

I parked my car on a side street four blocks from the house and took out a shovel from the trunk of my car. I carried it while Richard hefted the large orange flashlight that usually lived under his kitchen sink.

"So how did the guy die?" Richard asked as we headed west on the cracked and weed-studded sidewalk.

"Blunt trauma to the skull," I said and realized that the phrase perfectly described my own injury five months before. Was that the common denominator that connected me with the flannel-clad victim?

The streetlamps cast bluish shadows. We walked the rest of the way—side-by-side—in silence. If anyone saw me with that shovel, what would they think? Would they call 911 or just assume I was a nutcase on the loose? Luckily traffic was light and none of the cars that passed seemed to notice us as we trekked down the concrete path.

Finally I grabbed Richard's arm, pulling him to a stop, and we took in the psychic's residence. Except for a flickering blue light in one of the upstairs rooms—a rerun of Survivor?—the big old house was dark. I couldn't even see the sign that advertised the medium's services.

"Creepy," Richard whispered.

"You ought to see the inside."

We walked past the gravel drive and once out of the glow of lamplight darted into the home's weed-strewn side yard.

"Goddamnit, you didn't tell me the place hadn't been mown all summer," Richard groused as our arrival seemed to have rousted a swarm of hungry mosquitoes.

"What's a little malaria between friends," I said, swatting at my bare arms and wishing I'd worn a jacket. "And what are you bitching for anyway? All you have to do is hold the flashlight. I'm the idiot who's got to do the digging."

"So start digging."

Sound advice, but I had no idea where to start. "Give me a minute, willya?"

"A minute," he said testily.

I shut my eyes and cleared my mind, hoping I'd get some kind of vibe from the dead guy. I heard Richard slapping at mosquitoes and swearing under his breath.

Maybe I needed to roam around the yard. Maybe if I trooped across the area in a kind of grid pattern I would get weird vibes, literally stumble across the gravesite, dig down a foot or so, find the victim and—voila—justice would be served.

Of course the flaw in that plan was proving Madam Zahara or her son had killed the guy and buried him there. And what was their motive supposed to be, anyway?

"Have you got a plan or are we just going to stand here and be bitten until we come down with West Nile virus?" Richard asked.

"I'd better walk the property. Maybe then I'll know where to start digging." I could see Richard's form in silhouette. He shook his head as though perturbed. "Why don't you go stand on the sidewalk until I call for you. That way you won't get bitten as much."

"I'll do that," he said. "The last thing I need right now is another blood-born virus." He stalked off.

I looked around the shadowy yard wondering which way I ought to go. It didn't matter. I chose to start at the farthest, darkest corner and wished I'd asked Richard to hold the shovel while I used the flashlight.

No sooner had I gone five feet when the toe of my sneakered foot got caught in a hole. The shovel went flying and I fell flat on my face, wrenching my knee. "Goddammit," I swore as I grabbed at my leg, rolling onto my side. My movements had jostled a whole new swarm of mosquitoes, who seemed to zero in on my face and neck. I could feel them crawling all over me and slapped and cursed at them in anger.

"Will you shut up!" Richard whispered loudly.

"I just fell in a friggin' hole," I hissed back.

"Well, be more careful."

That was easy for him to say, he had the flashlight.

I groped for the shovel and used it to haul myself upright before gingerly putting weight on my throbbing knee. It let me know it was not happy, but it didn't give out on me, either. I took a fortifying breath to steady myself and opened my mind as I hobbled up and down the yard.

The night air was cool and damp—clammy—and I shivered. In fact, I stopped and felt downright frozen. The saying "cold as the grave" came back to me.

"I think I found it," I called to Richard.

No answer.

"Hey, you still there?"

"Oh, shit," I heard him say out loud.

"What's the matter?"

Before he could answer, a police car—with lights flashing—skidded to a halt in front of the yard.

"Oh, shit," I said as the officer jumped out of the cruiser, trained a light on the yard until he found me, and then drew his gun.

"Hands up!" he shouted.

I did as I was told, still with shovel in hand. "Something wrong, officer?" I asked, trying to sound cheerful.

"Yeah, you're trespassing. Put down the shovel and drop to the ground."

I tossed the shovel aside and fell to the grass, unleashing another horde of mosquitoes and wondered if the town lock-up provided Calamine lotion for its prisoners.

***

Brenda whacked a jumbo egg on the side of the hot skillet, then dropped its contents into the spattering butter. "Of all the stupid, lame-brained ideas…."

"Hey, as a person with a brain injury, I resent that remark," I said, and took a sip of my coffee. It was nine-thirty and I'd had to sit in jail until first thing that morning, waiting for a judge to set bail and for Richard to come and collect me. He'd been smart and ducked behind an arborvitae when the cop arrested me the night before. I didn't hold a grudge. Why should he get in trouble for one of my funny feelings? And I promised to pay him back…one day…for making my bail.

The toast popped up and Brenda grabbed it, first slathering butter and then raspberry jam on it before depositing it on my plate.

"Hey, what about me?" Richard complained.

I picked up one of the slices and dropped it on his plate. He nodded his thanks, scooped it up and took a bite—quite satisfied.

"And what's next on your agenda?" Brenda asked, sounding thoroughly annoyed.

I took another sip of my coffee before answering. "What I should have done first. Research the house. See who owns it. My guess is the dead guy. I've got a feeling Madam Zahara and her son have been squatting for some time."

"How can you prove that?" Richard asked, and took another bite of his toast.

"First I'd need to find out if the real owner has been seen in the past few years, which is what I should have done before we went blundering over there last night. I'll start with the county tax records to see who owns that house and who's been paying the taxes for the last few years. Next I'll see what else I can find out about the owner."

"Who says it was the owner that died? Couldn't it have been one of Madam Zahara's customers?"

I nodded. "If that's the case, I might be looking at a dead end from the start. My gut's telling me there's a paper trail to follow—but first I have to go looking for it."

"Be my guest," Richard said, polishing off the last of his toast.

"When I've pulled it all together, perhaps you'd like to be a witness when I present my evidence."

"And just who are you going to present it to?" he asked.

I picked up my cup. That was a good question. Clearly confronting Madam Zahara hadn't done the trick. But was a cop going to believe me?

Probably not.

But then I did have a friend at *The Buffalo News*. He might want to play with a missing-person story. And if he set the ball rolling, the Clarence PD might just pick it up.

I'd just have to wait and see.

But first, breakfast.

***

Since I wasn't scheduled to work, I spent the rest of that day on my computer in air-conditioned comfort while Brenda and Richard took off for the country club to sweat their way through a few rounds of golf.

First, thanks to the fact that the Erie County tax records were posted online, I found out the property on Route 5, which was also known as Main Street, was owned by one Fred Butterfield. Next up, I looked for every Fred Butterfield I could find, in case the owner was an absentee landlord. There were four of them in the greater Buffalo area. I had no idea how long the guy in the plaid shirt had been dead, so I wasn't sure which one I was looking for—at least at first. I discounted the one who was ninety-six and another who was six years old. That left two.

I Googled the name and came up with over five million, one hundred and eighty thousand results (in less than 2 seconds—not bad). I narrowed that down by adding Buffalo, NY to the search parameters, and winnowed it down to a mere seventy-two. It took another twenty minutes to go through that list. I found hits on only one of the guys on the tax records, who'd been a football sensation back in high school. Next stop: Facebook.

I had to go through a whole page of men by that name before I narrowed it down to two, but both of them were listed on that social network as living in the Buffalo area. Now to figure out which one was the dead guy. Not such an easy task, since one of the profile pictures was of Popeye the Sailor and the other was a 1989 orange Corvette.

Since I wasn't their "friend," their personal info pages weren't available to me. I couldn't friend them as myself—Madam Zahara knew my name and wasn't likely to approve my friendship request—so I went to Google and set up a phony email address, then went back to Facebook and set up a new account. And why hadn't it occurred to me to do this before now? I had a feeling I'd be able to use this bogus name and history for snooping in the future.

While I waited to see if my friend requests would be granted, I studied their info pages, but neither had allowed much information to be made available to non-friends.

Gut feeling told me the picture of the Corvette represented Mr. Plaid Shirt, although from the looks of his clothing and his hair, and the condition of the home on Main Street, he'd fallen on hard times long before his demise. That made the idea of someone killing him for that crappy house even more appalling.

To kill time, I friended a bunch of Buffalo institutions, including the library, the Bills, the Sabres, and any other sports-affiliated thing I could think of, a few restaurants, and microbreweries, figuring what the hell—it would give my fake persona a little credibility.

I Googled Madam Zahara and found her listed in the Buffalo online phone directory—she'd even paid for an ad—but that didn't tell me who she really was or what her connection to Fred Butterfield was.

It was after three and I already had twenty friends when I looked back to my profile page to see that Mr. Corvette Butterfield was now my friend, too. I clicked onto his pictures. Bingo! There he was in a number of shots, first looking some twenty years younger with said orange Corvette, and then a few of him looking pretty much as he had when I'd seen him at Madam Zahara's. He'd apparently never had the opportunity to become older.

I clicked back to his wall and found that his last post was made just two days before. "Watching the Mets on TV." I did a quick Google search and found the team had played two days before. (They'd lost—five to three.)

So, who was updating the dead guy's page—Madam Zahara or her long-distant trucking son? And when it came down to it—I had no proof that either of them had done anything wrong, and no real proof that Fred Butterfield was actually dead. Just that funny feeling in my gut that I had learned to trust during the past five months.

I figured I'd gone about as far as I could go on my own without doing some face-to-face interviews and possibly stirring up a hornet's nest, so I called my friend Sam Nielson at *The Buffalo News*.

Sam and I go back to high school days. He was the editor of the school newspaper and I took the photos. We didn't talk much back then, but we're now…maybe not friends, but we had a mutual understanding when it came to crime. He reported it, and I seemed to keep finding it. Since he'd helped me out a couple of times, there was no reason not to ask for his assistance once again.

"This sounds pretty lame," he said when I finally got hold of him late that afternoon.

"Have I been wrong so far?"

I heard him sigh. "No. Okay, what do you want me to do?"

"See if this guy has paid taxes."

"You got a social security number? Date of birth? Anything like that?"

"According to Facebook, he was born on April twelfth—no year given."

"And if that's a bogus date?"

"Then I'm shit outta luck."

"You'll be on *my* shit list, that's for sure." He was quiet for a moment, and I could hear the rustle of paper. "Okay, give me a day or two and I'll get back to you."

He hung up.

A day or two. It was going to seem like years. I just hoped he had things cleared up before my court date or I might find myself in jail—or doing community service. Maybe digging holes in parks for new trees instead of digging in yards looking for bodies.

But I didn't have to wait those two days because Madam Zahara called me. After all, I didn't have an unlisted number and she did know my name.

"Mr. Resnick?" she asked. "The one who visited a psychic on two occasions this past week?"

"That's me," I said as a chill ran up my spine.

"It seems as though we have more business to conduct."

"How so?" I asked.

"You want to know about Fred Butterfield, right?"

"Yes," I said.

"I'm prepared to tell all. And if you want to call the police after you've heard my story, I won't try to stop you."

Boy did that sound like a trap, or what? But she had me pegged and I did want to hear her story.

"I'm not prepared to go back to the house on Main Street. Can we meet on neutral ground?"

The connection was silent for long seconds. "I'm open to that. Where?"

Someplace crowded. "How about Eastern Hills Mall?"

"Where will we meet?"

"By the food court. Tomorrow afternoon. Is five thirty all right with you?"

"Perfect," she said. She sounded smug, which made the hairs on the back of my neck bristle.

"I'll see you then," I said.

"Damn right you will," she answered and hung up.

***

I was antsy at work all the next day, watching the clock and messing up drink orders. My boss is pretty forgiving and just chalked it up to me having a bad day. I was worried that the bad element was yet to come. I still wasn't sure what I had gotten myself into, but meeting Madam Zahara in a public place was the prudent thing to do.

I arrived at the mall's food court fifteen minutes before the agreed-upon time. Madam Zahara was already seated at a table near Subway, fidgeting. She was dressed in the same outfit I'd seen her in two days before. She adjusted her shawl, looked around, adjusted it again, looking decidedly nervous.

I scoped out the place, didn't see anyone who looked like a long-distance trucker hanging round, and walked up to her table. "Mind if I sit down?"

She waved a hand at the chair opposite her.

I sat down and folded my hands on the table before me. "You called me," I reminded her.

She sighed and leaned closer, keeping her voice low. "First, let me apologize. I shouldn't have taken any money from you, but old habits die hard." She reached into her skirt pocket and withdrew the ten spot and the ones I'd given her the previous times we'd met. She pushed the bills across the table, her bracelets rattling at the movement.

"Any other old habits you'd like to disavow yourself from?" I asked.

She ignored my question, studied my face, and finally spoke. "You were right. There was a horrific murder in my house."

"Fred Butterfield's house," I reminded her.

"It didn't always belong to him."

"Are you saying he bought it from you?"

"Cheated me out of it, more like."

"How?"

She sighed. "The bastard married me."

"How long ago was that?"

"The years aren't important. In fact, now they mean nothing."

Maybe not to her….

Her mouth drooped. She reached into her pocket once more and withdrew a slip of paper, which she set on the table. On it was written a name: Gary Madison.

"Who's this?"

"Our son."

I'd never had a kid with her, so I assumed she meant Butterfield. "Is this the long-distance truck driver?"

She nodded. "I was hoping you might try to get a message to him from me. Despite all my best efforts, I haven't been able to contact him."

"What makes you think I can?"

She laughed. "Mr. Resnick, we both know what you are."

"And what's that?"

"Somebody like me. A psychic. Only you're much better than I ever was."

"It wasn't just a game?"

She shook her head. "Reading the Tarot, consulting the crystal—that kept us off welfare and put food on the table while Fred drove around in that money hole of a Corvette."

"I take it he no longer owns it?"

She shook her head. "It's just a reminder of his so-called glory days. He never worried about supporting us."

"Mrs. Butterfield—"

Again she shook her head. "I never took his name."

"I can't say I feel comfortable calling you Madam Zahara."

"My name is Bridget Madison."

I nodded. "Bridget. Where can I find the body?"

"As I'm sure you surmised, in the side yard where the policeman found you the other night. You were so close, too."

"Yeah, well, I can hardly go digging there if you're going to call the cops every time I show up."

"Who says I called the cops?"

"Who else could it have been?" I asked.

"Who do you think?" She looked at me as if I was dense, and yet she was the one talking in circles.

"If I'm going to be taken seriously, I need proof to take to the police."

"I know, I know." She toyed with one of the rings on her fingers. "If you show up at the house later tonight, you'll have your proof."

"You wanna tell me what I'll be up against?"

"And scare you away?" She shook her head. "Now, about that message to my son...."

"Where am I supposed to find him?"

"He's around, and I suspect you wouldn't have much trouble locating him. His birth date and social security number are on the other side of that piece of paper."

I picked it up. Sure enough, the information was there.

She got up from the table. "I hope you'll come by the house to see me later."

"I'll be there."

She nodded, and stood. Her skirt was much longer than I'd thought, and as I watched her move away from the food court, a terrible chill came over me.

Under the filmy fabric, no feet touched the tile floor.

***

"Okay, now I'm totally confused," Richard said, and got up from the kitchen table to pour himself another glass of scotch. "Are you saying *she's* the ghost?"

"Can ghosts even show up in the middle of the day?" Brenda asked.

"They must. Because I'm telling you, whatever it was I saw had no legs and yet it glided right out of the food court. By the time I got over the shock and hurried after her, she was—*poof!*—gone.

"So it's her body that's buried beside that creepy old house?" Richard asked.

"That's what I'm thinking."

"But didn't you say Fred Butterfield disintegrated right before your eyes?"

"Maybe they're both dead," Brenda suggested, and cut a piece off the medium-rare steak on her plate.

"Somebody ordered a pizza the other night. Somebody called the cops on us, too. And somebody is updating Fred Butterfield's Facebook page."

Richard took his seat once more. "What about the son she wanted you to contact? Could it be him living in the house?"

"Maybe."

"Do you think he killed both of them?"

"What was it she wanted you to tell him?" Brenda asked.

"That's the thing. She never got around to saying it. She just said she hadn't been able to contact him."

"And what will you say if you do find him?" Richard asked. "'Hi. Did you kill your parents?'"

I wasn't sure how to answer. "I think I'd better get on the computer and start looking for him."

Richard shook his head. "No. If he killed his parents, you should go to the police."

"And how serious are they going to take me when I tell them I've seen two ghosts?"

"Can't your friend Sam write a story on the house or something?" Brenda suggested.

"I already called him about it."

"And?" Richard prompted.

I shrugged. "So far nothing."

"Then it might be time to start nagging, because no way do I want you to confront someone who might've killed his mama and daddy," Brenda said.

"Yes, ma'am," I muttered.

Brenda glared at me. "Don't you 'yes, ma'am' me like that. You listen to me."

"Yeah, listen to her," Richard echoed. I was beginning to feel like I was being bullied. The fact that I knew they truly cared about my welfare kind of took the sting out of it, though.

Calling Sam was a good idea. And I had Gary Madison's social security number, so that would make tracking him down a lot easier. If it was correct. I mean, did ghosts usually go around carrying their offspring's social security numbers? And how did a ghost write it down on a piece of paper? Could they hold pens and pencils?

I didn't want to think about it.

After dinner, I went back up to my apartment and called Sam at home. He wasn't exactly thrilled to hear from me so soon.

"Sorry, I've been busy at work—I didn't get a chance to look up that Butterworth guy."

"Butterfield," I corrected. "Mrs. Butterworth is syrup."

"Butterfield, Butterworth," he muttered.

"The story has taken on a new angle. I suspected the psychic to be the killer? Now it looks like she's dead, too."

"Oh my god. Someone killed her? Have you reported this to the cops?"

"No. She's been dead for a long time…I think."

"What a minute. She's a ghost, too?" Sam said, sounding incredulous.

"Yeah, but she asked me to track down and contact her son and she gave me his social security number to make it easier."

"Don't all ghosts do that?" he asked sarcastically.

"You could save me a lot of time by corking that number into one of your data bases."

"Okay. Let me fire up the computer and I'll do it now."

I had to wait a few minutes for Sam's computer to boot up, but the next thing I knew he was asking me for the number. I heard him tapping his keyboard and anxiously waited for him to report what he found.

"Hmm."

"What does 'hmm' mean?" I asked.

"The guy lives in Portland, Oregon. I've got a phone number." I already had my pen and a piece of paper out ready to take down any information he had. I wrote it down, plus the address.

"He is listed as a truck driver for RDC Equipment Supply. Looks like it's based in Portland."

"He could still be a long-distance trucker," I said.

"Or maybe he got a new job since the deaths of his parents."

"Oregon's a long way from Western New York," I agreed. "Is there any other information? Mother's name—father's name?"

"No father listed. Mother's name Bridget Madison."

"That's the name the fortuneteller gave me, all right."

"What are you going to do now?"

"Call the number, talk to the guy."

"And if he's uncooperative?"

"Well…there's the option of you writing about the house."

"And what angle do I use? Halloween's still more than two months away."

"I might have to go back to the house and start digging again."

"That'll only get you tossed in jail again," Sam pointed out.

"Yeah, by whoever is holed up in that house. But who could it be? Someone's squatting. They've got electric, and they must be paying the taxes on that place."

"Or," Sam said, and drew out the word. "You've imagined all this."

"I didn't imagine the cop that arrested me, or the name the woman gave me, or even the social security number you just looked up."

"Yeah," he agreed. "But something about this whole situation smells fishy to me."

"You and me both."

"Look, I gotta go," Sam said. "Keep me posted."

"Will do," I said with resignation.

I hung up the phone and stared at it. So, he thought I'd imagined all this, huh?

I couldn't have.

I didn't.

Richard had bailed me out of jail, but I had no witnesses for any other part of this whole situation.

I stared at the number I'd written down. If Gary Madison had a day job, it was way too early to call the west coast. I'd have to wait until later in the evening. But what the hell was I going to say? *Know any good ghost stories? Did you know your mother's a ghost?* Or how about, *Halloween came early—guess how?*

There was only one thing to do. I stepped up to my liquor cabinet and poured myself a shot of bourbon and hoped I figure out something more appropriate to say when the time came.

***

The eleven o'clock news had just begun with a lead story about a drowning in Lake Erie. I dialed the Portland number that by then I knew by heart, and hit the mute button on my remote control. The Channel 7 newscaster's lips moved as the line rang and rang. Maybe Gary Madison wasn't yet home from work. I had to work the next day and didn't feel like staying up until the wee hours to try calling again. I was just about to hang up when a voice answered, "Hello."

I sat up straighter on the couch. Suddenly my mouth had gone dry. "Uh, Gary Madison? Son of Bridget Madison and Fred Butterfield?"

"Yeah," he answered warily.

"My name is Jeff Resnick. You don't know me...but I've got a really weird story to tell you about your parents."

There was dead silence for several long seconds. "Yeah," he said finally.

"I've been to their old house on Route 5, and I had a really odd experience."

I heard him sigh, as though he was already bored by my tale.

"I've...I've seen them—talked to them both."

He sighed again and said, "Not again."

"I beg your pardon?"

"There's a reason I left Buffalo Mister...what did you say your name was?"

"Resnick. Jeff Resnick."

"There's a reason I left Buffalo, Jeff. To get away from my parents. Now I know every kid eventually says that, but they don't have to say it after their parents are dead."

"You've seen them since they passed?"

"Let me guess. My mother asked you to track me down. Even gave you my social security number, I'll bet."

"That she did."

"Did she make you think that a murder had taken place in the house?"

"Yeah. Was she murdered?"

"Only by cigarettes and vodka. I'd call that death by suicide."

"How about your father?"

"Fell down the stairs after a few too many beers. Broke his neck. That was fifteen years ago."

Damn. I should've checked the county records for a death certificate. "He's got a Facebook page."

"No, *I've* got a Facebook page and I post as him."

"Why?"

"Because that way I can find out what's going on with my friends in Buffalo without my ex-wife harassing me."

That made sense. Still.... "How long ago did your mother pass?"

"Four years."

Which explained why Butterfield looked so much younger than Madam Zahara.

"But I don't get it. Dead is dead. Why are they still in that house? What's keeping your parents from...moving on?"

"Probably pure spite. I mean, they sure got under your skin, and let me tell you, you aren't the first who's called me about this situation. I talked to a priest about exorcism, but he blew me off. It probably wouldn't have worked, anyway. They didn't respect the church in life, why give a shit about it in death?"

"I sensed there might be bodies buried in the side yard."

"It's where their ashes were scattered. It was a lot cheaper than buying a couple of cemetery plots," Madison explained.

So much for him being a loving son.

"Is there someone living in the house now?" I asked.

"Yeah, my cousin is there. I'm letting him stay there until the sale is final."

So that's who owned the Buick. "There's no sign up in front."

"Yeah, my real estate agent complained they kept disappearing. I figured it was either my cousin or my dad ripping them down. A developer has bought most of the property on that stretch of the road for senior living units. They'll take possession of the place at the first of the month. I figure caveat emptor. Razing the house should finally get mom and dad out of my hair forever."

No love lost among those three.

"I found an ad on the online white pages for Madam Zahara's psychic services."

"The Internet is forever," he said.

That was the truth. "Have you told them the house is coming down?"

"Nope."

"What about your cousin?"

"I told him to be out by the end of the week. He's resisting. I figure I'll tell him why closer to the date of the sale. I don't want him slipping up and saying something to warn mom and dad."

Somebody should.

"I'm sorry you got suckered into this," Madison said. "It shouldn't happen any more once the house is gone."

The restless spirits of his parents might not just be tied to the house, but attached to land it stood on, too.

Caveat emptor indeed.

"Thanks for speaking with me. I won't bother you again."

"And don't let my folks bother you, either," Madison warned.

"Thanks."

I hung up the phone.

Bridget Madison and Fred Butterfield might not have been the nicest people when they were alive, but did they deserve what their son had in store for them?

I had a feeling I should keep my nose out of this situation… but I was pissed at them for jerking me around, and determined to make one more visit to that dilapidated house on Route 5.

***

I put in another day of work at The Whole Nine Yards, but instead of heading home, I turned right and headed back for Clarence. Sure enough the neon sign proclaiming Psychic $10 was once again glowing. Apparently just marks like me could see it. Did Madison's cousin ever wonder about the people traipsing in and out of his temporary home, or was he just as oblivious about us as he was about the house's permanent residents?

I parked my car on the gravel drive and walked up to the house. Once again Bridget called out, "I've been waiting for you." No doubt she had been.

I opened the screen door and walked inside the house. The black floor greeted me once again. I crouched down to better inspect it. It sure looked like old water damage to me.

"What are you waiting for?" Bridget called.

I straightened and headed into the parlor where she sat behind the table once again.

"I talked to your son," I said, not waiting for her to ask.

Her eyes lit up. "And, and?" she asked, sounding pleased.

"He's sold the house."

Her expression fell. "He can't do that!"

I shrugged. "He already has. Your upstairs tenant doesn't even know. He's just been told to get out by the end of the week."

"No wonder he's been packing," Bridget said angrily.

I looked up. Fred Butterfield was again standing at the side of the room. He looked grim.

"Not only that, but as soon as the sale is final, a bulldozer will be here to knock the house down."

Bridget shot Butterfield an angry glare. "Did you hear what Mr. Resnick said?"

Butterfield nodded, looking worried.

"Where will we go?"

"Maybe it's time for you to move on?" I suggested.

She turned her head to face me. "To what? Oblivion?"

"Isn't that what we're all supposed to do…eventually?"

"Well, I'm not ready," she declared. She looked over her shoulder toward her common-law husband. "Are you?"

Butterfield looked resigned. He shrugged.

Bridget looked back to me. "Will Gary at least come back to see us one more time?" Her voice was a plea.

I shook my head.

Bridget's face screwed into a grimace and she burst into tears.

I had never seen a ghost cry before.

What the hell was I thinking? Until I'd met these two, I'd never seen a ghost before. I still wasn't sure what I was seeing was real. I could just be imaging all of this.

No I wasn't. I'd been arrested. I'd seen Bridget walk with no legs. I'd talked to Gary Madison. This was the real deal and if I hadn't already had a bunch of weird experiences I'd just say I was crazy.

Still, seeing a ghost cry was just plain weird, and yet I couldn't ignore the emotional turmoil going on in front of me.

"I'm sorry," I said at last.

I looked at Butterfield who once again shrugged. Then he stepped over to Bridget and pulled her hands away from her face.

"You're leaving, aren't you?" she asked.

He frowned and nodded.

"But then I'll be all alone."

"Not if you come with me," he said. I hadn't heard him speak before, and his voice was a lot higher than I'd anticipated.

"But Gary—

"Doesn't care."

Bridget's lower lip started to tremble. "But—"

"Besides, I'm bored hanging around here all the time. I'm ready to blow this pop stand and see what else is out there. Wanna come with me?"

Bridget's face was filled with indecision.

"Once this house is gone...there'll be nothing for us here anyway. Come on," he urged. "I'm ready for a new adventure. Let's go." He pulled her up from the chair. They stood there, or should I say Bridget hovered—she still didn't seem to have feet—and they looked into each other's eyes for a long, long time. And then they just...dissolved into nothingness.

I blinked and the room was different. The card table and its contents were gone. My nose wrinkled at the smell of moldering food, and the breeze rustled the fast food papers that littered the floor. Was Madison's cousin upstairs? If so, I didn't want to run into him and I got the hell out of that house as fast as I could. Gravel flew as I backed out of the drive and headed for home, clenching the steering wheel the whole distance.

Holy shit. There really were ghosts.

And I'd spoken to two of them.

***

For the next couple of weeks, every time I'd visit Maggie, I took the back route. It was about a month later when I finally gathered up my courage to drive by the house I'd come to think of as ghost central. Of course, it was gone. So were the trees. All that was left was level ground and a sign that said Donard Construction and Fine Senior Living at Donard Estates.

I will admit that I checked Fred Butterfield's Facebook page on a regular basis. As Gary had said, he kept it going, and presumably without a twinge of conscience. He had said his parents were con artists. I was their last mark. That they couldn't pull any more shenanigans was all for the best.

That is…if they were done conning people.

The last time I drove by it was night, and when I looked to the empty spot where the house had been, I almost swear I saw the outline of a woman with a filmy skirt and shawl smoking a cigarette.

Of course…I could have just imagined it.

***

About the Author

The immensely popular Booktown Mystery series is what put Lorraine Bartlett's pen name Lorna Barrett on the New York Times Bestseller list, but it's her talent—whether writing as Lorna, or L.L. Bartlett, or Lorraine Bartlett—that keeps her there. This multi-published, Agatha-nominated author pens the exciting Jeff Resnick Mysteries as well as the acclaimed Victoria Square Mystery series and has many short stories and novellas to her name(s).

Visit her website at: http://www.llbartlett.com/
(You can also find her on Facebook, Goodreads, and Twitter (@LLBartlettbooks).)

Made in United States
Orlando, FL
08 August 2022